# THE BUTCHERS OF BERLIN

# THE
# BUTCHERS
## OF
# BERLIN

# CHRIS PETIT

## SIMON &
## SCHUSTER

London · New York · Sydney · Toronto · New Delhi

A CBS COMPANY

First published in Great Britain by Simon & Schuster UK Ltd, 2016
A CBS company

1 3 5 7 9 10 8 6 4 2

Simon & Schuster UK Ltd
1st Floor
222 Gray's Inn Road
London WC1X 8HB

www.simonandschuster.co.uk

Simon & Schuster Australia, Sydney
Simon & Schuster India, New Delhi

A CIP catalogue record for this book is available from the British Library

Hardback ISBN: 978-1-47114-340-3
Trade Paperback ISBN: 978-1-47114-341-0
eBook ISBN: 978-1-47114-342-7

Typeset in the UK by Hewer Text UK Ltd, Edinburgh
Printed and bound in Great Britain by CPI Group (UK) Ltd, Croydon, CR0 4YY

*To Anna and Iain*

# PART ONE

# I

It was still dark as the old man dressed. The light would not come for another hour. Socks and suspenders. Trousers and braces. The underpants of which he was so ashamed, dish-wash grey and stained, for lack of soap, so threadbare they were in holes. His shoes, once good, barely held together and leaked at the slightest provocation. They smelled of the detergent used to wash the slaughterhouse floor. The medal deserved a collar, he thought. He had no cufflinks either and made do with rolled sleeves. The suit still had its waistcoat, which he wore for the little extra warmth it afforded, usually under his one sweater, which he discarded that morning, wanting to look his best. He took his overcoat, hat and scarf, which hung on the back of the door. As an afterthought, he folded his pyjamas and placed them under the pillow. He wanted the gesture to provoke some regret or nostalgia but felt nothing.

The pistol was an old Mauser C96. He appreciated the aesthetics of its distinctive box magazine in front of the trigger, the long elegant barrel and comfort of the wooden handle. His last companion of choice. His hands were cold but he would not wear gloves. He passed through the apartment, careful not to disturb the others because he wished to leave unobserved. He closed the door softly behind him, stood at the top of the stairs and stared into the descending gloom.

\*　　\*　　\*

The block warden was slow to arrive. He was a short man with a childish face and the insolent, spoiled look of minor authority. He didn't see the pistol in the old man's hand until he raised his arm. He gave a small yelp of surprise, followed by his characteristically unpleasant laugh, which he never had time to finish. He was in the middle of putting on his coat, with his mouth open, when the bullet entered his head, through the eye, at which the old man had been aiming. His head snapped back from the force. Blood and bone hit the wall, followed by the bullet. He slumped back and slid down, his blood a dark smear on dirty paintwork. The remaining eye fluttered, almost coquettishly, as he hit the floor sitting, paused and rolled over.

In the booming echo of the shot the old man thought he heard footsteps stop on the stairs. Female. He knew whose and regretted he could do nothing about that; perhaps she was his angel of death after all. At least he was her avenger.

The old man turned the gun on himself, grasped the barrel in his left hand to hold it steady and pulled the trigger. The bullet travelled upwards through the unresisting flesh of his chin and tongue, missing his false teeth, into the soft palate of his mouth, passing the nasal passage, to penetrate the brain where it lodged, causing none of the messy damage of the first shot. Such a neat, clean death; the old man was gone before he hit the ground, doing more tidily for himself than his victim, who jerked and twitched like a dog in a dream.

The young woman was still standing petrified when the second shot fired. A voice in her head told her not even to think and get out. She ran with her hand over her mouth until she reached outside and spewed in the courtyard as the door banged behind her, barely stopping before she carried on running.

# 2

August Schlegel woke up in a prison cell with no recollection
of how he had got there. Everything swam unpleasantly. He
wondered if he were still drunk. Like a man contemplating
white space on a map, he thought, 'My name is August
Schlegel and the street where I live is the same as my first
name, in the former Jewish quarter.' He opened one eye.
Had they thrown him in the drunk tank? There were many
things he disliked about himself, starting with his name. He
was only twenty-five but his hair had gone quite white, which
he also disliked, as he did the way it sat on top of his open,
ordinary face.

The air stank of stale drink. He had a memory of throwing
up during the party. The party. There had been speeches. A
big room full of boozed-up men. A group of the oldest and
toughest had decided to make him the butt of their lurid and
preposterous tales. Stoffel claimed to have dressed as a woman
for the S-Bahn murders, to act as bait. The idea was beyond
imagination. Stoffel was bull-necked with a boxer's nose and
a tobacco-stained moustache, which he claimed to have
shaved off for his drag act. Tears of mirth ran down everyone's
cheeks.

They were all reeling drunk by the end. He remembered
wondering if he would end up spending the night in the cells
again; it seemed to be happening more often. He recalled
standing swaying, trying to read his watch, and someone

saying, 'Ach! After eleven. Too late to go home. Everyone downstairs!'

Sleeping it off in the cells was standard police practice.

He must have dozed off. The next thing he knew, he was being poked awake. The reek of brutal aftershave told Schlegel it wasn't just a bad dream. He ran his furred and distended tongue around his teeth and tasted a horrible residue. He could feel his swollen liver.

'You'll do,' said Stoffel, continuing to poke him.

'What for?'

'A homicide.'

Schlegel couldn't find his hat and one glove was lost. His jacket and coat were wadded up under the bunk. At least the big leather waistcoat was still there. He kept repeating under his breath: I am not homicide. On the rare occasions Schlegel found himself drinking with the likes of Stoffel – at leaving parties, and there were plenty of those – he had a warning list in his head of subjects never to mention, however drunk. He hoped the image he had of himself regaling them hadn't happened. Stoffel's crowd were always laughing at things not in the slightest funny until someone said something really funny, when they made a point of not laughing at all.

He arrived in the garage hatless, his ungloved hand stuffed in his pocket. Stoffel was sitting in an Opel with the engine running. The garage was bitterly cold and it was no warmer in the car, whose heater didn't work.

'I am not homicide, you know,' he said to Stoffel.

'The rest are busy.'

Busy sleeping it off, he thought sourly. Where was his hat? It was a good one.

\*     \*     \*

There was a hole in the floor of the car and a chilly draught blew up his legs. He suspected Stoffel wore newspaper under his vest from the way he rustled. There was much discussion about what gave the best insulation. Stoffel smoked a foul cheroot. He was a wet smoker. Schlegel was aware of not having cleaned his teeth, not that it mattered. Nearly everyone's breath reeked these days. He tasted last night's alcohol. No shortage there. Outside it began to spit. To stop from feeling sick, he concentrated on the grinding of the useless wipers and the smeared vision through the greasy windscreen.

A lot of official traffic was on the roads. Trams were crammed with commuters. Those banned from public transport trudged past with their heads down. Another grubby dawn, another working Saturday and another of those filthy colourless days found only in Berlin in winter, in the year of our Lord nineteen hundred and forty-three.

A roadblock was set up where the street had been sealed off. They were in a run-down working-class part of Wilmersdorf. Schlegel saw soldiers on standby, their scuttle helmets silhouetted in the drizzle. There were a lot of ordinary policemen too and plainclothes, as well as special Jewish marshals with armbands.

The man they were referred to wore the usual unofficial uniform of snap-brim fedora and leather trench coat. He gave them a peremptory look and said, 'Gersten.'

Gersten's hair was worn unusually long over the collar. Schlegel remained preoccupied with his hangover as they were led through an arch into a deep courtyard surrounded by dilapidated barracks-like blocks with crumbling brickwork, dark with soot.

'Two Jews,' said Gersten. He pointed to a block entrance.

'You drag me out of bed for a couple of Jews!' protested Stoffel.

'Today the Jews are all busy getting arrested. We go in at full daylight, so you have five minutes to sort them out.'

Stoffel, still grumbling, said to Schlegel, 'You tell me what happened. Consider it part of your education.'

Stoffel was already nipping from a hip flask.

They were in a ground-floor corridor that ran from front to back, outside the block warden's quarters. The staircase took up most of the space. The hall stank of cordite. One man had been shot while putting on his coat and had fallen awkwardly. The eye was a gaping hole. The other by comparison appeared formally arranged, so neat he could have been laid out by an undertaker.

Schlegel passed Stoffel the pistol using his gloved hand. Stoffel looked at the weapon in appreciation.

Schlegel said, 'The old man shot himself after shooting the other man. There may have been a witness who ran away.'

'We're not looking to complicate this.'

'I stepped over a puddle of vomit by the door.'

Stoffel inspected the soles of his shoes, yawned ostentatiously and went outside. Schlegel followed. The yard was now surrounded by troops with submachine guns and attack dogs straining their leashes. He had heard nothing of their arrival.

Gersten beckoned them over. Stoffel insisted that Jews were not the business of the criminal police. Gersten ignored him and said Stoffel still needed certification of death.

'Get the bodies out here in the meantime. They're in the way.'

Gersten nodded to an SS corporal with a bull whip, who blew a long blast on his whistle. A squadron of Jewish marshals ran in and fanned out towards the block entrances. The corporal cracked his whip and the dogs pulled on their leads, followed by the noise of doors being hammered on and kicked in, then banging and screaming and people being yelled at.

Schlegel was quite unprepared for such controlled fury. It pitched him back to that other time, which he had trained his mind to blank, during the waking hours at least.

A man upstairs yelled, 'No packing. Get dressed and out!'

Stoffel was in no hurry to move the bodies by himself. He ordered a couple of marshals who were in the process of chasing out the first residents.

The men hesitated until Stoffel shouted, 'Unless you want to join the rest in the yard.'

A middle-aged woman tried to press money into Schlegel's hand, saying a terrible mistake had been made, her name should not be on the list. Schlegel looked at the pathetic amount and turned away. The woman moved on to Stoffel, who took the money and told her to wait outside. He asked her name and said he would have a word. The woman babbled her thanks.

'Go along, before I change my mind,' said Stoffel not unkindly, pocketing the money.

The sound of blows came from upstairs, followed by a sharp crack and glass being smashed.

'Dead body!' a voice shouted.

Schlegel thought perhaps the old man had been forewarned. As to where he had got the gun or why he'd shot the other man, he doubted anyone would care. Stoffel was smoking another of his foul-smelling cheroots. The tip, even wetter than the last, reminded Schlegel of a dog's dick. A steady crowd pressed downstairs. Some whimpered. Others complained about pushing. It was like watching a river surge.

Someone fell on the stairs. People started to get trampled. Schlegel tried to restore order, aware of Stoffel's sceptical gaze. The crowd seemed incapable of stopping. Schlegel was close to losing control of himself as he saw back to that flat horizon, marshland, huge summer mosquitoes, villages little more than a collection of hovels.

He pulled people up and shouted at others. A scream from under a pile of bodies seemed to act as a sign for the pushing to stop. Schlegel walked away, leaving them to sort themselves out. The air outside was absolutely still. It had stopped raining, not that it had done more than drizzle. His hands trembled in his coat pockets.

The corporal snapped his whip and ordered everyone to stop milling around. He separated the mostly elderly men. One who tried to point out his wife was screamed at. The crowd recoiled whenever the dogs showed their fangs.

The two bodies were now lying dumped in a corner by the bins, behind the rank of soldiers. The old man wasn't looking so neat now. Schlegel knelt down and put his hand inside the man's coat, like a pickpocket. The wallet he extracted was fake leather. The papers were stamped with a 'J'. Schlegel noted the name, Metzler, and the number of his apartment upstairs. The other man had no papers.

The corporal kept cracking his whip like he was Buffalo Bill. Anyone showing indecision was kicked into line by the Jewish marshals. An ugly pudding of a woman with orange hair let out a wail and ran across the yard, arms jerking like a wind-up doll. At the bins she threw herself on the body of the other man. The courtyard was momentarily stilled except for the woman's keening. The corporal stopped to look, then screamed at one of the civilians, 'You! Cockroach! Eyes front!'

Gersten had a stick of lip salve, used surreptitiously to moisten his mouth. He came over and said to Schlegel, 'The other man was the block warden, not Jewish, so it is technically a homicide.'

The woman paused her wailing to shout, 'We are German. I won't have my man touched by a Jew doctor. We were here years before this riffraff!'

Even for Stoffel this was too much. He snapped, 'What difference does it make? One dead man is the same as another.'

Gersten looked worried. 'In fact, one Jew didn't shoot another. She's right. You're going to have to get a proper doctor now.'

The block's only telephone was in the hall of the warden's apartment. Through the door to the living quarters Schlegel saw what looked like a comfortable set of confiscated furniture. The telephone was fixed to the wall, with a phone book underneath. He called a doctor and an ambulance. He then spoke to the Jewish Association and demanded a hearse.

When Schlegel went back outside the corporal was yelling, 'Do as you are told or the dogs will have you for breakfast!'

The purpose of his aggression was only to create more terror. A small boy duly wet himself from fright and stood transfixed by the expanding puddle at his feet.

An elderly Jewish medic had been found to pronounce the old man dead. He stood to address Stoffel. 'Take a look at the medal around his neck.'

Stoffel leaned in and whistled.

The doctor said, 'An old soldier deserves more.'

The medal, on a ribbon, had been hidden by the man's scarf: Iron Cross, first class. Not many of those, thought Schlegel.

The doctor said, 'A man prepared to die for his country.'

Stoffel, not usually short of an answer, was silent.

The widow yelled, 'Fucking Yids! You'll get what's coming!'

Stoffel ordered two policemen to get her out of the yard

before she caused trouble, then told Schlegel to take a look at the old man's apartment. His leg hurt, he said, and he didn't fancy the climb.

Locks were broken on many of the doors. Schlegel couldn't understand why the process had to be so destructive. He half-expected the building to take its revenge for being so violated, causing him to tumble downstairs and break his neck.

In the yard names were shouted. Abelman! Abendroth!

The old man lived on the third floor. The door was shut but unlocked. Schlegel pushed it open and saw bedrolls on the floor of the tiny living space and kitchen, and more in the corridor, making it more like a refugee camp than anything resembling a home. The old man would have had no choice about how many were billeted with him. Schlegel counted six suitcases. Nappies hung over the sink. No pictures or signs of personal possessions.

At the end of a corridor stood a tomblike bedroom, with space only for a single bed and chair.

Under the bed he found the man's military trunk with army postings stencilled on the top and old stickers for tourist steam-ships on the side. It contained only some tattered underclothes, a spare shirt, a threadbare green sweater and an empty collar box. The only two items of interest were a key and a notebook full of doodles and entries written in a minute old-fashioned Gothic script. Schlegel pocketed it, presuming it might be evidence.

The key was a small one, like those for lockers in cloakrooms, with a tag and the number, 2716. He took that too and thought had the old man not shot himself he would be waiting to be taken off.

Below in the courtyard he could see Stoffel smoking his cheroot while absent-mindedly kicking the foot of the dead warden. He turned away, and asked himself where the old man could possibly have hidden his pistol.

Behind a chest in what passed for the reception room, he found a chimney cavity where a stove had once stood. He got down on all fours and put his arm up the hole to see if there was a ledge. He wasn't sure if he looked round because he heard someone enter or if the woman had been watching him.

He stood up brushing his hands, like a man caught out. She was a tiny creature, stick-thin. He couldn't say if his presence frightened her. Her head was covered with a scarf, tied like a pirate's, a detail that took Schlegel back to games played in childhood.

The woman blurted out to ask why his hair was white.

Because that was the way it was, he said self-consciously.

She looked exotic, Oriental almost, quite old but interesting and attractive. She kept giving him odd looks.

He asked, 'Why did he shoot the warden?'

'Perhaps he intended to do something useful before he died.'

That made sense; block wardens were generally loathed.

Schlegel wondered if her real reason for being there was to frisk the place for anything useful. Why hadn't she been taken with the rest?

They were interrupted by heavy footsteps coming upstairs. At least three men, stopping on their floor. The woman paled, her terror palpable, and shrank back as they passed, followed by banging on a door further down, with shouts to open up. The woman's composure was quite gone. Schlegel turned away. She gasped as though he would betray her, and again as he stepped outside.

Three sweaty and dishevelled marshals stood in the corridor.

'We're short,' said the eldest, a little man who bristled with self-importance.

Schlegel recognised him as one of the men Stoffel had ordered to take out the bodies.

The door was unlocked. Schlegel led the way. The place was empty. Two tiny rooms, badly sectioned. Two beds, one made, one unmade. The same stale atmosphere of deceit and despair. The marshals seemed reluctant to leave.

'Well?'

The one who had spoken said, 'We have to fill the quota.'

'Show me,' Schlegel said, indicating the man's list.

Typewritten columns of names and addresses, nearly all ticked. Against the old man's name was written 'deceased'.

'What of those you can't account for?'

'We must search for them.'

'And if you don't find them?'

'They send us away to make up the numbers.'

Funk rolled off them in waves, on top of the prevalent smells of the building: the thin, sour stink of drains; lack of human washing; and something high and feral Schlegel put down to the greater fear left by the evacuation.

He studied the list again. The names for that apartment had two Todermanns not crossed off.

Schlegel said, 'They must have left early or are on a night shift.'

He returned the list, went out and waited for the men. He meant to leave with them but instead returned to the old man's apartment. The woman was standing in the same spot, shaking from head to foot. Schlegel raised a finger and waited for the footsteps to go.

It had taken – what? – thirty minutes to clear the place.

Schlegel mumbled he wasn't there to arrest anyone. He asked if the woman was living with her sister.

Her daughter.

She stepped forward and offered to read his palm, garrulous

with relief, saying she was a professional. She looked like she wanted to cling to him for protection. The situation was so ridiculous Schlegel wished he had gone downstairs.

He surprised himself by sticking out his hand, which he quickly withdrew, failing to hide his embarrassment.

The woman took it anyway. She grew calmer. Her hand was cool in his. The experience was disconcerting.

Schlegel hadn't touched anyone in two years, avoided even shaking hands.

'Do I have a future?' he asked, feeling foolish for playing along.

'Yes, not the one you expect.' She ran her fingers over his palm. 'But you have a past.'

He could not decide whether their strange enactment was in reaction to the brutality around them.

She gave him a stricken look and let go.

'You're different from the rest. Remember that, for you will see enough terrible things to turn your hair white many times over.'

He walked out without a word and went downstairs.

Outside it was trying to snow. The courtyard was empty except for the old man's body. The warden's was gone. Stoffel hadn't bothered to wait. A few snowflakes drifted down. The next set of incumbents would move in with their new habits and noises and smells, and it would be as though none of it had happened.

Schlegel looked at the old man again. There was a dignity to him, unlike his victim, but he saw nothing of the war hero, just an emaciated corpse keeping its secrets.

The old man's medal would get buried with him in an unmarked grave, preserved long after the body disintegrated; perhaps hundreds of years. Schlegel genuflected and touched the cold iron, unable to remember when anything had last aroused his curiosity. He undid the knot, his fingers stiff and clumsy. It came free. He stood up and stuffed the medal in his pocket, thinking of old recidivist habits.

Feeling he was being watched, perhaps by the strange woman upstairs, he looked around guiltily, aware that he was blushing, which was ridiculous.

An ancient, battered van drove into the yard. A tall, dark-haired man got out. The van was nondescript and had seen better days.

'Are you the Jewish hearse?' Schlegel asked.

The driver asked instead, 'Where did he get the gun?'

News spread fast along all kinds of unofficial channels.

'Can you give me a hand with the loading?'

That the driver had no help struck Schlegel as in keeping with the disjointed day.

He supposed he must look amenable; the driver certainly wouldn't have asked Stoffel. He bent down to take the dead man's heels. He regretted not having his hat. It was bitterly cold. At least it numbed the hangover. People usually stared at his hair but the driver seemed not to notice.

The corpse weighed so little, as though it barely consisted of matter at all.

Inside the vehicle looked like a converted bakery van, with shelves made of plywood. The casual way the driver closed the door afterwards made it seem the most normal thing to drive into a yard and collect a body. Schlegel found him handsome in a sardonic way, far more self-possessed than the men upstairs, who were always on the point of flinching, as if they expected to be hit.

He thought of cadging a lift, then decided he didn't want to ride with a dead man. As for the notebook, he had known upstairs he wouldn't hand it over. No one was interested. Stoffel would have snaffled the pistol.

The driver got in the van. Schlegel watched him go, thinking about the medal. Perhaps he shouldn't keep it. Maybe it was bad luck. What had the woman said? That he would see terrible things, enough to turn his hair white many times over.

# 3

Sybil still tasted vomit in her mouth. The fright of the shooting
continued to boom in her head and she had to force herself not
to run. Only she seemed to detect the strange, almost frenzied
tempo of official traffic as everyone else went about their business. Sybil saw police and military vehicles everywhere, and the
removal vans they used to take people away in waiting outside
factories and tenement blocks. For months things had been
quiet. A few had started to hope against hope, including Sybil,
however much her mother warned they would stop at nothing
in the end.

She passed through Olivaer Platz, crossed Mommsenstrasse
and went down Wilmersdorfer Strasse as it tried to snow.
Everything appeared normal: trams, buses, a policeman direct-
ing traffic. Cinemas, cafés, bars. A shoe-shine man with amputated legs, sitting on his box. A lorry with a flat tyre. A child
with a penny whistle. In a shop window, a toy monkey with a
drum. Pedestrian crossings. A big store looking forlorn. A
bookshop still with a Russian dictionary in the window. A
young woman, not unlike herself, in a cloche hat, glanced in
brief recognition. Caught in a flow of pedestrians, Sybil crossed
a busy junction, thinking she must speak to Franz. Franz worked
as an orderly at the Jewish hospital. She had known him since
she was at the school of design and fashion, not far from where
she was now.

Rather than use a telephone in the street, which attracted

patrols, Sybil marched into the Hotel Savoy in Fasanenstrasse and took a kiosk in the lobby.

It took ages to get through to the hospital, which was impossibly busy, and so long to fetch Franz that Sybil worried her money would run out.

At last he came, breathless, asking if she was all right because it was chaos at his end, with the hospital told to provide typists, marshals, doctors and nursing staff for hastily erected assembly camps for those arrested, and to prepare food for ten thousand.

'Ten thousand!' Sybil echoed.

Franz said, 'It's as though they mean to make a clean sweep.'

It no longer seemed possible to pretend. Such a level of arrest was unprecedented. Before a lull that had lasted several months, there had been only individual summonses for deportation, never any mass roundups.

Sybil also urgently needed to talk about the forged papers Franz was helping her get for her friend Lore, who was in hiding.

'Is Lore worth it?' he asked. 'It will be much more difficult and dangerous now.'

Sybil said yes.

'Call me the same time tomorrow.'

Sybil stared at the replaced receiver and feared she might altogether lack the courage to leave the booth, and would sit there until drowned in the tide of her rising panic.

She composed herself enough to walk through the lobby and smile at the ancient flunky dressed in his braided livery, whose sole job was to stand by the revolving door.

On the Ku'damm her nerve faltered at the sight of a street patrol checking papers. They had stopped a dark woman with frizzy hair.

Normally she swept past patrols with her blond head held high, secure in the knowledge that she did not conform to their stereotype. But that morning her legs disobeyed her and she knew she would soon come to a standstill, inviting arrest. Using the last of her energy, she marched into the *Konditorei* she was outside, thinking how much she wanted to share the security of its clientele, even for a few minutes. Smart women sat content and placid, drinking tea and eating artificial-looking cake, as if without a care in the world. Sybil was bone-weary and very frightened. Her feet ached and her chilblains burned.

She had to remember how to behave, ordering, looking around, gazing at passers-by. The white tablecloth, a pathetic attempt at luxury, was grimy. The thin tea was the usual herbal concoction. She got up and went to the toilet and rinsed her mouth and cleaned her teeth with her finger. There was no soap.

She went back, took a copy of the wretched Party newspaper, like a good little citizen, and drank her tea. The patrol was still outside, laughing and joking now.

The paper was full of such hate and rubbish. Now they didn't have their victories to crow about it made them hate all the more, as well as starting to feel sorry for themselves, which they seemed to be even better at than hating. Whenever her mother predicted they would come in great numbers to take their people away Sybil had refused to listen. For a start, there was a labour shortage, and they were told they were needed because of their jobs. Now this. It didn't make sense.

A voice came out of nowhere. 'Fräulein?'

Sybil jumped. She looked up at what appeared to be a pleasant, elderly gentleman, wanting to know if she had finished with the paper.

He wore a Party pin. She dreaded he would insist on sitting with her, pat her on the knee and talk about the Jewish filth being rounded up. Perhaps she should let him sleep with her, in exchange for his protection. But he paid her no attention, accepted the paper and walked away.

The lesson was salutary. From now on she could not allow for any more approaches made unawares. Next time the voice could be saying she had better come with them.

Sybil reached the conclusion she had been dreading. She would have to join Lore and go underground. The ones that went into hiding were known as U-boats, with reason; one might as well be at the bottom of the ocean. Many buckled from the pressure. Those with the discipline to forgo all outside contact had the best chance. That was not her, and probably not Lore.

# 4

Schlegel was coming up from the cells after searching in vain for his hat when Stoffel, standing by the main desk, collared him again and said, 'You'll do. We have another body.'

'Why me again?'

He had been looking forward to slipping off and going back to bed.

'You're fraud, son, I know that, but as of oh-six hundred hours this morning one slacker is requisitioned to the homicide department on my say-so.'

Schlegel knew the rest of the man's crew were down in the cells still sleeping it off. He had just seen them, lying on their backs, snoring, oblivious.

'Where's your other glove, boy?'

He didn't answer and followed Stoffel back to the car, confused because he was blushing for the second time that day. He supposed it must be to do with tired blood fighting the hangover.

They drove east, towards the poorer districts. Streets were empty, shops and bars boarded up. Schlegel stared at the surroundings and had trouble imagining what trees with leaves looked like.

Set on the edge of the city, bordered by the outer-ring railway, the meat district was a town in itself, a walled citadel, built fifty years before as a testament to civic pride, now fallen on hard times. It spread as far as the eye could see, a substantial complex of squat barracks, glass halls and sheds, dwarfed by the twin towers of the ice factory.

They parked on Landsberger Allee, by the north-west entrance. On top of the gate pillars stood two large statues of the Berlin bear. A line of low buildings led down to a railway siding where wagons stood. Weeds pushed up through the concrete.

Local cops, slaughterhouse and railway officials were waiting down below, looking green. A doctor and photographer were on their way. A cop led them to a cattle car, gestured to the ladder and stepped back. Stoffel's fat arse stuck out as he went up. Schlegel heard him say, 'Take a look at this, son.'

What he saw in the corner of the carriage more resembled something found hanging in a butcher's shop. No evidence was left of the pain inflicted, not even a head to register death's agony, just a flayed limbless torso, with the skin gone to reveal the muscle. What remained lay on its back, surgically treated to make it impossible to tell what sex it had been.

'Tell me what you see,' said Stoffel.

Dead meat was all he could think. A rack of meat.

'You would think they were going to eat it. No mess. No blood. Control. Precision. And where are we?'

'A slaughterhouse.'

'And what are we standing in?'

'A cattle car.'


The photographer arrived. They were still waiting for the doctor. Stoffel told the photographer to get on with it. The camera flashes looked like gunshots from outside the wagon.

Stoffel said to Schlegel, 'Here, take one of these.'

'What is it?'

'Grown-up pill. Make you feel better.' Stoffel put one in his mouth. He shook another out of the cylinder for Schlegel, who couldn't feel any worse.

'You're going to have to write up this one too,' said Stoffel. 'I'm short-staffed. It either came in on the train, which means it could have come from anywhere, and we bury it, or it was done by one of the locals.'

Stoffel asked the assembled men who had found the body. One of the railway officials said he had checked the wagon because the door was open. Old vagrants from the last war made a habit of sleeping there.

Stoffel whistled in the direction of the loitering civilians and demanded to know who was in charge. A tall fellow wearing a bowler hat and brown overalls wandered over in no hurry and announced he was Baumgarten, the slaughterhouse foreman.

Stoffel asked, 'Any of your boys been misbehaving?'

Baumgarten, an elderly, unshaven giant with a missing top front tooth and enormous hands, was slow to answer.

'It would be Jews,' he eventually said.

'What Jews?'

'Jewish butchers.'

'Excuse me,' said Stoffel. 'Since when did butchering count as war effort?'

Baumgarten agreed he was as surprised as anyone when they turned up. Most of his men had been drafted into army catering.

'Even our trainees were shipped off and the Dutch and Danish labour we were promised never showed, so we got Jews.'

Stoffel asked whether the Jewish butchers operated according to kosher practice. Baumgarten explained they didn't do the killing, they only prepared the carcasses afterwards. He laughed uncertainly.

'How many of these Jews work here?' Stoffel asked.

About a dozen, Baumgarten replied, counting on his fingers. They even had their own foreman.

'A dozen working here at one time with axes and knives!' exclaimed Stoffel. 'Whose bright idea was that?'

'The penpushers. They wouldn't listen.'

'You had better go and fetch these Jewish butchers.'

'They were taken away this morning.'

Stoffel gave a hoot of disbelief. 'In the roundup?'

Baumgarten said he'd heard it was happening all over. The least they could have done was warn them. Now they were short again. Over two thousand personnel used to work there before the war. Barely a hundred were left.

'Where were the Jews taken?' asked Stoffel.

They hadn't been told.

'Well, go and find out.'

The man lumbered off. Stoffel turned to Schlegel.

'Thirteen suspects, including the foreman. Take a look around while that shirker finds out where they are, see if anything comes to mind.'

Schlegel passed through huge separate compounds, the length of three S-Bahn stops.

He was given a map by the main reception in the central building on Eldenaer Strasse, where the talk was of that morning's arrests. The desk was staffed by three roguish old women who flirted clumsily as a matter of course. One marked for him where she thought the Jewish dormitory was.

'We didn't really know anything about them until they were taken away this morning.'

The dormitory was back up the end he had come from.

Outside, he rotated the map, using the towers of the ice factory as a marker. The dirty boundary wall he remembered from his one trip there with his stepfather, a dozen years before, to see a vet about a lame racehorse. He had been an impressionable age. The high wall didn't prevent those passing from hearing the bellowing of animals about to be slaughtered. It was, his stepfather laconically stated, where the animals went in and the meat came out.

The Jewish butchers' dormitory was a temporary wooden barracks like those crammed into every bit of city wasteland to house the growing army of foreign workers. Schlegel stepped straight into the sleeping area, with double bunks and a tiny cubicle which he supposed was for the supervisor. The building was freezing cold, without heating, and windows covered with tar paper. The space told nothing about its inhabitants. If they had been shipped out that morning taking nothing, then they had left nothing behind. When they were there it must have been like they had already gone.

The side of the barracks was overshadowed by a substantial hangar whose flank wall was blank, with low dormer windows set above. Ahead in the distance was Stoffel's parked car, and the clumsy figure of the foreman, Baumgarten, was shambling down the street in Schlegel's direction.

The smell in that part of the estate was a mixture of refuse and sewage, the full strength of which only hit Schlegel as he was confronted by a stench he thought came from some kind of septic tank until he saw the large slurry pit. There was no fence around it. Anyone stumbling into its black sludge on a dark night wouldn't get out in a hurry. Overcome by the fumes, he had to steady himself.

He became aware of a snorting and shuffling coming from inside the hangar. The first entrance he tried was locked. At the end of the building he found another set of doors, which gave at the shove of a shoulder. The place was awash with urine, which added an astringent layer to the general stink. The grunts and squeals sounded so human that Schlegel at first thought the mass of writhing, grimy pink flesh was people engaged in a bestial orgy. The pigs were rammed on top of each other, three or four emaciated animals wedged into stalls meant for one, which even then were too small to turn around in. Many were scabbed or had running sores. In one pen a mother had squashed her litter. In another, two pigs were eating a third which had expired. One pig chewed the tail of another too weak to resist. It paused and fixed Schlegel with its gaze. He noted pale lashes and blue eyes whose active intelligence appeared to find him wanting.

He saw at the far end of the hall, up in the roof, a suspended room with a large window. He could not say why he went up. He had already decided to leave. Perhaps it was the way the stairs ran up the outside of the building, inviting inspection.

It was a large empty room where the smell from downstairs was less evident. Schlegel stood before the big window and watched the herd squirm. At a distance it looked more like an army of maggots.

He grew dimly aware of another smell, coming from the corridor to one side.

The putrid odour reminded him of pus-ridden gauze and the sticky smell of butchers' shops. He should go. He had done what he had been asked. Yet he felt compelled.

The corridor was in the angle of the roof. The stench came from the room at the end. Its door stood ajar. Schlegel stepped into what looked like an old laundry. Tiled cream walls, a large sink with a long wooden draining board above an open gutter. An improvised shower had been fixed up above the sink, attached to the tap by a hose, which was tied to a high pipe with rope and a stick. The window was covered with brown paper. He peeled a piece away. It overlooked the Jewish barracks, which seemed almost close enough to touch.

A trolley like in a hospital stood in the middle of room, which was surprisingly warm.

His heart beat faster. The pill had made him focused and reckless, excited almost, in a hurry to take everything in. The shiny set of knives. A chain. Pen and ink. Stationery cards. A fat book, its pages open. A strange, crude drawing scratched into the plaster on the wall of a herd of animals throwing itself over a cliff into a broiling sea. And above all that stench. Slops in the tin bucket. That was the smell. What looked like offal floated in blood.

The lettering in the open book appeared to be Hebrew. His illogical thought was this was a room where the Jews performed their butchery in the traditional way.

A voice was calling.

It was Baumgarten, sent by Stoffel to find out where on earth he had got to.

Stoffel said it was clearly the murder room. Whatever had been done to the flayed body had been committed there.

'You have running water, the instruments, the table … I would say we are dealing with something more like ritual sacrifice, we're talking beyond normal murder.'

His voice sounded awed.

Baumgarten said, 'Fuck me, I've seen some stuff but nothing like this.' He stood with his fists clenched and face contorted. 'They probably placed the victim on all fours and cut her throat kosher-style, bashed the brains out afterwards, if you could find the head, then gutted her. That must be them in the bucket. Yids, for sure. All "yes sir, no sir" on the job but turn your back and they stick a knife up your arse.'

'What makes you say it's a woman?' asked Stoffel.

'They wouldn't do it to a man. They're animals. They can't even kill like men. They probably fucked her afterwards while she was still warm and rolled around in her blood before they got down to work.'

The rest in the room that had come to see looked spooked, including Stoffel. One remarked that all over soldiers were dying honourably in battle and now someone went and did this. Baumgarten was right. It wasn't natural. It was the work of savages.

Stoffel addressed the room and said what they had seen was not for talking about and should be kept between themselves. If he found anyone blabbing he personally would eviscerate them.

He told the local police he wanted the area searched for missing body parts. He turned to Schlegel.

'You've got a long day ahead of you, son. Go and find where those Jewish butchers are, because, as the man just said, we know what we're dealing with.'

# 5

It was the fourth winter of blackout. The city was shrouded in darkness for twelve hours. A lack of moon that night made the edifices of buildings indistinguishable from the sky. Sybil stuck close to the kerb where there was enough definition to guide her.

She had left Lore in the attic, calculating it would be safe there over the weekend, with no one around, while she went back to her block to find out what had happened and if anyone was left. Lore suffered from night blindness. She had lost her job because of it. Walking to and from work in the dark, Lore grew easily disoriented. After she punched in late again at the paint factory where she worked, the personnel officer told her it was impossible to argue with the clock.

Jobless, it was only a matter of time before Lore was deported. They both knew that. It was not a situation for which Sybil had been prepared. Were she caught sheltering Lore she too would be packed off. Lore affected insouciance, saying she could look after herself. Sybil considered life precarious and risky enough as it was, but a corresponding selfishness had overtaken everything, which amounted to a kind of death, and the wish to give beyond herself had played a part in her decision. Perhaps she was growing up.

Earlier that afternoon, Sybil had loitered in Savignyplatz, near the cutting rooms, not risking going in, in case anyone had reported her. At least one of the girls was reputed to be an informer. Everything had changed, irrevocably. Until then she had been protected. The company she worked for made clothes for export, listed as essential war work, and Sybil had a flourishing and unofficially endorsed black-market sideline tailoring couture copies for rich wives. The extra earnings from that she had calculated were enough, just, to accommodate Lore's survival.

After the other staff had gone, Sybil spoke briefly to her employer, Frau Zwicker, who knew nothing of the arrests and had assumed Sybil was ill and unable to telephone.

Sybil said she wasn't sure if she could come to work any more, until the authorities' position was clear.

Frau Zwicker was sympathetic but cautious, older, not given to demonstration. She had a political husband locked up somewhere. Sybil had already tested her goodwill with Lore, which had translated as asking if she could leave some things upstairs for a few days.

Now for the second time in a week she had become a source of uncertainty.

Frau Zwicker said, 'Those things you left in the attic. Regrettably . . .'

The workshop was in a low, old building, formerly stables, at the back of which was a cobbled cul-de-sac. The attic was reached by a rickety outside staircase. Hiding Lore there could only be temporary because the place was not secure. The door had only a latch and no lock.

Sybil found Lore sleeping peacefully. The image exasperated her, however unfair she was being. In hiding, Lore had little to do except sleep and read. The irony was had she not been fired she would almost certainly have been arrested that morning.

Lore's only false identity was a fake press pass, years out of date. Her official card named her as Hannalore Sara Dorfmann.

Both she and Sybil had been forced by the State to take Sara as a middle name. Both their cards were stamped with a large 'J'. They had by order to wear their star at all times in public. Neither did. Lore made a point of flouting the rules, insisting they dress up so she could take them to the Kaiserhof hotel, where Sybil sat timid among the black uniforms, lost in admiration as Lore chatted up two young bucks, saying they were secretaries at the housing ministry, and accepting their invitation to pay for tea. Afterwards Sybil's legs were so wobbly she clung to Lore for support.

Sybil considered Lore the cradle of her soul. Being reticent about expressing herself, she had carried the phrase in her head for a long time. Lore affected a coolness about anything so obvious as stated feelings. For Sybil life was something that happened to people and most had no say. Lore was her say.

Sybil thought of her as a butterfly about to be crushed. She worried too that Lore would grow bored of her, until she decided her reliability was probably what appealed in such uncertain times. In a freer life Lore wouldn't have looked at her twice.

Sybil was aware of Lore's inviting smell of fresh sleep compared to her own sour sweat when she arrived in the attic. Lore wasn't frightened on being woken, as she would have been.

They had to get out, Sybil said. It was too dangerous to stay.

Lore remained lying with her head propped lazily, as though what Sybil was telling her didn't affect them.

A train rattled past as it left Savignyplatz, enough to make the floor vibrate. The bare wooden boards were littered with shimmering buttons dropped by seamstresses in another age. They crunched underfoot.

'Look, I have started a collection.'

Lore scooped up those she had saved. The prettiest and the

best, she said. Veined, milkily opaque, some mother-of-pearl, like sea shells. Sybil started to cry.

She had not been looking to complicate her life by loving a woman. Lore said it was about seizing the moment, not least in the war against men.

'Look where they have got us.'

# 6

Schlegel lived above the old dancehall, Clärchens, in a small walk-up apartment on the top floor of a rundown building in the old Jewish quarter. Its angled windows looked down on a chestnut tree he had yet to see in leaf. He had two tiny rooms assigned through the housing ministry; he suspected his step-father of string-pulling. The novelty of having his own place was wearing thin. At this time of year every freezing return was unwelcoming.

His day had been spent searching for the missing Jewish butchers, starting at the main processing centre in the old synagogue in Levetzowstrasse, where Schlegel discovered everyone in a state of shock, from the arrests and the size of the task in hand. He witnessed chaos and incomprehension, a crush of desperate people like frightened animals, and just one German, a bored Gestapo man standing on an upturned packing crate in a huge and crowded hall, pointing to the left or right. When Schlegel used his badge to speak to a senior organiser, a completely overworked older female Jewish clerk, he had to wait for her to answer a stream of telephone calls, dealing with provision of food or medical emergencies.

'This is a murder inquiry,' he said.

There was no authority to his voice. Why should there be when it wasn't his job and the lot of them were being sent off anyway?

'They leave us in the dark then make us sort it out,' she said.

He showed a list of the butchers' names and presumed they were being held together.

She gave a look of exhausted disbelief. 'You want professions? We don't even have names.'

They had been ordered to house the thousands being held until they compiled new deportation lists from scratch.

Stoffel's pill had made Schlegel alert and unpredictable in a way that left him seconds from shouting. Its buzzing gave an accelerated clarity that was like running ahead of himself, a not unpleasant feeling, on top of which he was dizzy from not eating.

He annoyed himself thinking about the old man's motive when Stoffel had made it clear any old write-up would do.

In fact there had to be two motives. One for the shooting, and one for the suicide.

His irritation was increased by the compulsive fingering of the medal in his pocket.

At Rosenstrasse, a short walk from where he worked, the lobby was crowded with belligerent German women complaining that their Jewish husbands had been taken away when they should not have been.

One woman, louder than the rest, shouted, 'I am a citizen and my husband is protected by that!'

It was true, another said. There was a law.

The staff on the desk were unable to cope. One broke down.

Schlegel saw everyone was afraid, including the strident ones.

When he left others were starting to gather outside the building, forming a small but angry protest. Such things were unheard of. Schlegel wondered how long before troops were sent in.

The last centre he went to was in the street next to his. He walked past most days on his way to work without a second thought. He saw now there were bars on the windows.

He drew another blank on his butchers.

A male clerk, feistier than the rest, looked at him askance for even asking.

'It's a murder investigation.'

The man gave an incredulous hoot.

'A flayed body,' Schlegel insisted, knowing how unbelievable that sounded. He annoyed himself again by blushing. With his hair and pale complexion it was very obvious. The clerk appeared confused on his behalf.

He was fingering the medal again.

It was long dark by the time he got back to the apartment. The communal heating was off. He had no food but lacked the energy to go out, despite his growling stomach. Stoffel's pill was wearing off, leaving him listless and fuzzy.

Four dead bodies in one day, including the woman who had jumped from a balcony in the music hall on Mauerstrasse, one of dozens of temporary assembly centres, lying in the foyer, with a coat hastily flung over, stringy legs sticking out, one shoe missing.

The old man in his hat. The warden with his coat half-on. The flayed torso devoid of any human aspect. Five corpses, if he counted the one not seen, reported during the roundup. It was unbelievable, considering he shouldn't have been called out by Stoffel in the first place.

File the reports, have done and on Monday go back to his safe desk job.

He emptied his pockets, removing the old man's medal, notebook and key. He took off his gun, which he hated.

He picked up the notebook for want of anything better. The

handwriting was cramped and tiny, the arrangement of the letters tight and sinister, as though the man had allowed the angriness in his brain to spill directly onto the page. Doodles filled the margins, black scribbles, angry crossings-out, strange fractures, skulls. They were a mess, yet strangely professional and abstracted, making them hard to read. Like the handwriting, they contrived to be both meticulous and explosive.

'They give us nothing,' he read. 'Everything is filtered through our own associations and community organisations, which leaves us nagging and quarrelling among ourselves. They kicked us out of our homes. The revised tenancy laws certainly did their job. They register us. They rehouse us in impossibly overcrowded conditions where we forever squabble for the slightest advantage and space.'

Schlegel didn't usually think about such matters. He didn't have to.

He read on. 'Better, please, if you go now. Thank you for your assistance. The dog has teeth. We have yet to see them. But we shall.'

The entries grew sparser, the doodles scratching through the page.

Towards the end the tone changed.

'I have long ceased to exist, except as a husk, pausing only to note with heavy heart that suffering makes beasts of us all. Otherwise my days are filled with idle infatuation; the pathetic fantasies of an old man. Such beauty condemned. The nape of the neck. The turn of the hip. The delicate furrow between nose and lip (is there a name for that?).'

There were other mentions of this unnamed woman.

'A vision of radiance that only saddens. I see her wearing too many different outfits; she should be careful not to get reported.'

The last entry, in a shaking hand, was barely legible. 'I would rest my head on her bosom and die content. Other than that there is nothing to live for. Ten years of terror and we are dust already, waiting only for our bones to be ground, flesh reduced to the thinnest parchment, the spirit long departed. They have kicked the shit out of us.'

Schlegel didn't care to think about the old man because it forced him to think about himself. His cultivated neutrality put a lid on everything and the commentary running through his head distanced him further. It said: always look outwards, never inwards. It told him: this is you being plausible; this is you appearing engaged; this is you laughing, as you are supposed to, with that idiot Stoffel, throwing back your head and baring your teeth.

Music drifted up from downstairs. They would be dancing; he didn't.

He could not shake off a sense of personal crisis, as though within the morning's events lay a message. The accident of his being called out, the evacuation, the old man putting a bullet in his head, the woman telling his fortune, all seemed to be saying he was so far adrift he may as well not be there.

Were they telling him it was time to go and the old man's death was a sign to join him? He had thought about it, often.

Schlegel tested the barrel of his gun against the underside of his chin, in imitation of the old man. The fortune-teller had more or less told him his life wouldn't be worth living.

Too serious about everything else, he always lacked the resolve to end it.

He threw the gun down in disgust.

The old man's medal seemed both to berate him, for his funk, and to be telling him he should investigate the mystery of its owner's suicide, as a way of bringing him back to life.

Sometimes Schlegel thought of himself as a Lazarus figure. No one in the Bible had asked Lazarus how he felt on his return from the dead. What was the point when there was nothing come back for?

He picked up the gun again. His life teetered in the balance, between following the old man into the great nothing and asking that simple and most dangerous question: why?

# 7

The house lay deep in silence, the only sound the scuff of her cautious tread as she felt her way upstairs. None of the block's communal lights worked. Sybil could not tell whether the building had been evacuated or some residents remained hiding. The enveloping darkness, blacker than outside, made it feel like her eyelids had been stitched shut.

On the third floor the moon came out briefly, bathing everything in a barely perceptible silver. The door to her apartment was wide open.

She felt her way inside, sparing her torch, and sat on her mother's unmade bed, thinking about obligation, worry and how they didn't get on.

She still couldn't believe they had made a clean sweep. There were always exemptions. Her mother had important clients, top people, influential men who valued her service. In the current euphemism, she knew people and, unlike Metzler, was a survivor.

Sybil looked in pathetic secret spaces to see if her mother had left a message. Finding nothing, she went down the corridor to Metzler's flat. She had never seen inside. It was like looking in a mirror: the same troubled rooms with their fusty residue of anxious sleeplessness and worn nerves, constant bickering and shame brought about by a demeaning lack of privacy. Clothes strewn around, half-packed suitcases.

The changing laws had taken away with remorseless logic until only the people were left; then they took them too.

Sybil stood in awe of the power capable of sucking them out of their lives.

When her torch died she stood in the dark, weeping. She wanted only to lie down and pretend there might be such a thing as a lazy afternoon, or holidays, with her and Lore lying around in bed then stuffing so much food into themselves that clothes had to be loosened.

Several vehicles pulled into the courtyard, followed by doors slamming.

Sybil daren't leave now.

They worked systematically, starting downstairs, checking apartments. Somewhere in the distance a child gave a long wail. Sybil heard them move up a floor, followed by another set of vehicles arriving. A man with an overbearing manner shouted, demanding to know who was there. Boots clumped upstairs. The man announced the block was off-limits and they were sealing all apartments.

A woman told him to stop shining his flashlight in her face and said they were social workers, sent because mothers had been arrested at work and children left behind.

The man threw the women out, telling them any more children would be forwarded to the collection centres.

The night became full of the sound of hammering.

Sybil stood fearfully by Metzler's front door. The building's only exit was on the ground floor. The fire escape to the roof had long been nailed shut.

The banister guided her back down. Sybil was congratulating herself on her nerve and luck holding when the telephone rang and the block warden's widow emerged to yell someone was wanted. Sybil watched the woman's torch beam flashing around until it landed on her face and remained there, followed by an ear-piercing scream.

She launched herself, aiming for the torch, hit a cushion of flab, barged the woman aside, and, heart pounding, stumbled down the corridor as she had after the shooting, passing where she had been sick. She ran out of the building into the icy night, only to find her exit blocked by the arrival of another set of vehicles. Behind her men's boots rang in the corridor as they gave chase.

Sybil thought of the bins as the only possible hiding place, then remembered the boiler room. It had been a common trysting space. A key was kept hidden behind a loose brick.

She felt her way along the wall. The vehicles' cowled lights were like angry slits, too dim to reach her. The men in pursuit ran out into the yard.

Darkness masked Sybil as she fumbled for the key, cursing inwardly until her shaking hand found the lock and she cracked open the door and slid into pitch-black.

Feeling awkward and foolish, stuck alone in his apartment after deciding not to blow out his brains, Schlegel felt compelled to go downstairs to the dancehall where he drank one beer, listened to a tinny combo, saw sad people guiding each other around the floor and watched a woman sitting on her own. She was not so young but still beautiful and looked around as if waiting for someone, in between accepting invitations to dance. He would have asked, had he been capable.

The whole thing should have been plain, yet wasn't.

The old man's diary also made reference to a palm-reader who told the fortunes of senior Party members, who must be the woman he had encountered.

And the old man's vision of radiance, was she the daughter

mentioned, whose name had not been crossed off the arrest list?

The puddle of vomit at the scene of crime suggested the shootings had been witnessed. That much he'd told Stoffel. Was this witness the old man's mystery woman?

Todermann. Schlegel did not recall any first name.

The palm-reader had said he was different. Not in any interesting way. If he were honest with himself, he found the world a bewildering place.

One side of him decided nothing was worth the bother.

Yet back in his rooms he wrote: Murder is a single-minded business.

And next to it: Suicide is a single-minded business.

And after that: The two don't usually go together.

Schlegel looked at the medal again, then the book. Some pages had been removed, so neatly sliced that their absence was almost undetectable.

That night he dreamed of sheep's bells and dusty roads, somewhere he had never been, a biblical landscape, he decided, even as he dreamed. The sheep moved in comfortable formation, led by a goat. In these days of hunger, he often dreamed of animals. Hogs. Bullocks. Pheasant. Plump turkeys. Horses. Perhaps his stepfather ate his knackered mares. He dreamed of the knife slash to the throat of the sacrificial offering and woke in the night with a start, to find himself drenched in blood, then woke again properly, aware of being famished before even fully awake, soaked from his own sweat.

When the men came and searched, Sybil squeezed herself into the narrow space between the cold boilers, hardly daring to breathe, until they made themselves nervous with talk of rats and left.

Listening to the relentless hammering coming from the

block, Sybil drove herself half mad imagining it was her own coffin being nailed shut.

A few people found hiding were brought down and made to stand in the freezing cold until there were enough to fill a vehicle. Sybil listened to cries of despair and the occasional blow, followed by a scream of pain.

She hugged herself in an effort to preserve her body heat and reviewed her dwindling options. She was supposed to see Franz's forger but still had no idea where, or if the arrangement still stood after yesterday's arrests. According to Franz, the man had some kind of job with the Jewish Association, which meant he was probably protected, though who could say any more.

She needed Franz. The gamble seemed worth the risk of crossing town, as he was their only hope.

Sybil sensed dawn as an almost imperceptible grey under the line of the door. Her exhausted body gave no indication of having slept, though she must have because the hammering had stopped. She cracked the door open, her joints so stiff she could hardly stand. The yard was empty.

The warden's apartment was silent. The man's blood was still on the wall, dried to brown. Sybil left by the back way. Reaching the street, she experienced such giddy relief she thought she might keel over.

At the station there were telephones. Sybil called the hospital switchboard, which put her through to the night orderly room. She was in luck. Franz was there.

She spent the journey fighting panic, however much she told herself patrols wouldn't operate so early on the week's one day of rest. At Westkreuz a returning night-shift piled in and fell into a collective stupor. At Kaiserdamm two soldiers with rifles got on and Sybil had to make an instant decision about whether to get off. When one smiled she saw they were little more than boys. When she reached her stop they stepped aside. Their greatcoats smelled of mothballs. The walk to the hospital took ten minutes. Empty streets played havoc with her mind. There were only main roads, which left her exposed. She imagined patrols appearing from nowhere. She heard police sirens she was certain were coming for her.

Franz was waiting at the back by the kitchens. He gave her a salute like they were old comrades, which they were, in a way, although they had not kept in touch. He looked exhausted and wore scruffy overalls when he had always been such a sharp dresser. Sybil had once made him a double-breasted suit of which they were both especially proud, with a nipped waist and flattering trousers. He was thinner now, sallow, cheeks hollow, the spark dimmer.

She confessed she was at a loss to know what to do about his forger. She had spoken to the man once, the day before the roundup, on the direct number Franz had given her, along with a name so common she thought it almost certainly false.

'What did you say?'

'What you told me – that our mutual acquaintance Rosamund Hecht wished to invite him to her birthday party.'

'And?'

'He said he had heard. It was at two o'clock on Sunday and it was necessary to bring a large present as it was an important birthday. I said I wasn't sure where to come or how large the present should be. He said that was for me to work out.'

She asked Franz how well he knew the man.

Franz gave a dismissive suck of his teeth. This is going badly, Sybil thought.

'It doesn't work like that. People keep everything separate now.'

'What should I do?'

The blatant way he stared left her uncomfortable.

'Go to the Association's headquarters in Oranienburger Strasse at the time he told you. Ask at the main desk if there are any messages for Fräulein Hecht.'

Sybil thought she should have been able to work that out for herself.

'Even so, you can't walk in there without a pass.'

'It's a lesson. You are on your own. I know only what I have told you. If you want to find him so badly you will work out a way. That's how it is. He knows that too. No one can afford to make it easy any more.'

On the train back, she realised her mother's suitcase had not been in its usual place by the chest beside the bed. The luggage left in Metzler's apartment indicated that their owners had been forbidden to pack. Only now did it strike her that her mother's possessions, including her Tarot cards, were gone.

# 8

Schlegel spent Sunday at his mother's, for the sake of a hot bath and a couple of square meals. It was a kind of normality he detested, but never enough to stop taking advantage of its comforts. This is you being hypocritical, said the voice in his head. Why not; everyone else was.

His mother was by contemporary standards horribly rich, with a big house in Westend. She drove herself around in a Hispano-Suiza, claiming that managing without a chauffeur was her contribution to the war effort. Schlegel's stepfather came from a family that manufactured ball bearings, fitted into almost every conceivable moving part, on top of which he had made a fortune on the stock market.

Schlegel's real father had been a Roman Catholic. His earliest memories were of being taken to Mass in Shanghai. His mother was English. It was an unusual alliance at a time when Germany and Great Britain had been at war for three years. Schlegel was the single result of the union, born 1918.

His mother was what she called English aristo, her mother half-German, a reflection of the complex intermingling of Anglo-German minor royalty. His father had been a civil official. Schlegel remembered only bay rum in jet-black hair, a pair of monogrammed brushes in a dressing room, cheeks that smelled of shaving soap, and polished shoes, black in the week,

47

brown otherwise. His mother was always vague about what he did. 'Something terribly boring, darling.'

His father's subsequent whereabouts were almost never discussed, apart from his mother claiming he had gone to Argentina and was possibly dead. There was no death certificate, only a report of him having drowned, which had been passed on by the embassy in Buenos Aires.

'In a river,' his mother said, as though such an end were somehow vulgar. 'And not even fishing.'

Schlegel could not decide to what extent his mother and stepfather were really married: the separate bedrooms; her society life; his racehorses, which took him away most weekends. He was a strange man, rather anonymous, not unlikeable, who rarely ventured an opinion. Unusually he was at home that Sunday, closeted in an enormous study where he spent a lot of time on the telephone.

Schlegel was sitting with his mother in the morning room. She had got up late and was eating breakfast and sucking a sugar lump – a luxury in itself – for a hangover.

They were briefly joined by Schlegel's boss, Arthur Nebe, head of criminal police. His mother pulled a face when he was announced.

Under normal circumstances of rank and order, Schlegel would never have had to address Nebe, being so far beneath him, but Nebe was bound to acknowledge Schlegel because his stepfather was one of his oldest friends.

Nebe wore his uniform even though he was off duty. He ostentatiously kissed Schlegel's mother's hand.

'Dear Arthur,' she said.

Nebe smoothly made excuses to join Schlegel's stepfather. Once he was gone and over cups of Darjeeling, which was brought in by a complicated smuggling process involving

Japanese diplomatic immunity, his mother told him that Nebe had a reputation as a playboy, which he knew; that Frau Nebe remained invisible, which was certainly true as no one had ever seen her; and that Nebe was referred to behind his back as Top Dog, which Schlegel hadn't known.

'Why?'

'Pedigree looks and attention to grooming.' She took another sugar lump from a silver bowl. 'Arthur has a very large nose, what one might call in certain circles a real Jewish conk.'

Schlegel conversed with his inner voice, which said, this is you stuck with your mother who always insists you behave more like friends.

She subjected him to her full range. The sniggers. The smut. The gossip. The peals of laughter. The risqué. That bitch Riefenstahl. Wallace Simpson as a sexual contortionist. Those ghastly Mitfords. His mother's breakfasts were like runway rehearsals for her in later full flight. If nothing else, she always turned up immaculate and fully rehearsed. Even in a dressing gown she made sure her hair and make-up were perfect.

Schlegel pointed out how she had kept the English habit of putting her butter on the plate first rather than spread it directly on the toast.

'You can hardly call this toast. They barely seem to know what toast is.'

Schlegel knew Nebe had a fondness for summoning underlings by telegram, usually to the Adlon, and stiffing them with extortionate drinks bills.

'I do find his style rather too American,' his mother said. 'All that eating out, staying in hotels, even here in town, with rooms taken by the hour for his secretarial flings.'

Schlegel added that Nebe was known to go to the Fatima club, whose novelty feature was interconnecting telephones on all the tables.

49

His mother rolled her eyes. 'So American. Is he seen talking on the telephone?'

'Yes.'

'In uniform or out of uniform?'

'I have no idea. Out, I suppose.'

'Uncomfortable in a civilian suit, I would imagine. He would have been talking to a call girl.'

'How do you know?'

'They're all call girls there.'

'That's just another of your sweeping statements.'

'He talks disparagingly enough about you.'

He couldn't tell if this was her mischief or true.

'They're all such terrific intriguers. None is satisfied until things achieve Venetian proportions. Does any of that reach down to you?'

She was being disingenuous. It was a loaded question. His lack of ambition disappointed her.

Schlegel was reminded of her remark when he found himself standing soon after in the garden for what was known as one of those little talks. Nebe used a cigarette holder, which he held cupped from underneath, a dandy's touch.

Nebe had found him in the morning room and asked for a word. His mother had just gone upstairs to change. Schlegel suspected the timing was deliberate.

Nebe wanted to speak outdoors, which struck Schlegel as unnecessary.

They didn't even walk but stood on the lawn.

Nebe asked, 'Do you think it wise that you should be running around with homicide?'

He made it sound like the choice had been Schlegel's.

It was cold, the grass damp underfoot. Nebe's smoke hung in the still air. A ragged chorus of crows came from the nearby woods. Two gunshots sounded. The crows flew up into the grey sky. Schlegel supposed it was his stepfather seeing what he could bag. The last time he was there his mother said, 'I would rather starve than eat more rabbit.'

'Tell me about this flayed body,' Nebe went on. 'What did it look like?'

'Like something out of a butcher's shop.'

'Any closer to finding the Jews that did it?'

'No one has got around to compiling their lists.'

'Why don't the bloody Jews just use the arrests lists?'

'I don't know, sir, but they were quite adamant about having to do their own.'

'Bureaucracy! Nobody's happy until everything is done twice. What's with the other case? Stoffel tells me you are writing the report on that too.'

Schlegel said the only outstanding feature was why the block warden had been shot.

Nebe appeared to find that funny. 'Because most of them are ghastly little tinpot dictators.'

It was an odd statement. Was Nebe being critical in a wider sense? Was he making a veiled political remark?

Schlegel saw what his mother meant. Slippery slope.

'Don't waste time on it.' Nebe looked at Schlegel archly. 'It is not as though homicide is your beat.'

'They were short, sir. I had to fill in.'

'Good party, was it?'

He should have guessed. Nebe had spies everywhere.

'That flaying, are you telling me the suspects are all in custody, even if you can't find them?'

'That's right, sir.'

'They'll be gone soon. Save yourself the paperwork.'

He gave Schlegel a light touch on the shoulder to signal their chat was done. Casual superiority was the man's style.

Nebe paused on the terrace as they prepared to go back in through the French windows. 'That double shooting.'

Schlegel said there was a shortage of character witnesses. It was too complicated to explain about the palm-reader. He could picture Nebe's look of incredulity if he told him how the woman had read his fortune in the middle of a roundup.

'Nevertheless, go easy. The man may have been someone's agent.'

Schlegel presumed he meant the block warden.

'No! The Jew. Don't go digging up skeletons.'

'Can you say whose agent, so I know where not to dig?'

Nebe became vague. The question went unanswered. His gaze was that of a born dissembler, leaving Schlegel uncomfortable at the prospect of being drawn into his web. The floated initiative, rather than anything resembling a straightforward order, was typical.

If the old man had shot himself because he had been spying on his own people that changed everything.

# 9

They were on the S-Bahn to Börse for Oranienburger Strasse, passing the giant flak tower, followed by the street camouflage, hung like circus safety nets over main thoroughfares, as if waiting to catch something. Sybil was more than usually aware of the money belt strapped to her waist. Life from now on would become a series of erasures, eaten away by the constant gnawing in the pit of the stomach.

She whispered that she was for abandoning the meeting. They should get off. It was too dangerous. Too much had happened.

The train stopped at Tiergarten. Most trees were gone, cut down.

Sybil saw how useless her previous way of thinking was. Untrammelled imagination was of no use now. Everything had to be stripped down. Raw animal instinct was needed. Their bodies had to become like antennae that learned to calculate the exact moment when to cross a road or leave to avoid getting caught.

Lore whispered, 'We take a look. Too dangerous, we leave. Don't worry.'

They became synchronised after that. Sybil knew Lore would get off a stop early. Lore seemed to enjoy the risk.

She made them wait at a bus stop across the street from the Association, housed in an old synagogue whose dome was a local landmark. They watched for ten minutes. Those allowed in and out wore a special armband which they didn't have. When one young man left the building Lore set off after him.

Once around the corner of Auguststrasse she approached the young man, gave her most charming smile, and explained what they needed.

He wanted to know what was in it for him.

Lore pointed at Sybil and said, 'My friend will show you a nice time.'

Lore winked at Sybil and Sybil winked at the man.

Lore said, 'For two minutes of your time.'

When he agreed and went off Sybil asked, 'Why him?'

'He was the first one that looked enough of a mug.'

The young man returned with an envelope addressed in the name of Hecht, inside of which was an address to the south towards Kreuzberg in Lindenstrasse. Sybil thought it about a thirty-minute walk.

When the young man asked for his reward, Sybil surprised herself by telling him to fuck off. Her language shocked her as much as her decisiveness.

Ten minutes later they were laughing about it.

Lore said, 'Look at all the couples out on their Sunday stroll. That's us.'

The address turned out to be a gramophone shop. This being Sunday, it was closed. Sybil feared a trap. Lore was relaxed.

'Hang around ten minutes, then we go.'

They left after five. As they did, a tall man of cadaverous appearance approached and pointed down the side of a building to a garage with a door inside a larger one. His gestures were economical. Seeing Sybil hesitate he turned on his heel. She was forced to grab his sleeve to prevent him leaving, which was when she committed them.

The man ushered them through the door after unlocking it. Inside was an empty space, apart from a motorbike and sidecar stored under a groundsheet.

Sybil said, 'There are two of us now. We need papers.'

He asked if she had money. He ignored Lore.

She said she had even though he could produce a gun and take everything she had.

With that he seemed to take pity and asked if she could type. She couldn't.

'I suggest you learn. We can give you papers that say you are a secretary. Then you will always be able to find work. I only need your photographs now. Regrettably there is a fee.'

Lore could have taken the photographs. She had a camera and tripod. Not being told anything seemed to be part of the process.

The man named his price. Sybil complained it was too much. He said she was free to go elsewhere. He did it this way because the police kept a watch on commercial developers.

The man looked away while Sybil fished in her underwear. His shoes didn't quite match. Sybil felt at the limits of her identity, watching two young women on the point of abandoning their previous life, with everything dependent on a squalid and possibly untrustworthy financial exchange.

The man made a point of smelling the money before taking them to a small studio room with a photographer's lamp and a camera on a stand.

Sybil took off her hat and tidied her hair as best she could. There was no mirror. She stared at the lens, trying to look cheerful. Signing away her life, she thought. When it came to her turn, Lore contrived to convey inner amusement.

The man looked like someone with too much on his mind. Could they even be sure they would see him again? They were like babes in the wood.

He said, 'Go to the Café Bollenmüller tomorrow in the lunch hour and I will deliver the developed photographs and tell you where to go for your papers.'

On the way back Sybil thought about what they were committing themselves to. Flop houses and dives must exist, but she knew nothing about that world. She feared she might have to sell her body. If that were the price of survival, would it be so awful? This new kind of thinking surprised her.

Lore said, 'I have an idea.'

# 10

Nebe was back at Schlegel's mother's that afternoon, which was no surprise, for one of her Sunday dos. These select parties, for all their impromptu air, were rigorously planned. Nebe came in uniform again and sat drinking mint tea, chatting to a contingent of select wives, who were allowed to be attractive but not as beautiful as Schlegel's mother.

This time Nebe was the master of cordial distance, raising his tea cup in acknowledgement of Schlegel. They spoke briefly, not about work, as was the form. Nebe's talk was along the lines of 'How are you, dear boy?' as if they hadn't seen each other in months, and 'Doesn't your mother look wonderful?' She did. Svelte and feral, with her perfect figure, however much she complained of being flat-chested.

Francis Alwynd also came. The Irish poet was seen as a big social catch, being wild and mystical, with a romantic background that included republican insurrection and internment by the British.

Schlegel hadn't seen him in a while. He turned up with an attractive young woman.

Alwynd greeted him with a knowing smile and a mock salute. 'It has been far too long. Fine nights we had.'

Schlegel had once been deputed to look after him because he had English when Alwynd spoke no German, other than a phonetic nonsense. They had knocked around together, listening to jazz and getting drunk, until Schlegel decided Alwynd was more interested in his students, bedded in quick succession. The university was almost all girls, and it let Alwynd teach writers banned in Ireland. He told Schlegel he thought he had died and gone to heaven.

He came to the party dressed as usual in a fisherman's polo neck and corduroys. After looking around at the assembled dignitaries he announced in his usual roguish and tactless way that these days you had to go to concentration camps to hear the best jazz.

'Fritz Weiss plays regularly in Theresienstadt and I am reliably told the Ghetto Swingers offer an outstanding form of Nigger jazz without objection from the SS.'

Alwynd grinned and recalled long drunken nights they had spent at his apartment playing and trading jazz records, which young soldiers on leave brought from abroad.

'One came from Amsterdam, remember?' Alwynd reminisced in his distracted way. 'He told us of first-class jazz clubs, with a black music scene from Surinam. Mike Hidalgo was the musician's name, that's right. He had a big German following.'

They had played his records and clicked their fingers, and drunkenly argued over whether Surinam was in the Dutch East Indies or the Caribbean.

Alwynd made a point of including the young woman in his stories. The talk was just skating, Schlegel saw. The real conversation lay in the meaningful looks passing between Alwynd and the girl. He was jealous.

Schlegel thought of the flayed body, the dead man's medal, as he listened politely to Alwynd explain to her how they used to dine together.

'Sometimes we went to Stockler's and sat among the prosperous businessmen and their well-dressed wives.'

Schlegel supposed there was little for Alwynd to do except

fuck and Berlin offered plenty of opportunity with its men away.

'You used to complain about everything being slathered in mustard sauce.'

'*Mea culpa*. Never again. Even the embassies these days are pushed to turn out a decent meal. Alas, no more. Such fine nights.'

His expression grew dreamy. He put his arm around the young woman.

'Time for Francis to lie down. My fondest to your mother. She's busy. We'll slip away.'

His mother was having one of her floating afternoons. Whatever combination accounted for her heightened state, it was a fine balance. Schlegel listened to his stepfather making a date with Nebe to attend the Arc de Triomphe. His horse had come fifth the year before.

'We've never gone much for rice, on the whole,' said one of the wives.

The voice in his head said: Pick up the gun. It makes more sense than this.

His stepfather announced he had a stallion with a terrific tool he was putting out to stud. His mother said the Hungarians were all right if you got enough drink down them.

Later she said, 'You seem more cheerful these days.'

Schlegel could not be bothered to disagree. His diffidence so annoyed her that he made a point of it. 'Your dress looks nice. New?'

'Not so new.'

'I seem to have lost my hat.'

'Not the one from Jermyn Street?'

It had been shipped from London via Switzerland, probably picked up by his stepfather on one of his visits to Zurich. Schlegel wondered why when he couldn't see the difference between a hat from Jermyn Street and one by Mühlbauer.

As for ending up in the RKPA Financial Crimes Office, he dimly suspected his career had been taken care of by unspecified spheres of influence and if forced he would say his stepfather had gone to his old pal Nebe and asked him to help out with his troubled stepson. As a teenager Schlegel had gone through what was referred to as his delinquent phase, culminating in arrest for shoplifting in KaDeWe, which his mother considered not quite beneath her as a department store.

Prison was avoided. He was ordered to get a proper haircut and be examined by a psychiatrist. He was sent away to construct roads and learned to cope with being picked on and beaten up because he was thought Jewish, being circumcised.

He was supposed to enlist in the cavalry after that but failed the medical.

When he told his mother he was working in financial investigations she tried not to sound disappointed. 'I suppose you always were good at figures,' she said, which was not true.

That afternoon, as he was leaving, a woman said to his mother, 'I have a seamstress near Savignyplatz. I suspect she's a Yid.'

'Can you tell?' his mother asked in her most offhand manner.

'I couldn't care either way. It's not my job to catch them but she does lovely work and I would be sorry to lose her.'

# II

Francis Alwynd's visitors were a surprise, to say the least. The girl Lore had been one of his brighter students, keen on Lawrence and Joyce. She spoke good English and professed to share his love of poetry. She remained one of the few he hadn't had. Her sexual preference did not extend to men, which made her all the more desirable. The other young woman he knew only enough to assess her as amenable.

He was drily amused to find them standing like a couple of waifs on his doorstep. Because he encouraged students to drop round he was used to the unexpected. To most he appeared an exceptionally privileged figure, with his own large apartment overlooking Hochmeisterplatz.

For all his otherworldly air, Alwynd viewed his sexual liaisons as commercial transactions. Frequent food parcels from Ireland were a luxurious booty that gave him bartering power in his conquests. He dressed the transactions with good manners and consideration. The rich English woman with the dull manufacturer husband, redeemed by his love of racing, whose guest he had just been, called him a soft predator, offered in admiration.

Lore knew the back of Alwynd's apartment had a servants' room, with its own stairs. Alwynd was casual about letting people stay, for reasons of loneliness, she suspected. She also had a hold over him because those he used were quickly discarded. He had confided to being homesick, in spite of loathing everything about the old country. He said the Germans had produced nothing of note since the nineteenth century. The current regime accommodated him well enough as it let him teach writers banned in Ireland. His own references, he cheerfully told Lore and anyone else who would listen, lay in pagan myth, early Christian mystics and the sexually explicit.

He was a head taller than his visitors. He stood barefoot, in a shirt hanging out and trousers. He could see the other woman had guessed he had a visitor in his bed. He was done with her for now, which left him in the mood to entertain.

'Well, it has been a long time. Come in. There may even be some real tea. I have supplies from home.'

Because he always spoke English, which Lore had to translate, Sybil tended not to go when Lore and Alwynd met, thinking herself a burden. There was something else. Alwynd was a tall, big-boned man with a shock of dark hair, handsome in a brooding Celtic way, whose faraway look occasionally snapped into a gaze of blatant sexual demand.

Lore had told Sybil they should come clean with Alwynd, admit they were Jewish and ask if they could stay a few days. She suspected Alwynd had guessed anyway. In discussions on Joyce's *Ulysses* he had repeated several times, 'Of course, Leopold Bloom was a Jew. Yes, that's right.' He said it took a brave man to make a hero of a Jew in Ireland.

Furthermore, Alwynd accepted that he and Lore had poetry in common, which he considered rare, and declared he cared nothing for social convention. The man marched to the beat of his own drum, Lore said, on top of which he was always laughing at Germans as sticklers for social observance.

Sybil sat on an upright sofa and wondered how Lore would broach the subject while Alwynd made tea in the kitchen, and talked easily between the rooms, saying only the other day he had been thinking about one of his conversations with Lore.

Sybil found the easy pleasantries grated after the tension of the last forty-eight hours. She considered Alwynd probably indiscreet and tactless. She was prepared to defer to Lore, who said Alwynd was indifferent to racial and religious distractions, apart from hating the British. His propaganda broadcasts against them made him something of a local star, otherwise he seemed studiedly indifferent to his past, the war, and whatever woman he was with. There were stories of an abandoned wife back in Ireland.

Alwynd served them awkwardly, his social skills minimal. He was still barefoot. He said to Lore, 'I expect you're short of a bob or two.'

'Always, and hungry too.'

Alwynd looked aghast and said, 'My God, there's cake!'

He disappeared to the kitchen and returned with mismatched plates on which lay thick slices of moist, compressed fruit cake.

Lore protested that she hadn't intended for Alwynd to feed them. Alwynd waved his hand, and said he couldn't stand cake anyway.

Sybil had never seen anything so succulent and inviting. It would be sweet too. She almost dared not start eating for fear of cramming it in her mouth.

She looked at Alwynd in awe and asked if it had real sugar. Alwynd's sparse German seemed to extend to understanding her.

'Sugar or golden syrup,' he said, amused by her reaction. 'And dried fruit too. Wednesdays at school was a half-day and you could order a packed lunch. You used to get a slice of the same cake wrapped in greaseproof paper. It was called sudden death.'

Lore as usual had to translate for Sybil's benefit.

Alwynd added, 'Schoolboy humour.'

He seemed as entertained as if he were watching a show as

they inspected, savoured and devoured the cake, telling each other to take it slowly, making noises of ecstatic appreciation with every mouthful, then using their fingers to wipe the last of the sticky residue off their plates.

The effusiveness of their thanks became embarrassing, until Alwynd said, 'Drink your tea now, children,' and Sybil appreciated he was older than he looked, perhaps forty, a man who made sport with girls half his age.

Alwynd slopped his tea into the cup's saucer and drank from that, with an air of childish disobedience. The sight saddened Sybil. Individual flourish and such civilised values as eccentricity were beyond them now. She thought she heard the click of the front door, signalling the departure of Alwynd's unseen guest. He caught her eye and smiled, whether shy or superior she couldn't tell.

He got up and put on a record whose strange primal rhythms were unlike anything Sybil had heard.

'Proper jazz,' he said. 'None of that anodyne rubbish with strings that passes for it here.'

He turned to Lore and said, 'I get asked to write quite a lot, for newspapers and so forth. Rubbish, really. What a tyrant Cromwell was. How the British invented the concentration camp. Not rubbish as such, but they accept any old nonsense. You could say the Welsh are all three-legged and no one would question it. The point is the text has to be translated. The real point is it has to be written in the first place. You see, I'm thinking you could write it for me then translate it so we can bill them for the cost of writing and a translation fee. Split fifty-fifty. The girl who did my translations is no longer around.'

Another one bedded, another gone, thought Sybil, presuming Alwynd escaped unscathed from his romantic encounters.

'Feel free to stay the night,' he said, and Sybil saw he had known what they'd had in mind. 'Plenty of room at the back.'

The music progressed in a crescendo towards the end.

'That old "Black Bottom Stomp",' Alwynd said, looking at Sybil provocatively. He stuck his hands in the pockets of his baggy corduroys. Lore looked around happily. Sybil wasn't sure. She had seen how Alwynd looked at her with that dangerous and attractive combination of merry glance and hard stare.

## 12

Schlegel made his way to headquarters for his turn as night-duty officer. The appointment was supposed to be by rota but seemed to include him a lot more than others. Stoffel almost never did it. The job only mattered in an emergency, which usually didn't happen, leaving the desk sergeant in charge and the duty officer free to help himself to an empty cell.

He told the sergeant the shop would be open for half an hour if anyone wanted any business. Shop was the name of the storage cellars for requisitioned goods, a long narrow space that ran under the street. As a lot of Schlegel's cases involved black-market confiscation, he was expected to sell on to colleagues at bargain prices, a standard arrangement from before his time.

The boring stuff was named for the record and put in store. The deal included a warehouse in Moabit where anything large of interest was got rid of on the quiet, with the profits going to what were known as office emergency funds. Smaller stuff – watches, jewellery and personal effects – was available at nominal rates for staff to sell at a profit. The briskest trade was in bicycles, liquor and tobacco, for which they could get four times what they paid.

Many of the night staff came down to the shop. Some shuffled in sideways, with a wink and a nudge. Others were brazen, producing their lists. The most unusual items he sold that night were a stamp album and fifty new umbrellas.

\* \* \*

Schlegel telephoned the main Jewish administrative office in Oranienburger Strasse. He was right to think that in the present crisis they would have a night staff. A woman eventually answered, sounding elderly and frail. He heard her intake of breath at his mention of criminal police.

He said he needed someone to look up a dead man's work record.

She said the office was closed until the morning.

'We can either sort this out between us now or I will have to send someone over, which will be less pleasant for everyone.'

The woman agreed to do it. Just the one card, he said.

He called back and was told Metzler used to have a job with the railways.

'Until three months ago.'

'As what?'

He was listed as a cleaner. Schlegel asked for dates.

'January 1941 until November 1942.'

'And before?'

'He was originally a teacher.'

It didn't say where. Wasn't there supposed to be a full record?

'There should be. Most have two or three cards. Perhaps his are lost.'

'And after last November where did he work?'

'At the slaughterhouse.'

'Excuse me?' asked Schlegel, not sure what he was hearing.

'At the beginning of December he was moved there.'

His skull tightened. Coincidence? Or a connection to the flayed body?

He asked whether the card gave a job description of Metzler's last employment.

'He is first listed as a bookkeeper. But that has been crossed out and someone has written cleaner.'

'Whereabouts?'
'It just says shed twenty-seven.'

Schlegel went upstairs to the room where maps of varying sizes and sorts were kept. Maps of sewers and waterworks; maps of the city's electricity and gas grids; insurance maps, showing which buildings had firewalls; small-scale maps and large ones. The first he looked at showed mainly the railway yard, like a huge artery.

He came across an atlas-like book devoted to the district, published to coincide with the completion of the project fifty years earlier. The pages had public spaces in green, residential in ochre, the commercial zones in grey and the slaughterhouse, including the yards and railway, which took up several pages, in pink.

Scale drawings of the long halls showed how the animals were sent on precise, individual routes, into holding bays and pens and corridors leading to their respective slaughterhouses, after which they were taken through to the adjacent cleaning and butchering sheds, to be turned into inert product in preparation for their final destination, the wholesale commercial market.

The actual slaughter rooms had individual numbered doors. The floor plan showed the separate entrances through which they were driven: 26, 27 and 28. Number 27 was the pork room.

Was that what was meant by shed twenty-seven? Was it where the old man ended up? A Jew sent to work in a pork room; someone had a nasty sense of humour.

The man's tagged key that looked like it belonged to a locker began with a twenty-seven.

# 13

Schlegel worked in a small, gloomy office in Alexanderstrasse, tucked away in a wing at the back of the main building that overlooked an inner courtyard. Its lack of importance was underlined by an absence of any corridor connecting the main building to his, leaving him having to cross the yard in all weathers. A sick-looking plane tree struggled to reach the level of his window on the third floor. In the time he had been there it failed to grow and in summer barely managed to leaf. The outside wall opposite was blank. The office was horribly brown and sunless. The furniture consisted of filing cabinets and a couple of identical chipped bureau desks facing each other, with rolled lids and numerous drawers and cubbyholes. Down the corridor sat the secretary he was supposed to share with others but the desiccated Frau Pelz had taken a huge dislike to him, for reasons he could not fathom. It was impossible to get her to do anything; another addition to his list of what not to talk about to homicide: that he was reduced to doing his own typing.

That morning Schlegel signed off after an uneventful night duty, walked across the yard and went up to his office, meaning to telephone the slaughterhouse before going home, only to find a stranger sitting there. This was a shock in itself, as the room had few visitors, and more ominous because of the man's uniform.

Schlegel thought he must have done something badly wrong to attract the attention of the SS.

The stranger asked if he was Schlegel. He said he was.

'We have been assigned to work together.'

He looked at the man and asked if he really was meant to come there.

'You just said you were Schlegel. What have you done to offend Frau Pelz so?'

'I wish someone would tell me.'

'My name is Morgen. Who's Stoffel?'

'Homicide.'

'He telephoned. He wants you.'

Schlegel was disconcerted by the way Morgen sat there, looking at home. He failed to understand why an SS officer was being assigned to work with him. The man's kitbag in the corner suggested he had come straight from the station. Schlegel wondered where before that.

'Is this yours?' Morgen asked, reaching down to produce Schlegel's hat. It was like watching a conjuring trick.

'Where did you find it?'

'In the locker they gave me downstairs.'

Schlegel stared in astonishment. 'How did you know it was mine?'

'It has your name inside.'

Schlegel turned the hat awkwardly in his hands, thinking the man must have him down for a fool.

'An English hat too,' said Morgen.

Schlegel gave an unnecessary account of the hat, all the while thinking he couldn't even be sure what rank Morgen was. SS insignia were notoriously hard to read, even among the SS.

Schlegel hoped the uniform was more frightening than the man. Morgen appeared neither good-looking nor other-wise, somewhere in between, with hair already thinning on top, a cleft chin, the beginnings of a jowl, round wire-framed spectacles, and a pendulous lower lip that gave him what

Schlegel could only think of as a disappointed way of looking at the world. He suspected the slothful manner was deceptive.

Morgen's ashtray was already full. Schlegel's asthma meant he didn't smoke. He envied smokers the way women leaned in when a light was held. He supposed Morgen about eight or nine years older, thirty-three or -four. He wondered how the man managed to smoke so much with cigarettes in such short supply.

The slither of sunlight began its daily twenty-minute crawl across the blank wall opposite.

Morgen reminded him, 'You have a dead body waiting. Stoffel.'

Not again, he thought.

'Dead bodies are Stoffel's department, not ours.'

'This one has money stuffed in its mouth.'

Schlegel could have ignored Stoffel's request. He was technically off duty but his life seemed to have taken on the illogical air of an unpleasant dream. Morgen insisted on accompanying him.

Schlegel usually took public transport, not being eligible to use what was left of the motor pool. Morgen would have none of that and hailed a taxi. He sat filling the cab with smoke.

Schlegel asked him to open the window. Morgen obliged by lowering it a crack.

Schlegel crossed his legs and was aware of Morgen staring at his shoe. It was tied with a broken lace, long enough only to string through a couple of eyes. Laces and razor blades were among the latest shortages.

He asked where Morgen had been. Morgen returned the question, asking if Schlegel had ever been to Russia.

Schlegel said he hadn't. He was uncomfortable lying, and presumed Morgen could tell. It seemed quite possible that

Morgen had been sent to shake the place up because they were all on the take.

Morgen lit another cigarette, opened the window to throw out the butt and rewound it so the crack was even more infinitesimal.

Whatever else the man was, he was a smoking machine.

A dead man in a long overcoat lay on his back. He had been found on the floor of a large reception room in a substantial ground-floor apartment near the zoo, after local police broke into the already sealed premises, following a report of lights showing in contravention of blackout regulations.

The dead man was tall, over six foot, of sallow complexion and probably in his late thirties. From the neck down he didn't appear much disturbed and his state of repose reminded Schlegel of the way the old man had lain. The shoes had large holes in the soles. Unlike the old man, his hat had fallen off and rolled on the parquet floor.

The only extraordinary feature was the wedge of money spilling out of the gaping mouth. Schlegel had imagined a neat roll inserted like a cork, not stuffed in anyhow, in what looked like a frenzy, leaving the dead man's eyes appearing to protrude in disbelief.

Stoffel, a man rarely surprised, did a double take on seeing Morgen's uniform. Two more men walked in. The younger was Gersten, the Gestapo man from the roundup. Schlegel didn't know his companion, an elderly consumptive with bitten cheeks, who, despite walking a deferential pace behind, had the air of a sadist. Gersten grunted at Stoffel and asked if he was in charge.

They immediately began squabbling, taking up from where they had left off. Stoffel said he was dealing with a murder and had no need of Gestapo assistance.

Gersten said he was there because the apartment was Gestapo property, having been requisitioned.

Schlegel took in the room. It was large and spacious and its owners would have been rich. The walls had been stripped of their pictures, leaving faded spaces where they had hung. Empty bookshelves in glass cabinets indicated a once considerable library.

'What's your theory?' Gersten asked Stoffel.

Stoffel shrugged. A couple of lowlifers had come to loot, prior to the property's contents being sold off. With the place empty it was a safe break-in.

'Presumably the murderer stuffed what he could in his pockets before he left.'

'But what happened?' asked Gersten, looking as though he thought Stoffel could try harder.

'An argument. No honour among thieves. One ends up killing the other. The only real issue is the money.'

He asked if Gersten recognised the man, as he was dead on what was now Gestapo property. Gersten tapped the corpse with his toecap and observed the shoes didn't match.

Stoffel announced to the room that one advantage of everyone going hungry was dead men tended not to crap their pants.

Gersten ignored him. 'Black market, I would say, which puts the ball in your court. You'll find the money is counterfeit.' He turned to Schlegel and said lightly, 'No one can afford these days to donate good cash to a dead man's cake hole.'

Schlegel was aware of Morgen in the background, saying nothing.

Stoffel addressed Schlegel. 'Since you're here, son, go through the man's pockets.'

'Didn't someone do that?'

'Waiting for you, dear,' said Stoffel. 'Be our guest. Bad knee, can't bend down.'

He proffered an old biscuit tin he used to store the dead's personal effects.

Schlegel recognised the fine line between acceptance as one of them and being the butt of their cruelty. He didn't want to appear squeamish, while knowing he could also be seen as weak for giving in.

There was nothing in the coat. Nothing in the rim of the hat. Nothing in the jacket pockets. The jacket was double-breasted and still done up. He wondered what to do about the back trouser pockets because it would mean disturbing the body. He unbuttoned the jacket. The crotch was stained, about the size of a large coin, presumably from a small last involuntary release.

Schlegel grew aware of Morgen standing closer, and he said to Morgen rather than Stoffel that on second inspection the stain looked more like blood.

'Then you'd better take a look,' said Stoffel.

'That's the doctor's job.'

Schlegel stood up, surprised by his decisiveness. He handed the biscuit tin to Stoffel. Stoffel grunted and signalled to the doctor who had been hovering in the doorway to carry on.

Like the rest of them, the doctor smoked. Schlegel watched ash fall and land next to the dead man's nostril where it lay undisturbed. The doctor made a clumsy job of opening the fly.

Blaming his arthritis, he turned to Schlegel and said, 'Do it for me, son. My fingers are too stiff.'

Suppressed sniggers greeted the remark. The doctor's cheeks were a drunk's network of broken veins.

Schlegel knelt down and undid the buttons and parted the waistband. The shirt was in the way, then the underpants. The dark stain was no larger. He separated the fly. The doctor opened his mouth in surprise. The cigarette fell out and landed on the man's crotch.

'For God's sake. Get out of here,' said Stoffel.

The doctor staggered to his feet. He didn't look well.

'And take your bloody cigarette!' said Stoffel.

The doctor mumbled to Schlegel, 'Would you? My fingers.'

Gersten's sidekick leered. Schlegel pinched the cigarette between his thumb and forefinger and passed it to the doctor, who didn't want it. He flicked it aside for someone to pick up. Stoffel was laughing hard as he did.

'Give us a proper look, boy. Tell us what you see.'

Schlegel pulled the fly wider.

Gersten said in disbelief, 'He's got no cock!'

Stoffel found the whole thing side-splitting.

Where the man's penis should have been was a bloody hole. A clean cut at the shaft indicated surgical precision, in contrast to the money stuffed messily into the mouth.

The doctor was about to keel over. Gersten's eyes bulged like the dead man's. The doctor sat down, breathing hard through his mouth. The rest of the crew stood around in varying degrees of disbelief. Only Morgen appeared unconcerned.

Schlegel found the sight not frightening as such. It didn't involve smashed bone or enormous gouts of blood. The disturbing aspect was what these highly personal acts represented, one seemingly spontaneous, the other so calculated.

Stoffel interrupted to ask crudely, 'Have the balls been cut off? Are we talking castration too?'

Schlegel had had enough. He stood up, failing to provide the smart answer Stoffel required. Backchat was seen as essential to the job.

Stoffel told the orderlies to remove the body. Morgen puffed away. Gersten continued to look put out. Maybe he was squeamish. Most of the men were standing protectively with their hands in trouser pockets.

Morgen said, 'You realise the body was probably killed else-where and dumped here.'

'What makes you say that?' said Stoffel, looking not at all pleased.

'There should be much more blood, and it would have been impossible to get such a clean cut if the man had been struggling.'

Stoffel looked unimpressed. 'Strangled here first, I would say, and a sharp knife. What's the point of bringing him here?'

Morgen didn't bother to answer.

Stoffel said, 'In that case you and your albino friend can do the door-to-door.'

Outside Stoffel asked Schlegel, with a poke of his thumb in the direction of Morgen, 'Who the fuck is he?'

'I've no idea. He turned up this morning.'

'More to the point, who does he think he is?'

Schlegel shrugged. Stoffel leaned in confidentially. 'Find out what he's doing here. That's an order. It can't be anything good.'

Schlegel excused himself and went over to Gersten.

'About the old man who shot himself, who telephoned us about the shooting?'

Gersten patted his pockets for his lip salve. 'It must have been a Jewish marshal.'

'The shooting occurred before the area was sealed. We think there was a witness.'

'We had other things on our minds.' It was said in a vague, confiding way.

Schlegel wasn't sure. Gersten, for all his affected air, struck him as a man to be in full possession of the facts.

Schlegel asked if Gersten knew any more about the old man.

'That he worked at the slaughterhouse, for instance.'

Schlegel was aware of Morgen coming over and staring as Gersten said, 'Are you sure? That's not what we heard.'

'Did you know he might have been working for us?'

'Really?' Gersten repeated his act with the lip salve. 'Who says?'

'We've had a tip-off that he was an informer.'

Schlegel wanted to see Gersten's reaction. Informers invariably worked for the Gestapo. Not a flicker, which left him wondering how reliable Nebe's information was.

Morgen appeared endlessly interested in the idea of the dead body turning up in an apartment that had been sealed by the Gestapo, especially if it had been taken there after being killed.

'Why there?'

Schlegel wanted to ask why on earth should he know.

They spoke to the local district warden, who confirmed the original complaint had been over a blackout infringement, an anonymous call. It was the sort of place where people kept to themselves and were quick to inform on any irregularity.

'Respectable, in other words,' said Morgen.

Schlegel couldn't tell if Morgen was being sarcastic.

Once dignified, the area had become shabby and too deathly quiet even for such a discreet address. Few cars were parked out because no one could afford to run them.

They knocked on doors to no effect.

Either people were out or those that were in had nothing to report and were eager to disappear back inside rather than be seen to be talking to the police.

Morgen asked if Stoffel was as obtuse as he looked. Schlegel wasn't sure how much to volunteer and answered economically. Morgen asked about Gersten. Schlegel said he'd only come across him once before.

Morgen asked why Gersten wore his hair so long.

Schlegel suspected he was going to spend a lot of his time telling Morgen that he didn't know.

'Why cut a man's dick off? I've never come across that before.'

'I don't know.'

'What's so funny?'

'Nothing.'

'I don't understand why people laugh when something isn't funny.'

They came across a forlorn message fixed to a tree. A local resident was asking for help finding her lost dog. Morgen said the woman was stupid to have a dog.

'Expensive when there isn't enough food to go round. I hear oysters are in from Holland, as if I can afford them. I suppose you can see cutting off a man's dick being part of a crime of passion.'

'It's not our case.'

'We're the ones knocking on doors. It's also a classic locked-room mystery.'

Schlegel had read his share of detective fiction. 'It's not. The back window was smashed. That must be how they got in.'

The remark earned him a look.

'A man with a mind of his own.'

With Stoffel the remark would have been mocking. Again with Morgen, Schlegel couldn't tell.

They got around to the address of the elderly woman with the missing dog, which she went on about. When they managed to ask if she had noticed anything unusual she knew immediately what they were talking about. Her beloved pet had failed to come home and she had sat up sleepless with worry. There had been noise in the garden a few doors down. She pointed to the back of the crime scene.

'What sort of noise?' asked Morgen, revealing a considerateness new to Schlegel.

The woman reduced her voice to a loud whisper. 'I heard voices, not German. And they had a vehicle.'

'Yiddish?'

'No, not Yiddish, at least I don't think. Yiddish sounds German.'

'What sort of vehicle?'

'Am I supposed to see in the dark? It was pitch-black. Big engine, small engine. They sound the same to me.'

'My goodness, you need handling with kid gloves,' said Morgen cheerfully. 'Just tell us in your own words.'

The woman seemed to be enjoying herself now. She remembered seeing an unprotected light on in the house. 'Which of course isn't allowed.'

Something was being carried that involved a lot of grunting and swearing. She couldn't say how many men there were. More than two, she thought. She had been too afraid to go and look.

'Did you think to call the district warden?' asked Schlegel.

The woman looked nervous, sensing the question could lead to trouble. Schlegel was sure she had reported the blackout infringement.

'What did you think was happening?' Morgen asked.

She was very certain in her answer. Things were being taken out of the apartment.

'Why do that?' Morgen asked.

She grew indignant. 'Fine policemen you are! Rich Jews lived there. But when you go to such places for the auction preview all the decent stuff is gone. They had a piano because the daughter took lessons and you could hear her in summer when the windows were open, banging away at her scales. Tell me that's still there.'

They left her to it.

\* \* \*

'What were they talking?' Morgen asked. 'Hungarian? Romanian?'

Plenty of outside labour came for the work and overtime, according to reciprocal agreements. Morgen thought it unlikely that the woman would have heard a language from any of the occupied territories – Poland, the Soviet Union, Czechoslovakia and so forth – because their workers tended to be locked up at night.

'Norwegian? Danish? Greek?' asked Morgen, in an apparently good mood for the first time. 'I have a theory about the dog.'

They went back to the apartment garden and found it in the bushes, throat cut.

Morgen said, 'Why didn't they take it with them? You would eat a dog these days.'

Neither was inclined to return to the woman as the bearer of bad news. Schlegel saw her watching from her window.

They went back inside as it started to rain, via the back door with its broken pane. Morgen led the way.

'If the body was brought here after being killed they would have taken him in this way.'

Schlegel had a flash of the murder room in the slaughter-house, with its knives and strange drawing. Could the dead man have been taken there to be killed? Or somewhere like it? He had an intimation of other such places. He couldn't get the Jewish butchers out of his head. Another neat, surgical cut. Anatomical.

Even with the apartment stripped, Schlegel could see the place would have been a beautiful home. There would be a lot of competition to become the next tenant. In a few weeks it would no doubt look as it had, with comfortable furnishings, tapestries, paintings and carpets, maybe a piano for some nice little girl of correct breeding; would she play with better timing than her predecessor, hitting each note just so?

Morgen's voice came from down the corridor. 'The fact of the man being left could be seen as a message for its present temporary owners, the Gestapo.'

Then money stuffed in the mouth had to be because the dead man had been paid to talk. He was an informer. Schlegel wondered about his new companion and thought how life had got a lot more complicated in the few hours since his arrival.

# 14

The Café Bollenmüller was a large and dowdy establishment near Friedrichstrasse, crowded with professionals and secretaries having lunch. Outside it was raining hard and the place smelled of damp clothes. Sybil and Lore turned up bedraggled, neither having an umbrella.

They took a corner seat with a street view, which was being vacated as they arrived. It was just an ordinary lunchtime Sybil told herself as she inspected the busy room. There was no sign of their man from what she could see. Newcomers tried to share with them and were disagreeable on being told the seats were taken.

They were waiting for someone, she said, smiling at Lore, like they were meeting for some normal reason.

A waitress came and stood rubbing her leg with her foot. Varicose veins, thought Sybil, whose attention to detail helped her keep her nerve. The black uniform had been washed so many times it had gone grey.

She opened the menu and found a single strand of greasy hair she supposed was the waitress's. Everything had been crossed out until only potato soup and sausage and cabbage remained.

She told the waitress they would order when their friend came.

She kept glancing at the street, hoping to see the figure of the tall man.

Ten minutes passed. Sybil got up and did a tour of the

crowded room, to check in case they had missed him. When she got back Lore was defending the table from other diners trying to take it over.

Sybil sat back down, shrugged at Lore and looked out of the window, which was when she saw.

She leaned forward and whispered, 'Don't turn your head. Take my hand. Act normal.'

She told her that reflected in the shop window across the street she could see the furniture van the Gestapo used.

'Move In, Move Out with Silberstein?' Lore asked.

It was how the Gestapo took people away, in disguised civilian vans. Sybil looked sideways again.

'A car is drawing up in front of the van. Three men in hats and coats.'

'Three plainclothes men in a car can only mean police,' said Lore. She had gone very pale. 'He must have betrayed us.'

'He will have shown them our photographs.'

'He must have been working for them all along.'

The three men entered the restaurant. The tallest one with long hair was clearly in charge. They surveyed the room. Sybil calculated there must be over a hundred in, which gave them a slim chance. She even considered throwing a chair through the window and making a run for it, except the plate glass looked too tough.

The one in charge remained by the door, checking those leaving. His accomplices started going round the tables, clearly knowing who they were looking for, sometimes asking for papers for the sake of inconvenience, sometimes not bothering. They were in no hurry.

Sybil said, 'We have to split up. They will be looking for two of us.'

Was there a back exit? She couldn't remember. She hadn't been in years. They would probably have a man there anyway.

They weren't stupid. Was there anywhere to hide? Cloakrooms. Kitchens. If they stayed they would get caught.

It was a split-second decision.

Sybil said, 'We leave separately. You go first.'

'I don't look like a secretary. They'll stop me.'

It was true, though Sybil resented the inference.

Lore said, 'I stay, you go.'

'What will you do?'

Lore made a show of unconcern.

'Hang around. Have tea. Stroll out.'

The two men were still over the other side of the room, moving among the tables. Sybil calculated maybe three or four minutes before they got to them. She said Lore should get up and go to the newspapers, which hung on wooden rods next to the coat rack.

'Take the *Völkischer Beobachter*.'

'No thanks.'

It was the Party rag Sybil had taken in the café on the morning of the roundup, for the simple reason that she was more likely to be taken for one of them.

'Don't take your hat off. No one will question you if you are seen reading that. It's our only chance. We'll see each other back at Hochmeisterplatz.'

'Wish you luck,' said Lore.

She offered her cheek to be kissed like old friends, then turned at the last moment and kissed Sybil briefly on the lips.

'Till later. Wish me luck.'

Sybil stood and her nerve failed her. The man by the door looked too knowing and imposing. He made a point of talking to those leaving, a comment here and there, checking them out. Sybil went to the toilet instead, to compose herself, aware of Lore reflected in the café's big mirror, apprehensive as she followed Sybil's progress across the room.

Downstairs she sat on the toilet without using it, thinking she might as well give up and wait until they came for her. She pulled herself together, to set a proper example to Lore, went back out into the washroom and stuffed her hair inside her hat as much as possible, to appear less obvious to anyone using the photograph, in which she was hatless.

How transparent and scared the woman in the mirror looked.

She decided to make a beeline for the door, and somehow bluff her way past the man. She would say she was going to see her SS lover. She could even give a name because a woman she had sewn for was married to one.

As she came back up, Lore was walking exposed towards her, on her way to the newspapers. One of the two Gestapo men started to look at her. There was no way to warn her. An insignificant little man in a shabby raincoat stood up and started to walk out, crossing Lore's path. His exit was cut off by the second Gestapo man, who asked for his papers. Lore veered towards the newspapers as the little man panicked and tried to run. She grabbed the newspaper and quickly sat down, gesturing to Sybil that she should take advantage of the altercation. The little man was being wrestled to the floor and thumped.

Most people carried on as though nothing were happening. Some craned their necks and one or two stood to see better what was going on. The man started sobbing.

Sybil walked fast to the exit. The Gestapo man on the door was distracted and held it for her automatically. She thanked him with a brief look; another secretary on her way back from lunch. Their eyes met briefly. She saw them shift from indifference to a flicker of recognition, but the moment was broken by his colleagues shouting to him.

'Your lucky day,' he said in an easy way. 'Catch you later.'

He laughed when she stood rooted to the spot and said, 'Hurry along now.'

Sybil ran out into the rain, losing herself among the umbrellas, dazed with relief. One glimpse of the man's sensuous mouth was enough to warn her his cruelty would be complicated.

Her adrenaline was flowing. It wouldn't last. Doubt already chased at her heels. Had they been betrayed? It made no difference. They were no nearer to getting papers.

Iranische Strasse was four stops and a walk. Regarding Lore, Sybil reassured herself that the Gestapo hadn't been checking everyone's papers and the Party rag amounted to virtually a passport.

At the hospital she went to the kitchen entrance where she found Franz supervising several trucks that were backed up to the door. He said she was fortunate; he should be off duty but had been called back to organise food distribution to the holding centre in Rosenstrasse.

He said he was dog tired because they had run out of the pills they usually took to get them through.

Sybil asked to talk in private for a couple of minutes.

'Two minutes, no more.'

He took her through the kitchens, where huge vats of cooking vegetables smelled like dishrags, to a tiny larder where they had to stand too close.

She said she and Lore had been betrayed or the Gestapo had arrested the man Franz had sent them to. Fearing for Lore's safety, she broke down and was not altogether comfortable when Franz took her in his arms. He said he would try to find out what had happened. Sybil said they still needed papers and were compromised because the Gestapo would have their identity photographs. She asked if there were any way he could smuggle her and Lore into the hospital, even for a few days. She had no idea how realistic their current arrangement was. She couldn't see it lasting another week.

'If Lore or you were ill we might.'

'She suffers from night blindness,' she said lamely.

He asked what if Lore were to break a leg. Sybil thought he must be joking.

'You could pay to have it done. I could do it.'

Was he saying he wanted to break Lore's leg because he had heard gossip about them and was jealous, or was it a sign of how tough everything had got? She regretted having to stand so close, did not want to be held. It felt like he was taking advantage. She stared at the floor, seeing herself on the edge of a strange new area of barter and transaction, in which people were both her friend and not.

She asked Franz if there was any chance of a lift back into town.

'I can drop you near Hackescher Markt. Better still, come and dish out our stinking soup, then you can see if your mother is there.'

Sybil knew she was obliged to look, however much she told herself her mother had the necessary connections to ensure her own safety. But she couldn't be sure. There had been no time to check anything. Her life had felt split since she'd run away from the shooting. Her flimsy belief that her mother had managed to escape now struck her as irresponsible and fanciful.

Franz found a pinafore and a white coat, and as an after-thought plonked a cook's cap on Sybil's head. He promised it was safe because no one asked food distributors for papers and inside there were no Germans.

Thinking of Lore, she hesitated.

Franz said, 'In our situation it is hard not to see danger every-where, but the Germans are actually remote. It's why they don't know what to do with the demonstration. Their fear rules. They themselves are lazy penpushers, worried about making a decision. We are dealing with dross not the elite. The best are away fighting.'

She sat in the cab of the lorry between Franz who drove and another man who kept his mouth shut. After a while she ignored their silence. She had never been driven before in a private vehicle. From her elevated position the streets looked shabby, frighteningly ordinary and remote. An S-Bahn train ran above them as they drove alongside. There was even blue sky.

The cowl running down the middle of the floor of the cab grew warm and vibrated through her shoes. She had to move her knee whenever Franz changed gear.

Even more unbelievable than her being there was what was going on outside their destination. A crowd spilled into the street, reducing the lorry to nudging its way through. Franz returned the many thumbs-up.

They went in the back where a single guard waved them through.

While they waited for a trolley Sybil looked up at the daunting building with its soot-blackened stone. She heard the rumble of the S-Bahn, even with the noise of the protesting crowd. According to Franz, the nearest station had been closed, to discourage people from turning up to the demonstration.

The S-Bahn ran directly from the attic where Lore had been hiding to where she was standing now, yet she could see no connection between the two points in her life. She forced herself to believe that Lore had stayed in the Bollenmüller behind her newspaper until the men left with their trophy catch, then strolled out as cool as you like. The man had seemed amused to let her go, after all.

Franz told her to stick with him. Their entrance into the building was entirely unquestioned, as he had promised. They took a service elevator. They wheeled the heavy trolley into a large assembly room where a long line of forlorn and famished men stood waiting, supervised by marshals. The whole process had to take place in silence. Someone muttered that the marshals were Jews like the rest of them.

The soup smelled like pigswill yet Sybil was so hungry that the prospect of dishing it out and not being able to help herself was torture.

She saw tables and benches and bowls, not nearly enough. This was the case. Most had to stand and dirty bowls were left for others to use. There were no utensils.

The queue shuffled past. The smell of rank, unwashed bodies combined with that of the unpalatable soup. A few tried to ask for news from outside and were shouted at by the marshals.

Sybil developed the habit of sticking her thumb in the bowl and ladling soup over it, just to get a taste between servings. She managed to pocket a piece of bread for later, and asked Franz if they got fed as part of the job.

If there was any left, he said. Her helpings became more meagre.

She saw no women. She supposed they were on another floor. She had thought they would take the soup to the prisoners, pushing the trolley, which would allow her to look properly. Perhaps women were served second.

What would Sybil say if she saw her mother? Worst would be to see her and be unable to talk.

Whenever the chanting started up outside, with the women shouting for their husbands to be returned, some men in the queue stood straighter, but most continued to look dejected, as though they considered the demonstration hopeless.

The marshals pushed off early, leaving her and Franz to feed the stragglers. Sybil's arm ached from ladling.

There was no soup left by the time they were done. She asked Franz to give her ten minutes while he packed up. In the corridor a marshal asked where she thought she was going. Upstairs, she said briskly, because they were short-staffed.

There the real nature of conditions became apparent. Hundreds of silent people crammed into rooms. Franz had said over a thousand. Floors so crowded there was no space to lie down. Befouled air like a physical presence pervaded everything. The stink all over of shit and unclean bodies. Toilets without doors; more queues; a man holding his head in his hands, noisily emptying liquid bowels. All utterly demoralised and demeaning. Part of Sybil was angry that these people allowed themselves to be treated like that. She saw the dead eyes of those who had abandoned hope; with reason.

In the women's rooms Sybil was reduced to holding her nose to stop from gagging. Many were menstruating and had no sanitary towels or the wherewithal to clean themselves.

Although Jews, these people were technically citizens, protected by law thanks to their marriages. And all this within yards of those going about their business, trams and buses, cafés and cinema shows; all dignity lost. Words failed her.

Out in the courtyard she went and crouched in a doorway, hoping no one could see, and wept dry, racking sobs as she devoured her crust of bread.

Franz found her, and seeing the state of her took her in his arms again, saying they must go. She said he smelled of tobacco. He said that for extra day shifts he was now paid in cigarettes because the money was running out. He asked if she would help tomorrow. He could pick her up nearby on Dircksenstrasse to save her the journey to the hospital. Sybil nodded. Everything was like it was down the wrong end of a telescope: her thoughts, Franz, the courtyard.

She was shakily relieved not to have found her mother under

such conditions, however scant the consolation. The fate of those wretches awaited her too if she put a foot wrong. Ten minutes that had seemed like a lifetime left her swearing never to let anyone force her to become so degraded. She would kill herself first.

# 15

'Which of you is Detective Schlegel?'

Schlegel looked up from his desk and saw a thin man of Slavic appearance in the open doorway of the office, with his hand up like he was pretending to knock.

'You have a visitor when I expect you don't have many,' said Morgen, not looking up and doing what Schlegel couldn't tell, apart from endless smoking.

The stranger wore rimless spectacles. His hair was like a black skullcap. He had on a fur-collared coat that Schlegel coveted. The riding boots were in good condition and highly shined.

'Lazarenko.'

'So not German?' said Morgen, again not looking up.

'Ukrainian. Working as a consultant and translator for the Gestapo. I will show you my card.'

The card was printed, with a Gothic typeface.

Morgen ignored it. 'Be our guest.'

Schlegel saw he was going to have to be the polite one. He offered Lazarenko the only spare chair. The man smelled of cheap cologne and had one of those moustaches that failed to grow beyond a faint smudge.

Lazarenko crossed his legs and produced an envelope. From it he took a crumpled strip of paper, which he smoothed out before passing over. Schlegel wondered how he could afford his coat on a translator's pay.

The paper strip was a wage slip from the big paint factory out in Treptower-Köpenick. The amount was pathetic. Schlegel understood why when he saw the payee was Russian. He was rather surprised forced labour was paid at all.

'That's the thing,' said Lazarenko. 'It's notification of wages. They don't actually get the money.'

'Who does?'

Morgen interrupted. 'Their employer, the economic division of the SS, the WVHA, which leases its workforce to the factory.'

Lazarenko nodded.

'Do they get anything?' asked Schlegel, feeling behind.

'A bit of cash each week from the firm's float.'

'Enough to live off?'

'Everything is provided anyway. Food, accommodation, clothing. The rest is down to scavenging, which they are very good at.'

'No love lost between you and them then,' said Morgen.

Lazarenko agreed. Like many of his countrymen he was not a Bolshevik and happy to take sides against its tyranny.

Morgen said he'd had Ukrainians fighting alongside him.

Lazarenko asked where. Morgen didn't care to answer and asked, 'What is this about? You didn't come here to discuss our *entente cordiale*.'

Lazarenko offered an unsteady smile. The obedient under-dog, thought Schlegel, all manners, in perfect imitation of his masters. Lazarenko's problem was the gestures were skewed. He held eye contact longer than was necessary, so it turned into presumptuous staring. The manners looked like a front. The secretive smile, to suggest superior knowledge, was a further irritation.

He offered the pay slip as a possible clue to the murder the day before. 'It was found by local police when they searched the garden.'

'Not well enough to find the dog,' muttered Morgen. He asked to see the wage slip.

'Is it likely? A Russian wandering around a smart suburb at night, miles from where he should be.'

'They are allowed out unsupervised on Sundays.'

'Even so. What's it got to do with us?'

'Inspector Stoffel asked me to address you because he is busy.'

'Smart man.' Morgen sighed. 'And before Stoffel? Just so we know.'

'Inspector Gersten. Local police brought it to his attention and he referred it to Inspector Stoffel because of the homicide.'

'And does Inspector Gersten have any theories?'

'He agrees with me that the Bolshevik-Jewish conspiracy might not be confined to the east and has managed to smuggle agents into Berlin.'

'Is Gersten an expert?' asked Morgen.

'He seems to have considerable knowledge but accepts that I have first-hand experience, so can offer valuable advice.'

'So you are Gersten's consultant?'

'I would like to think so.'

'So who killed the man, according to this theory?' asked Morgen.

'Either a secret gang of Bolshevik Jews that has managed to disguise itself as part of the workforce, or it has teamed up with the last Jews in Berlin.'

'And your grounds for thinking this?'

Lazarenko ventured that many Soviet commissars and party officials had escaped detection by murdering their rank and file and stealing their papers.

'Their ruthlessness and cunning cannot be underestimated.'

He pulled a sad face and produced a wallet, taking from it a small photograph which he passed to Schlegel, who was not prepared for what he saw and quickly passed it to Morgen.

'The bodies included my wife and children,' said Lazarenko. 'Thank God they weren't desecrated. Many were.' Lazarenko raised his spectacles and pinched the bridge of his nose. 'Senseless, senseless mutilation.'

Lazarenko explained how in the Soviet retreat of 1941 Bolsheviks had teamed up with Russian Jews to lay waste and carry out terrible reprisals among the local Ukrainian population. The photograph Morgen was holding showed the results of one such action: a distant view of low foreign houses, a dusty square, plane trees in leaf on a hot day, and a dark stack of corpses, their blood pooled on sandy ground.

Morgen handed the photograph back to Lazarenko and said the Russians were a formidable enemy. Sheer force of numbers made them fearless. And with a history of cruelty too.

Schlegel wondered about Lazarenko showing the photograph. It had sounded a wrong note. It was too shared a moment for a stranger, more a bid for sympathy or attention than sincere. But Morgen seemed convinced. He told Lazarenko his theory made as much sense as anyone's.

'But I am surprised they didn't take the dog, given the skill for scavenging you refer to.'

Lazarenko looked uncomprehending. Schlegel explained. Lazarenko feared they were joking at his expense. His German was passable but Schlegel wondered how much he missed. Once it was clear they were serious, he expressed his relief with a fanning gesture.

Schlegel decided Lazarenko's behaviour seemed to depend less on imitation than copying, without a full understanding of what was involved. He was reminded of the phonetic nonsense Francis Alwynd resorted to when drunk, in the belief that it passed for German. But Alwynd had enough sense of himself not to care.

Morgen told Lazarenko he needed him to come and speak Russian to an old woman, then they would go to the paint factory where he could translate for them. Schlegel thought Lazarenko looked grateful out of all proportion to what was on offer.

Morgen turned out to be an expert scrounger in his own right.

He protested he was not going anywhere without a car. Schlegel said they wouldn't get one.

'That's because you don't drive,' said Morgen. Schlegel wondered how he knew.

The desk clerk in the motor pool couldn't have cared less. He scratched his backside and refused. Morgen asked for a telephone. The clerk pointed to his. Morgen told the switchboard to connect him to SS headquarters in Prinz-Albrechtstrasse. He asked for an extension, gave his name and rank and said, 'What authority do I have here?'

He paused to ask the desk clerk his details. The clerk, nervous at how things were going, reached into a drawer and produced a set of keys.

Morgen said into the receiver the problem was now solved.

The clerk contrived to look churlish and chastened. Morgen told him to fill in the paperwork. He nonchalantly raised his arm, obliging the clerk to stand and return the salute.

The car was the one Stoffel had taken, with the hole in the floor.

Lazarenko suddenly told them he wasn't allowed to travel in police cars. Any more than we are, thought Schlegel. Stoffel would have a fit. Technically it was a pool but Stoffel always got the Opel.

Lazarenko droned on about how his job restricted him to

public transport, for which he had a pass. He produced it, seeming to think they might doubt him.

Morgen said, 'We can always arrest you and throw you in the back.'

Lazarenko waved his hands and Morgen explained he wasn't being serious, however much it looked like he wished he were.

'Have it your way,' he said, and told him which station to meet them at.

They drove in silence, Morgen humming and smoking. Schlegel was no closer to fathoming the man. They passed down a broad road in an affluent section with detached houses, discreetly screened behind trees.

Morgen slowed down to examine this strange, still world and said, 'You have no idea how unbelievable this all looks.'

The business with the old woman took five minutes. Lazarenko spoke Russian and the woman confirmed that was what she had heard on the night.

Morgen said, 'Interesting.'

The woman bestowed upon them an ecstatic look and said her dog had returned. Schlegel and Morgen looked at each other. Lazarenko put his foot in it by saying he thought the dog was dead. Morgen quickly said that they had been talking about another dog. He needn't have bothered. The old girl was away in a world of her own.

'He's sleeping now,' she said. 'Otherwise I would invite you in to say hello.'

They left Lazarenko to his public transport and drove to Treptower-Köpenick. Morgen lit cigarette after cigarette, leaving Schlegel to wonder if the man drove while he smoked or smoked while he drove. When they passed a gang of sturdy, shoeless women working on a building site Morgen grunted, 'Russians.'

Schlegel asked if he didn't like them.

That wasn't what he had said, he replied and asked, 'Did you know you can tell a Jew by the way he walks?'

Schlegel answered carefully that he wasn't that observant.

'Someone said, the other day. Even from behind.'

The Russian whose pay slip it was appeared reeling drunk, so incoherent he could barely talk, and kept clutching his stomach in obvious discomfort.

Lazarenko explained that the man worked with chemicals in the vats, which accounted for his state.

They spoke in the yard beneath an austere gigantic box of brick and glass, constructed in the style of twenty years before. Its main feature was an enormously tall chimney that made Schlegel dizzy just to look at.

The Russian was obviously harmless, probably brain-damaged and certainly too addled to make sense of their questions. The idea of even going to another part of town seemed beyond his comprehension. What would he do there and when would he go? They were marched to work, worked all day, and were marched back.

In his eagerness, Lazarenko appeared to have miscalculated, Schlegel thought. He even felt a little sorry for him, however irritating the man's unctuous aggression.

Lazarenko produced the pay slip. The Russian stared at it and rattled off something that embarrassed Lazarenko.

'Well?' asked Morgen.

Lazarenko said the slip was meaningless. They all threw theirs away. He had no idea how it got where it had.

Morgen asked if that was all.

Lazarenko squirmed and mumbled that the man had said the slip wasn't large enough to wipe his arse with.

Schlegel thought Lazarenko's discomfort was more about making a fool of himself with them. Even if he had been told to follow up on the pay slip by Gersten, Schlegel was sure he had puffed up his own importance.

Lazarenko continued to push hard on the fact that workers were let out unsupervised on Sundays. The Russian spoke fast, his contempt plain.

Lazarenko turned to them, his expression one of impotent anger.

'He's a lying bastard. It's clear. He pretends he stayed at home all day playing cards. He says anyone can confirm that, but that's because he knows they will cover for him.'

Morgen dismissed the Russian and addressed Lazarenko. 'Don't waste my time. You're going to have to come up with something better than this.'

Schlegel watched the Russian staggering off like he'd had a skinful.

Lazarenko, crestfallen, promised more. He hoped they would make a good team yet. Morgen whistled at the sky. Schlegel saw who he reminded him of. It was the actor Charles Laughton. He had been a big star before the war. Schlegel had been with his mother to see *Mutiny on the Bounty*. His mother complained about the actor they used to dub Laughton's beautiful speaking voice into German. It was a quality he shared with Morgen.

Morgen said little on the drive back other than he thought there might be something to Lazarenko's theory. There was more. The underbelly Lazarenko inhabited was riddled with informers. Almost certainly he had come to them as someone's spy.

Schlegel supposed Lazarenko was Gersten's man, sent to sniff them out. He supposed even he, Schlegel, was Stoffel's spy because he had been asked to report on Morgen. He wanted to ask whose spy Morgen was.

Morgen said, 'It would make perfect sense for the Russians to kill anyone they found spying, and be brutal, but I can't see them leaving the money. They're dirt poor. And why transport the body across town?' He added, 'I wonder if Gersten knows Lazarenko calls himself a consultant.'

Schlegel asked whether Morgen was going to carry on wearing his uniform.

'What you mean is, you don't want anyone thinking you are SS.'

*Touché*, thought Schlegel.

'It is the authority with which I am invested,' said Morgen, deadpan, leaving Schlegel wondering about him again. Sometimes he seemed deadly serious, at other times dangerously flippant, as with the sloppy salute to the motor-pool clerk.

'I don't think I have a suit. The moths got them.'

# 16

Night had fallen as Schlegel walked up to Hackescher Markt. He cut under the railway and what sounded like chanting at a football match came from the direction of Rosenstrasse. By the sound of it, the gathering of the few he had seen on Saturday was now a sizeable crowd. They shouted for their men to be released.

As he neared the scene, Schlegel saw that some carried torches. He was reminded of a dutiful congregation at a religious observance. No rowdy drunks sent in to wreck things, which was the usual procedure.

That the police weren't breaking it up meant the situation must be delicate.

They seemed eager to have their story heard, being naive enough to believe anyone among them was sympathetic. They also possessed the certainty of those in the right.

Schlegel presumed a significant armed presence was assembled nearby.

He saw the pale upturned faces of those around him. It had grown bitterly cold again. He sensed doughty women, so wrapped up as to be shapeless; middle-aged and older. An exception was a young woman, who looked up at the building with an expression of almost ecstatic yearning.

A car drew up, sounding its horn. Men got out and went inside. Their arrival set the crowd off again. Schlegel watched the young woman shouting with unwavering fervour.

A long blast on a whistle sounded. Everyone ignored it. A man shouted through a megaphone for them all to disperse.

Silence fell. Schlegel heard a line of soldiers step forward, followed by the snap of rifle bolts. The sound threw him back, and filled him with dread.

The crowd melted away down side streets.

He thought it unlikely they would start firing in the dark, massacring civilians in the middle of the capital. They saved that sort of thing for elsewhere.

Fifteen minutes later the women started gathering again, their silent disapproval palpable.

Schlegel went and stood where he was before, near an advertising pillar. His ungloved hand was freezing in his pocket. The young woman took up her position next to him. She looked defeated, her face pale in the moonlight, her tears frozen to her cheeks.

About a ten-minute walk from where Schlegel was standing in the crowd, another woman sat and waited in the dancehall in Auguststrasse that occupied the ground and first floors of the building where he lived. It was the second evening she had gone and waited there. She had in fact noticed Schlegel on the Saturday night, watching her.

She did not know what the man she was assigned to meet looked like. He, however, knew her from her identity photographs. The arrangement had been made through a go-between, who left a message in a particular café explaining where to go.

The waiting woman, as the photograph for her false papers showed, was still beautiful, if no longer young. It crossed the minds of most men looking at her to wonder what she was like in bed. She had the air of someone who could pick and choose in a way that would make any man feel special.

That may have been the case once. Now life had become a matter of seeking protection, not on her own terms but for survival. She had been an entertainer and actress, not a very successful one. Since meeting the man in the leather coat, with his questionable mouth, everything had become shrouded in fear and uncertainty.

The story in her mind for that evening was she was seeking romantic attachment in exchange for protection, and the obvious excellence of the man's papers. Her hope was to throw herself at his mercy so he would take pity and hide her, in return for being given the ride of his life. She wished him no harm. She would, in the language of romantic magazines, beguile him.

Nothing had happened on the Saturday. She sat in the large room at the back, near the kitchens, with a view of the floor. She got asked to dance and wondered each time if it was him. There weren't many in, apart from pimply youths and aged lotharios, a few soldiers on leave and what looked like a contingent from Prinz-Albrechtstrasse slumming it. For a while she watched the strange young man with stranger white hair staring like he had seen a ghost or experienced something equally unsettling. She thought of asking him for a dance because he looked so lost.

'There is something pleasantly old-fashioned about this place without it being frumpy,' she announced to one of her passing companions. It seemed as though someone were speaking through her, in a voice that came from a different time. 'I suddenly feel like being in another world, compared to outside.'

She was light-headed yet had drunk no alcohol. Nothing else mattered other than dancing for the moment. She spoke more solemnly than usual, with what she believed approached wisdom.

She watched women and girls dance with each other for lack of men. The music was a combination of the over-jolly, schmaltz and sad. The three-piece combo probably had become reduced over time from a proper band; two were old men and the drummer little more than a boy who had trouble keeping the beat. A sad place after all, she thought. A sad life. The movement of the dancers made her think of the rise and fall of the sea, which she had seen only twice in her life. She dreamed of its impossible openness, and of the opportunity to give herself freely, without condition and all the usual romantic and physical nonsense, which was never fulfilled by the fumbling and hasty transaction of fluids, and left her thinking of crude scientific tests and inadequate exchanges of information. However well she had trained her body to respond, her head was a million miles away, like an astronaut looking down on those clumsy, red-faced men who grimaced terribly at the end, and thought their balls were the world and were so proud of their ugly cocks.

When no one came for her that first night she went home. Sundays the place was shut like everywhere and she reviewed her diminishing options. She spoke with two actors she knew. One was in a chorus line and said he was about to be called up. The other, older, of whom she remained fond, held her hand and said all of them at the Schaubühne lived in fear of their contracts not being renewed. The woman could not tell if she was being spurned because she was not as vivacious as she once was, or whether everyone's choice was reduced to having none.

On the Monday evening she returned with a heavier heart. She sat by a yellow stove, on a little platform by the stage.

She feared that the man in question would not come. She would dance with others. She would allow them to buy her drinks this time. They would get her tipsy and she would grow maudlin. She would be barely aware of whatever man was sitting opposite her. She would watch the dancers. The same souls, coming together. She fancied the music would be more sentimental than on the Saturday; the start of another long week. She would wonder about all the people who had placed their glasses on the scarred table top and sat on those chairs. She would think about all the invitations to dance. She would see past and present mix, her mind lulled as she considered the swirl of time and think: This is a place where one can come to forget.

The man watched her dance – noting her distant yearning – and watched her go back to her table alone.

The low wail came from far off, growing louder. Everyone stood in disbelief. Sirens! Air raids had not played a part in their lives for nearly a year. A woman said in wonder, bombers are coming, and a ripple ran through the crowd.

To Schlegel's ears that whooping ululation, somewhere between a lament and a screech, filling the skies with dread, was the most frighteningly modern sound. He wouldn't put it past the authorities to be sounding a false alarm to get the crowd to disperse. Two women discussed how they had better go as it was forbidden to be out during a raid.

Sybil knew she should have gone home but drifted back to Rosenstrasse, drawn by the extraordinariness of the event. The women took her for one of them, offering smiles of encouragement. She took comfort from their toughness and resilience. Men sent off to fight just did what they were told. Their lives were ordered and they were looked after. They did not have to find food or keep everything together. These ordinary women were the real heroes of the war. They gave her hope. She had a clear image of describing the scene to Lore and Lore would not begrudge her lingering.

She left when the troops threatened to move in. She took the train from Friedrichstrasse to Charlottenburg, hurried down streets still crowded with workers going home, ran up the back staircase of Alwynd's apartment, only to find their room empty.

She supposed Lore was with Alwynd but his side was dark too.

She returned and lay on the bed, trying to block any thought of Lore in the hands of the Gestapo.

Her heart shrank when the sirens started. In among their wailing she heard footsteps on the back stairs and thought it had to be them coming for her.

She turned out the light and hid under the bed.

The door opened. The light went on. Sybil held her breath and shut her eyes, then knew she was being a fool. There had been no banging on the door.

Lore looked amused more than surprised as Sybil embarked on the undignified business of extricating herself.

Sybil asked where she had been, annoyed by her own behaviour.

The cinema, Lore said casually.

Before that she had read the paper at the Bollenmüller from cover to cover and Sybil was right; no one bothered her. 'I never would have thought of that,' she said in admiration.

She still seemed excited by the whole episode.

'And then?' asked Sybil.

'I went to the cinema after coming back and finding you weren't here.'

Sybil thought Lore should have waited. She would have and said so, accusing Lore of being insensitive, trying to ignore her own guilt about not returning straight away as promised.

Lore appeared unbothered.

'It never crossed my mind you weren't safe. I thought you were probably looking for your mother. I went to the cinema for the sake of watching something mindless, until they switched the lights on, right in the middle of the film, and a sign came up saying an air raid was on its way, so we all got up

and trooped out. I looked back and saw great clouds of cigarette smoke and dust trapped in the light of the projector.
That's what we'd all been breathing, and I thought it so unfair
that someone decides one person is allowed to breathe that
foul air and another is not.'

Sybil thought she didn't know Lore at all really.

'The break in the film was like reality had intruded. I thought
of our lives as celluloid unwinding through a projector, and our
film not being allowed to continue, like those jerks in the
Bollenmüller coming in and cheerfully announcing, 'We're
switching the lights on now. Off you go.' But at the same time
as having these strange thoughts, I felt so sure of myself I asked
the cinema manageress for a refund.'

Sybil looked at her in astonishment. 'Did you get one?'

Lore laughed. 'No, but she said come back any time and see
the film for free.'

The first defence guns started in the distance.

'The planes are coming,' Sybil said. 'I just want to go to bed
and be held.'

It was too cold to get undressed. Lore remained in her strange
mood, an almost morbid exhilaration she tried to share.

'I hear the blast kills more than the explosion. The body
can be quite undamaged afterwards. Maybe we'll be found
quite preserved like those entwined couples in the ruins of
Pompeii.'

The dancehall waiter presented the woman with a drink she
hadn't ordered. The glass was placed in front of her with such
certainty she didn't think to question it. Before she could ask
he was gone. She'd barely glimpsed him in the time it took.
She watched his departing back and thought him so suave in
the way he moved he could have been an actor. Perhaps he
was. Next time she would ask. They might have friends in

common. Why hadn't she noticed him before? She considered going after him but that was not her style; men came to her. She looked at the glass of bright green liquid and saw the message written on the drink mat to meet outside a house number down the street. She wondered whether the waiter was merely the messenger or the man that wanted her. She could do a lot worse, she thought. She blocked out any intimation of what she called the other business; the man in the leather coat with his seductive voice and insistent demands, always making out there was a choice.

They would be watching the door to see if she left alone or with a companion. She went to the toilet. The window was too high to climb out of. When she came out a waiter was hurrying from the kitchen. She slipped through before the door stopped swinging and walked quickly towards where she hoped the exit was. There it was; her luck was in. Her eyes took time to adjust to the dark. She made her way through the garden and climbed over the low wall that divided it from the street.

She turned left and went and stood in the sheltered doorway of the number she had been given. The street was empty. It wasn't as dark as most nights. The cloud had lifted and the sky was clear. She waited and no one came. Shadowy figures drifted past not seeing her. At one point she heard distant laughter and a little later a man and a woman shouted at each other. She grew anxious. The sirens started up and she was leaving when a figure came towards her out of the dark, addressing her, and she couldn't tell if this man was her waiter. She wanted only to feel safe and attractive and appreciated. The loneliness got to her most. She found herself smiling for the first time that evening. This prospect of love with a stranger, like a romantic interlude in a corny song. A line came into her head, from a play, she thought: Let the devil take the hindmost. She could not remember what it meant. She hoped he would be a practised seducer and in the dark she could forget about the other brute.

The sirens chased Schlegel all the way to the fortress-like shelter in Reinhardstrasse, a colossal concrete block that rose into the air, an invitation to be hit, rather than going underground because of the insubstantial substrata. The sirens sounded in waves and in between an expectant hush settled over the city. In the fifteen-minute walk along the river he saw cars abandoned and trams halted between stops. The only noise apart from the electronic wail was of hurrying footsteps. There was still time. The bomber fleet would have been spotted by the coastal defences and had yet to penetrate the outer ring.

Wardens checked the papers of everyone entering. The prospect of apocalypse did nothing to improve anyone's manners and Schlegel was caught in a scrum of pushing and shoving. People spoke in hushed terms, apart from the few who speculated in loud voices about a false alarm. The interior of the shelter offered a grim set of endless rooms, overcrowded with nervous faces, some already babbling. Rudimentary ceiling lights cast a sickly glow. Some rooms were mainly families. In others children were kept away because the occupants were noisy and drunk. Schlegel settled for one less full than the rest. He wasn't sure he wanted to be there when the bombs fell. It was too much like waiting to be buried alive. Several couples around him took the prospect of their demise as an excuse to grope each other. A women's skirt was yanked up, exposing white thigh above stocking top. Sex and death, Schlegel thought. The man's hand worked away at the woman, who rolled her eyes. Schlegel wanted to tell them to slow down or they would be finished long before the bombs came and have nothing to do. Others squirmed and writhed. He did his best to ignore the dog-like in-and-out of a panting, grunting couple on all fours in the corner. A woman with a small boy entered the chamber and slapped a hand over his staring eyes before dragging him off.

Schlegel decided he'd had enough of this death in waiting. It was like being in an Egyptian tomb. He made his way back to the entrance. No one was supposed to leave but he showed his badge and was allowed to go.

He had the streets to himself. He walked fast. At least I have my hat back, he thought. He wondered where Morgen was. Perhaps a bomb would fall on the man. He wished him no harm but life would be less anxious without him. Perhaps the bomb would land on him and make everyone's life easier. He saw his mother at his funeral, weeping crocodile tears behind a becoming black veil, throwing the first scoop of earth onto his coffin; a silver scoop at her insistence because the dear boy deserved nothing less. That he was somehow alive and sentient in the coffin was another matter.

The moon came out to welcome the bombers. The first searchlights switched on, casting an eerie light. Friedrichstrasse, utterly deserted, resembled an empty stage set. He cut through to Oranienburger Strasse. Distant gunfire sounded from the north in dry, hacking coughs. The sky began to glow. He was back in his apartment as the first bombs fell on the outskirts. After turning off the gas, he sat in the kitchen. He supposed he ought to go down to the cellar but instead went up to the roof. Darkness was transformed as hundreds of searchlights swept the sky, the night ahead a mass of flashes from bursting shells. He learned to distinguish between the angry sound of flak guns and the heavier anti-aircraft batteries. The drone of the planes grew. Concentration of fire provided a magnificent, terrible sight.

Searchlights chased in desperate search of planes, their beams catching puffs of smoke from exploding shrapnel.

The sky became full of red flares, like falling chandeliers as they burst and continued to burn on the ground. Then it was the turn of the green flares. Schlegel tried to make sense of what he was seeing. The first planes must be the pathfinders. He braced himself for the main force. He heard their heavy engines, a mighty roar coming in low. It was orchestrated chaos, the percussion of the heavy bombs, the staccato of the defence guns. Sticks of incendiaries drew incandescent streaks across the sky. Bright lines of tracer fire shimmered. What a spectacle! Four years of blackout and it was like someone had switched on the entire city's conserved energy supply. Schlegel was too mesmerised to be scared, even grew exhilarated at the thought of his exploding, disintegrating body. Everyone should be out watching. A herd of spooked cattle stampeded down the street beneath, their bellows distinguishable over the noise. They would be from the nearby dairy and the white drayhorse that followed, sparks flying from its hooves, would be the local brewery's. One, two, three bombs fell near enough to make his building shake. It must be the heaviest raid yet. Now they seemed to be coming in barely higher than the housetops. He lost count of how many. There would be rubble and ashes tomorrow and burst pipes and mains. Half the department would phone in to say it couldn't get in because of transport disruptions. Parts of the city close by were starting to burn, perhaps streets he had walked down that day. An explosion bigger than the rest sounded as something fell with an enormous blast. The aftershock came seconds later. The roar was so deafening he clapped his hands to his ears. He looked up and still the planes came. Hundreds if not thousands. He saw one trapped in the cone of a searchlight. It started to twist and turn as it tried to lose the light, which hung on for the tracer to zone in. The big machine became like a ponderous four-engined beast of death, thrown around with such abandon that Schlegel thought it surely must shed its rivets and fall apart. The pilot succeeded in losing the searchlight, which chased the darkness after it, catching the aircraft's silhouette briefly then losing it for good. Schlegel had hardly been aware of the ear-splitting drama while watching the chase. His building shook again as other bombs fell, enough to make the windows rattle. He saw the first starburst of flame as the aircraft started to burn. The searchlight pursued and picked it up again, subjecting it to its pitiless gaze. The hit plane fell, majestic and lumbering, flames streaking from its fuselage and wing. He heard the engine stutter, even amid the cacophony. Guns zeroed in and blazed away long after it was obvious the bomber would not be limping home. Schlegel watched the aircraft's burning descent in awe. Every blast and tremor and window rattle told him that he, and not they, was the one who was alive.

# 17

Yellow smoke hung over the city, giving everything an opaque glow. Schlegel's impression was of a shocked hush, combined with a ringing in his ears. The morning's transformation was akin to that of an occult visitation: a cow shaking in a crater; those bombed out wandering by dazed, carrying bundles; the strange, corny image of a crone singing a nursery rhyme in a cracked voice; someone saying half the transport system was bust; roads flooded where water mains had broken; fire engines and ambulances racing, sirens blaring. The army surplus shop in Kleine Hamburger Strasse was having its windows boarded up while the owner complained half his stock had been pilfered. Metal lay everywhere, debris from shells fallen back to earth. The body of a car sat upright alongside its chassis, as though it had been lifted rather than blown off. Shopkeepers swept broken glass. Queues formed as usual, for the long and relentless business of waiting. Despite the devastation, cheerful outrage was the tone most heard. Gangs of kids ran around collecting souvenirs. Schlegel saw one whooping boy carrying a large spent shell case. He presumed school was off. It was a fine day for a change, with the palest blue sky discernible behind the smoke haze, as though the bombs had chased away the worst of the weather.

The city's governor and Minister of Propaganda, Dr Joseph Goebbels, was out of town on his way back from Bavaria, delayed in Halle in his private railway carriage. With all the latest telecommunications kit he could speak directly to his liaison team, which informed him the suburbs to the south and west were still burning, as was the centre. The dome of St Hedwig's cathedral had collapsed into the nave. Unter den Linden had received a number of hits, as had Friedrichstrasse. In Wilhelmstrasse his own ministry had been spared but Goering's Luftwaffe building had suffered bad damage, which Goebbels thought only fair, given how the fat marshal had boasted the city's air defences were impregnable.

All talk in the street was of a new super-bomb capable of demolishing whole blocks. They had arrived at the state of total war, and he welcomed the fire of their apocalypse as the ultimate test before victory. He ordered a full report. He would make an immediate inspection upon his return. He would go to the people and confirm his presence among them, secure in the knowledge that he was the only leader to show his face these days while the others skulked in their tents.

In the centre at least the transport seemed to be working. One building was already being boarded up, to preserve the line of the street's facade and cover the damage.

The pounding seemed also to have provoked the first signs of spring. A few snowdrops had appeared next to some trees on a muddy stretch of grass.

At one big intersection a building had engorged itself onto the road, the facade sheared off, leaving the interiors exposed. On some floors all the furniture had been blown out and on others it stood intact, turning the exposed rooms into a bizarre display of people's lives. Schlegel had a flash of the murder room transposed there. How much brutality and how many beatings and fights had that building seen before meeting its own violent end?

The whole city stank of shit, Goebbels was told upon his train being met at the Anhalter Bahnhof. A further delay had done nothing for his mood. On being told the full extent of the damage he raked his hands down his face and exclaimed histrionically, 'Dear God.'

He sat behind a glass screen in his carriage, on the other side of which telephones rang and young aides busied themselves. He travelled with only pretty secretaries. His wife was in a clinic in Dresden suffering from nervous exhaustion.

When told that both the Scala and Winter Garden variety theatres had been hit, Goebbels was reduced to gnashing his teeth.

'What! No more Baby the elephant and her high-wire act?'

Via intercom, he ordered telegrams of condolence be sent to the two Swiss brothers that ran the shows. He dictated that they had done more for the image of the circus than anyone since Hagenbeck introduced new methods of wild-animal training; then in an aside to a secretary, 'Just to show I know what I am talking about.'

Who could forget the horse that went to bed using a huge pillow to rest its head? There were ponies and camels besides, trumpeting sea lions with their clowns, cattle, bears and chimpanzees, and only the gentlest and most exemplary methods employed, for the brothers could not abide cruelty to animals. Cabaret and theatre stars were enlisted as well, for which reason Goebbels kept a close eye on upcoming female talent in need of a leg up.

He remained a great public advocate of wholesome variety entertainment. Perfect for families, and the best antidote for troops on leave from the front. He had taken his own children and watched in delight as they stared up, eyes blazing with excitement, necks craned and little mouths agape as the trapeze artistes flew high above the crowd. Goebbels watched with a more discerning eye; he'd had the female flyer, for the simple reason of fancying hard muscle as a change from the usual soft contours.

As he was passing close enough to the central revenue office in Jüdenstrasse, only a short walk from his office, Schlegel stopped off and spoke to a corpulent young man with whom he had worked on several cases and whose jovial air hid a sharp mind. Otto Keleman's other distinguishing feature was glasses so smeared Schlegel wondered how he managed to see through them. Keleman's myopia and flat feet were enough to keep him from being conscripted, though he hinted that the tax office looked after its own, providing false medical certificates. Accounting was deadly dull but not as bad as being shot at.

Despite his background and modest appearance, Keleman was an unlikely party boy, with an inside track on every reception and embassy bash going. He had even managed to wangle invitations to some of Schlegel's mother's parties, which were notoriously hard to get into.

Keleman worked in an enormous room where hundreds of officials sat at rows of desks.

'I slack, you slack, we slack,' he said on seeing Schlegel. 'I've no windows in my apartment. Spectacular, no? How's yours?'

'Intact.'

'What can I do for you?'

'I want to see a man's tax file.'

'That's what we're here for!'

Keleman wrote down Morgen's name, saying a man's tax

returns, true or false, told you everything you needed to know about him.

'Any reason?' he added.

'He sits opposite me. He's SS.'

Keleman looked surprised. 'Working with you?'

'He turned up yesterday.'

'They stick like anything to themselves usually. Barely ever mix.'

'That's what I thought.'

'Either you are very privileged or you're in trouble.'

'Can you get his military record too?'

'Shouldn't really; not impossible.' Keleman paused. 'He will have been sent to spy. Everyone's at it now more than ever. It's this season's fashion.'

'We're very dull. We keep our heads down.'

'Both the SS and Ministry of Propaganda – that's quite a big and – have been all over us in the past months, involving us in endless tax investigations into the Gestapo. They were getting too pally with the Jews, cutting deals and so forth. Big scandal. Dismissals for embezzlement and corruption. Don't you know about this?'

Schlegel shook his head.

'Gossip, man!' said Keleman, eyes bright. 'Jungle drums. Doesn't any of that reach you?'

'Not in my backwater.'

'Same here, until six months ago. We could have been a posting in Outer Mongolia. No one would have been seen dead co-operating. Tax investigations were virtually unheard of. What was the name of those stables in Greek myth?'

'Augean.'

'Shit sure is getting shovelled now. Revisionism is in the air. Maybe your turn next to get turned upside down.'

'That's what Stoffel says. Who's doing it?'

'It has Goebbels written all over it. Short, sharp and austere, and very gnomic. On the other hand, the SS has its oar in too, and SS and Propaganda aren't usual bedfellows. It's not only the Gestapo being turned upside down.' Keleman pointed to a pile of files on his desk. 'There's a civilian offensive. August Nöthling?'

'As in the food store?'

The man's delivery vans were still a common feature of everyday life. Schlegel knew from his mother that those with money paid to circumvent the increasingly bothersome matter of rationing cards.

'Shopping Bags is up to his neck.'

'Shopping Bags?'

'That's what we call him. Everyone's known for years Nöthling is the back-door man to the golden pheasants. Two months ago nobody gave a toss and now his case is top of the list, and I can tell you nothing has been that high priority in this office since 1941 when we were sorting tax breaks for the new territories in double time.'

Keleman flicked through a file.

'The man is certainly well endowed when it comes to clients. Interior Minister Frick. An army C-in-C and a naval one. The Minister for Science Education and National Culture. The list goes on. Remember Walter Darré?'

'Food and Agriculture?'

'Former Food and Agriculture. Currently on sick leave.' Keleman made a drinking motion. 'The thing about Darré is that when he ran the Food Estate it was not subject to public audit of accounts. These boys have very deep pockets. Listen to this. Eleven kilos of chocolate, one hundred and twenty of poultry and fifty kilos of game, and that's just Frick's delivery list.'

Keleman sat back. His pullover had moth holes.

'Have you heard about Horcher's?'

Everyone knew Horcher's and almost no one could afford it. Schlegel remembered formal meals on special occasions, usually birthdays, normally with just his stepfather, who held an account. His mother found the restaurant's baronial panelling and heavy oil paintings too reminiscent of provincial English hotels and preferred Kempinski's.

It was so protected it could virtually afford to advertise its scorn of the very idea of ration cards, and its staff were exempt from conscription.

Keleman said, 'There's a ding-dong battle between the Poisoned Dwarf Goebbels, who eats only spinach like Popeye, and insists on closing everything so he can mobilise the civilian reserve, and Fatty Goering whose favourite dining table it is. Dr G has already asked us to take a look at Horcher's books, which I can tell you now won't bear inspection. It always makes for amusement when the gods fight among themselves. Do you fancy a drink tomorrow? I've scrounged a ticket to a press screening to Dr G's latest epic, and in colour to boot. Starts at eight, so shall we say six? As for Horcher's, red caviar and sturgeon is what I'd have, if anyone were offering.' He gave a burst of laughter and said, 'I'm still buzzing from the bombs. Give my best to your mother.'

Schlegel had to smile. They had shaken hands maybe twice. 'Naturally. She always asks after you.'

# 18

Lore's only extravagance was buying 35mm film for her camera. It was in short supply and expensive. She used it to take clandestine photographs of abandoned Jewish sites.

Her one piece of identification was an out-of-date press pass whose photograph showed her looking boyish. She told Sybil she had bought it on the black market, replaced the photograph and a friend had touched up the stamp. By friend, Sybil presumed Lore meant former lover. Lore rarely talked about her past but Sybil gathered that she had moved among a freewheeling set of women who all slept with each other out of a disrespect for what they called the baby-making machine, their dismissive term for male genitalia.

Lore knew the pass wouldn't stand up to inspection, nor would a false letter she had on Agfa notepaper certifying she was an important worker employed as a camera assembler. It could be easily checked she wasn't. Yet Lore remained optimistic about her chances where Sybil thought only a proper false identity and an actual job would offer security, which Lore dismissed, saying she didn't want to be a secretary.

On the morning after the raid, Lore asked Sybil to do her a favour, as Alwynd was already putting her to work. She had her photographs developed at a particular shop in Pankow whose owner, Schmidt, she had known for years and trusted. Sybil would need to take a 51 tram. Lore had three rolls she wanted developed.

\*　　\*　　\*

The tramline's direct service was interrupted because of track damage. They could only go so far, then everyone had to get out and walk a short distance to pick up another.

Schmidt, thin and balding, was a morose type who didn't become any friendlier when Sybil mentioned Lore, except to say she was always cadging cigarettes.

Sybil said he must be mistaken because Lore didn't smoke.

Schmidt said, 'I know.'

Sybil supposed she had passed some test, until the man asked to see her papers as it was security regulations now. Sybil said she had left them at home. The only thing she had on her was a library card from the tobacconist in Turmstrasse that lent books on the side for a small subscription.

Schmidt made no further mention of the papers. Sybil thought he seemed preoccupied.

As she turned to go, he said, 'I might be able to help.'

Schmidt moved from behind the counter, switched the door sign to closed, slid the bolt and pulled down the blind. He motioned to follow him through to a shabby room comfortably furnished with old pieces. He said he had an unusual proposal. For a terrible moment Sybil thought he was about to make a pass.

'I don't have to spell out your situation. Papers and so forth.'

Sybil presumed he was offering his services, but couldn't be sure.

He asked if she would be interested in modelling work.

Seeing which way the conversation was going, she asked what kind.

'It pays well. We sell to soldiers.'

'Do you have any samples?'

Schmidt cleared his throat and stood up.

He showed her a photograph of a woman stepping out of a bathtub and several more lying naked on a rug. The poses were suggestive rather than blatant. The woman wasn't glamorous or beautiful.

Sybil supposed if she agreed the papers would be more forthcoming. She might even be able to trade the cost of one against the other. It didn't seem much of a price.

'Does Lore know?'

'I never knew how to raise the matter. I have known her a long time, since she was almost a child.'

'Who takes the photographs?'

'I do. But in your case it might be easier perhaps if she considered taking some of you.'

She and Lore laughed about it later, moving from saying they were not that desperate, to agreeing it would be deliciously subversive to have hundreds of soldiers unwittingly beating themselves off over a racial inferior.

'Of course, I knew,' said Lore. 'Everyone knows about Schmidt's mucky pictures. I'm sorry. I hoped Schmidt would raise the matter with you because I knew he wouldn't with me and would have been too embarrassed had I asked. If the money's that good we should both do them.'

They were laughing so hard that Alwynd came to see what was going on. Sybil wasn't sure Lore was doing the right thing telling him, but Alwynd laughed along with them and asked in apparent innocence if he could watch.

# 19

'Otto Keleman sends his regards,' Schlegel said to his mother.

'Who?'

'Never mind.'

He looked at Morgen. It was not a lunch or location he could have predicted.

His mother had shown no surprise when he turned up with Morgen. Her first question was whether Morgen's uniform was tailored. Unfortunately not, he said. He had been sent off wearing only a summer one in the middle of winter, so had made do with what he could find.

'It still has the bullet hole.'

It was the type of remark guaranteed to endear him to Schlegel's mother. If Schlegel had said it she would not have found it the remotest bit funny.

That morning no one had done any work. The canteen was full with staff comparing damage. The rest of the time was spent on the telephone checking on friends and relatives. As it became clear that no one had been lost the mood became relaxed.

Morgen was sitting in the office with his tie undone. A pall of smoke hung above him in perfect imitation of the sky outside. He seemed strangely energised but mentioned nothing of the bombing. He seemed to have adopted a new habit of alternating his cigarette between different sides of his mouth with each drag. Schlegel wondered if that was his own particular nervous reaction. Everyone seemed to be behaving out of character. The forever sour secretary Frau Pelz could be heard gossiping away outside. Morgen, however, did not call anyone, perhaps because he had no one. Schlegel wondered if there was a Frau Morgen.

Even Stoffel stopped by, mainly to look askance at Morgen and raise his eyebrows behind his back.

Stoffel asked Schlegel if there was any joy with the Jewish butchers. Joy was not the word he would have used. He came up with a vague and complicated excuse that went on long enough for Stoffel to interrupt.

'Let me paraphrase. The holding centres are still in the process of compiling their own registers.'

Schlegel blew out his cheeks in a show of frustration. He could see Stoffel suspected he was being given the runaround. To make matters worse, Frau Pelz shouted from outside saying his mother was on the telephone and she was putting her through.

Schlegel knew Stoffel could hear the bloody woman's crystal tones as she put on an excruciating display of self-serving concern.

'Of course, my heart is torn,' she said, with British bombs being dropped on her, who was English.

This led to Stoffel announcing as Schlegel replaced the receiver, 'I didn't know your mother was English. Do we have a spy in our midst?'

He smirked to make it clear he meant Morgen. Schlegel was still cringing from them having overheard his mother's offer to buy him lunch. 'No one's going to be working today. I'm paying. Let's say the Esplanade.'

It was a top hotel. Stoffel grunted before leaving, as though dismissing him as a mummy's boy.

'Missing butchers,' he said pointedly. 'The pathologist says the flayed corpse is beyond identification. No fingerprints to speak of and the head so smashed in to make a nonsense of any dental records. I could have told him that just from looking.'

'A head?'

'The local police found it under the wagon behind the wheels. No sign of the rest. *Buon appetito.*'

His mother had one of the best tables overlooking the Esplanade's courtyard garden. On impulse he had offered to take Morgen, thinking that if anyone could prise anything out of the man it would be her, who was fearless in her questioning. Her second question was, 'Where are your people from?'

Frankfurt, she was told. And what did they do, she asked. Worked for the railway, he said. Schlegel was impressed his mother showed not a flicker of disappointment. She probably knew several families who owned railways. Did he think state ownership was a good thing? Morgen looked like he couldn't care less.

There was trouble over the order. His mother made out she was vegetarian when Schlegel knew she was not. Dining in public she invariably insisted on some form of eggs Benedict, which after negotiation and regretful discussion about short-ages, became reduced to poached eggs. That day there were no eggs and the only vegetarian plate was cabbage.

'Three chicken, then,' she sighed. 'Just this once, and breast only.' She turned to Morgen. 'It's all propaganda anyway, this business of certain people not eating meat and refraining from the hard stuff. I hear our leader retains a fondness for bratwurst and is known to take a beer now and then. Hard to know who to believe these days, don't you agree, certainly not that sawn-off megaphone Goebbels. You don't look the sort of fellow to report defeatist talk. I'm the last person to give up, but when you look at some of our glorious leaders you begin to wonder. Not exactly the greatest human specimens. Have you seen Lammers? He looks like he has two glass eyes. Heydrich was a blond beast, no longer with us, and most of them are foreign. I am allowed to say that, being one myself. I expect the food was ghastly in Russia,' she said, turning again to Morgen.

Schlegel was impressed she had worked out that much.

She had her own imperious tick list of subjects. The bombing. 'Utterly awful. We were spared damage, thank God.' Shortages. Morale. The rudeness of waiters, shop assistants and domestic staff. 'Such a liverish lot. They make Parisians seem sweet by comparison and they're bad enough. They're all being called up now so it serves them right. What's wrong with plain old-fashioned good manners?'

She turned to Schlegel and said he wasn't adding much to the conversation.

'Monologue,' he corrected, then before she could complain added that he was entertained enough as it was.

He was surprised she hadn't picked up anything of the impending Nöthling scandal. She knew the man slightly as he aspired to mix socially with his clients, and dismissed him as common and pushy, in keeping with those he served.

'I can't say it surprises. They've all been living off the most enormous gravy train and so brazen it would put Nero to shame.'

On the other hand she knew the Horcher's story, saying it was more amusing than the version passed on by Keleman.

'Oh, him!' she said, reminded. 'The moon-faced one with the smudgy glasses. Very good at buttering up. I expect it gets him into more knickers than you would think. Anyway, Horcher's, in one corner you have that runt Goebbels, who is thin and stingy, and in the other Goering, who is a fat glutton. From what I understand it's a question of interpretation, now things aren't going so well. Not much of a show of support for our troops if the guzzlers are stuffing their faces at home. You will see, by the way, I am not drinking.' She turned to Morgen. 'I expect you would cheerfully machine-gun the place, given half a chance.'

He still might, Morgen said, which made her laugh.

Schlegel was surprised at her understanding of what was going on at the top, who was in and who was out and what alliances were forming. Goebbels, having taken delight in putting one over on Goering by closing down his favourite restaurant, which included sending a gang of provocateurs to smash the windows when Goering tried to keep it open, had been forced to make a huge U-turn.

'The trouble is, none of them can get close to Adolf any more. The ghastly Bormann guards his kennel like nobody's business. Goebbels can't get near him and dear Albert, who was Adolf's greatest pet for ever so long, can't either.'

'Why not?' asked Morgen, looking properly interested for the first time.

'Because the so-called gang of three is pulling the strings. We all know Keitel is a fat zero, so it comes down to Lammers, who controls the purse, and Bormann. Of course Goebbels wants Foreign Minister but he's not going to get it, and to make out he's not as much out in the cold as he is he forms an alliance with Speer and his Ministry of Armaments to give substance to all that hot air he talks about total war. Now, the trouble is Albert needs Goering back on board. Hermann, as fond of him as we all are, is lost in a world of his own – the rouge, the mascara, the morphine, the lipstick and Chinese dressing gowns – but he still holds considerable powers that Speer wants to use to work around Bormann and all those other shits in the Chancellery.'

She looked at Morgen and said, 'I hope you're not taking

notes. This is straight from the horse's mouth and utterly confidential depending on whom I am talking to.'

Morgen smiled charmingly. 'So Speer told Goebbels he had to go and eat humble pie with Goering?'

'Which was why he was in Bavaria when the bombs were falling. He made a big show afterwards, being seen to be seen, and the Horcher's punchline is quite delicious.'

Goebbels had done a deal with Goering to let Horcher's reopen as a private Luftwaffe dining room.

For the first time Schlegel saw Morgen laugh properly, at the excellence of the intrigue.

'Enough to make the Borgias' eyes roll.'

*Plus ça change*, agreed his mother. 'If they put half the effort into winning the war that they invest in their scheming they would have had it won years ago. Their big mistake was England. There for the taking. I could have told them, if only they had asked. Now what is it exactly you do in the black order?'

'I was a serving officer in the Wiking division for six months.'

'Active duty?'

'Very. We were wiped out three times over. Only eighteen of us from the original company survived.'

'How many in a company?'

'About two hundred.'

'Eighteen out of two hundred!' She laid a consoling hand on Morgen's arm. 'I am so sorry, and there's me telling silly stories.'

'Not at all. Anyway, I am back now.'

'And working with my son. How come?'

'I have no idea.'

'You must have some.'

'No, honestly. I haven't a clue. I expect I have been sent here to stay out of trouble.'

'You don't look like a troublemaker.'

She had no time to pursue the point, having seen the time

and remembered her hairdresser. Schlegel thought it unusual to see his mother so puzzled about anyone.

'What did you do before?' she asked, settling the bill.

'I was a judge.'

'My heavens! What kind of judge?'

'A prosecuting one, Internal Affairs.'

'Really?' she said, without missing a beat. 'What's to investigate? I would have thought you were all such good boys. Code of honour and so forth.' She thought for a moment and said, 'I expect you're like Jesuits, God's storm troopers.'

Before Morgen could answer a waiter interrupted to say Schlegel was wanted on the telephone. He thought it must be a mistake. Nobody knew where he was.

But it was Stoffel.

'Just to spoil your lunch,' he said.

## 20

Half an hour later they were standing in Treptower Park, not far from the Russian paint factory whose chimney stuck up like a peremptory finger. A body had been found partly hidden in bushes.

On the journey Morgen had resorted to his usual taciturn silence, deflecting Schlegel's questions. The only thing he expressed interest in was the previous flayed body and what was called the murder room.

'Pigs throwing themselves over a cliff, you say?' And of the drawing scratched on the wall, 'Gadarene Swine. New Testament. Demonic possession.'

A devil expelled from a man took hold of the pigs.

Morgen's uniform drew looks. People avoided the SS. The cultivated image was sinister and mysterious, and it fostered the myth of being the bright, cruel flame at the heart of everything.

Schlegel wondered how esoteric Morgen was, given that the black order was the new Freemasonry, within which it was said existed an occult clique.

Schlegel looked out of the window as the train crossed the river and the flat expanse of Treptower Park came into view. He made out the cluster of official vehicles, and a line of police and their dogs moving forward in a slow search. The dome of smoke still hung over the city.

\*     \*     \*

The park was bleak and windswept, with bronchial trees and intersecting paths with no one on them. The snowdrops here had understandably resisted putting in an appearance. Flowerbeds had been dug over and left. There had been no planting in public spaces for a couple of years now.

The line of searchers moved forward in the distance. A pathetic-looking tent had been put round the body. Stoffel, pulling grimly on a cigar, his nose blue, dismissed the photographer, a different one from the slaughterhouse, and said they were still waiting for a doctor, which was a waste of time because what they had was nothing but dead.

'As bad as last time,' he said, with a grimace. 'Save it for the battlefield.'

'Man or woman?' asked Morgen.

'Hardly matters. Woman, probably.'

'Why are we here?' asked Morgen.

'I don't need you,' said Stoffel. 'It's him.'

Schlegel guessed he was about to inherit Stoffel's latest problem. He now had another flayed body, after writing off the previous one on the grounds that it wouldn't happen again.

Stoffel prodded his lapel and stood so close Schlegel could smell meat on his breath.

'This means the one or ones doing the murders must have avoided arrest.'

'Are you saying same killer both times?'

Stoffel famously had a sixth sense for such things.

'You can put your tongue in my mouth if it isn't. Get me the names of any Jewish butchers not arrested.'

Schlegel wanted to say bureaucracy didn't work like that. Without saying so, Stoffel made it plain he didn't care. He was concerned only with avoiding a personal reprimand, and was giving the problem to Schlegel.

Stoffel moved on to chew the fat with the generally shifty

bunch from the local station, about how this case was like a nastier version of the one where some Kike kid had dismembered a female and disposed of the bits. Legs in the stairwell of a block in the same street that Schlegel lived in, arms in a yard elsewhere, torso in a restaurant bin.

'The head we never found because the kid baked it in his oven. Nor were her breasts and internal organs. And what did the kid perform his surgery with? A penknife!'

Stoffel gave a shrill bark, a signal for the rest to join in.

Stoffel stared back at Schlegel, inviting him to laugh. Schlegel smiled with difficulty, feeling useless.

Stoffel pointed at the body tent. 'At least your man here uses the proper tools. Clean cuts. Surgical precision.'

The light started to fade. Feet and hands grew numb. They all slapped themselves to keep warm and passed a flask around. Morgen was standing smoking on his own. The moment seemed right for Schlegel to pass on what Morgen had said about being Internal Affairs.

Stoffel's exaggerated double take put Schlegel in an unexpectedly good mood. He wondered what Stoffel's misdemeanours were for him to look so worried.

A car approached across the grass. Three men got out. One was the useless doctor from before. Schlegel was surprised that the second man was Gersten and even more when he recognised the smart whipcord coat of his companion.

Stoffel jerked his head in Morgen's direction and said, 'Get ready for the cold wind of retribution,' and went off to sort out the doctor.

Schlegel's good mood survived being taken aside by Gersten to tell him Lazarenko might be able to help with this latest body.

'Tell Stoffel. It's his case.'

Gersten said, 'We would rather speak to you and your friend.' He meant Morgen. 'Confidentially.'

Schlegel supposed Lazarenko was Gersten's lapdog. Entourages were popular. He decided Lazarenko probably had more influence than he had credited. The Gestapo wouldn't have many Russian speakers.

Gersten beckoned Morgen over. Schlegel saw Stoffel watching. Gersten was keen they give Lazarenko another chance.

'Intelligence we're picking up from the Russian community says these killings have a Bolshevik angle. We're only trying to help. Stop panic in the ranks.'

Community, thought Schlegel; was that what they called it?

Morgen said, 'It has nothing to do with us, other than Stoffel being too idle to do the work himself.'

'Exactly. He's only interested in his stories.' Stoffel was cracking up the men again. 'He retires in two weeks anyway.'

Schlegel didn't know. He was surprised. Most of the older ones hung on because of shortages, unless they were ill. Talk of any leaving party usually started at least six weeks before. For the last one there had been a futile search for an old-fashioned stripper.

Gersten said to Lazarenko, 'Show them.'

Lazarenko had a briefcase. He stooped to rest it on his knee so he could open the lock. What came out was a malevolent object of frightening design, more the size of an axe than a household hammer, though a hammer it was, with a black metal spike and a wedged striking edge.

'I have kept it as a reminder of what happened to my people. A bad souvenir, you might say.'

On 25 June, two years before, retreating Russians quelled a local uprising with extreme cruelty.

'They were not satisfied with just killing. They cut off women's breasts and men's genitals. Jews crucified children to walls and slit their guts so they stared at their insides spilling out as they died. This mallet is for slaughtering cattle, but its blows killed many men and women and smashed their bones. They did it to German prisoners too. Tied them up and cut off their noses, tongues, cocks and balls, then beat their brains out with this.'

Schlegel stared at the horizon as he struggled to imagine the conspiracy Gersten had in mind, how it really worked and was transmitted.

Gersten said, 'A rogue agent. Someone with the knowledge of that experience. I would say that's what we're dealing with.'

Morgen said, 'Today's Tuesday. Herr Lazarenko said the Russians can only kill on Sundays, and we don't believe his previous suspect was up to the job.'

He doubted if this new body had been lying there since Sunday.

Gersten said, 'We think they work at night and have access to transport.'

'Prove it then. I thought they were all locked up after work.'

'Not in any meaningful way,' said Lazarenko. 'There are women in other barracks.'

He thrust his hips obscenely and said guards made use of them too. They were all in it together.

Gersten stepped forward, assuming a confidential manner. 'You were in Lublin when it was known as Dodge City.'

Morgen looked irritated.

'You know the score. We know your reputation.'

Morgen turned to go. 'See Stoffel.'

'You know the terrain. He doesn't. He's barely interested. They're all as thick as shit. This needs someone with your skills.'

Morgen walked away.

Gersten didn't appear greatly put out and said to Schlegel, 'He won't be able to resist a challenge like this.'

'What happened in Lublin?'

'He was known as the bloodhound. He had an eye for big, sensitive cases. But he always ended up offending someone. That's why they got rid of him.'

Lazarenko claimed to have seen Morgen in Lublin.

'He wouldn't remember. I was just a refugee. I worked as a barman in the mess where he ate.'

Schlegel considered Morgen's new reputation as a super-sleuth. He was damned if he would tell Stoffel.

Gersten said Morgen had a habit of getting into trouble. A big investigation into a racket involving stolen Jewish furs became an embarrassment when it was discovered the main suspect was the brother of the mistress of a top official and she was fencing the goods in Berlin.

'He'll come round. He needs it as badly as we need him.'

## 21

'In four days, gentlemen, four days, we have had a double shoot-ing, two bodies butchered beyond any hope of recognition, and a corpse with its penis cut off. Five bodies in four days. What are we to make of this?'

They were in what Nebe called an emergency conference and everyone else just another boring meeting. There were about ten detectives in the room, the stale old farts; all the good ones had either volunteered or been conscripted.

Despite the indifference of his audience, the occasion showed Nebe at his best: rhetorical, sarcastic, difficult to fathom, possi-bly vacuous. His best trick was to keep everyone guessing.

Morgen interrupted Nebe's flow by strolling in late, sitting down and lighting up. Nebe watched with exaggerated disbe-lief before reasserting himself.

'This is what Minister Goebbels said to me. "Why, just as I am about to declare the city Jew-free, do the police allow a Jewish maniac to go on the rampage?" '

Nebe looked around. No answer was forthcoming.

'I was told this was unacceptable on top of the public rela-tions disaster already faced because of the SS arresting a load of the wrong Jews. These botched arrests have led to an unprece-dented demonstration, and Minister Goebbels will not toler-ate a second scandal, with news getting out of a Jewish mass killer. Already he has been asked by a Swedish journalist if the city now has its equivalent to London's Jack the Ripper.'

Schlegel thought it might secretly suit Dr Goebbels to have his Ripper, because it would serve to underline the dangerous and unstable nature of those he wished to be rid of.

Nebe went on to say it had been Dr Goebbels' greatest wish to declare the city Jew-free after the latest action, which was now not the case because thousands had avoided arrest and gone into hiding.

'The SS has been given a deadline of six weeks to round up all the strays. Jew-free means what it says. You have a lot less time. Dr Goebbels will not have his plans for a clean sweep under-mined by rumours of this Jewish Ripper.'

A wag at the back asked if anyone had found the missing penis. Faced with suppressed titters, Nebe sensed an uphill battle.

'Help me here. Is this man killing for sadistic pleasure or in desperate protest against the deportations? How many killers are you talking about anyway?'

'One, sir,' said Stoffel, quickly.

Morgen said no. While the first two killings – the old man and the warden – cancelled each other out, the others had involved transportation and extra hands to carry the bodies.

Stoffel wanted to know what Morgen and Gersten had been talking about in the park. Morgen said Gersten was given to wild theories and he had told him to take them up with Stoffel.

Nebe held up his hand. 'One, two, three killers, I don't care how many. Forty-eight hours to sort it out before you explain yourself in person to Dr Goebbels, who will not view the matter lightly. I want a daily update and you'd better have some news. Dismissed. Schlegel and Morgen to remain behind.'

Nebe didn't invite them to sit. He placed a fifty-mark note on the desk in front of him.

'This note is counterfeit. Find out where it comes from.'

Schlegel presumed it came from the money found in the dead man's mouth, but he deferred to Morgen as the ranking officer, who said nothing and stood looking insolent.

'You are Financial Crimes, aren't you?' asked Nebe, with an attempt at his usual sarcasm.

Morgen fielded with blank sincerity. 'I believe so, yes, sir, as of Monday morning.'

'With a history of rank insubordination.'

'Six months' Prussian amusements and another six at the front. In winter, sir.'

Schlegel watched out of the corner of his eye. Prussian amusements meant penal colony. Such detention wasn't unheard of but for it to be followed by combat duty meant Morgen must have annoyed someone very much.

Nebe said, 'Find out where the money is coming from. That's all.'

Morgen continued to stand there. Nebe gestured to say they were dismissed.

'Permission to speak, sir,' Morgen finally said. 'To find out we will almost certainly need to know who killed the man, as I presume we are talking about money found about his person.'

Nebe did his best to look stupid.

Morgen said he had no expertise in forgery and it would be helpful to know what they were dealing with.

Nebe consulted a file on his desk, making a show of opening the folder a crack. He said the forgery was passable to the untrained eye. Fifty-mark notes had a portrait of a woman in a headscarf on the front and Marienburg Castle on the back. Half a dozen flaws pertained to both images, including a missing window in the detailing of the castle.

'A speck, but absent nevertheless,' said Nebe. 'The print dye doesn't quite match. Some of the tailing of the italic lettering is shorter than the original. The clearest error can be found in the frame around the woman's head.'

Its detailing included a series of points along the edge of the frame. In the original there were none at the corners, but in the forgery there were.

'And the verdict, sir?' asked Morgen.

'The overall quality is very good and would be much harder to spot were it not for the basic error of the corner points.'

As they were leaving Nebe said to Morgen, 'I hear your reputation is for rocking the boat.'

'Isn't that what I am supposed to do, sir?'

Morgen looked bored. The impression Nebe gave, for all his slipperiness, was of an ineffectual man.

'Not here. Not with us. What is the real purpose of your assignment?'

'I have no idea, sir.'

'Well, we didn't ask for you.'

'Nor I to come here.'

'Can we be honest for a moment?'

That was rich coming from him, Schlegel thought.

Nebe went on. 'Can we hypothesise?'

Schlegel wanted to say that Morgen did not look like a hypothetical man.

Nebe ploughed on. 'Do you think it's possible you are in a situation where you don't know yet on what it is you are supposed to report?'

Morgen shrugged and said he couldn't possibly say.

Nebe seized on that. 'Can't or won't?'

Morgen sighed. 'Are you saying I might be on one of those assignments where the investigator goes in essentially clueless, apart from being nudged to stumble across whatever it is he is supposed to investigate?'

'Precisely!'

'I can't say I have ever heard of such an assignment, but thank you for warning me.'

'Life would be much easier if I knew,' Nebe said with consummate vagueness.

'Me too, sir.'

'Here's what I think. All you know is you have been allowed back from Russia on condition you do nothing. This you will ignore because your reputation is as a trouble-maker. We both know that. What worries me is that whatever you dig up will be on your own initiative, which will be of benefit to others, possibly this department's enemies, but you will not find out who they are. Do you understand what I am saying?'

'That I will get into trouble without understanding why.'

Nebe nodded, looking pleased. 'Yes, I can work with that. Be careful you don't turn out to be the mad dog that bites us in the pants.' He gave a strange whinny that passed for a laugh. He seemed very taken by the idea. 'Keep me informed of your every move on this and if you discover who you are answering to, tell me immediately.'

'Who are your enemies, sir, so I know?'

The remark was delivered with sufficient deadpan insolence for him to get away with it. Nebe laughed unexpectedly and waved them from the room.

Outside in the corridor, Morgen looked at Schlegel intently and asked what on earth had Nebe been on about. Schlegel could honestly answer he had no idea.

Morgen left. A man of abrupt transitions; none of the usual hello and goodbye, no formal saluting. There and not there. Schlegel enjoyed watching him go.

As the urinals in that part of the building were better appointed than the smelly toilets on his floor, Schlegel took advantage. He was going about his business when Nebe joined him, leaving a diplomatic space. They stood in a show of attentive silence. Schlegel stared intently at his vanishing piss. It was common gossip that Nebe was inordinately proud of his cock and his opening line in any seduction was quite simply, did they want to see it?

'Enough to make them goggle,' was the verdict of his mother, who regarded herself sufficiently well-bred to make a point of vulgarity. 'But not as big as he thinks.'

Schlegel got away first but Nebe finished quickly and joined him at the basins where he asked whether there might be a connection between the old man who had shot himself and the Jewish butchers, through the slaughterhouse.

Schlegel said carefully that he had been asked to file a report on the old man, and as far as he understood the search for the missing Jewish butchers was a separate issue.

'That's your decision,' said Nebe, sounding lightly sinister. 'I quite understand.'

The remark was typical of the man's mind games.

'What do you make of Morgen?' Nebe asked, drying his hands and doing up his jacket. Schlegel noticed he hadn't finished up properly and there was a spot on his trousers where he had dribbled.

He said it was too early to say. Better to volunteer nothing, he thought.

'Has Morgen said anything?'

'Not about why he is here. No, sir.'

'Find out and tell me.'

How many people was he expected to spy for now? He volunteered that Morgen was not showing any signs of being there for underhand reasons. That much was true, for all the speculation. Everyone was projecting onto Morgen, including himself. The man might be odd and mysterious but so far he had not shown his hand, if indeed he had one.

Nebe grew exasperated and asked Schlegel if he had been born yesterday.

Schlegel held the toilet door for Nebe and they went their separate ways until Nebe suddenly turned round and came back.

'What wild theories of Gersten's?' he asked with restrained aggression. He appeared upset.

Schlegel carefully rehearsed his lines in his head first before reciting that Gersten had an unreliable Ukrainian translator who believed the killings had a Bolshevik connection.

'Russian Jews or Russians *and* Jews?'

'He's not clear. I think it's more to do with them having killed his people in a similar way.'

Schlegel at first avoided looking at Nebe, addressing the medals on his chest. Now he saw the man's face was white with anger.

'Categorically not. I will not have you going down that route. Absolutely forbidden!'

Schlegel wondered what he had said wrong.

Nebe repeated what Stoffel had told him: the hunt now was for any missing butchers.

Schlegel decided to stand up for himself. He had been given the job of finding them because no one was interested. If it was now so important then homicide should take care of its own cases, because he did not have the necessary experience.

His remarks verged on the insubordinate, and he lacked Morgen's indifference, but he calculated he could get away with it because Nebe deferred to his stepfather. Stoffel would give him hell but it was only for another two weeks.

# 22

Sybil's afternoons continued to be spent at Rosenstrasse, help-ing Franz, without knowing why, other than feeling safe because she had no fear of being unmasked there. Lore anyway seemed content at Alwynd's, writing the man's copy and translating it so Alwynd could bill for two fees. Lore and Alwynd were always chuckling together or talking about stuff that went over Sybil's head. She knew Lore was safe with Alwynd and decided it was easier when she was out of the way.

She felt protected by Franz's coping. Time to do the job, he said, and they got on with it.

Otherwise she tried to make the most of the isolated pockets of tranquillity that came her way. Sitting alone quietly sewing while Lore slept, until interrupted by the grunting of one of Alwynd's students being noisily fucked and a bath being run afterwards, the pipes wheezing and hammering as the ancient system tried to cope. Sybil amused herself with the thought that the clanking and sighing was what Alwynd's fornications would sound like by the time he was an old man. She was as usual a little shocked by the language she sometimes used to herself.

Where Sybil thought about the future and was too paralysed to do anything about it, Lore insisted their luck was holding and they should ride it. She said Alwynd was a great believer in the drift of currents. Lore once shook Sybil and told her to appreciate what she had. They couldn't have been more fortu-nate stumbling across the apartment.

They inevitably quarrelled more, which was compensated for with lingering reconciliations. Sometimes Sybil felt too stupid for Lore and feared she got on her nerves. She felt unsettled about everything: not telling Lore about Rosenstrasse; pretending she was out searching for someone who could find them papers; not getting around to having her pin-up photos done; not making a greater effort to look for her mother. The fate of her mother continued to nag which was perhaps only to be expected; theirs always had been a shrewish relationship. All this Sybil normally would have taken in her stride, but she was often too exhausted to sleep.

To his surprise, as Schlegel was leaving the office he received a call from Francis Alwynd asking what he was doing. Nothing, he said.

'Come over. We'll have a jazz evening.'

It was the first time in as long as Schlegel could remember that anyone resembling a friend had extended an invitation.

They played jazz, got drunk and chatted about art, which Alwynd knew about.

He stood up suddenly, and said, 'There are a couple of girls in the back. We could turn this into a party.'

Sybil heard Alwynd prowling the apartment, standing and listening outside their door. He opened it. They were in bed and the light was out. He had once said to her in his unsubtle way that what he liked best was waking in the night with his cock hard and being able to put himself in a woman and drift off again, feeling truly safe.

Lore stirred in her sleep as Alwynd left. Sybil lay there, thinking about Lore and the give and take of their desire, which was something wholly new after the strange and unsatisfying business of taking a man into her body. She feared Alwynd would yet find a way of insinuating himself. She listened to the world outside, with its weather and traffic, knowing that without Lore next to her life would make no sense.

Alwynd came back pulling a face.

'They might. Not in the mood, I suspect. One's a lesbian. The other isn't really, but is completely under her spell.'

Alwynd turned up the volume on the record player.

'I was talking to one of my acquaintances at the Foreign Office who was saying that the leadership, for all its fear of decadence, is obsessed by it. Is that your view?'

Schlegel said he had no access to the leadership other than what the mass media told them and that was very controlled.

'I will show you what I mean,' said Alwynd.

They stared together at pale female nudes in suggestive and sinful congress with a succession of animals, especially muscular black pythons.

'Black, no less!' exclaimed Alwynd. 'Hitler's favourite, von Stuck. You'd get away with nothing like this in Ireland, however much you dressed it up in religious metaphor.'

They were looking at a large art book of colour reproductions.

'Here's Paul Mathias Padua's *Leda and the Swan*.'

The image, both suggestive and specific, showed a naked young woman lying tilted upside down on a bed with her legs apart, waiting to receive a rampant swan.

'It caused a scandal when Hitler chose it for display in a day of German art.'

Schlegel hadn't known.

'It's terrible art,' said Alwynd. 'Come and look at these.'

He crossed to a chest of drawers and got out two sheets wrapped in tissue.

'Banned here now. I got these in Vienna when you could

pick them up for nothing.' Alwynd unwrapped the pictures and showed Schlegel two stark, half-undressed female studies, with graphically displayed genitals. Schlegel stared at the parted vaginas, not at all sure what to make of the drawings. Their fluid, confident lines seemed to offer an unsettling combination of the cold and the forensic, amounting to a clinical curiosity that transcended voyeurism, but he didn't really understand what he was looking at, not in terms of the subject, which couldn't be more plain, but its interpretation. He decided they probably represented everything they had been taught to fear.

They got a lot drunker. Alwynd said it was nice to be able to get stocious once in a while in agreeable company.

'The Germans are such relentless drinkers. The Irish too but they are more relaxed, though they probably end up the drunker. I rather miss that. The relaxation I mean. Well, time to stagger off to bed.'

Schlegel looked at his watch. Too late for a train, he said.

Alwynd waved airily. 'Help yourself to the sofa and in the morning we'll have breakfast with the girls.'

Schlegel thought about the drawings Alwynd had shown him. He supposed them passionate; he could not imagine anyone displaying herself like that for him. He slept briefly and woke up. The sofa was uncomfortable. He was about to get up and walk home when he saw Alwynd's typewriter on the table.

He put down a blanket to muffle the noise of the machine and started to type one-fingered:

*On the morning of Saturday, 27 February 1943, at approximately seven a.m., a Jewish male (Metzler, W.), aged 64 years, proceeded to shoot in the head and kill a German male (Schmeisser, J.), aged 47 years, warden of the former's residence at Brandenburgischestrasse 43. The Jewish male Metzler then immediately shot and killed himself. As far as we can ascertain, he used his own pistol (Mauser C96), kept illegally since his time of military service. It is believed the incident was witnessed in part or whole by a passer-by who then fled. The witness, probably female (Todermann), remains unavailable for questioning. The Jewish male Metzler was due for deportation on the day of his death. It has not been possible to ascertain whether, or how, he knew of his impending arrest, or to talk to witnesses about the man's character or mental constitution, and so forth.*

He drunkenly thought the tone caught the right balance of dull precision and dry facts. He decided to omit the military record. All he lacked was a motive for killing the warden. He was obliged now to talk to the widow. He would do that tomorrow. After that it would be done.

He turned off the light and opened the blackout curtain and sat in the window and watched the street. The moon came out. There was still some movement, one or two cars, a few passers-by.

He thought about the other deaths, the murder room, the flayed bodies and money stuffed in a dead man's mouth. Instinct told him to file the Metzler report as quickly as possible. The enigmatic presence of Morgen told him he wasn't dealing with something straightforward.

He woke after dreaming of the same dusty roads as before, standing in an empty landscape, waiting for nothing. He had a dry mouth and a hangover, which felt like someone had shoved grit into the inside of his eyelids.

When no one appeared he left. It was still early. He was too hungover for Alwynd's breakfast.

As he had time he decided to walk home via the tax office where two dossiers on Morgen were waiting at reception.

On the way he heard a woman at a tram stop say, 'It's the idea of things falling from the sky that you can do nothing about that really gets to me.'

He read Morgen's file. The man's age he had guessed right, nine years older than himself. He was listed as told: an investigative judge with prosecuting powers. The transfer to military action, and his serving rank in the Waffen-SS, was noted in pencil at the end of the report. In the margin someone had written in a different hand, 'This one won't be coming back,' under which was written in ink, 'Wrong!' followed by details of his transfer to Financial Investigation, Criminal Police, Berlin.

An early report noted expertise in international law, and a controversy over Morgen's chosen subject for his thesis: pacifism. That was a surprise, though Schlegel supposed the result must not have been so subversive for it was passed for publication by the censor. More controversial was Morgen's objection to Hitler becoming Chancellor, on the grounds that it invested too much power in the hands of one man. The report was vague on the outcome, other than to indicate a scandal which was prevented from coming to trial by the influence of powerful friends.

'This man needs careful watching,' concluded the first part of the report. 'That said, lack of compromise and principled behaviour make him a valuable asset, if used correctly.'

Schlegel could not decide whether this meant Morgen was considered a liability or a useful tool. Whichever, several accounts followed of superiors' mounting exasperation at his intransigence. Despite a roving brief to investigate internal affairs in the new eastern territories, he was, as reported by

Gersten and Lazarenko, accused of indiscretion and persisting after prosecution became unrealistic. The most damning assessment had him as tenacious and possibly stupid in his inability to obey orders.

The report noted several cases closed for lack of conclusive evidence. Morgen's downfall came after refusing to make a prosecution in a routine case of homicidal drunk driving, because he didn't believe the evidence, followed by detention and six months' combat.

It was a considerable fall from grace followed by a dubious rehabilitation that made little sense, unless it involved an ulterior motive, such as everyone feared, insinuating him into the criminal police to expose internal corruption, which would not be difficult.

On reflection the most disturbing assessment Schlegel found was a handwritten addition to the section covering his career in Lublin, which noted, 'This officer makes a habit of getting himself beaten up.'

Schlegel laughed before deciding he didn't want to become a candidate for getting beaten up too. The few times it had happened he hadn't liked it at all.

The warden's blood, still on the corridor wall, had gone almost black. The block felt like it had remained empty. Schlegel rang the bell by the hatch. The widow didn't recognise him at first. As he followed her into the apartment he saw the backs of her slippers were trodden down. They slapped the floor as she walked; thick stockings still bunched around ankles displaying deltas of broken veins. The room smelled of inadequate personal hygiene. He wasn't offered a seat. He said he needed to know why the old man shot her husband.

'Spare me a rookie cop. How old are you anyway?'

'Twenty-five.'

'You should dye it.'

She meant his hair. He wanted to say hers disqualified her from any pronouncement on the subject.

'Ask that Todermann bitch, if you can find her. My trap's shut on the matter.'

She crossed her arms, obviously dying to tell. Schlegel threatened to drag her down to the station. She shuddered and said she couldn't face those photographs of the drowned in the entrance hall. It was true. No one knew why they were there. Schlegel made a point of avoiding them too.

In the end, he had to pretend he was going to hit her. She started to cry in an entirely false way, and Schlegel saw the whole thing had been about her being able to talk up the story to her friends afterwards.

She huffed with indignation then did as she was told, now clearly wishing to shock.

'That lump of lard used his authority the better to position his cock. "Oh, I will have to report you . . . unless you are extra nice." ' She made a masturbating gesture. 'Didn't like to sully himself. They did it to him, it didn't count as a race thing. Tell that to the bishop!'

Her husband and Sybil Todermann had such a relationship, of which Metzler was jealous.

Schlegel supposed he had his motive.

Would he put this in his report? It would only complicate and he didn't fancy being assigned to two months investigating corruption among block wardens.

The woman said the reason her husband didn't fuck them was because he didn't want to feel their tails.

Schlegel let it pass and asked whether Sybil Todermann's mother had been subjected to her husband's attentions.

'Are you kidding? That witch! I bet she cast a spell on that fool Metzler, stuck pins in her wax doll. There was that nuisance of a child that fell downstairs and broke its neck.' She contorted her face. 'Tell me that wasn't her.'

He said he had heard Todermann's mother told fortunes. The remark provoked phlegmy laughter.

'She could no more read the cards than I can, but that didn't stop her – "beware of the tall dark stranger" – as if sucking up to a bunch of superstitious Party bosses was going to save her a one-way ticket.'

The old man's door was nailed shut, not very effectively, and the Gestapo seal applied. A couple of hard kicks and it gave way.

If a gun had been safely hidden up the chimney, other things could be too.

He took off his coat, jacket, waistcoat and shirt to save them getting filthy. It was freezing cold but better that than a fortune in cleaning bills. He spent a dirty fifteen minutes feeling around as far as he could reach. A loose brick came flying down, narrowly missing his head. He lay breathing hard, staring up into the black chimney. A second loose brick he managed to retrieve. He scrabbled around with his fingers trying to explore the hole but his reach wasn't long enough. It occurred to him how tall the old man must have been. Schlegel found a wooden spoon in the kitchen and used that to poke around in the recess. Nothing. Perhaps someone else had got there first. Maybe Metzler hadn't keep his secrets up the chimney. Where would he hide something? Under the floorboards? Schlegel inspected the trunk again. The green pullover was gone, confirming that anything hidden up the chimney would have been taken too.

Schlegel tried to picture what he was looking for. Some sort of secret text that filled in the gaps and explained everything? He couldn't see it. People weren't that neat about loose ends.

What he found was not what he had imagined. He stared at his discovery for the longest time, thinking. It wasn't a lot but all the old temptations were there.

# 23

The bombed house was only about a five-minute walk from Alwynd's apartment. Sybil passed it a couple of times before realising it had taken up residence in her head. It showed there was such a thing as retribution and their persecutors might not escape unscathed.

It was easily entered in spite of the door being nailed closed and warning signs declaring the building unsafe. There was too much damage for it not to be accessible and after quickly checking no one was around she slipped inside.

Later on, she came to think of what she found as her refuge. It was hard to reach because part of the stairs had come away and she had to find damaged floorboards to make a walkway across the drop. The first time she crossed she was frightened by the darkness that went all the way down to the basement. Fall and she would break her neck. She wobbled in the middle of the planks, thought about the moment of stepping off into space and hurried on.

The ceiling had crashed in on most of the first floor but at the back behind the rubble lay a perfectly preserved space that had served as someone's reading room, with a little open fireplace and an armchair and small table. A window overlooked the back, the garden now full of blasted masonry. The walls were lined with bookshelves, even the one with the door. It was silent and peaceful in a way she had never encountered before. She wanted nothing more than to come every day and work her way through the books until life became normal again. They were good books too. Classics. Books she had never got around to reading. Names she had never heard of. Poetry too. She promised to teach herself to read it. She imagined holding her own with Lore and Alwynd. At first she was happy to sit and indulge in the luxury of undisturbed thinking. She switched the table lamp on not daring to think it might work. It did. She started to read a story about a man named Biberkopf who haunted many of the places she knew. He had just got out of the prison in Moabit and his first meeting was with a strange rabbi. Biberkopf seemed quite mad, stir crazy perhaps, a persecuted ox of a man, but not in the way people were now, just another loser looking for a break. It seemed he had strangled his mistress.

When she got home Lore was humming the hit tune 'You Shall Be the Emperor of My Soul'.

Over the next few days, Sybil searched the rest of the house as much as she was able. It must have been lodgings because upstairs there were different bathrooms and kitchens and a series of bedsits, all covered in dust. She even found some food, only carrots, just the right side of mouldy, which she took downstairs and pretended was a feast. She supposed her little library had belonged to the landlord. The layout there was different. It seemed more a man's space than a woman's but she couldn't tell. What she thought had been the bedroom was too damaged to enter. She searched in vain for a pipe or a coat or a pair of shoes that might say. The carrots gave her as much pleasure as anything she could remember. She imagined she was a castaway. She couldn't remember when she had last had a game of her own. When she was ready she would share the space with Lore, although superstition played a part in not showing her. Her growing fear was of their being taken together. Sybil had started to think her own arrest would be bearable so long as she could believe Lore was still free.

She did the obvious thing and looked for valuables and identity papers. At first she found this rooting around distasteful, then decided she should extend her search to other places in the hope of finding a dead person's papers. Why pay when you can get it for nothing? The observation struck her as so funny she laughed until she had a stitch, and then even more at the thought of herself laughing alone in this strange, damaged place. After that she went downstairs and quietly carried on reading the story of Biberkopf.

# 24

Schlegel was relieved to see Morgen wearing a civilian suit. Out of uniform he looked less threatening. The suit must have been in mothballs for years. Even with his cigarette smoke the room smelled strongly of camphor. Morgen described it as diabolical and he was not sure if he could live with it.

'But perhaps not so inappropriate if Nebe thinks I am the devil in disguise. Isn't that what you are all saying?'

Schlegel denied it but was a terrible liar, and Morgen told him so.

Schlegel stared at his desk top in embarrassment. Morgen seemed more amused than offended. He stubbed out his cigarette and said as though addressing a dim pupil, 'Paranoia is the operating principle of our system, top to bottom. It's not a rampant paranoia, more one of stealth. It's an extension of the leadership principle, which works on initiative and interpretation rather than direct order and command. Are you with me so far?'

Schlegel said he hadn't thought of it like that. A case in point was Nebe, who for all his seniority seemed as worried as the next man.

'Like the Carter Family says, "It takes a worried man to sing a worried song".'

Schlegel was astonished by the reference. He hadn't thought of Morgen like that.

'Yes, yes. Hot jazz boy!' He laughed. 'Not any more. One learns to move on from such dalliance. I was a fan of the method more than the product. Classical music never sounded good on gramophones and jazz did. It was the right music for that technology. Yes, the Carter Family. Recorded in 1930 for the Victor Talking Machine Company. The story of a man imprisoned for unknown reasons, therefore legitimate for us to discuss in terms of American paranoia.'

Schlegel suspected he was being played with and waited for the pounce. His own paranoia extended to Morgen flicking through *his* file and cackling wickedly at all the references to ineffectiveness, backsliding and questionable decadence; the rest didn't bear thinking about.

Morgen carried on, apparently unaware of Schlegel's discomfort. 'From my modest observations of human behaviour, I would say this paranoia has two main outcomes. In spite of all the assertions of strength, the system is flawed, perhaps fatally, because the only legitimate responses are panic and inertia, masquerading as efficiency. I know we swept everything before us in the conquests of 1940 and '41 but it was effortless. A perverse reading could hold that mass mobilisation was really concerted inertia because the machinery did all the work and the war machine is the perfect product of paranoia, wouldn't you say?'

The man's thesis had been on pacifism, Schlegel remembered.

'Anyway,' Morgen continued, 'as of this January we have officially entered the new age of panic. Blame what you like, the army's failures in the east, the alignment of the planets . . . but with panic comes superstition.'

'Why are you telling me this?'

'Because I see you as the perfect representative of panic and inertia. You are a paradigm of the system. And you know it's true, which is why you don't take offence. You are, Schlegel, a fascinating specimen.'

Schlegel sat there incapable of thinking, other than admiring how effectively the tables had been turned.

'As for me,' Morgen continued, 'let us for the moment play Nebe's game. You are all terrified of your corruption being exposed, and corruption is the last resort of inertia. I could deny that I am a spy with powers of judicial enquiry – perhaps I already did, I no longer remember – but I may be lying, because lying is the cornerstone of the edifice. This is not criticism but fact. And I would go further to say that sometimes the virtues of lying are underestimated. Of course, if I am lying now you will find yourself answering for that shop in the cellar you run.'

Morgen waited for Schlegel to deny it. Schlegel said nothing. He had never heard such strange talk. From Morgen it didn't sound defeatist or subversive. Schlegel wondered if it came from some condoned higher level, dedicated to a constant re-evaluation of the entire project. Perhaps, far from being the outsider, Morgen operated at the heart of the system, in some rarefied strata, beyond the usual strictures and propaganda control, secretly dedicated to philosophical enquiry. But if it were really the case, he wouldn't be sitting in Schlegel's backwater.

Morgen resumed smoking and became businesslike, moving papers around his desk.

'That's all for you to decide. However, I will throw this in for free. No one has asked me to investigate your little shop.'

'Who told you about it?'

'Stoffel, of course. He wants to get you in trouble. He doesn't like you. He's crafty though. He slipped it in very well. Stoffel is such a good representative of inertia that he should be made its formal ambassador. I doubt if we will see Stoffel go through the necessary evolutionary stages to reach a state of paranoia, but I may be wrong. As for friend Stoffel, I suggest you tell him that

I am a spy because it is always good when men like that are made to sweat. And in the meantime, please note that I have just raised your paranoia levels, by giving you confidential information in the guise of a favour that is more of a poisoned chalice.'

Morgen, pleased by his bamboozling, went back to his papers before quietly announcing, not looking up, 'To tell the truth, I don't know why I am here, but it is always possible someone will ask me to make a report of the sort you are all so afraid of.'

They worked in silence. After some time thinking about it, Schlegel volunteered to Morgen that he thought the dead man's penis had been amputated because he was circumcised.

Morgen sat back and said, 'Do explain.'

'As a rule, all Jewish men are circumcised.'

Schlegel was too, thanks to his mother being English where the practice was not unusual. German boys never were, he had found to his cost. During his compulsory labour service he was regularly taken for a Jew and beaten up in the communal showers, being told that a Jew couldn't hide when it came to his cock.

Morgen switched his cigarette to the other side of his mouth. 'Are you saying the man's cock was cut off to hide the fact that he was a Jew?'

'Or as an act of desecration because he was.'

'No one will bother to identify a dead Jew.'

Morgen stood up abruptly, put on his overcoat and announced he was going out.

Schlegel read over his report. His efforts struck him as pathetic. For whom was he writing? It would be filed unread and never referred to again. It was, in Morgen's assessment, a perfect product of inertia. Morgen had analysed him more effectively in two minutes than anyone else had managed in years.

Show some initiative, he thought.

Metzler was someone's agent, according to Nebe. Whose? Schlegel suspected Gersten's, which meant murky waters. Yet could he afford to ignore it? The hard question everyone had to ask, probably even Nebe, was have I done enough to cover myself? In dealing with superiors, the point unconsidered was invariably the one that was exposed, however thorough in other respects. Plenty of stories circulated of innocent parties sent to punishment camp under the amorphous charge of professional negligence.

He called Gersten's office, thinking if he couldn't reach him he would leave it at that; let chance decide.

Gersten disappointed him by answering. Schlegel explained why he was calling.

'Yes, the old Jew,' said Gersten enigmatically.

'I'm told he was your agent.'

Gersten laughed. 'Says who?'

The block warden's widow, Schlegel answered, thinking serve her right, she could deny it all she liked. He said he feared the case was not as straightforward as everyone assumed.

'You'll find it is. The old man was a fantasist.'

He pointed out Gersten had not mentioned knowing Metzler at the scene of crime.

'Because I hadn't seen him.'

'You must have realised. He was brought into the yard. He was identified.'

Gersten insisted it was of no consequence to Schlegel's report.

'The only issue as far as you are concerned is his motive for killing the warden. The rest is irrelevant.'

'Why?'

'Because the man had nothing to sell.'

'Did he offer?'

'Yes, but they all do and he was as bad as the rest, saying he had this and that, he could help, but when you call their bluff they give you nothing.'

Gersten was too clever for him. According to Morgen's new categories, Schlegel could not work out the man's operating method at all. Not paranoia or inertia. Something slipperier.

Gersten, patronising, said, 'I expect he was trying to sell information in exchange for his safety, but nothing came of it. I wouldn't waste time. No one is interested.'

Schlegel had overplayed his hand. He was about to hang up when Gersten appeared to relent.

'We're not in the business of being obstructive. If it helps, say that aspects of the report are off limits because of their confidential nature. Everyone will know what that means and you will have covered your bases.'

It was a putdown; the favour of the senior party on behalf of an incompetent junior. Gersten was probably only a few years older but outranked Schlegel by several levels.

'And is Morgen interested yet?' asked Gersten.

'I think you will find him too paranoid,' Schlegel replied, amused. Gersten asked what was funny and Schlegel hung up without answering.

'You're right,' said Morgen, taking off his hat and coat. 'He was a Jew. By name of Abbas. He worked in the Jewish picture library.'

He sat down and passed over a copy of the dead man's identity card, showing a fellow with a long equine face, recognisably that of the one lying on the parquet floor.

Schlegel looked up in surprise. 'Where did you get this?'

'The Jewish Association is obliged to keep a copy of all identity cards. I had no idea what I was looking for. There are thousands to look through. I was lucky. There aren't many As before Abbas.'

Schlegel was equally impressed when Morgen produced cards for the old man and Sybil Todermann.

'We can confirm from his work card that Metzler ended up in the slaughterhouse, and the Todermann woman worked as a seamstress near Savignyplatz.'

Schlegel said, 'I think I know what this is about.'

It was Morgen's turn to look surprised.

'I think it's Gersten.'

'Who killed Abbas? You can't be serious.'

'Of course not. I think Abbas was his spy. Gersten is an active intelligence gatherer. Lazarenko calls himself a consultant but he's really his spy. Nebe says Metzler was someone's agent.'

'Except Gersten denies it is him?'

'A colleague of mine in the tax office was telling me the Gestapo was turned inside out last year for corruption, with a lot of dismissals.'

'If Abbas was Gersten's agent, it would explain his shock at seeing him when he wasn't expecting to.'

'But why cut off the man's penis?'

'Perhaps we are dealing with a psychopath.'

'There's something else,' said Schlegel, reaching into his desk. 'We now have a direct link between Abbas and old man Metzler. I found these fifties.'

He counted out the notes. Ten fifties. Five hundred marks. Brand new and all with the telltale points to say they were forgeries. Morgen picked up a note and inspected it.

'Exactly the same as the others. Where were these?'

'Behind a ventilation grille in Metzler's bedroom, more or less hiding in plain sight.'

'Did you think of keeping them?' asked Morgen, reading him perfectly.

'Of course. I have a history of recidivism.'

There seemed no point denying it. He told Morgen about his shoplifting sprees.

Morgen said, 'Boys will be boys.'

They found Stoffel in the canteen, wearing his bowler hat and reading a newspaper. He looked at Morgen's worn flannel suit and said he looked better out of uniform.

Morgen said, 'The dead man in the apartment was a Jew named Abbas.'

Stoffel gave a couple of slow handclaps, returned to his newspaper and licked his finger before idly turning the page.

'Jew cases are not priority.'

'Quite,' said Morgen. 'What's to investigate if they are all being packed off?'

'Quite. The only thing Herr Abbas did was to be inconsiderate enough to die on our patch.'

Stoffel looked at Schlegel with opaque, watery eyes, his dislike evident.

'Your Metzler report?'

It was on its way, he said.

'Are you being told not to investigate the Abbas case?' asked Morgen.

Stoffel made an equivocal motion. 'Nothing active.'

'Who told you not to?'

'It doesn't work like that.'

'How does it work?'

Stoffel turned to Schlegel. 'Educate the man.'

'I want to hear it from you,' said Morgen.

Stoffel considered the challenge. 'It's no skin off my nose. Just because there is a flap on doesn't mean anyone has to do anything. Besides, there's no budget for dead Jews.'

From Stoffel's studied indifference and the comfortable

spread of his haunches, Schlegel suspected the man had a card up his sleeve.

'You know the old joke about murder,' Stoffel went on. 'If you have to commit one, kill a Jew because no one will investigate.'

Neither of them laughed.

'How are we supposed to interpret Nebe's panic?' Morgen asked.

'Biggest boy hits bigger boy, bigger boy hits big boy, big boy hits biggest of the small boys and so on down. Nebe will tell you if you ask nicely that he has to be seen to bang the drum for the sake of his superiors.' He sat back and looked at them wearily. 'Everyone knows the problem is about to go away. Soon no Jews will be left.'

'And those in hiding?'

Stoffel went back to his newspaper. 'They are jumping off buildings and throwing themselves under trains and drowning in rivers faster than we can pick them up.'

He flicked over another page and carried on reading as he said, 'The money's your problem, I believe.'

'Can we expect any sort of help?' asked Morgen.

'You're on your own with that.' He gave Schlegel another nasty look. 'I will sort you out later for telling tales out of school.'

They were climbing the stairs back up to the office. Schlegel was already out of breath when Morgen paused on a half-landing.

'About Gersten. Let's say he's at the top of a triangle and at the base you have Abbas and Metzler. And in the middle you have the money. Agreed?'

'Agreed.'

'You also have Gersten trying to send us off on a wild-goose chase by using Lazarenko. I think Gersten doesn't want us to make any connection between him and the money.'

'But he was the first to mention it was fake, when we were all standing around looking at Abbas. He sounded very certain.'

'I think it was an involuntary admission. He was in a state of shock, finding his agent stretched out on the floor.'

Having inadvertently instigated the investigation, Gersten was now perhaps in a position of having to thwart it.

Schlegel asked if they should confront the man. He didn't confess to his own failed effort. Morgen said they had nothing and for the moment Gersten was probably capable of running rings round them. What they were going to do was what they had been told.

'We're going to follow the money.'

Schlegel told Morgen he was meeting a friend that night who might be useful.

'I have to return your files to him. They made interesting reading.'

Morgen had the grace to concede this subterfuge, and they carried on upstairs with Schlegel thinking it probably wasn't too often that Morgen was caught out.

# 25

Sybil was optimistic when Franz said a vacancy had come up in the hospital laundry room, and there might be a job for Lore working in the grounds. Sybil thought her luck might be changing, until she understood from the way Franz looked at her that his benevolence had a price.

He wasn't unpleasant about it and smiled attractively.

'This is the way it is now.'

Franz was in a flirtatious mood and Sybil realised he intended to make his demand after they were done with serving and unless he got what he wanted now he wouldn't do any more to help. Be philosophical, she told herself. The stakes were high enough to make what he wanted meaningless by comparison.

Franz said they could go downstairs. He knew the building.

Sybil thought back to when they were students and how much she had liked him, if not physically. He wasn't so bad, she told herself. He wasn't some monster. He took care of himself. He was one of the few whose breath wasn't terrible.

He took her to a storeroom in the basement. Once the door was shut he told her to get in the mood. Sybil knew she was too passive when they kissed. He grew impatient. Then he couldn't get hard and made her suck him. She had to kneel down. She thought how easy and natural it was with Lore, compared to Franz's flaccid dick slipping in and out of her mouth. She felt nothing. She said to herself, this is how it is now. Then he got harder and told her to help push him inside her because he still wasn't properly stiff, and there was the demeaning business of lubricating him with her spit. After that it was over almost as soon as he started. She despised him as another man taking advantage, and felt a little sorry for him for being so pathetic. He hadn't even lain her down, just fucked her standing. His thighs quivered when he came while he cursed for being too quick. She tried not to show her contempt and even kissed him, as if to say it would be better next time, hoping it would never come to that.

Sybil Todermann's work card described her as a seamstress. Schlegel suspected this was a rather modest description because he knew from his mother's friend of the young woman who copied fashions and he doubted if there were many women's tailors around Savignyplatz.

On the train he brooded on all the machinations he had got sucked into since Morgen's arrival, the latest of which was Stoffel's enmity. He remained puzzled by Stoffel's lack of concern over Nebe's impending deadline. Not only could he not be bothered to do anything, he couldn't be bothered to be seen to be doing it.

The place where Sybil Todermann worked was smarter than her job definition implied. From the front it appeared a fancy shop where it was necessary to ring a bell to gain admission. Immediately inside was a well-appointed if dated reception with cubicles for clients to try on clothes.

When he said who he was to the woman who answered she went pale.

'Frau Zwicker?'

The woman nodded, frightened. He reassured her it was a routine enquiry. He only needed to speak to Sybil as a witness to something else.

Frau Zwicker said Sybil hadn't turned up all week.

He asked to see where she worked.

She took him through. The space was bigger than the front of the shop suggested. Two dozen women worked in rows and the air was full of the hum of sewing machines.

'What can you tell me about her?'

Frau Zwicker said she was a good worker who kept to herself.

'What do you make here?'

'Clothes for export mainly.'

A seamstress who had lived with a crazy mother, he thought; end of story. Except for his mother's friend and her Jewish seamstress.

'Show me some of the stuff she makes for the important wives.'

Frau Zwicker tried to pretend they did no such thing.

'I am not here to cause trouble. I only need to follow up on Fräulein Todermann. Your business is of no concern to me.'

Frau Zwicker mumbled for him to follow. She led the way down a corridor with a glass roof, at the far end of which stood a studio where clothes hung on rails.

Frau Zwicker gestured and said nothing, still expecting trouble.

Schlegel fingered his way through the hangers. Winter coats mainly, some evening dresses.

Frau Zwicker showed him a smart woman's suit. He knew enough about clothes to know it was both à la mode and well made. He also knew fashion was becoming scarce.

'It's very good, isn't it?'

'She was the best.'

'What else can you tell me?'

Frau Zwicker hesitated.

'Perhaps you could give me a list of her clients.'

'There isn't one. It was done through personal contact.'

'You must know who these women are.'

'I trusted her to make her own connections. She needed the money.'

'Is it legal for her to have her own clients? I am thinking of her Jewishness.'

'She had a special work permit.'

The woman was hiding something. She resisted a little longer, then collapsed and admitted that Sybil had come back there on Saturday as they were closing.

'Did she say anything about a shooting?'

'A shooting! Of course not.'

He gestured at the suit. 'I need to borrow this for a few days.'

The woman knew enough not to ask.

'If you have a bag.'

She found one.

'Have you the name and address of the client who this is for?'

'It's pinned to the suit.'

'Is it ready to go out? No more fittings?'

He looked at the address. It was near his mother.

'Why don't I deliver it in person? I have to go that way.'

Frau Zwicker looked at him as though he were mad, and he wondered too.

'There's nothing else you have to tell me?'

She stared at him miserably.

'Such as where she might be now.'

'She wouldn't want to get me in trouble.'

'Anything at all. I can always come back with others.'

'There's the attic,' she said.

It was up a flight of stairs at the back of the building, quite unprotected in terms of security. Frau Zwicker's story was Sybil had kept some items there. He saw from the old buttons on the floor that the place had once been used as a sweatshop. It didn't explain the discarded typewriter ribbon. An S-Bahn rumbled past, making the building shake. It would make a good safe place. Had she stayed there? Was there someone else?

# 26

They were in what was known as the bar with the green door. Its elderly barman was from another era, with a central parting and Kaiser moustache. Otto Keleman, certified accountant and unlikely party boy, was possessive of his haunts, and this was his favourite. He appeared put out when the barman made a point of welcoming Morgen.

'Haven't seen you for a day or two. Thought you were dead.'

Morgen had already got the evening off to a bad start by referring to Keleman as the man who had been showing his file around. Schlegel tried to explain, which only made matters worse. Keleman believed a confidence had been betrayed when all Schlegel wanted was for everyone to be open for a change. He dreaded Morgen following that with his mother's remark about Keleman getting into women's knickers.

Morgen asked if his bottle was still behind the bar. Privileged regulars could leave theirs. By no means everyone was invited to and it was a sign that one had arrived. Keleman admitted he had been trying for years.

Dozens of bottles, showing different levels of consumption, stood on shelves in front of the mirrored wall behind the bar.

Seeing Schlegel for a newcomer, the barman said, 'Sometimes ten years can pass before the owner comes back to claim his.'

He treated Morgen with impeccable insolence that was clearly affectionate.

'Been anywhere interesting?'

'Not really. You know how it is.'

'East, I would say.'

'Any reason?'

'You have the look.'

'Which one is that?'

The barman sighed. 'Think of something funny to say. People have been trying to get me to laugh for years.'

Keleman weighed in with an unfunny joke about fucking a nun.

Schlegel spotted Francis Alwynd sitting in a corner with what looked like a couple of young Foreign Office pals. He was in his fisherman's jersey and a tweed coat. He gave a lazy wave and saluted with his glass.

There were no women in. The atmosphere was one of masculine clubbability, with a clientele of professional suits who looked like lawyers, and a few uniforms. A lack of windows cast the place in a greenish light that made it resemble an underwater cocoon. Keleman was now on best behaviour, quizzing Morgen on how long it had taken him to get his bottle.

Schlegel produced one of the false notes and gave it to Keleman, who inspected it.

'It's a fifty-mark note.'

'A forged fifty.'

Keleman looked again, then got out a real one. Schlegel pointed to the discrepancies. Keleman agreed it would be much harder to spot without the telltale points at the corners of the frame.

'Even so, you never really look at the stuff. It's just a transaction. Short of it having "funny money" written on it, most people wouldn't notice. But that's not your point.'

'We want to know who is producing it,' said Morgen.

'Much in circulation?'

'Haven't got that far.'

Keleman looked at them knowingly. 'But you are required to go through the motions. I know all about that.'

'We are at least supposed to come up with a plausible report on who is producing it,' said Schlegel.

'Don't you have stool pigeons?'

Keleman seemed amused by his slang.

Schlegel said not really. Crime in wartime had become petty.

'There are no gangs left. There's not much murder. No cat burglars or jewel thieves. It's mainly about nicking food now. Nothing sophisticated.'

'It's pretty sophisticated in terms of corruption,' said Keleman. 'But that's quite close to the surface and often brazen.'

Morgen interrupted to say, 'It would make sense if the forged notes belonged to some pre-war operation and were only just reaching the market.'

Keleman said, 'Are you saying it's not in people's interests to forge now?'

Morgen inspected his empty glass and shrugged. 'Opportunity. Wherewithal. Expertise. Everything is dispersed. There is also the black market. We live in an age of barter. Solid goods.'

'Let me pour you another,' said Keleman, the ever-gregarious host, availing himself of Morgen's bottle. The round finished it.

Keleman knocked his back and said, 'Then you have to ask in whose interests it is to forge money.'

'Opportunity. Wherewithal. Et cetera,' repeated Morgen.

'Exactly,' said Schlegel, who was already having trouble focusing.

Keleman said, 'A criminal gang seems unlikely because, as you say, people are away. There is one obvious answer. I'll tell you, but first let me buy you another bottle.'

As Keleman stood up, Morgen said to tell the barman to put

the bottle in Keleman's name. Keleman stood beaming, saying it had to be one of the best evenings of his life.

While Keleman was at the bar Schlegel went to the toilet and paused to chat to Francis Alwynd. They exchanged pleasantries until something struck Alwynd as funny and he beckoned Schlegel closer. The Foreign Office boys were talking money among themselves.

Alwynd seemed barely able to contain his mirth and in a loud stage whisper announced, 'Those girls staying with me, I might be harbouring a couple of Jews.'

Schlegel quickly looked around. They were speaking English, but even so. The Foreign Office boys were still discussing expenses.

Alwynd behaved like a man who had no inkling and grinned like he had come up with the funniest remark. He mouthed the word 'Jews' again.

'Be careful who you say it to, Francis.'

Alwynd made a show of behaving like a reprimanded schoolboy, shrinking down in his seat. He was completely drunk, which he confirmed by saying, 'I am altogether bladdered, but you're right. Mum's the word!'

'Seriously, Francis,' Schlegel said, thinking he must sound like the man's maiden aunt.

Alwynd put his finger to his lips and said, 'Shh!' and collapsed into giggles.

Schlegel left him to it and rejoined the others. Keleman filled their glasses and saluted them.

'Well, cheers. I can't tell you how happy this makes me.'

Schlegel found it difficult to see the real difference between having a bottle behind the bar and buying drinks over the counter. He wondered meanly whether Keleman really did have much luck with women.

Schlegel saw Alwynd continue to put his finger to his lips and make shushing noises. He hadn't known the man was such a liability.

Keleman picked up the forged note and said, 'I should have paid with this.'

'Be our guest,' said Morgen. 'Schlegel was going to avail himself of it anyway.'

Keleman looked at Schlegel, who turned to Morgen and said, 'That was in confidence.'

'No, it wasn't. You placed no conditions or terms when you told me so I am free to tell who I like, for the purposes of entertainment, social lubrication, or whatever.'

He made the point so amiably that Schlegel was forced to concede. He supposed it hardly mattered if Keleman knew of his old habits; it would probably make him think more of him.

Keleman looked at the note again. 'You need to ask yourself who's left and who needs the money.'

'We all do,' said Morgen.

Schlegel said, 'Cigarettes probably have more buying power than money these days. Where's the sense in forging?'

'Unless,' prompted Keleman.

'Unless what?' Schlegel prompted back.

'Unless you really need the money. Again the question is who does? Most forgers working at the moment make a good living providing false papers. I expect your forger is one of them.'

'You mean Jews,' said Morgen.

Keleman nodded. 'Though I would have thought it's getting a bit late for them.'

Morgen said, 'Everyone knows Jews are clever with money but if you're saying they're the forgers we're going to have to show it.'

'Get yourself a stool pigeon, that's what everyone else does.'

The remark struck everyone as funnier than it was. They were sliding fast into drunkenness.

Keleman said Jews and money went together. During the big inflation crisis local Jewish presses turned out money round the clock. Printing, money and Jews belonged historically. The point now was all their money had been confiscated, but they were still expected to pay for everything.

'They're being charged for their own roundup and cost of deportation. I've seen the books. Even concentration camps, which were previously tax exempt, are having to file returns, as part of the new initiative to turn them into proper economic concerns.'

Keleman stared uncertainly at his glass and leaned forward.

'How much do you know of what goes on? Or went on. I am not sure it still does.'

Schlegel pointed out that such affairs did not fall into their domain.

'It's the fleecing that counted as much as anything.'

'Meaning?' asked Morgen.

'Those that could afford it were allowed to buy their way out for exorbitant sums. The practice still exists, or did until very recently.'

'How does it work?'

'On a ransom basis, more or less. Perhaps it is still possible to buy people back or bribe the right official to stay off the list.'

'And how would one go about this?'

'Through the correct Gestapo official.' Keleman sniggered. 'Or rather the *incorrect* Gestapo official.'

'Names?' asked Morgen.

Keleman shook his head. 'My information is not first-hand. Besides, I believe there has been a cleanup, so I'm probably out of date.'

They ended up completely drunk. Keleman missed his film preview and didn't care, being too excited about getting his own bottle. Schlegel asked Morgen whether Keleman was inert or paranoid, according to his theory. Keleman took a while to grasp the basics then said, 'That's brilliant. I am inert *and* paranoid.' He slid down in his seat.

Alwynd had fallen asleep in his corner, a beatific smile on his face, his companions gone. Morgen sat like a buddha, amused by the chaos.

Keleman briefly rallied to say, 'Actually, I am completely paranoid.'

He gave a rambling account of the corruption he was investigating.

'Huge slush funds. Names you wouldn't want to know about. Big, big stuff. They're all paying each other off. I need help.'

He frowned and looked morose, then perked up, saying he had another party and did they want to come. They made their excuses and stood out on the street, trying to work out the best way to get where they were all going, until Schlegel was left with Alwynd, who joined them and said he didn't know how to get home. The two staggered off together in search of taxis, gave up and stood waiting for a bus.

Alwynd said, 'I shouldn't have said what I did about the you-know-who.' He appeared unrepentant. 'I reserve the right not to like Jews, but your people should not be doing what you are doing, do you know what I mean? Bonny girls, but I know they have to go. I am just a way station on their road to Calvary. We each have our cross to bear. And there's my bus.'

He was gone, leaving Schlegel befuddled. He had missed the others leaving. He lurched drunkenly home; the night before sober by comparison. The walk seemed to take forever.

# 27

The sky remained the colour of sulphur. Schlegel was nursing the usual hangover, his mood not helped by oversleeping. Morgen had hauled him out of bed, banging on his door with news of another body.

'With money.'

The crime scene was nearby, only about five minutes, past Rosanthaler Strasse in a bomb-blasted building, not far from the cattle shed from which the rampaging cows had escaped. A guard stood outside. The rest were down in the basement.

They were taken down by a uniformed policeman with a torch. The hall and stairs were strewn with rubble. Wafting up came the aroma of decomposing corpse.

The way down to the basement grew dark. The electricity had gone.

To access the murder scene they had to crawl through a hole. There in a dark cave Schlegel sensed the presence of several men.

'Good afternoon, girls. Better late than never,' said Stoffel. 'Save your batteries. We're waiting for the light.'

They stood around in the darkness, apart from the occasional flare of a match and flash of a torch as the electricians fed cables down. Schlegel held his nose. Boots crunched on rubble. Stoffel told everyone to move as little as possible in order not to disturb the evidence.

'Money stuffed up the vagina of this one,' he announced, as though he were a tour guide. 'Female, obviously. Not so young.

Hard to say with the bloating. She may have been a pretty one. Two or three days since death, at a guess. Rigor mortis subsided. Black putrefaction setting in. A nice bouquet. The pancreas will be in the course of digesting itself. The flies, such as they are at this time of year, are having a feast. Probable cause of death, strangulation. Whether sexual intercourse took place remains to be established, but she has been interfered with.'

He switched on his torch and gave them a brief glimpse of splayed, mottled legs, the exposed thatch of pubic hair and money, a few notes lying crumpled between the legs, the rest stuffed into the vagina.

'Who found the body?' Morgen asked.

'Rescue workers. Alerted by the bruising to the throat. They must have been too scared to help themselves.'

'Is the money the same as before?'

'Don't know yet.'

Gersten spoke up for the first time. 'I would still say we are talking about acts of terror perpetrated by a Bolshevik Jewish slayer.'

Schlegel was surprised he was there. He supposed Lazarenko was lurking one step behind.

'Says you,' said Stoffel.

Their voices echoed in the dark. There seemed to be none of the usual crime scene activity in terms of doctors or medical orderlies and general police. It was as though they were being granted a special preview.

'Has the body been cut, like the other one?' Morgen asked.

'Not obviously. We must wait for an examination.'

The lights arrived and didn't work so they continued with torches, pointing half a dozen at the body, whose top half was clothed. The head was turned away, russet hair covered in dust. Schlegel saw livid bruising on the throat. The hands were thrown up, as if in surprise. One shoe was gone, the other half off.

The dimly lit scene, within the greater destruction, was too bleak to invite comment, other than Stoffel saying she looked like a great big rag doll, which prompted him to add with a guffaw that the children in the house must have been giants.

Nebe put in an appearance and looked irritated at getting his boots dirty. The mood remained strangely lethargic until he clapped his hands and said the clock was ticking. They had until four o'clock to come up with a presentable theory for Dr Goebbels, otherwise he was cancelling all leave.

He lectured them about how the Jewish maniac had struck again. He demanded to know whether this latest lot of money was forged like last time.

No one had looked because of rules about disturbing the scene of crime.

'Fuck the crime scene!' Nebe screamed. 'Schlegel!'

Schlegel stepped forward while someone shone a torch. Not wanting to look, from modesty as much as revulsion, he saw one of the crumpled notes that lay outside the body was a fifty. He passed it to Morgen who confirmed it was fake.

Nebe put his hands on hips, looking expectant.

Morgen said, 'We are working on the theory it was Jews that printed the money.'

That set Nebe off.

'Jews printing their own money! Jews running around killing people! What next?'

Nebe was at his most insufferable, throwing his weight around because he hadn't the faintest idea what to do. He was notorious for getting others to do the work and taking credit or attributing blame accordingly.

Morgen said, 'Perhaps you could advise us, sir, as it is not clear whether you want these cases solved or for them to go away so they don't become part of some underground propaganda.'

'Both! Both!'

Morgen said, 'In that case, you should hear what Herr Lazarenko has to say.'

'Who's Lazarenko?'

Lazarenko was produced out of the shadows and Gersten explained who he was. Lazarenko, ever pushy, immediately offered his translation services to Nebe.

'Get on with it, man. Has anyone got a cigarette?'

When no one else volunteered Morgen got around to offering one of his. Schlegel thought Nebe, usually so impeccable, looked haggard in the match flare.

Lazarenko gave a practised little speech. Bolshevik atrocities committed in northern Ukraine the summer before last overlapped with the current spate of killings. As a result of his latest intelligence he believed a killing gang was at work, and it was part of an internecine civil war among the last of the Jews, in which Russians were also involved.

It was the last thing Nebe wanted to hear. He rounded on Lazarenko.

'How can you know this? A civil war! Are you saying there is a chance of rebellion among these slaves?'

Gersten had to step in. He drew attention to himself by shining his torch upwards to show his face, unintentionally making himself look grotesque. Stoffel tittered.

Gersten reassured Nebe that there was no chance of any uprising among what remained of the Jews, or the Russians.

'They are in hand.'

'He said civil war.'

'An exaggeration. Think of it more like a Sicilian vendetta. A tiny group killing out of betrayal and revenge. It will soon burn itself out. Such death throes are typical of Jewish behaviour in general. When threatened from outside they fall to squabbling among themselves.'

Stoffel clapped his hands in ironic applause.

Nebe took Morgen aside. Schlegel heard him say Morgen was making the case too political. Then he announced that he didn't want to hear another word about vendettas or historical connections.

'Dr Goebbels is a very busy man. He is only interested in headlines.'

Morgen was only interested in the money, and where that took them. If Abbas and this new body were killed in retaliation for something specific, then dressing the bodies was a message.

He speculated the length of Auguststrasse. 'Hunter and hunted. Hunter uses agents but the hunted is too good. The bodies become trophies.'

'Is Gersten the hunter?'

'No names for the moment. We seek only the pattern.'

Morgen stopped, looking suddenly deflated. He took something from his pocket and slipped it in his mouth, a gesture reminiscent of Gersten's chapstick flourish.

'What's that?' he asked, thinking of Stoffel's grown-up pill.

Pervitin, Morgen said.

Schlegel knew about it from his mother, in connection with slimming; she spoke of its aphrodisiac qualities. Morgen said it would give him stamina and concentration. It was the official wonder drug.

'You sound like an advertising salesman. Will I find myself down the rabbit hole?'

They walked on.

Morgen said, 'For argument's sake, let's assume the hunted is the forger.'

'How do we find him?'

'Wait to see what bait the hunter sets up next and follow that. Is there anywhere to get a drink round here?'

Schlegel thought it a bit early. That wasn't what Morgen meant.

'I am thinking of the dead woman being used as a soft trap, to draw the hunted. You could see, despite her state, she was a looker. A siren.'

Given the whereabouts of the body, he thought it likely they had met locally.

Schlegel said there weren't many bars left. The dancehall downstairs from him didn't open until later.

The bars didn't either and they had to get the owners out of bed. Morgen insisted on inspecting every one and each time he walked away without a thank you, which was left to Schlegel, in return for sour looks. In the last bar the owner was up and changing his barrels. Morgen was more interested. The premises was less of a spit-and-sawdust affair than the rest, with tablecloths and candles stuck in empty bottles.

Outside, Morgen stopped again.

'You be the hunted and I the hunter. A woman wants to meet you but you can't be sure. Would you choose that last bar, or any of the rest?'

They were all too small, Schlegel said, with no escape if there was a trap.

'That can only mean the dancehall.'

It was still officially shut, but the kitchen staff were in. The manager had yet to arrive and the waiters were not in until later. The kitchen staff weren't any help because there was a second evening shift. Schlegel followed Morgen through to the dancehall where a female cleaner was swabbing the floor. He had been there only a few nights ago. The place had the depressed air of all out-of-hours joints dedicated to false cheer. Quite the little philosopher, he thought, when it came to hackneyed observations.

He couldn't resist sitting behind the drum kit on the low podium. He worked the bass pedal and flicked the cymbal. It must be the pill, he thought. He would amaze them with a spontaneous drum solo.

Morgen was talking to the cleaner, who said she had been doubling up on the kitchen's evening shift on Monday night when a well-dressed woman hurried through the kitchen just before the sirens and left by the staff door.

Her appearance matched the dead woman.

Morgen asked when the manager would be in. His name was Herr Valentine and he lived upstairs. Schlegel went to fetch him.

Valentine turned out to be a presentable if threadbare elderly man with silver brilliantined hair that smelled of violets. He said he was about to go down as it was.

He vaguely recognised Schlegel, turning to ask over his shoulder where he knew him from. Before entering the dance-hall, he paused on the threshold and shot his cuffs.

'You're asking a lot,' he said after Morgen finished. 'My memory isn't what it was.'

He cheerfully admitted most evenings were spent in his office getting sozzled.

'Not much else to do these days. The clientele is no fun. The girls don't come in as much. I can't pay the musicians what Kurt Widmann does. The last man we auditioned for a drummer had a wooden leg.'

Nothing turned out to be wrong with the man's memory. He remembered the woman being in on the Saturday and the Monday for the obvious reason of her being on her own when her kind usually came escorted. He had spent a long time trying to decide whether she was on the game.

'Was she?' asked Morgen.

'Not obviously. She wasn't looking to pick up just any man.'

Herr Valentine turned to Schlegel.

'You were in on Saturday as well. Not for long.'

Schlegel supposed it was his hair again.

'You're Kripo, aren't you?' Valentine asked. 'Not the other lot.'

Morgen said yes, criminal police, not Gestapo.

'The other lot were in on Saturday night.' He asked if Schlegel had spotted them. 'They're not subtle.'

Schlegel shook his head. But the dead woman sounded like the one he had happened to be looking at. It was starting to resemble the sort of trap Morgen was talking about.

'And on the Monday?' Morgen asked the manager.

'I would say she left with the waiter. Perhaps not *with* the waiter but around the same time.'

'What waiter?'

'He was in for a couple of evenings, filling in.'

'Do you think they're connected?

'Human nature. They fuck in the toilets given half a chance, especially the ones coming back from the war. Monday was the night of the bombers so we had to close. I made the announcement when the sirens went and she was gone by then. I know the waiter left early.'

'Are you sure?' asked Morgen.

'I settle up each night when the staff go home and he didn't come for his pay, which is a first during my running of the place.'

'What was he like?'

'Tall. Handsome. Dark. Only in for a couple of nights.'

'Name?'

'I don't remember. I doubt if it was real.'

'You must have a job sheet,' said Morgen.

'It doesn't work like that, not down at this end. Cash on the night, no questions asked. Report me for all I care.'

'Do you remember hiring him?'

'I didn't. He turned up to fill in for someone who was sick. Which was fine. He was presentable, didn't trip over. I would have kept him and fired the other fellow.'

'What about the other fellow?'

'In this evening. Come back and ask him. Have a drink on the house. Crème de menthe. It's pretty revolting.'

After the dancehall Morgen said they must draw up a list of possible forgers. Jewish professional records would list all printers, graphic designers, anyone with access to etching tools, the ones who had been to art schools before they closed.

'It will be someone with the right kind of training.'

They had no lead to speak of on Abbas, apart from a dubious Russian connection.

'But I can't see that turning up anything about money. To switch for a moment, what do we really know about Metzler, since the money links him to both bodies?'

Schlegel admitted the man was an enigma.

'He does rather become *our* enigma. What was his profession?'

'Teacher, I think.'

'Do we know where?'

'No. Some of his files have been mislaid.'

'It doesn't matter. Jews have been banned from teaching for years.'

Schlegel remembered the little key from Metzler's apartment, which he had attached to his own key ring.

'There's this. It looks like it belongs to a locker.' Morgen read the tag.

'Two-seven-one-six.'

'He worked in something called shed twenty-seven.'

'Now no one can complain if we look,' said Morgen, turning round and walking back up towards Rosenthaler Strasse.

Schlegel pointed out the station was the other way, but Morgen had something in mind. When they reached the scene of crime, Stoffel's Opel was still parked in the street, with the keys in the ignition.

# 28

'Proper meatballs too,' said Morgen. They came with noodles and a sauce that was hard to identify.

'Gherkin, maybe. Mustard. Onion. Too much flour. Not bad all the same. They look after their own.'

They were in a large dining hall, full of clerical and secretarial staff and workers in overalls from the slaughterhouse. Food was dished up by kitchen helpers from a stainless-steel counter. Schlegel supposed some enterprising manager worked hard keeping the place supplied with meat sidelined from the wholesale market.

They had been bounced around different offices in search of Metzler's job record, starting with the downstairs reception where the old girls were now as disobliging as they had been previously jolly.

'We're disinclined to help if it involves Jews, after what they did to that body. Try upstairs. You might have better luck there.' It was the woman who had given Schlegel the map. 'We're not a filing cabinet down here.'

Upstairs they visited dull rooms staffed with disagreeable clerks. Metzler's name could not be traced. Schlegel presumed his work record had been removed after his death. The young, sourly pretty female clerk dealing with them looked washed out and disgruntled.

Schlegel stared, mesmerised by the dandruff in her parting.

He saw her again in the canteen, chatting animatedly.

Both men ate fast and used their fingers to lick their plates clean, after which Morgen lit up and flicked his ash into the tin lid provided.

Outside was sunny for a change, with a rising wind. They walked past empty halls that attested to a lack of business.

'Odd that none of them upstairs had heard of Metzler,' said Morgen.

They were on their way to try the rail depot where Metzler was supposed to have worked before his transfer to the shed.

Morgen said, 'Agatha Christie at least gives you clues and suspects.'

Schlegel's mother was an avid reader of Christie. *The Body in the Library* had come out the year before. Morgen had read earlier Christie translations in Russia, where her domestic murders worked well as a counterpoint to battlefield massacre.

'Almost delicate, you could say.'

Once peace came Morgen would dedicate himself to expanding his waistline. He stuck his hands in his pockets and recited, ' "Let me have men about me that are fat, sleek-headed men and such as sleep a-nights. Yond Cassius has a lean and hungry look, he thinks too much; such men are dangerous." *Julius Caesar*, act one, scene two.'

Turning to Schlegel, he asked, 'Any relation?'

Not as far as he knew; his namesake was Shakespeare's first translator.

Morgen said, 'I bring culture to the slaughterhouse. "Upon what meat does this our Caesar feed that he is grown so great?" ' He strolled on, saying over his shoulder, 'And upon what meat do we feed? And such talk of sedition.'

Schlegel again mentioned the idea of Metzler as possible agent for Gersten, thinking how people didn't repeat themselves in Christie. For all the red herrings, things proceeded along well-oiled lines.

The rail depot stood at the opposite end of the pig district, beyond the S-Bahn with its enormously long elevated walkway that spanned the whole of the estate, down to Eldenaer Strasse.

Metzler was at least remembered at the depot, by the single clerk in a moss-green suit who sat in a hut in the big storage shed. He made a point of having to be prompted before grudgingly conceding that Metzler had not been a bad worker.

'For a Yid.'

All the same, it must have been a relief when he left, said Morgen.

'He minded his own business,' conceded the clerk.

'What was his job?' asked Schlegel.

'Checking deliveries. Dry goods mainly into one warehouse. Imported machinery into the other. For collection.'

'What's the strangest item you might get sent here?' asked Morgen.

'I have no idea what you could mean,' said the clerk with suspicion.

'Do you know why Metzler was transferred to the slaughterhouse?'

'Where?'

As the man seemed not to know, Schlegel explained.

'As far as we were concerned, he just left. It didn't bother us to know where.'

'Nevertheless, now you know, would you like to speculate why?'

'He must have crossed someone.'

'Not you?'

'I don't have the power.'

'Where's your boss?'

'On leave.'

'So there's only you?'

'Just me. They bring in labour as and when it's needed.'

Morgen turned away then back again. 'Was Metzler in fact your superior?'

'He was here before me, but once I came he couldn't be my boss because of what he was.'

'But he had to teach you the job.'

'Ticking things on and off lists, you don't have to be taught that.'

'These minor functionaries with brains the size of hamsters,' said Morgen as they walked off, loud enough for the man to hear.

'Isn't that being unfair to hamsters?'

'Why isn't he in the army? He looks fit enough to be cannon fodder. Why aren't you, come to that? Not that you look fit.'

'I have a doctor's chit to say I am a liability.'

'In that case they should make you a general. Now, show me this murder room.'

They passed the pig shed. The stench was as bad as before but the eerie silence told Schlegel the animals were gone. Morgen insisted on looking. The enormous space appeared more disturbing for being empty.

'It looks like the piggies went to market,' said Morgen.

Upstairs, all Schlegel could think was nothing was as before. The room had been stripped. The sink was smashed. The draining board was gone, as was the improvised shower and paraphernalia. There was no bucket. The knives had been taken. The crude drawing on the wall had been smashed away with a chisel; the plaster remnants lay on the floor. In the middle of the room stood a small pile of ashes – what was left of the book, Schlegel presumed – on top of which lay deposited a huge turd. Shit had been smeared over another wall in huge, angry swipes.

Baumgarten, the slaughterhouse foreman, was casual about the destruction of the murder room, saying some of the boys had gone a bit wild, being so disgusted by what the Jews had done. They thought the place evil. He added, what could you expect from Jews and their revolting practices.

Baumgarten recognised Schlegel and called him Whitey.

He had his own hut, on wheels, with steps up, near the porter's lodge on Thaerstrasse, which marked the start of the pig district. A long cobblestoned street ran in a straight line to the Landsberger Allee gates at the other end.

Baumgarten grudgingly allowed them in, helped himself to tea and offered none.

'What about Metzler?' Morgen asked. 'Did he have anything to do with the Jewish butchers?'

Metzler he hardly knew, Baumgarten said. It was a repeat of his earlier performance. Schlegel, not caring about Baumgarten, told Morgen they were dealing with a classic stonewaller.

Baumgarten glared, hands twitching.

'Did all the Jewish butchers work in the pig shed?' asked Morgen.

Baumgarten scoffed. 'Refused absolutely. Jews and pigs. Probably didn't like killing in kind. They did sheep and cattle.' He pointed behind him. 'Over the road. Cattle and horses at the far end. Sheep in the middle. At this end mutton and pigs.'

'Yet the old man worked with the pigs,' said Morgen.

'It seems so.'

'What did he do exactly?'

'No idea. You can go and ask.'

Like Stoffel, Morgen was incredulous that Jews were allowed to work with offensive weapons.

'What was to stop them running amok?'

'They were guarded. Strict rules. They didn't mix with our butchers.'

'Guarded by?'

'Hitler Youth.'

'Fourteen-year-olds?'

'No. Strapping lads, tough as they come.'

The telephone in the hut rang. After hanging up Baumgarten addressed them with the air of issuing a dare.

'Two sows. Come and see how it's done.'

Baumgarten was more forthcoming once he was giving the guided tour. The Zentralviehhof remained one of the world's most advanced slaughterhouses, with every stage calculated for speed, efficiency and lack of waste.

Schlegel asked about the state of the pigs they had seen. Baumgarten wasn't responsible for the pens. His duty began once the animals started their final journey. He pointed to a ramp that led down to several doors, which accessed the tunnels known as runs, taking the animals to the last stage.

'They die with their own. Let's go this way,' he said, gesturing towards the run. He grinned, showing his missing tooth.

Was it a joke in bad taste? Schlegel asked.

'We use it all the time. Saves having to go round.'

Impatient with the man's nonsense, Schlegel went down, followed by Morgen.

They entered a long, badly lit, narrow tunnel that disappeared into the distance. If it was anything like the length of the street above, Schlegel calculated it would take them at least five minutes; a long last journey for any pig.

A smell of death permeated the walls. The passage rose slowly. Schlegel grew attuned to all the terror experienced in that corridor.

Baumgarten lectured them in a loud voice. 'As the process unfolds it becomes less bloody. It is a miracle of modern efficiency that a live animal can be reduced in minutes to a carcass and butchered into the parts we are familiar with eating, and all under one roof. When my father worked here public visits were so popular special guide books were printed.'

He carried on spouting facts and figures for the length of the passage. Broken lights sometimes made it almost too dark to see. Pervitin now seemed like a bad idea, its quickening effect indistinguishable from panic. It made Schlegel want to run back and check there still was such a thing as sky and daylight.

He remembered a devilish trick in one Agatha Christie involving the pig-like squeal of a murdered man, and someone quoting Lady Macbeth saying who would have thought the old man had so much blood. Schlegel's breathing grew ragged. He feared an asthma attack.

At last Baumgarten, still droning on, said, 'Here's the blue door.'

It took them through to a large hall whose walls were full of complex and infernal-looking piping.

'This side of the door the animals continue in single file. Here's the bar I told you about. Step over it carefully, please. At this point the floor usually falls away, but of course not now, ha-ha! The bar becomes the mechanical process that moves the now-helpless animal forward until it reaches Haager, who is standing there waiting to render you brain-dead with his hammer.'

Haager was waiting on the platform above.

Baumgarten called out, 'Or are you using the stun gun today?'

'Always the hammer.' Haager brandished it and made a pantomime of hitting them on the head. The opaqueness of Haager's eyes made Schlegel very much not want to pass under his waiting hammer. They were being sized up the same as any other animal awaiting extinction.

He was spared by a service gate which Baumgarten led them through.

'So, gentlemen, the killing floor.'

Morgen looked like he wanted to hit the man. Schlegel was certain that the whole exercise had been done as a way of telling them to get lost. Or perhaps Baumgarten had grown so coarse he considered such conduct normal.

'And what does Haager think of as he swings his mallet, time after time?' muttered Morgen.

Probably of nothing but his mother and his tea, thought Schlegel.

Haager brandished the stun gun. 'Perhaps one of our friends would like to do the honours.' In his other hand was a bottle of brandy. 'The butcher's swig. Well, gentlemen. Aim between the eyes. Compression does the rest.'

'Do your job,' Morgen called out. 'Or I will come and fire it in your knee.'

Haager laughed uncertainly.

The first sow emerged through the blue door, blinking and uncertain, refusing to play her role, visibly petrified, rooted and shitting herself. Baumgarten had to prod her until she stepped across the bar and the floor fell away, causing her to scream uncontrollably as the mechanism jerked her forward into the death stall where the hammer swung and Haager grunted and the cracking of the skull sounded like a rifle shot, and the sow fell stunned and thrashing, and her squeal transferred to the next pig, waiting unseen, whose wails of terror told them she knew exactly what lay in store.

Schlegel saw Morgen had forgotten to smoke.

Baumgarten said in civilised countries they believed the animal should be insensate at the moment of slaughter, unlike the Muslim and Jew whose religion demanded the throat be cut.

'A cow bled to death standing can take six minutes to die, from the cut to when the eyes roll back and it starts to collapse. We have seen film of kosher butchers ripping the tracheas and oesophagi from the throats of fully conscious cattle, and animals writhing in pools of their own blood, while struggling to stand for minutes afterwards.'

Everything happened much quicker than the time it took to tell. They had been laboriously informed how chains were attached to the animal's hind legs so it could be lifted and worked along a pulley system. Once hanging, she was bled and then would be completely dead.

A second man stepped forward with a long knife which he stuck in the sow's aorta, a practised thrust, a lateral tear to the throat. The knife made a sucking noise as it was extracted. The man stepped aside as the pig gave a great sigh and steaming blood shot from the incision, splashing into a bath underneath, in huge dark, sticky bursts until the jet's pump faded.

The sweet smell of blood filled the air. Schlegel thought how they were all just sacks waiting to be pierced.

The attendant pig's screams built in a crescendo. Schlegel was almost forced to clap his hands to his ears as he had with the bombs. Morgen looked pale.

Despite the speed of the process, it seemed to go on forever. Squelches and farts emerged from the expiring animal. Haager leaned casually against the stall, a cigarette dangling from his fingers. When the beast was quite still, the man with the knife, watched by Haager, slit the belly from ribcage to anus. The body defied the cut for a moment, then gravity did its work and steaming entrails spilled out in a hot mist.

The second pig's squealing was silenced with a blow more violent than the first, provoking a final angry scream of pain.

The adjoining hall room was full of steam from an enormous vat of boiling water that had been prepared. A figure came at them out of the mist, a stunted man in a dirty apron. A thick fringe and unlined face made him appear boyish.

'Here's Sepp,' said Baumgarten. 'Tell these gentlemen about Metzler.'

'The Jew. What he was doing here is anybody's guess. He turned up with a chit, that's all I know, saying he had been transferred.'

'Whose chit?'

Baumgarten said, 'The railway's.'

'Whose chit specifically?' asked Morgen.

'The Gestapo representative in the railway office for the marshalling yards.'

Morgen asked why Baumgarten hadn't told them before. Because he had only just remembered, Baumgarten said insincerely.

The first dead pig joined them, dimly visible, hanging by its heels, waiting to be lowered into the vat.

Sepp had a strange way of staring with his mouth open.

Morgen said to Baumgarten, 'Come on, you can do better. Reason for the transfer?'

'Generally, it was said he'd behaved like an idiot and fallen out with someone. In actual terms, it wasn't necessary to know.'

'Why not?'

'We figured he wouldn't be around long.'

Morgen asked for the name of the Gestapo representative at the railway office.

'Webel,' said Baumgarten after some thought.

'Weber,' said Sepp.

'Either way, don't stand too close.'

Baumgarten waved his hand to indicate the state of the man's breath.

It was as hot as a Turkish bath in the room. Schlegel felt the sweat soaking into his clothes.

He asked what the old man's job had involved. Scraping the epidermis, Sepp said, pointing to the vat into which the animal was immersed to soften the skin before it was cleaned with a combination of a wooden paddle and a scraper.

'Can you say anything about him?' asked Schlegel.

'There's steam here most of the time. You don't see the others.'

Sepp struck Schlegel as simple. He walked away. It was like being in a real fog, except hot. Voices became muffled. He could see nothing. He supposed somewhere in the vicinity butchers had then worked on the carcasses. Baumgarten had explained the job in his grisly, pedantic manner in that endless tunnel: decapitation, cutting off hooves, severance of tail, splitting of the animal, followed by general butchery into larger sections, prior to further cuts, usually made by the purchasing retailer. Schlegel regretted the meatballs.

He turned round to see a figure creeping up on him out of the mist. It was Haager, the executioner, stun gun in hand, aimed at him. Haager quickly laughed, raised the gun and fired into the air. The fixed bolt shot out of the barrel and remained there like an obscene metal finger. He laughed again, raucously, and said, 'I wanted to show you this.'

He proffered the gun. 'You develop a funny sense of humour working here.'

If the man had intended to scare him he had succeeded. Yet the way he proudly showed off his gun was docile, demure even.

Haager followed him back to where the others were standing.

Schlegel asked, 'Do you know any more about what happened to the Jewish butchers?'

'Oh, yes,' said Sepp. 'Shipped straight out. Put in a wagon and sent east.'

'What? Last Saturday morning?' asked Schlegel, astonished. Had Baumgarten known?

Baumgarten replied it was a big place and no one had told him. He was obviously lying. Schlegel asked Sepp what time this had happened.

'First thing. Before first thing. It was still dark.'

'How do you know?'

'We were asked to form an armed escort.'

'Who's we?'

'Me and some Hitler Youth.'

'Who asked?'

'Two men I have never seen before.'

'Officials?'

'Obviously.'

'Plain clothes or uniform?'

'Plain.'

Schlegel asked for a description. No one he recognised.

Sepp wasn't even sure whether the butchers were taken away as part of the official roundup. They were told they were being transferred as the result of a shortage of proper butchers where they were bound.

The usual big camp, said Sepp when Morgen asked.

'Where are the changing rooms here?' Schlegel asked.

In the back, Baumgarten said.

'Did Metzler have a locker?'

'Ask Sepp,' said Baumgarten. Sepp didn't know.

'Show us,' said Morgen.

The two men took them into a large tiled area with a row of lockers. Through an archway two naked men padded around after using showers hot enough to steam, a luxury these days.

Sepp said, 'Metzler as a Jew would have been forbidden to use the showers. Jews stink as it is, even when they wash.'

Locker number sixteen opened with the key Schlegel had.

Metzler's work overall, cap and apron, gauntlets and rubber boots were still there, along with a stack of newspapers and an empty sack.

Sepp and Baumgarten stared in suspicion as Morgen chucked everything in the sack.

They telephoned from Baumgarten's hut to speak to Weber, the Gestapo official responsible for Metzler's transfer. He had gone home early, ill, so they called him there. Weber came to the telephone sounding perfectly well, but faded when Morgen said who he was.

Yes, he told Morgen between bouts of artificial coughing, he recalled Metzler, but had no memory of having anything to do with his transfer to the slaughterhouse, apart from being surprised to find him gone because a lot of strings had been pulled to get him a job at the rail depot in the first place.

'Would that be Gersten?'

The man affected vagueness. Pressed, he thought it had something to do with Metzler having an old army pal in the police force.

After speaking to Weber, Morgen insisted on looking around. He couldn't decide whether Metzler's transfer to the pig room was punishment or deliberate. Why hadn't he been sent to work with the other Jews?

Because he wasn't a butcher, Schlegel suggested. Morgen conceded the point.

'Usually they herd the Jews together, yet Metzler was a unique case.'

Weber and the depot clerk had both told them Metzler was the only Jew working there.

As usual, no one seemed to be around, until they heard distant yelling from one of the buildings. Morgen moved ahead to investigate. Schlegel thought him like a tramp in his shabby coat, carrying Metzler's sack over his shoulder.

The din came from a glass-roofed shed much higher than its surroundings. A lobby and double doors took them into a huge hall, stripped of features. The roof was smashed and water formed in large pools. At the far end, Schlegel saw the back of a crowd in a huddle. The raucous shouting sounded like some sort of contest.

Whatever was going on seemed typical of the latent threat of the place.

Brawny lads with closed-off, ecstatic faces focused on the violent spectacle, their shouts and cheers primitive and guttural. They wore shorts and singlets and their sweat suggested strenuous exercise. Some fingered their genitals in excitement at the sight of two tall youths hitting each other without gloves. One's eye was swelling and the other had a bloody nose.

Some of the boys started to stare at them suspiciously. The man refereeing noticed too. He was an athletic type with a closed face, a boxer's nose, cropped hair and he wore a tracksuit. Schlegel had seen the look before: always mean and very hostile.

The youth with the upper hand unleashed a flurry of punches to the head of his opponent, and Schlegel found he could not help but be excited. At least the spectacle was human, however primitive, compared to what they had just seen. The lad punched was hit so hard Schlegel thought his head might come off. The light went out of his eyes and his legs turned rubbery. Morgen watched impassive, smoking, as the boy hit the deck, to be counted out by the referee, who then walked over and demanded to know what Schlegel was doing. The crowd closed in, anticipating its next thrill. The herd mentality was different from anything he had come across before; boys who had grown up with nothing but war. He was aware of Morgen watching to see how he acted under pressure. He showed his badge to the tracksuited man and said they were conducting an inquiry. The man asked if it involved them.

The man stood, threatening, staring Schlegel down.

Morgen said loud enough for all to hear, 'Here is the little man in control of his space, with his little wolf pack.'

'Excuse me?' said the man, turning on Morgen.

The next thing, he was down on the floor, clutching between his legs and whimpering. Whatever trick Morgen had performed, it was done too fast for Schlegel to comprehend and hadn't even involved dropping Metzler's sack.

The crowd goggled. One or two bristled. Morgen waved them away.

'Disperse.'

He held up his badge and the recently baying unit grew surly. Morgen singled out the winning boy whose celebration had been spoiled.

He said quietly, 'Stand to attention when you talk to me.'

The boy slowly did as he was told, doing his best to put on a front.

'What have we here? Another young man with a prominent Adam's apple and obedient, if insolent eyes, in thrall to male camaraderie and the competitive edge? Had I been the other lad I would have punched you in the throat. Do you have anything to say?'

'No, sir.'

'Then to the victor the spoils.'

He threw him Metzler's sack and told him to follow.

Morgen walked ahead. The young man remained undecided. Schlegel watched his humiliation take hold as tears pricked his eyes. Morgen stopped and beckoned. The crowd watched, morose.

They made an unlikely trio as they returned to the car. What Morgen was up to Schlegel had no idea. Had the attack on the tracksuited man been specific, or akin to his own accumulated frustration? The fury with which the boy had gone about his business was as shocking as the sight of the last of the blood being pumped out of the sow's failing heart.

Morgen ordered the boy to put the sack in the boot. He inspected him again and asked his greatest wish.

To die for the Fatherland.

Of course, said Morgen, producing his pistol.

'We can take care of that now.'

Schlegel said, 'You can't do that!'

For a second Morgen seemed barely in control – then the moment passed and the gun was back in his pocket. He became genial, telling the boy he would have a black eye tomorrow.

Schlegel was certain had he not been there Morgen would have pulled the trigger.

# 29

Nebe had them all in for his forty-eight-hour deadline meeting. The tension was palpable because word had got out about cancelling leave and introducing consecutive twelve-hour shifts.

Nebe marched in looking brisk, followed by Stoffel, trying not to look smug.

'Well, gentlemen, what do you have for me on the subject of our Jewish maniac?'

Stoffel stood up and said there was in fact another murder to consider.

'Another murder!' exclaimed Nebe, sounding rehearsed.

To judge from the winks and nudges, half the room was in the know. Stoffel grew sombre as he announced a murder they had overlooked.

'On 31 January, a woman was found strangled in woods near Köpenick.'

The location was significant. It was near where the body had been found in Treptower Park. The attack was of a sexual nature.

'Am I supposed to warn Dr Goebbels a Jewish maniac is working the length and breadth of the city?' asked Nebe.

Stoffel said the victim, like others, showed signs of postmortem sexual abuse. He looked pleased with himself.

'Though why anyone should want to fuck around with her, dead or alive, is beyond me.'

Nebe cracked up. Stoffel as unofficial court jester was allowed to be as crude as he liked. At one of the drunken parties,

Stoffel had taken delight in poking Schlegel, who was forced to take it in good humour, showing which parts of the body could be hit without leaving a mark. 'There, bruising. There, no bruising. The kidneys are always good.'

'The old cunt was sixty-three and her purse was missing.'

Nebe said, 'But Jews aren't allowed to drive and those still with us are being worked too hard to take time off to murder. What are you telling us?'

Morgen interrupted to ask Stoffel if he intended to link the three killings: the woman in the woods, the dead man with money in his mouth and the most recent female victim.

Stoffel recited, 'Strangulation. Strangulation. Strangulation. Money left at two scenes and taken from the other. In all three cases gender parts interfered with.'

Morgen said, 'I thought the Abbas case was considered of no consequence.'

'We were told not to waste time on a Yid, but if the case gets solved as part of another investigation that's different.'

He made a tick in the air with his finger.

'How much money was stolen from this woman?' Morgen asked.

'A mark.'

'One mark!'

'That's how much she had when she left the house.'

'You're building a case on one mark! Do we ask if the mark was forged?'

'Gentlemen!' interrupted Nebe. 'We are here to put our heads together, not bang them!'

Stoffel, refusing to be outdone, pointed out that the notorious Dusseldorf Vampire had changed weapons and methods all the time.

Morgen looked incredulous. 'Is all this because homicide is nostalgic for the golden age of Weimar murder?'

Stoffel said the case reminded him of Ogorzow, homicide's biggest case of the last years, with at least eight women bludgeoned, raped and murdered. It had become part of his legend and endless repertoire.

'It's a psychological game of cat and mouse. We don't just beat it out of them. The way we turned Ogorzow we could have charged tickets, it was that good.'

Morgen added, 'Are we throwing in the flayed corpses for good measure?'

'When it comes to dealing with the sickness of human imagination there are no limits. Kürten, the Dusseldorf Vampire, asked the prison psychiatrist if after the guillotine had removed his head whether he would still be able to hear, at least for a moment, the sound of his own blood gushing from his neck. Imagine a mind capable of coming up with something like that, let alone his answer when told he probably would: "That would be the pleasure to end all pleasures." '

Schlegel remembered the Kürten case. The newspapers had been full of it, with photographs of the cage that held him during his trial. He had been an impressionable fourteen. It was the first time he had come across the word psychopath, after secretly reading *The Sadist*, bought by his stepfather and written by a psychiatrist who had interviewed Kürten. Schlegel couldn't get over the man's ordinariness, compared to the unpredictable viciousness of the crimes. Even his defence counsel had given up. Kürten was quite unlike other dedicated murderers. Haarmann only killed men, Landru and Grossmann only women, but Kürten was a riddle that did the lot, men, women, children and animals. He killed anything he found as well as deriving sexual pleasure from setting things alight.

Schlegel had gone through a troubling period wondering whether he too was a psychopath, based on what he later dismissed as the pathetic premise of not finding much to excite him.

'Are you saying you are looking for another Peter Kürten?' asked Nebe, looking suitably grave.

Stoffel hinted he already had a suspect in mind that would far outstrip Kürten's notoriety.

Nebe went on, 'Kürten was intelligent and well turned-out. He had a job and a wife. So did Ogorzow. A Party member and a wife too. Might your man be like that?'

Schlegel noted how Nebe in the course of the meeting had gone from describing the killer as a Jewish maniac to Stoffel's man.

Stoffel was too fired up to answer, saying Ogorzow had the perfect job where he was free to move around. That was the kind of detail they had been chasing in this case too.

'Ogorzow had a uniform,' said Nebe, picking up the thread. 'Yes, a railway uniform.'

No one bothered to point out nearly everyone had a uniform by then.

'There's another thing,' Stoffel said. 'Ogorzow had a normal sex life with his wife. With his victims he sometimes achieved full intercourse but otherwise did not bother, so we presume he failed to get hard or tugged his pudding.'

Morgen asked, 'Are you telling us the amputation of the penis may be inspired by a desire to emasculate the victim because of the perpetrator's inability to achieve an erection?'

Stoffel's cronies made a point of not laughing.

Stoffel protested. 'Don't take me seriously! Semen was found outside the old woman's vagina, suggesting he was incapable of penetration.'

'And the woman in the bomb site, if intercourse took place?'

'We are not talking about consistency.'

After the meeting Morgen said to Stoffel, 'So you are not looking for a Jewish maniac, it's official?'

'I can tell you something for nothing, it's not a fucking Russian.'

Franz suggested they go down to the basement again. Sybil told him she had her period. She presumed he would insist on some other form of satisfaction, but he left it at that.

'For the moment,' he said.

After finishing work she stood in the crowd. The first prisoners were being released. A cheer went up as a group stumbled into the last of the light. She drew on the crowd's strength, trying not to think about Alwynd cornering her in the kitchen to announce that he was drawn to transgression and it was his nature to betray.

Sybil was aware of his disconcerting habit of starting conversations in the middle, without preamble, then watching the effect of his detonating remark. She presumed he was talking about women, and it was the start of his move on her.

He was washing dishes when he said, apropos of nothing, 'I am not against the Jew as such, of course not, but I am against the money he stands for.'

Had he guessed, she asked herself, nearly dropping the plate she was drying.

Money wasn't exclusive to Jews, she said, and left it at that.

Feeling soiled by Franz, she dealt badly with Lore, and lay awake for a long time thinking about Alwynd. As with Franz, there would be a price to pay.

Morgen requested to see copies from the evidence section of the photographs taken in the slaughterhouse boxcar and murder room, as well as the forensic report. Taken with a flash-bulb and in stark black-and-white the images looked even more graphic.

Morgen studied them for a long time.

'A human body butchered to look like an animal prepared for eating. Knives for kosher killing. Hebrew writing on the wall. Pig guts in a bucket.'

'Not from the body?' asked Schlegel.

Morgen tapped the forensics report.

'It says bucket contents animal rather than human. A pig's, in fact. Yet to the Jew a pig is an unclean animal, which they refrain from eating. There's Metzler too, cleaning his dead pigs.'

'Jews have been passive until now. Why start?'

'Rage perhaps on the part of a stronger character or group at the submissiveness of the herd.'

'Herd?'

'We may be rational but our group instinct remains animal. Or perhaps it is intended as a kind of human sacrifice.'

Schlegel, helpless, said, 'I am no expert.'

'Perhaps we should take Lazarenko more seriously.'

'Are you saying now the killings are linked?'

'Not the old biddy in the woods.' He trailed off. 'The trouble is we all stopped listening to each other years ago. Maybe we should take account of Stoffel too, who believes they are connected, even when they are not the same.'

Morgen pointed to the drawing on the wall in the photograph and asked what it was saying.

It was about exorcism, Schlegel said, and featured pigs, a recurring theme.

'Hurled themselves over a cliff to perish in the waters below.'

Morgen turned his attention to the details on the draining board.

'A sacrificial offering, with Jewish symbols. Candles. The dead animal, in this case human. Perhaps the situation is allegorical. Or intellectual. The product of an educated mind.'

The murders struck Schlegel as pretty real.

'What do you know of the Cabalists?'

Next to nothing, Schlegel admitted.

Morgen was smoking furiously, lighting another cigarette when he already had one smouldering in the ashtray. His eyes assumed a dreamy expression.

'The Cabalists taught that the allegorical is far superior to the literal. The literal is practical, the allegorical speculative. The practical is restricted – embarrassed even – by circumstances of place and time. The speculative exalts the soul to the knowledge of temporal, celestial and eternal objects, which are the images of the Divine immutability.'

Schlegel wanted to point out they were not homicide, or a university department of philosophy, but an obscure backwater. He wanted to say life had been much easier before, which wasn't altogether true. The trouble had been there from that first shot on Saturday morning, like the starting pistol that marked the race.

He now could think of a dozen ways to have avoided being dragged out by Stoffel – by standing up to the man, for a start – but he hadn't.

'In plain speaking?' he asked, desperate for a handle.

'Acts of desperation to appease an angry god. Or despair and desecration at being abandoned by that god. The difference between kosher and ordinary butchering is the animal has to be consciously killed in a precise manner with a special knife by an expert, and the blood not gathered, in contrast to old forms of idol worship. There are calibrated regulations, down to what parts of the animal can and cannot be used.'

Morgen exhaled, suddenly flat. 'I don't know. Sometimes I see this hunted figure as a cornered rat, devoid of imagination, a tool, with someone else's brain running the show. What I do think is we will soon expect to find a mother and child killed within the same space and on the same day because their rules of animal slaughter prohibit the offspring being killed with the parent.'

'Are you saying this is all deliberate?'

'Nebe is terrified someone wants it to get out. Jews are being relocated. A man or group are doing this because they want people to know, so they seek damaging publicity in the form of sensation.'

# 30

Although Gestapo undercover operations were off-limits to criminal police inquiries, Morgen was curious to test Gersten on the question of forged money. Gersten, affable but brisk on the telephone, told them to come over, but not for long as he was off to the theatre.

'With Frau Gersten?' asked Morgen politely when he met them in reception.

'Not, as it happens.'

Gersten led the way upstairs, at home in his manor. The cleaner, a middle-aged woman, was finishing up as he led them into a room smelling of furniture polish. She was a Jehovah's Witness.

'One of the bible bees. Terrific workers. I wish they were all like that.'

The woman could have been deaf too for all her reaction. Seeing Schlegel looking at a framed photograph on the wall, Gersten said, '*Emil and the Detectives*.'

It showed a recognisable younger version of Gersten as a gang member in a scene from the film.

'Aged fourteen, playing eleven.'

He looked proud. Seeing Morgen was not charmed, he admitted he hadn't been a very good actor.

'Too ironic for romantic leads. I got cast as the fifth or sixth gangster, once in an Edgar Wallace as the murderer, until I fell out with the boss of the business over an actress we were both seeing.'

Boss of the business being Goebbels, Schlegel supposed.

'My career came to rather an abrupt end when I realised if you can't beat them . . .'

Morgen looked no more persuaded and said, 'You were right, some of the notes found in Abbas's mouth were fake. How did you know?'

'Heads up, I was in a state of shock. Abbas had taken a long time to cultivate and just when he was about to yield results . . . Bang! Curtains! The first thought that came to mind was people nowadays can't afford to leave good money lying around.'

'We found more from the same batch in Metzler's apartment.'

'Really? I know nothing about that.'

Morgen grew distracted, feeling down the side of his armchair. He found something. Schlegel couldn't see, though he caught his expression of puzzled disgust as he palmed it.

'What about Metzler?'

'What about? We all try to do small favours. Metzler came to my attention through an older colleague who was in his regiment. He had gone to complain to him about having some nasty little job. We arranged a move to a clerical desk. Favour to an old comrade.'

Schlegel said, 'We think Jews were responsible for the forging.'

Gersten recrossed his legs, relaxed. 'Your department, not mine.'

'Have you heard anything about why Metzler shot himself?' asked Morgen.

Gersten waved his hand vaguely in the direction of the east and got up saying he didn't like to be late for the theatre.

'To be continued another time.'

He paused at the door, thoughtful.

'It only occurs to me now – with this business of fake money – that Metzler might have been using us.'

'How?' asked Morgen.

'That his approach had an ulterior motive. Perhaps he played me for a fool.'

Morgen fished in his pockets and said, 'I found this down the side of your chair. It must have been left for the tooth fairy.'

He opened his palm to reveal an incisor with the root attached.

'Gestapo property?'

Gersten took the tooth, inspected it with studied distaste and threw it towards the nearest wastepaper bin where it missed and lay on the rug.

'There is a place for that kind of thing. Not guilty. Not my style.'

Back at the office there were urgent messages from Lazarenko. Schlegel was inclined to ignore them. Lazarenko beat them to it by telephoning again.

He was at the paint factory where three workers had been found dead in a vat, overcome by noxious fumes in an apparently routine accident. One was the Russian they had talked to.

Schlegel motioned for Morgen to pick up his extension so he could listen in.

Lazarenko said he had been put in charge of the case because it involved Russians. The Gestapo didn't usually bother with such lowly business.

Schlegel was sure Lazarenko was overstating his position. Unctuous and untrustworthy.

Lazarenko whispered down the phone in his sibilant accent, 'There is more to this than meets the eye.'

'Tell Gersten.'

The silence was pregnant enough for Schlegel to understand that Lazarenko had reasons for not doing so.

'I wanted to warn you such accidents are easily arranged.'

'We don't deal with alien crime. There are appropriate channels.'

'No one will listen. There are rope marks where the dead men were tied.'

Schlegel wanted Lazarenko to talk to Morgen, who took over while he carried on listening.

Lazarenko sounded increasingly desperate as he insisted Morgen come and inspect the site. Morgen told Lazarenko to file a report and he would look at it.

Lazarenko muttered in his own language for a while, before coming out in a rush. 'It will be said among the Russians these men were killed as a result of internal feuds over gambling.'

'How, when they don't have any money?'

'They are crazy. They run up huge speculative debts and fight over them.'

'And gambling debts are not the real reason?'

'The gang leaders don't want their men disclosing their involvement in the murder of a Gestapo agent.'

'Did you tell this to Gersten?'

Lazarenko didn't answer. Morgen asked if Lazarenko was out of his depth.

All he would tell them was Gersten had found another interpreter, female and attractive. He sounded miserable.

'They think I know too much, so they will pack me off like all the rest.'

When they spoke to the waiter at Clärchens that evening he was concerned about being reported by them to the labour office for having an unregistered job. They inspected his papers, which showed he was an ethnic German from Poland. Morgen asked why he wasn't in the army.

Because he was a deserter, thought Schlegel. The dealers and hawkers around Alexanderplatz could usually provide a good set of papers. The waiter's were especially impressive, stating he was a theology student. He told them with a straight face he was going to become a minister.

'You were off last week and sent in a replacement,' said Morgen, unimpressed.

The waiter didn't have more than a first name. Schlegel was surprised the man knew that much. Socially these days it was common not to know people's names for the simple reason that if it came to answering to the police it was better not to.

The waiter said the man was an acquaintance he had met through a cinema club, shortly before. All he knew was he was a mature student, of Russian background, from one of the original anti-communist refugee families going back to the 1917 revolution.

'And his first name?' asked Morgen.

'Grigor.'

The waiter had been paid by Grigor to stay at home. Two packets of cigarettes and a wristwatch that had since bust.

Morgen dismissed him. He seemed keen to stay on. Schlegel said he was tired. Morgen offered him one of his pills. Schlegel declined and wished he hadn't after going upstairs and dreaming of grown men on the point of death, screaming for their mothers.

# 31

Morgen was already in when Schlegel got to the office and he looked like he had been there all night.

'While babes sleep vampires do their homework.'

His desk was a mess of papers, with more strewn on the floor. The ashtray was overflowing, the room a fog of smoke. His eyes were artificially bright and bleary. The magic pill made him seem worked up and excited where Schlegel felt wrung out, the day hardly begun.

'I kept the Jewish archive up until after two. Let's start with a possible shortlist of forgers. I came up with three. One turns out to be dead, so two. On grounds of probability, I assume we are not looking for a woman. I have settled on men under forty, given job requirements of a steady hand, nerve and stamina. I have also made up a long list for those aged between forty and fifty-five, mainly from the print trade.

'The Jewish professional registry is not very up to date. However, a preliminary check showed three out of five of the forties to fifty-fives are gone, deported last year.

'Of the three under forty, the dead one was called Plotkin. I list him because he committed suicide after a robbery at the printing works where he was employed. He jumped off the roof while the Gestapo was in the building.'

Or was assisted in his jump.

Morgen raised an eyebrow then hurried on. 'The other two went to the same Jewish art school before it closed. One is

Franz Liebermann. He works as an orderly at the Jewish hospital. Also an authorised driver, so he has freedom of movement. The other is Yakov Zorin, who despite his name was born here in 1918. This almost squares with what our friend the waiter told us, except Zorin isn't called Grigor. Zorin incidentally has breeding. His mother was a Borodin, a famous Russian family that included Ashkenazi Jews. I only know this because—'

Schlegel witnessed the extraordinary sight of Morgen falling asleep in the middle of a sentence, like a man overcome by narcolepsy.

He snapped to and carried on, unawares.

'Next there's this,' he said. 'I spoke to the waiter again and did it after you went.'

It was a drawing of a man's face. Despite its rudimentary nature Schlegel thought he looked familiar.

'My impression of the waiter's description of his replacement.'

'You could have got a police artist to do it.'

'You don't like it?'

'That's not what I mean. Just that there are people to do this.'

'He wouldn't have turned out so late, and I wasn't going to risk the waiter discovering his religious vocation had deserted him in the night and vanishing. It's a passable likeness of what he described.'

'It's quite good actually. It's the Jewish hearse driver. I helped him load Metzler's body.'

He was sure. Morgen had caught his aloof, self-contained manner.

Morgen was already on the telephone to the Jewish centre in Oranienburger Strasse. He asked for the transport division. The telephone operator said they had no such thing. After Morgen explained, Schlegel heard her say, 'Oh, you mean the hearse drivers.'

They were based at the other centre in Grosse Hamburger Strasse. Morgen asked how many drivers. The operator wasn't sure. Morgen hung up in a hurry and stood up.

'Come on. I don't want to telephone and warn them.'

Morgen half-ran with Schlegel struggling to keep up.

'I see why the army turned you down. The magic pills mean I don't sleep and am ready for anything.'

Morgen lost his temper when they were referred on by reception to another centre in Auguststrasse next to the former Jewish girls' school.

He shouted, 'Don't any of you people know where anyone is?'

The woman he was addressing flinched and Schlegel felt obliged to apologise. She said no one could keep up any more with everything happening so fast. The hearse drivers had been transferred only in the last week.

Morgen asked if she knew any of the drivers' names. One she knew, called Fredi.

'What about Yakov?'

The woman looked blank.

'Grigor?'

Morgen was out of the door before she had finished shaking her head.

In Auguststrasse they flashed their badges at the gate. The hearse was parked in the yard. Morgen checked his gun and told Schlegel to do the same. The guard pointed to where the drivers waited for calls. Schlegel wondered if they should not be getting backup but Morgen marched across the yard and threw open the door to the drivers' room. The man inside stood up, terrified, hands half in the air. He was squat and bald. Morgen subjected him to a rapid interrogation. What was his name? How many of them worked there? What were their names?

'Come on, you can do better. You must know their names.'

The man blurted he had only been on the job a day and the other drivers worked different shifts.

'Names?'

The man shook his head and said people didn't have time to learn anyone's names these days.

Morgen asked who else might know the other drivers. Was there a personnel office?

The driver didn't have a clue. There wasn't even a street map in his van, he said.

The main building they found run by a staff that seemed barely to know each other or what they were doing.

Morgen lost his temper again. Schlegel told him to calm down. The woman they were talking to fled in tears, saying she would try to find someone.

'You can't keep making them cry.'

Morgen sniggered, snapping his fingers.

The man was the limit.

The woman came back with a nervous type, competent-looking but downcast. He took them to an office where he searched a cabinet, trying to find information on the hearse drivers, always on the point of giving up.

'Does anyone know how to do their job around here?' Morgen asked.

'No one showed us how anything works.'

'What are you talking about?'

'We were in Rosenstrasse until just now. This is our first day.'

'Where's the old staff?'

'Gone.'

There was no doubt what he meant.

'What? They released you to work here?'

The man said they had spent the week in a state of suspense, presuming they would be deported. No one had said that was never the intention. They were just being held. The demonstration had been quite unnecessary.

Schlegel was slow to understand. Morgen was impatient to explain.

'They were arrested so they could be put into the system.'

'They already are.'

'No, no, not like the other Jews because they are married to Germans. Experienced staff were needed to handle the administration of the roundups. Now these are done they can be packed off with the rest and untrained half-Jews inducted in their place, now there's almost nothing left to administrate.'

The reason it had to be kept secret was for fear of alarming the former administration of its imminent redundancy.

The man said in the meantime no one had shown them how anything worked.

Morgen smacked his forehead and said how stupid he had been. He ran out and had already reached the drivers' room as Schlegel reached the yard. The hearse was gone.

'German efficiency!' he shouted as Schlegel ran in.

He pointed to the duty list, showing the times and names for different shifts. He cursed the driver for not showing them.

Schlegel said the man was probably too confused to know.

There were three listed drivers. Their names meant nothing to them.

Schlegel had to pacify Morgen after he started kicking the furniture.

'The waiter said the man's name was Grigor. The man he described was the hearse driver I saw. The driver we spoke to has only just started. The man upstairs says everyone has been shipped off. That must mean the drivers, and Grigor too.'

They could find no Grigor on the deportation lists for that week. It meant checking every name. They were back at the

Grosse Hamburger Strasse centre in the administration office, which was now looked after by one person, also responsible for two other offices.

Morgen said it was like one of those liners found abandoned at sea.

They did however find Zorin, Yakov; sent the Tuesday before to Auschwitz.

'Cross him off.' Morgen threw up his hands. 'Grigor, where are you?'

Schlegel picked up the telephone. Morgen asked him what he was doing. Calling the Gestapo.

'No, no, no, it's too soon to talk to Gersten.'

Schlegel said he wasn't calling Gersten. He asked the Gestapo switchboard for the number of the camp in Auschwitz.

'And the area code?' He wrote down 2258.

He used the association's switchboard and asked to be put through. The operator reported trouble getting a line. Schlegel told her to keep trying.

Morgen, still racing, used his extension to get the switchboard to dial Kripo headquarters. He got through straight away and asked to speak to Nebe, via his secretary, who put him straight through.

He explained the situation and Nebe spoke back for several minutes until Morgen hung up in exasperation.

'No extradition,' he said to Schlegel. He got up in a rush and returned five minutes later, just as Schlegel managed to get through.

Morgen came in shouting, 'Zorin *is* Grigor!'

Schlegel refused to be interrupted as someone had just answered. He asked to be put through to the labour office.

Morgen called Nebe back and said the man they wanted to interview was not only the forger, he was responsible for at least two murders.

From Morgen's thunderous expression, Schlegel guessed

Nebe was saying if the forger was out of the picture the problem was resolved.

It took Schlegel five more minutes of waiting while Morgen threw his hands in the air. The only surprise was that the woman who picked up sounded young, friendly and cheerful.

Yes, she said, she had the work register to hand.

He gave Zorin's name.

'That's easy. It'll be at the end of the index.'

She said there was no listing for Zorin.

'He will have just arrived.'

The register was updated daily, she said, and if Zorin was a skilled worker he would have been processed straight away and signed on.

'Threatening to rain,' he said, on being asked what the weather was doing. He tried to picture her. 'Do you have your workers registered by name or by profession?'

'Both.'

'Have you had a delivery of butchers recently?'

'No.' It was said with certainty.

'How do you know?'

'Because we are desperately short.'

'Could they have been sent elsewhere?'

'Lublin perhaps, but everyone knows we have been advertising for them. We have far more agriculture and farming than Lublin.'

She sounded like she wanted to pass an idle ten minutes chatting. He supposed she was a long way from home. Kiel, she said.

Schlegel presumed Zorin was the forger, had killed Abbas and the woman, then fallen victim of a relentless bureaucracy and nobody was going to bother to extract him.

They were chasing nothing.

Except where was Zorin now?

And how did that fit with him being Grigor as well?

Schlegel complained to the young woman that the system didn't sound very efficient. She agreed and told him how a whole blast furnace had gone missing the year before.

Morgen, impatient, ended the call by depressing the receiver. He asked why he had told the woman it looked like rain when it was sunny out. Schlegel said he didn't want her to feel she was missing anything.

'How did you find out about Grigor?'

'Easy,' said Morgen. 'The switchboard operators were the first ones today that sounded like they knew what they were doing, so I presumed they hadn't got rid of them yet.'

The switchboard took the calls reporting all Jewish suicides. It relayed the information to the hearse drivers.

'The drivers are known by their first names. The one called Grigor matches your description, and the waiter's. Everyone called him Grigor, though on the actual drivers' list he was down under his real name, Yakov. A gentleman with an eye for the ladies, she said.'

'Except he is not where he is supposed to be, and nor are the butchers.'

# 32

Sybil and Lore watched from the window as Alwynd crossed Hochmeisterplatz on his way to his classes. They went to the back of the flat where Sybil posed nude. She was self-conscious because it reminded her of the demeaning business with Franz. She complained of the cold. Lore said at least it made her nipples stand up. Sybil said she didn't want to do it, so they went back to bed. Lore told Sybil she was beautiful and held her face. She said she didn't know what she would do without her. Afterwards they got tipsy on plum brandy of Alwynd's they found in the kitchen.

'And before ten in the morning too!' said Lore.

'Cheers!' said Sybil, flushed from sex.

They took photographs of each other; for each other, they told themselves, though that was not the case.

When Sybil was a student some of the girls had posed as artists' models. Lore insisted she be photographed naked too, so they would be even. She showed how to work the camera, standing with her arms round Sybil, saying all she had to do was wait for a moment she liked and press the shutter.

Afterwards they agreed they were even looking forward to the results.

Lore saw there were some frames left on the roll and said she wanted a photograph of them together. They had never appeared in the same picture.

Lore had a self-timer. Sybil stood waiting in front of the

camera, trying to make herself as tall as possible, like she had as a child having her picture taken. Probably fewer than thirty photographs of her existed altogether, all lost, apart from three: one showing her as a baby in a perambulator; one as a young schoolgirl with her first satchel; and one of a student group in a café, all mugging to camera, apart from Franz trying to look cool in dark glasses.

Sybil stared into the lens and watched the camera iris open and shut. For the first they stood next to each other. In the second Sybil took Lore's hand and in the third she impulsively reached for Lore and kissed her as hungrily as she ever had.

They both grew awkward when Lore took the finished roll and handed it to Sybil. Still feeling the effects of Alwynd's brandy, they stood kissing for a long time in the doorway. Sybil wanted to go back to bed. Lore said later; she had to work. Lore said in a self-conscious way, 'Sweet kisses as we part,' and gave a salute like a matelot. Sybil was conscious of Lore watching as she left, as though wishing to retain the moment.

She wondered about not going to Schmidt's, while perfectly aware she had little choice. She compromised and decided to go after spending an hour in the sanctuary of her little room, only to find Polish workers in the process of boarding up the house.

She tried to negotiate with the German supervisor, saying it was her home and she had come to retrieve the last of her belongings. The man showed his order sheet saying the property was condemned.

Sybil took the 51 tram as before, depressed at losing her refuge.

The track had been repaired so she didn't have to change.

Schmidt was no more or less friendly than before. Come back in two days, he said.

That was a Sunday. Sybil took it to mean Schmidt intended

to subject her to his lens. They could discuss any other business then, he said.

She ventured to ask how long it took to get papers. He said it depended, implying that the acquisition of illegal papers was like everything else and worked according to influence, position and usefulness.

Taking the initiative, Sybil said they could try some photographs now.

Schmidt had a studio across a courtyard, with proper lighting and a series of painted backdrops. She had to wait wrapped naked in a blanket for the mark of her brassiere to go. Schmidt was remote and professional. A little to the left. Head up. Sybil displayed herself as naturally as she could. Only at the end did he say if she were more adventurous he could pay a lot more. Sybil knew she had been naive not agreeing a price. She had assumed it was a test and part of getting in with the man. Only the fact of Lore trusting him had stopped her walking out. Schmidt's unthreatening manner had probably tricked a lot of women into taking their clothes off.

'How much do you pay?'

He told her. It was a small fortune.

'Next time. Not now.' He had to keep the shop open in the day. 'Think about it.'

A man tried to pick her up on the tram on the way back, sitting behind and resting on the back of the seat so he could keep up an insistent monologue. She got off and walked.

Lore had never been interested in the tedious demands of male desire. The few men she had tried it with were all sprinters or non-performers. Girls had more fun, she said, and it didn't end with getting pregnant.

Had they been ordinary citizens they could have lived as a couple, for the simple reason that the law hadn't got around to sending them off to a camp for loving each other, as they did men.

Outside of motherhood, women were deemed irrational and irrelevant. Their role was proscribed. Even so, she and Lore could have lived hiding in plain sight.

But had they not been persecuted they would never have met and being on the run together was preferable to a safe life alone, Sybil decided. It seemed absurd how this medieval witch hunt made a dirty secret of everything. The enemy included Alwynd, for whom they represented a prurient interest to be treated with amused but latent hostility because they fell outside his masterful gaze.

# 33

They were in the staff day room of the Jewish hospital, a big room with tall windows and angled sunlight, beyond which lay a bare expanse of neglected garden, its lawn full of last year's weeds. Franz was dozing in an armchair. Seeing them standing there he knew he had been seconds too late waking up. He seemed resigned, as though he knew someone would come for him sooner or later.

'We're going for a drive,' said Morgen.

Franz looked at Schlegel and clutched the arms of the chair, as if about to change his mind and make a run. Morgen pushed him back and said he had nothing to worry about.

'Think of it as an excursion.'

They drove across town to the western edge. They were in Stoffel's Opel again. The motor pool clerk had given them the nod, saying Stoffel was in the tank sweating a suspect and had been for the last twelve hours. Morgen watched Franz in the rear-view mirror, handcuffed in the back. Franz asked where they were going. Morgen said to relax, it was nice weather and spring was coming.

'What do you think of this war?' Morgen asked, as though making conversation.

'Which? The one against us?'

'A man with spirit, that's what I like to see. At least you don't have to go into the army and get your head blown off.'

Franz grunted. 'We're all dead one way or another.'

He gave a good impression of sangfroid. Schlegel wondered how long it would last.

What was left of the afternoon sun blinded them as they passed down the Kurfürstendamm with its once-smart shops depleted and shabby. 'Can you still get milkshakes at Kranzler's?' Morgen asked.

They drove on into Koenigsallee, past smart houses and little lakes through the district known as the Gold Coast.

'Where a lot of your people used to live,' said Morgen.

'My people weren't rich,' said Franz.

Everything looked softened and reduced through the dirty windscreen. Schlegel sensed the purpose of the drive was to stretch the tension until it snapped.

Morgen turned off the main road, drove for a few minutes and stopped on a long straight avenue by the railway tracks and big goods depot. Morgen suggested they stretch their legs. Franz looked reluctant.

Morgen rested his backside against the warm bonnet and smoked. Past the avenue of trees a long line of covered wagons stood in a siding.

Morgen said, 'You should ask yourself what you know. Prove useful and you won't find yourself on that platform.'

Schlegel watched Franz swallow. Morgen appeared serene. He produced Sybil Todermann's identity card and passed it to Franz.

They had been students together, it turned out, Franz at the Jewish art school and Sybil at the equivalent of fashion and design. They had all hung out at the Café Quik.

Morgen said, 'I remember the Quik. Joachimstaler Strasse.'

He asked where Franz had lived. Mitte, he replied.

Morgen said, 'I once availed myself of a tart in Münzstrasse before the war, when it was still a red-light area. Do you remember the Jewish baker that sold the onion pies with poppy seeds?

'He was Polish. In Rochstrasse.'

'With the fruit and veg market, and the model railway shop I once saw Goering coming out of. It was where he bought his train sets.'

Schlegel would not have been surprised if he and Franz hadn't attended the same parties during his Bohemian phase. Boys with long hair, drinking beer out of bottles, jazz records, girls in lipstick. He had been to a cellar bar once with a three-piece combo and the drummer openly smoked a reefer.

Morgen showed him Abbas's card next. Franz glanced at it and handed it back.

'All I know is the rumour mill says he was someone's agent, in exchange for his daughter going to a soft camp, and he may now be dead.'

'Did you know him?'

'Not to speak to.'

'Whose agent?'

'It doesn't do to learn their names.'

'That's all right. It's not our investigation. What about Grigor?'

Franz frowned and eventually said, 'You mean the one I was at art school with? He was two years above me. He had his own crowd. I didn't see him in years.'

'He drove the hearse. You work at the hospital.'

'We have nothing to do with them. The hospital has its own pathology department.'

Franz had a stiff right hand that he frequently massaged. Morgen asked to see it. Two fingers had been broken and badly set.

'No forging for you. Another one off the list.'

Nor did Franz admit to knowing the strangled woman, in as much as they were able to describe her. He did remember that Grigor was a great one for dancing.

Across the tracks a group of men in blue coats emerged from a hut and prepared the wagons, setting ramps and unlocking doors. Schlegel could just make out the stoker firing the boiler in the cab of the engine. The men seemed in good spirits, calling out, followed by bursts of laughter.

Morgen said, 'Are we clear about this? What's going on over there and what's going on between us?'

Franz said nothing.

'Information is all we need. Not much of a price. Or we just as easily stroll over the tracks and put you on the train. There's always room for one more.'

Tinny, soothing music started to play over the station loudspeakers.

'Who chooses the music?' asked Morgen.

They got back in the car and drove a short distance into the forest beyond. Morgen said it was time for a walk. Schlegel couldn't be sure if Morgen was aware of what he was implying.

Franz sat there, his hands driven between his legs.

'Out,' said Morgen.

They walked into the woods. Morgen kept his hand in his coat pocket. Franz looked pinched and worried. It was muddy underfoot. The sun had gone and the first chill was settling after the unexpected warmth of the day.

Schlegel thought that for Franz they must resemble an absurd and sinister version of a classic double act: the beanpole who looked about sixteen with white hair and the shorter, rounder one who despite his clownish air was the deadlier.

They passed through the trees and came to an open space with a little bench. Morgen suggested they sit. They must have appeared even more ridiculous, three men crowded on such a bench.

Franz eventually asked, 'Am I saving my skin here?'

Morgen said, 'Part of my job is to investigate the internal affairs of bodies that include the SS, Gestapo and criminal police.'

Franz looked at them, calculating.

Morgen went on. 'We know with regard to Jewish matters there has been a history of financial wrongdoing on the part of the Gestapo, which led to suspensions at the end of last year.'

Morgen lit yet another cigarette and addressed the glowing end. 'Were any untoward activity to come to my attention I would be bound to investigate it.'

'But if I open my mouth and word gets round.'

'It won't. I don't divulge my sources.'

Schlegel tried to imagine himself in Franz's position. They were about the same age. Franz was involved in a dangerous trade: saying too little was as fatal as saying too much. Schlegel knew he would be hopeless.

He said, 'Todermann witnessed a shooting last week. Can you tell us anything about a man named Metzler?'

'Ah, Metzler,' Franz said, exhaling. It was like watching the air go out of a balloon.

Metzler, Franz said, had turned up the previous spring claiming he might be able to arrange a deal to get some out.

Franz professed no knowledge of the details, other than a general mistrust of Metzler, who seemed aware of his own questionable trustworthiness.

'What do you mean?' asked Morgen.

'He was in a difficult position as he technically answered to the Gestapo but was recommending we cheat on them, at the same time as warning us we needed to ask ourselves if he was being sincere or setting a trap.'

'What was supposed to pay for all this? Private equity?'

They had arrived at a point of trade. Morgen made his understanding clear by offering Franz a cigarette.

'I was at one meeting with Metzler, only one of two I attended, where he said it would cost a lot of money, but he thought the risk worth it. He was the one who suggested if there wasn't the money we should think of ways of finding it.'

Dangerous waters, thought Schlegel.

'Why only two meetings?' asked Morgen.

'I had a feeling about Metzler, so I dropped out.'

'What sort of feeling?'

'He was too good. He made it look like he was playing for us but I worried it was a trick to sell out those who became involved.'

'And what about them?' Schlegel asked.

'All moved on, which supports what I am saying.'

Morgen interjected. 'You are bound to say that even if they weren't, to protect them.'

'I am telling you what I know.'

'Is any of what we have talked about still going on?'

'If it ever started. People said Metzler was a bullshitter and the plan to make fake money was a Gestapo scam in the first place.'

'Did anyone get out, as far as you know?'

'No one ever said. The Austrians came and took over from the Gestapo, which ended anything that might have been going on.'

'Why?'

'Unlike the Gestapo, the Austrians didn't take meetings.'

'When was this?'

'Last October.'

'Tell us how things changed.'

'A lot of Gestapo faces disappeared. The Austrians increased security massively but suspended deportations, which led people to hope they would not be sent away.'

'How did the Gestapo take this?'

'As you would expect when outsiders come in and take over.'

'Was there any specific reaction?'

'Are you kidding?' Franz exclaimed without thinking. He corrected himself and explained how in the week before the Austrians came the Gestapo conducted a big clearout at the Jewish Association. Several hundred were fired and deported.

Schlegel took that to mean they had got rid of those that knew too much.

They arrived at the crucial area. Franz sat looking like he might say more. Morgen persuaded him, with a second cigarette.

Franz took his time composing himself, the cool customer again.

'Would you be able to give us a name?' asked Morgen.

'Gersten.'

Metzler's sack lay neglected on the floor in the office until Frau Pelz asked if it could be thrown out.

'I suppose we should look,' said Morgen. It was an unedifying prospect. The contents smelled awful. The newspapers turned out to be just random, from what they could tell, rather than collected for a reason. The boots were boots, the gloves were gloves and the hat was a hat.

The stiff and grubby waterproof apron was the only item of interest. It had a large pocket across the front. Morgen felt inside. There was something.

'A photograph.'

It was regular snapshot size with a crinkled border.

'Well, well,' said Morgen. 'Friend Franz again.'

Schlegel looked at the picture, taken in a café with a group of youngsters sitting around a table. Students. There was a time when Schlegel could have found himself sitting among such a group: vaguely rebellious, quietly dissident, stylish but scruffy; he too had aspired to that look in his younger years.

Franz was at the front of the picture, wearing dark glasses and with his collar turned up.

Opposite was Sybil with shorter hair, looking dreamy and unconcerned in contrast to Franz's scowl.

She and Franz were the most stylish of the crowd.

'It was taken in the Café Quik,' said Morgen. 'I recognise it. But why does Metzler have it?'

'Metzler's notebook hints that he had a crush on Sybil, but it also suggests Franz knew Metzler better than he made out.'

Morgen turned the apron over. It was made of a stiff material that was awkward to handle.

'Sybil was a seamstress, am I right?'

He went out of the room. Schlegel heard him talking to Frau Pelz. He returned with scissors and snipped at the hem of the apron until the backing came away.

'See,' said Morgen.

Sewn into the apron were more banknotes, all fifty marks, all fake.

# 34

When Sybil went to wait for Franz he didn't come. He had said he thought it would be the last or second-last day serving at Rosenstrasse. They had been releasing prisoners in batches and now there were only a few hundred left. Apart from wondering where he had got to, she was relieved. Franz seemed altogether callous about what had happened, and continued to manipulate, claiming he was desperately short-handed, with the dangled carrot of a possible job at the hospital. Sybil suspected he was getting ready to renew his demands.

The S-Bahn was open again, a sign the crisis had passed. Knowing she was unlikely to witness anything like it again, she returned to the crowd.

Given what Franz had told them, they were within their rights to request a formal interview with Gersten.

'Let's surprise him. I want to see his face when we tell him,' said Morgen.

According to his office he was down at Rosenstrasse, supervising the last of the releases.

The crowd was still gathered. People talked openly, in defiance of the inevitable clampdown. A story was circulating about how when the releases were announced a Gestapo man had presented himself to the crowd with a clenched fist of solidarity, as though between them they had achieved something.

Morgen asked the crowd if the Gestapo man had long hair. As he sounded chatty he was taken for one of them. Yes, came back the answer.

The arrests were now being officially referred to as an error and a violation. Morgen, yawning, made a joke about how awkward it must be to eat humble pie while climbing down at the same time.

The atmosphere grew stranger and more carnival-like, full of cautious celebration and foreboding.

Morgen announced he was fading fast and needed to sleep. Gersten could wait or Schlegel take care of it.

'They don't warn you about the crashing tiredness.'

Sybil watched the tall white-haired young man and the shorter one who constantly smoked, and she couldn't decide if they were dangerous.

The women's persistence had won the day. Their struggle made her more optimistic about her and Lore's chances.

She told herself: We will learn to live on the run; we will lie, cheat and steal, do whatever it takes to survive. I will not let the way Franz used me happen again.

Start with what you know, she told herself. She would find or make uniforms for herself and Lore. A nurse's would be too obvious because they might get asked to help.

They would keep moving. There were lofts, basements, empty trams, parks, houseboats, even brothels, a whole city of hidden courtyards and secret spaces. The Jewish Cemetery in Weissensee had remained open. Tomorrow she would go there with Lore to check for buildings that could be used as refuge. Lore could carry on working for Alwynd, but continuing to stay there was out of the question.

She and Lore had discussed damaged apartments and fresh corpses, both offering a potential crop of the right stamps and cards and papers. It would be no test of her nerve to explore these abandoned blocks. She would scavenge. She would not flinch from touching dead flesh. She would do all this for Lore and Lore in return would make her special. They would become vixens by day and she a creature of the night.

Lore had asked what of those bombed out of their homes who had lost everything. The authorities would have to make provision. If they went and said their papers had been destroyed there would be no way to prove them wrong. There was bound now to be a certificate for such people.

It was a windless night. As darkness started to fall candles were lit. A waning moon hung in a clear sky, turning faces ghostly in the dark.

After Morgen had gone, Schlegel looked in vain for the young woman with the frozen tears.

Part of him wanted to shout out that this truce would be forgotten and everything would continue to be relentless.

He thought he spotted Gersten and his henchman.

There was no reason to go home. He could always go to his mother's and sleep in his childhood bed, with the guarantee of a hot bath and a decent meal. She was forever telling him in her provocative way it made no sense to live in that ghastly hole when he could be comfortable with her. 'Safer too when the bombs come.'

It was her way of saying he was a hopeless case. She had once deigned to inspect his apartment and pronounced it a slum, saying she knew of rooms belonging to White Russians living in Woyrschstrasse. 'Impeccably connected. Stunning daughter.' Schlegel had met her; a princess, no less, achingly beautiful. The last he'd heard she worked for the Foreign Ministry's Office of Information. At more formal parties he still occasionally saw her, drawing a clear circle around her by conversing in

French, Russian or English. Schlegel had been briefly admitted, until stumbling before company much cleverer and more politically daring, and, here was the warning, dangerously careless in their dismissal of the regime for its lack of class, which they by contrast had in spades. Schlegel's mother was frowned on as a fellow traveller because she didn't hang out with the diplomatic crowd, which was the accepted way of social agnostics and passive resisters.

A male voice asked gently if she was Fräulein Todermann.

Sybil thought of Lot's wife turned to a pillar of salt. She tried to run. Others were waiting.

The man strolled over. She couldn't see his face.

'You slipped past me last time.'

The crowd started to melt away, as though her taking was an abrupt signal that normal service was resumed. No one looked at her or the men around her.

A hand took her shoulder and gripped it until she winced. The man addressing her appeared in excellent spirits, like he had run into an old friend he was delighted to see. He produced a chapstick and greased his lips.

Schlegel derived satisfaction from surprising Gersten, making him spin round. He had an impression of two other men folding a third party into the back of a car, which, incongruously, was a regular taxi.

Gersten had his chapstick in his hand.

'Split lips,' he said with a nonchalant grin.

'Morgen needs to talk to you. Officially.'

'Bad timing. You just spoiled the pleasure of arrest.'

Gersten recomposed himself to assume an air of amused tolerance.

'Oh, all right. I'm intrigued. My place, noon tomorrow.'

He gave a cheery wave and moved briskly into the taxi. Schlegel could see enough to make out the silhouette of a woman. The car departed. She turned and looked through the back window. He recognised her from the identity card Morgen had showed him, and the photograph they had found in Metzler's apron.

Driven away in a taxi of all things. The officer in charge got in and patted her knee, making her instinctively recoil. He noticed and she knew she would be punished for it later.

She was too numb to feel afraid. She dreaded the moment when Lore's anxiety turned to certain knowledge that she wouldn't be coming back. Reckless kissing in the dark, for their pleasure only: Sybil prayed the strength of that memory would be enough to block out the men surrounding her.

'There's a twist,' said Gersten. 'I have you in mind for something. You still have a choice, but this is different from what I can usually offer.'

Sybil had to remind herself to be scared. This was not what she was expecting. The consideration. The politeness. A sense of talking as equals. The lazy, even effeminate turn of the man's wrist to indicate an unfortunate twist of fate. The possibility in a raised eyebrow of a different course being offered. The man was frightening for not being frightening.

Nor was the room the expected interrogation space.

The ride had lasted a couple of minutes. They could have walked it in five. Gersten told his man to pay.

It was the most feared address, once part of the stock exchange, where Room 23 was known as the gateway to the east.

The imposing entrance gate had dwarfed them and opened of its own accord. Sybil felt herself starting to shrink. Gersten smelled of 4711.

She was reminded of that when he placed a bottle of perfume between them.

'Chanel Number Five. Consider it an introductory gift.'

She stared in disbelief.

He said the room had a view of the river by day.

Taxis. Armchairs. Perfume. Unbelievable luxuries. Riverside views. She was being seduced, not sexually, though she could not discount that.

'Tell me about yourself,' he said, as though she were applying for a regular job.

She stared at her scuffed shoes and thought there was no point in pretending. She had lost Lore.

'We're not animals,' Gersten prompted. 'We can be heartless when dealing with our enemies, but I am sure we can be friends.'

He offered a cigarette from a silver box. Sybil wanted to say she wouldn't touch anything of his were it the last thing on earth.

She said instead, 'I work for many influential women. I am a dress designer.'

'Yes, it's important work.'

He knew where she lived, and who her mother was.

It was warmer sitting there than anywhere she could remember. Gersten seemed fond of his hair, constantly running his fingers through it.

'Where is your mother now?'

Sybil said she didn't know.

'I know.'

She feared the worst. It meant Gersten had her.

'Is she safe?'

He stared back enigmatically before remarking matter-of-factly, 'I know people who pull out nails with pliers, teeth too sometimes, but that's not my style. One colleague doesn't even bother with the pliers. He smashes teeth with a hammer. Not personally, of course. Thugs do that.'

Gersten let the remark hang.

'Pretty girl,' he murmured.

She couldn't tell if he meant her or a previous victim.

He went on as if discussing nothing serious. She asked about her mother. He ignored her.

'There's this room and there are other rooms. It's nice here. Let's say, I offer you a choice where it's possible to stay in the equivalent to this room.'

He explained what he could normally offer – 'could' thought Sybil, as he said it. People came and worked for him. In exchange for their freedom they took on the job of seeking out those that had gone underground.

She could always watch them slam her fingers in the door and call her a Jewish whore before doing whatever they liked. If she said yes? Or she could pretend to go along then disappear like others, out near the lakes perhaps.

'I want you to look for one man. This is almost certainly the one you were due to meet next in the process of acquiring your new papers.'

He offered another cigarette, which she accepted without thinking and repressed a shiver when he said, 'Let me match you.'

She leaned forward into the flame and hated herself, then, playing the game, thanked him and blew smoke out of the corner of her mouth. She couldn't remember when she had last had a cigarette.

'He's dangerous. He's a psychopath. He rapes and kills women. We need you to find him so we can put an end to his killing spree. What I ask is dangerous but it's better than the train.'

He looked at her calmly. 'Poland is death. We both know that.'

'What's to stop you sending me later?' The cigarette was making her sick.

'You'll get your new papers. You don't look Jewish. We are realists. Life remains negotiable for the lucky few.'

'Am I lucky?'

'Do a job for me and you'll get a nice set of papers.'

'And my girlfriend?'

Gersten looked surprised, deliberated and said, 'I will throw her in too, if you are successful. She doesn't look Jewish either.'

The idea seemed to strike him as funny.

It wasn't as if she was being asked to betray anyone, she reasoned, and asked how she was supposed to track this man.

'That's your job. We don't know what he looks like or his name but there must be those that do.'

'Such as the man who was supposed to meet us.'

'Regrettably, he is dead now.'

'He was alive last Sunday.'

'Not by the time he was supposed to meet you on Monday. The one we want was responsible.'

'He rapes and kills women, you said.'

'That too. He selects from among those whose papers he is forging. He may well have chosen you if your photograph had reached him.'

He flicked Sybil's photograph on to the table between them.

'Undeniably pretty. We think he's good-looking too. He makes his approach via his go-between.'

'You said he no longer has a go-between.'

'There'll be another. You found the last. I am sure you can find the next. Think of it as a challenge.'

He scribbled out his cigarette in the ashtray.

'Do well for me and everything will go swimmingly. I must say the elusiveness of this man is getting on my nerves so forgive me if I get tetchy from time to time.'

He stared at her levelly, inviting her to share in his game. Sybil found him very frightening and knew she must not let him see that.

'Can I ask a question?'

'Please.'

'Why do you care if he is murdering Jewish women?'

It was not the right question.

Gersten answered sharply, 'We don't want him moving on to German women. Isn't that obvious?'

He became amenable again and said he needed her signature on documents for a pass that would let her move freely around the city.

'Everything by the book,' he said lightly as he showed her where to sign. The old-fashioned pen required an inkwell. Sybil had a violent image of driving the pen into the man's eye, then throwing herself out of the window.

'As for your terms, I can pay the same as your previous job, plus per diems. Keep receipts. Avoid previous company. Tonight you stay here. Tomorrow you will be given a private room in the Grosse Hamburger Strasse centre, in your own wing and with your own exit. You will live a private existence away from the rest of the building, apart from your immediate colleagues and myself. You have your own staff room where you can eat. You personally are not subject to curfew or travel restrictions. I will use the photograph I have of you for your pass card, which will show you work for us. You will report to me on a daily basis between nine and ten in the morning. I will be at the office which is in your quarters. If not they will know where I am.'

Her first thought on being told how few restrictions she had was Lore, and how they could still spend time together after all. Her spirits lifted.

'You're in this building tonight. You needn't worry. It's a

room not a cell. But first come with me. I want to show you something.'

They walked down empty corridors past closed doors. The only sound was their footsteps. Sybil clung on to when she would next see Lore. Otherwise she was wandering in the forest, utterly forsaken. They went down two flights, through a series of doors, into a darker part of the building. Gersten led her into a room. She gasped in surprise. It was her mother seeming not to see her back. Then she understood. The space was divided by a two-way mirror.

'She's quite safe. She will be taken back tomorrow.'

Gersten stood with his hands in his trouser pockets, absent-mindedly fiddling with himself. He answered Sybil's next question for her.

'From my side your mother was not difficult to find. Her seances or whatever you want to call them are hugely popular with important men who are insecure about the future.'

The sight of her in that glass cage nevertheless knocked the stuffing out of Sybil. She had been negligent in looking, however much she suspected her mother hadn't been searching that hard in return. Whatever she had imagined, it was never that her mother would end up being played by Gersten as a pawn in his game. As he gauged her reaction, she knew he could apply as much leverage as he liked because she was, in the end, too dutiful and conforming to break the taboo of betraying her mother.

'There she is, protected, as long as you don't get ideas above your station. I will give you the address of where she is staying. Go and see her. You must have a lot to catch up on.'

'Can I see her now?'

'No. I don't wish her to know of our arrangement. She thinks she is here because a prospective client wishes to broker an arrangement through a third party, i.e. myself. As I say, she has official protection, highly placed. She performs a fashionable service. She will be secure as long as you and I understand each other, and you tell her nothing of our arrangement. Do we understand each other?'

Her room that night was on the top floor. There were bars on the window but otherwise it was like a hotel, with soap in a dish, a new toothbrush, toothpaste, a metal-framed bed with a mattress, with proper sheets, blankets and a floral bedspread, two pillows, a rug on the floor, and a lavatory behind a screen, with the almost unheard-of luxury of real toilet paper.

Gersten unlocked the door, stood back to let her in, gave her the Chanel and, without another word, shut her in.

Sybil sat on the bed, unscrewed the top of the Chanel and wondered how her life had come to this.

# 35

Schlegel was surprised to find Otto Keleman sitting on his doorstep, smoking and drinking a bottle of brandy. He said he'd forgotten to leave it behind the bar. He had been with Schlegel's Irish friend but as they lacked a common language there had been more drink than talk.

'Lovely man, dirty fingernails. Bottoms up!'

Keleman giggled and slapped his backside. He looked a mess. Schlegel was surprised he knew where he lived.

'Of course I know. I work for the fucking tax office.'

'Are you all right?'

'We need to talk.'

Keleman bowed with mock pomposity. Schlegel thought if he invited him up he would never get rid of him. He suggested the dancehall. What was so important that it couldn't wait? He wanted an early night. Keleman lurched and stumbled and Schlegel saw how drunk he was.

They stood in the yard outside where Keleman was less afraid of being overheard. Inside a lugubrious waltz was being played badly. They had passed a one-armed dancer on the way through.

Keleman stood close enough to brush Schlegel's lapel as he murmured, 'Go easy, if I were you.'

'What makes you say that?'

Keleman prodded him in the chest. 'Leave it, all right?'

Keleman looked around melodramatically, as though eaves-droppers lurked.

'Tell me what you know about Nöthling.'

'Nothing apart from what you've told me.'

Keleman sniggered. 'Refresh my memory.'

The man was being so tiresome.

'Shopkeeper. Corrupt. You should go home. I'll walk you if it's not far.'

'Ah ha!' Keleman pointed wildly. 'I know where you live but you don't know where I live!'

His eyes widened and he quickly excused himself. Schlegel listened to him spew in the dark. He returned, swigging from his bottle. Schlegel caught a wave of alcohol and vomit.

'Come on. You can clean yourself upstairs.'

Keleman had to stop several times on the way. Schlegel showed him the bathroom and listened to him piss noisily before retching again.

He emerged chastened, more like his normal self. He sat down in Schlegel's only decent chair, arms dangling between his knees.

'The big fish never get caught,' he announced morosely. 'Let's really mix our metaphors. I predict a big shit storm coming.'

He rambled on, saying there was a series of wars going on in the upper leadership.

Schlegel said he'd heard as much.

'Do you remember how they got the Chicago gangster, Al Capone?'

'Tax evasion.'

'Exactly! You couldn't think of anything less fashionable in our office until six weeks ago. Now they could all go down. Give me a name.'

'Goering.'

They laughed. Everyone knew about Hermann's corruption.

'Goebbels.'

Keleman made an equivocal gesture. Schlegel said he wasn't sure he wanted to know.

Keleman agreed. 'There's nothing worse than finding yourself caught between the upper and lower jaws of bureaucracy when they are about to snap shut.'

'Your meaning seems plain, but I still don't see.'

Keleman sighed. 'It's very different from the Bolsheviks. Step out of line, you get shot. Even if you don't step out of line you get shot. If you have your snout in the trough here the chances are you never get it taken away completely. It's the underlings, you and me, my friend, who get shafted.'

'In that case lose whatever it is you need to lose in the system.'

'Not good enough. They nail us for losing it and they nail us for not losing it. *Capiche?*'

'Us?'

'It might be wise for me to keep a back channel open, so you are aware of what is going on.'

Keleman reached into his coat pocket and handed over several sheets of paper. It was a typed list of names and, next to each name, different figures running into the thousands.

'What is this?'

'Famous names, some very much so.'

'I can see that. And the figures?'

'Money probably. Lists it's better to be ignorant of, unless you compiled it.'

'How did you get it?'

'A little birdie.'

'Anonymous?'

'What do you think?'

'Why do I need to know?'

'I am being quite selfish in that respect. Sorry. When they fish me out of the Landwehr Canal I would like someone else to be aware of why I was put there. Consider it a case of being forewarned. It's financial. You're financial.'

Swim in murky waters and you probably did end up in the canal, and what Keleman had showed him certainly did affect him.

Nebe's name was on the list, with a figure of '2000' next to it.

# 36

Schlegel watched the scene unfold through the two-way mirror. They were in the downstairs tank. Stoffel was on the other side of the mirror, jacket off, sweating, stubbled, bowler hat tilted back, cigar on the go. The scene was being watched by a bunch of homicide cops that barely moved to let them in. Already the flask was being passed around.

'Celebration,' one said dourly, not offering.

Stoffel gave sly looks to his observing cronies, and at one point gave a thumbs up behind the suspect's back. Stoffel wore garters on his sleeves and looked unintentionally comic, having removed the front stud of his stiff collar, which stuck out either side of his neck. A bright light shone in the face of the suspect, a sorry specimen with a pudding-basin haircut, a dullard's look and a mouthful of crooked teeth.

'Going well?' Morgen asked the cop standing next to him, a grey little ghost of a man with a reputation for unstinting use of blackjack and knuckleduster.

The cop took his time.

'A classic, if you ask me. Axel Lampe. Has one of those invisible jobs that allows him to move around, driving the family laundry van. Repeated cruelty to animals. Reported for beating a horse and molesting a woman. He was sterilised for that, but it didn't stop him from carrying on raping and killing. He says he's been at it since he was eighteen.'

'How old is he now?'

'Forty-six. Sometimes the animal fucked them when they were dead.'

'How many is he admitting to killing?'

'As many as eighty.'

'Eighty! The man looks incapable of tying his own laces.'

'Down the years. Think of it as once every four months.'

'What's he doing here now?'

'Pulled up for a traffic offence, went crazy and attacked the cops. When they hauled him in he said he wanted to talk to homicide. They thought him a time-waster and didn't bother until he tried to hang himself.'

'Why does Stoffel want to see us?'

'You'll have to ask him.'

Stoffel took a break after twenty minutes, by when his method was clear. Carrot and stick: the cigarettes with which the suspect was plied; the strategically placed knuckleduster on the table, which Stoffel fingered occasionally. Lampe had the air of a clumsy innocent who would smash things without meaning to. Stoffel's focus on his subject was total and flattering and the man basked in the attention while volunteering nothing, waiting for Stoffel to suggest the answer, then agreeing.

Morgen was furious when Stoffel came out, confronting him for trying to frame the man as some kind of super-murderer.

'You're wrong. He has huge animal cunning.'

Axel Lampe's case-history folder had been left in the anteroom. Morgen waved it and said he had just read it.

'Lampe is a simpleton. He doesn't know how many days in a year or minutes in an hour. He thinks Silesia is a city. Is there any forensic evidence?'

'I am doing you a favour. Come and talk to him and he will tell you. Strangulation! Strangulation! Strangulation!'

\*　　\*　　\*

They went into the stifling tank. Lampe resented their intrusion and looked at Schlegel with sulky eyes.

'Tell these gentlemen about the Jew you killed last week,' said Stoffel.

'Which one was that?'

Before Stoffel could prompt him, Morgen snapped, 'Let the man remember for himself.'

Lampe accused Morgen of spoiling his train of thought.

Stoffel said gently, 'In your own time. Tell the gentlemen what you told me.'

Lampe furrowed his brow in a show of concentration and at last asked, 'Is this about Abbas?'

Morgen gave Stoffel a warning look not to interrupt.

'I am not stupid. It's important to get it right.'

After another silence, Lampe said in a rush, 'I killed Abbas because he was an interfering Yid.'

Morgen asked how Lampe knew Abbas was a Jew.

'This woman told me she was being pestered by this Yid.'

'What is this woman's name?'

'I met her in a bar. I come up to town on my days off. She said she didn't want to take the Jew's money. That's why I stuffed it in his mouth.'

'Where did you leave the body?'

'I don't know. The last thing I remember was cutting off the Jew's tool.'

'Remember that then you must remember where you were.'

'I just went along. I can't remember where.'

Lampe started to whine.

The story was full of holes and contradictions, yet he seemed to believe what he was saying. He and Abbas had spent the day drinking, with the woman at first. In one version they both fucked the woman, which was when he realised Abbas was a Jew. Abbas also boasted of having lots of money.

Challenged or contradicted, Lampe said he could only tell them what happened according to what he remembered.

He broke down, shouting, 'Why should I be telling you this when it's going to get me the guillotine?'

'Tell them what happened next,' said Stoffel.

Lampe looked as though he was facing an examination question where he had no idea of the answer.

Schlegel could no longer tell what was true. Stoffel had clearly fed Lampe his lines and worked on him, but through a willed act of absorption Lampe had made them his own, and volunteered several versions.

By one account, he had stayed up in town overnight, in a daze, and on the Monday carried on drinking and looking for the woman who had complained about Abbas.

Stoffel interjected to say they had checked. It was Lampe's day off. There were no laundry deliveries on Mondays.

The woman he strangled that night was the first woman. They had gone on a bar crawl and he had no idea where they ended up. Or it might have been another woman he had picked up along the way.

'We agreed a price then she refused, so I did her anyway and the money was the price we agreed.'

Lampe was sweating and shaking as though reliving the experience.

'Please don't let them kill me,' he mumbled to Stoffel, who laid a reassuring hand on his shoulder.

'You know that won't happen. You're clause fifty-one. That makes you exempt.'

'I know. I mean these gentlemen. They are going to take me out and shoot me.'

Lampe's story started to take on a ghastly plausibility. He and Stoffel argued over what he had done with the money in the second murder.

'You didn't,' said Stoffel softly. 'You stuffed it up her cunt.'

'No, I shoved it up her arse.'

That was money he had taken from the Jew. Five minutes later he said it might have come from money stolen elsewhere and used to finance his bar crawl. He admitted to stealing frequently.

Stoffel said, 'Tell them about the job you did last year.'

Lampe puzzled for a long time as his features composed themselves into a play of remembering. He and a friend had done the job. A print works in Gesundbrunnen.

He suddenly announced as though he had just remembered, 'The man's cock I made a present of to the first woman. That's why we argued.'

He put his hand to his mouth and giggled.

Schlegel asked if he remembered anything out of the ordinary happening on the night he killed the woman.

Lampe went blank, then brightened and said, 'Apart from killing her?'

'The bombs?'

He smirked and quickly came back with, 'There are bombs going off in my head all the time.'

He stared at Schlegel with a beguiling emptiness.

Thinking he was supposed to add something, Lampe recited, 'I found pleasure in killing animals. I began doing humans at the age of eighteen. For years I stalked, stabbed and strangled as many women as I could, raping them before and sometimes after. I killed men too. The dick I cut off should have been my own. I understand that now.'

# 37

Gersten was waiting for them in a large and impressive room, as before. Big windows showed the river. He was alone, sitting with an accordion, playing it idly.

'The old squeezebox. This is probably out of order, but would you like to come to a party tonight?' He looked at them brightly. 'Says he, about to face a formal questioning.'

He appeared beguiled by the situation, a man with nothing to hide. He gestured at the accordion. 'A hangover from my days as a child actor. I am playing tonight with a bunch of Ivans. I can't resist showing off.'

'Russians?' asked Morgen in surprise.

'Yes, a wild foot-stomping band, not a hundred per cent approved, but music one can let one's hair down to, and the *Untermensch* off its collective head is something one should experience at least once. That they might stick a shiv in you adds a certain spice. Of course, they know we'd shoot the lot of them.'

He unstrapped the accordion and laid it down.

'Actually, such fraternisation is not altogether discouraged by more progressive schools. It opens channels. What those humourless cunts from SS Vienna don't understand is you need an understanding of the enemy, you need to play with him. That bandy-legged idiot in charge considered it his duty to show us so-called Prussian swine how to deal with the Jew bastards. My arse! Look at them. A fuck-up from day one!'

He turned to Schlegel.

'About tonight. I am to meet a particular Russian, who wishes to speak to me about a confidential matter. I have no Russian, he has no German or Polish but has a bit of English, which I believe you speak with your Irish friend.'

Schlegel was surprised Gersten knew about his association with Alwynd.

Gersten said Alwynd was bound to be watched. 'You must know that. The thing is, we've been trying to cook something up with the Foreign Office using Alwynd as a conduit to the Republicans, but they are such lazy bastards, the Irish. Anyway, perhaps I could borrow you? Think about it. I guarantee you a mother of a hangover.'

'Why not Lazarenko?'

'Because this is about Lazarenko,' Gersten muttered darkly. 'What do you want to grill me about? I understand we are here for a frank and free-ranging discussion. Shall we be needing a stenographer or are you just taking notes?'

'This is a preliminary questioning,' said Morgen. 'Should we need a record of any part of the discussion we will ask for a separate statement.'

'Does he have to be here?' Gersten asked, not so friendly, pointing at Schlegel.

'I work with him.'

'On whose authority? He has nothing to do with internal affairs.' In a smiling aside, he said to Schlegel, 'No offence.'

'On my authority,' said Morgen.

'Are you still empowered to carry out such investigations? I heard you are in bad odour.'

'Unless one is stripped of one's authority, an investigative judge remains one regardless of circumstances.'

Gersten laughed. 'Well, that's me put in my place. Before we begin, can I get either of you gentlemen anything?'

They refused. Gersten said to Schlegel, 'Nothing personal. I just like to be clear about where we stand.'

Morgen said it had come to their attention that Gersten had an agent who bribed him to look the other way.

'Is that all? Ask away.'

They were investigating aspects of the Abbas case and had been told he was Gersten's agent.

'I don't deny it.'

'We have been told that the fake money was being forged by Jews to pay for stuff.'

'What stuff?'

'We will come to that. I repeat the question.'

'I heard that too.'

'That's not what you said last time.'

Gersten gave a booming laugh. 'I was lying. We have our interests to protect.'

Morgen stared back, stony. 'You accepted that money or its equivalent—'

'That part I didn't hear.'

'We are also told you stole or confiscated this money.'

'I didn't hear that part either.'

Nor had Schlegel. Franz had said nothing about that.

Gersten leaned forward. 'Cards on the table time. How much do you two know about Jewish affairs?'

Morgen replied, 'For the purposes of this conversation, nothing. Go on.'

'They used to own everything and now they don't. To put it bluntly, it has been an exercise in asset stripping. We take what they have and ask them to move on. It's not the prettiest but it's policy. Yes, I accepted money but I handed it over.'

Gersten picked up a table lighter and fiddled with it.

'However much Jewish circumstances were reduced, the clever ones clung on to diamonds, jewellery and gold, put aside for a rainy day. Unofficially it has always been the case to let those that could afford to pay through the nose buy their way out. For us the question was a simple one of how to relieve them of what they still had hidden.'

'How do you draw the line between negotiation and blackmail?'

'How indeed? What is being undertaken here – as far as I understand and in as much as anyone bothers to inform my level – is a highly complex and modern reshaping in a social equivalent to the hygiene reforms of the last century. Wouldn't you say?'

'Go on.'

'That was how it was explained in one of the few lectures we received on the subject I didn't fall asleep during. The point I'm making is they didn't issue us with a how-to manual. Most curtailment was by legislation, which was unequivocal and withdrew rights to a point where anyone with the nous and money skedaddled, as intended. Even last year, it was broadly suggested those with the wherewithal should get out. It was easier when the Yanks were still neutral. Be that as it may, the Jews are traders. It's in their nature to bargain. They're still bargaining at the station. "Oh, I don't like this carriage." For a packet of cigarettes, which miraculously appears, "Can I have a better carriage?" It's human nature. Sorry, I've lost my thread.'

'Negotiation and blackmail.'

'The Jews are always trying to negotiate. If an elephant steps on your foot you ask nicely if it could transfer some of its weight to the other foot. Do you see what I'm saying? Some days the elephant might take some of the weight off, and on others even lift the foot altogether, and on yet others stamp down harder. If the elephant lifts its foot you might consider making an offering in the hope that it won't put it back down again.'

'A fine parable but elephants aren't in the business of blackmail.'

'We offered a service in exchange for a fee,' Gersten said bluntly.

'What service?'

'Our orders were to take them for everything they had. Actually, that's an exaggeration. There were no specific orders. The general understanding was they should be left with nothing, and it was up to us. For those evacuated, a declaration of assets form had to be signed, donating all possessions to the state. But as a nomadic race, the Jew is adept at self-subsistence and hiding. It is impractical to conduct full body searches of everyone who passes through our hands, but if you offer a service, it is surprising what is forthcoming in the way of payment.'

'What sort of service?'

'In their position, there are places you would not wish to be sent and there are others which constitute the cushier option. Being in the business of travel agency, we were able for a fee to fix the softer arrangement for those that could afford. One camp is a holiday resort compared to the rest and, of course, those that could pay wished to go there . . .'

'You speak of it in the past.'

'It is a service I can no longer provide. Perhaps others can . . .'

The silence hung.

'You're right,' Gersten went on. 'In any business involving confiscation of assets, some will go missing. There were those among us that were lax when it came to helping themselves. It is why the Austrians were sent for, because it was said we were too venal. They said we became corrupted by the Jews and their deals. There are those that said we turned our headquarters into the equivalent of a souk.

'I will be honest with you, hand on heart. I don't have to tell you this, but I am rather proud of it. Like anyone, we are subject to budgets and funding and money is tight now with all priorities dedicated to the war effort. The problem we had was the increasing amount of those due for deportation that failed to report and went into hiding. It was our idea more than a year ago to create an agency of Jewish recruits, setting a fox to catch a fox. As a formal body it needed a budget, not much of one, but we decided to pay the agents, to make them feel better about themselves and therefore more efficient and useful to us. It's not easy asking people to be traitors for the sake of saving their own skins, which is what it comes down to. You need to offer certain foundations and infrastructure, a business model so to speak, with targets to be met and so forth. Life has to appear normal.'

He flicked the table lighter off and on, distractedly holding his finger to the flame as he talked.

'But could we get anyone to pay for it? Even the modest sums we were asking? We tried everywhere. Even the mayor's office, which was the main instigator of ridding the city of these people. Deaf ears. And all the usual little pots in reserve gone. Who would fund our modest operation? Of course, the cynical answer is make the Jews pay, but they really were pleading poverty, saying there wasn't even the money to perform their minimum duties. You have to keep asking yourself, is what they're saying true or are they being foxy? But they really were strapped. Never negotiate with a Jew. It goes on and on and they have four hundred and ninety-three excuses. Given they know it's the eleventh hour, they do everything within their power to procrastinate, these merchants who have nothing left to barter except their souls. One grows weary of their excuses. At first it was amusing seeing how tricky they could be and what they could come up with but that has long grown boring. So, we decided—'

'Who's we?'

'OK, I decided – if we could liberate hidden Jewish assets by advertising a service, then we could use those funds to finance the other project.'

'How did you advertise this service?'

'Cards on the table again. I used the old man Metzler. I can tell you, no one was more surprised than I when I saw he was the Jew that had shot himself. I knew him quite well.'

'Then he was your agent,' said Morgen.

'If you mean someone who skulked in doorways and reported what he saw then no. If you mean someone I spoke to who then spoke to other people and reported back, then yes, he was an agent.'

'You used Metzler to inform them of this service you were offering.'

'I thought of him as someone who could state our case to his people. He was smart enough not to be under any illusions but worldly enough to see a difference could be made.'

'When was this?'

'I suppose from about last April through September.'

'For about six months until five or six months ago.'

'That sounds about right.'

'This was to offer people able to pay a choice of which camp they went to?'

'I see what you're thinking.'

'Go on.'

'Why bother to honour the obligation when they're in no position to ask for their money back?'

'You said it.'

Gersten scorched his finger, snapped the lighter shut, winced and laughed.

'That'll teach me. I think one has to deal straight at a certain point and not cheat.'

Morgen looked at Gersten blandly and closed his notebook. Thinking the interview over, Gersten started to get up, blowing on his finger.

'I haven't finished,' said Morgen. 'We are told the whole operation was much bigger than you acknowledge.'

Gersten gave an earnest look to say he didn't know what Morgen was talking about.

'Money was being paid to smuggle people out while you looked the other way.'

Gersten snorted. 'That old chestnut! If I'd been given a mark for every time I have heard that story. I am sorry, it's mischief on the part of your informers.'

'They were forging the money to pay for that. In other words, Metzler was conning you.'

'Who's telling you this? It's a trick to set us against each other. Of course the Jews want to believe that some get-out or a fairy-tale ending exists. It's a nightmare trying to sort out transportation as it is. Now you are saying there are other trains!'

'Goods trains move all over Europe. I am sure many carry contraband. Human traffic would be an extension of that.'

Gersten frowned. 'On second thoughts, I think I may have been responsible for the forged money, without knowing it.'

'Cards on the table time?' asked Morgen ironically.

'Ha-ha!' said Gersten. 'Metzler complained the Jews had no money and I said – as a joke – tell them to forge it, not thinking he would take me at my word. It comes back to me now. Anyway, he told me although they had excellent document forgers there was no one of sufficient expertise to fake money. That was the end of the matter, as far as I was concerned, but from what you are saying Metzler went ahead. I admit it has been nagging at the back of my mind. That's what I must have been hinting at the last time we talked when I wondered if Metzler hadn't played me for a fool.'

Schlegel wondered how good Gersten was on the accordion. Listening to him play them was like watching the improvisations of an accomplished musician.

'And stealing the money?'

'I heard they fell out among themselves.' Gersten paused. 'Metzler was very good and wasted in many ways. Most of them you can read like an open book, but he was different and I admit I spent much of my time trying to double-guess him.'

Gersten stood, looking no more ruffled than if he had been strolling in the park.

'I hear Stoffel has pulled the cat out of the bag and Lampe's endless confession is being referred to as the crowning glory of his career.'

'What else did you hear?'

'Lampe is about to be given a grand tour of the sites of unsolved murders all over the country and will sign off on each and every one. I have to say, from what I've heard, the man gives sadism and necrophilia a bad name. Not the sharpest knife in the drawer. All made up, wouldn't you say?'

Morgen changed the subject. 'I think my colleague has a question about Fräulein Todermann.'

Gersten's slight recoil, tilting back on his heels, reminded Schlegel of a boxer riding a punch.

'We would like to speak to her.'

Gersten produced his chapstick.

'Fräulein Todermann is engaged in confidential work.'

'Ten minutes.'

'She is not available. Later, perhaps. I will tell you when. I don't mean to be difficult.'

Schlegel wanted to take issue but Morgen said, 'Have it your way.'

As they left the building, Morgen said, 'I have an idea about Fräulein Todermann.'

# 38

It took all morning for Sybil's papers to be put in order. Later Gersten appeared and issued her a laminated pass, using the photograph taken by Abbas, and a certificate of passage. The card carried the Gestapo stamp and stated: *Fräulein Todermann is permitted to take measures in Jewish matters. The authorities are asked to support her in this.*

Sybil was hard-pushed not to weep with shame.

'This is a standard card. Normally you would have to check a quota of fifteen addresses a day. As agreed, you will concentrate your search entirely on this one man. Now what clothes do you have?'

Only what she was standing in.

He took her to a room that had more than any shop. She should select three wardrobes.

'Help yourself to silk underwear. I like the feel of silk next to skin. It's a small luxury we will permit you. Call it our secret. The rest should be modest and unostentatious without being threadbare or dowdy. I recommend practical shoes because you will be doing a lot of walking.'

She knew he would stay and watch. He insisted on inspecting everything down to her choice of underwear.

She understood she had to make a show of getting undressed, revealing everything while retaining a becoming modesty. She calculated the man was too full of himself to do anything more than observe, for the moment.

He confirmed as much, saying he liked to watch. Feminine beauty was the great single wonder of the world.

'How can so few parts result in such infinite variety?'

He grew philosophical contemplating Sybil's body, wondering at what point beauty ceased to become beauty, not that she had anything to worry about. Most women had ugly feet but hers he could gaze at all day.

'A shame about the chilblains. We'll give you something for those.'

He confessed that he always found a woman dressing after sex almost unbearable for its erotic tension. The act became the repository for what had gone on before.

'Try the stockings with the corset and garter belt next, not that you need a corset, but let's see it anyway. You are lucky you haven't ballooned like so many women on this atrocious diet we now have. Perhaps as a treat you could come out with me one evening. I could take you to a restaurant where we can still get a good meal, as unbelievable as that sounds.'

Gersten kept it light and hid his threat. He seemed to possess too much irony for that, making out the whole show of her dressing and undressing was a foible for his decadent amusement. Because she didn't feel afraid, Sybil started to feel safe with the man, which was exactly what he wanted. She considered him extremely dangerous.

She presented herself wearing a suit with a tighter skirt than normal.

'When does the cat show its claws?'

Gersten was puzzled.

'What am I supposed to do when I find this man?'

'That's up to you.'

'Am I supposed to seduce him?'

'Up to you, dear.'

He tilted back in his chair, legs straight out, feet crossed, jacket undone, hands in trouser pockets. Sybil saw he had an erection.

'It's good if there is a tension between us. Try on something else.'

As she undressed again, he said, 'You have nice areolae,' as if inspecting a broodmare.

He preferred a green coat to a blue one and helped her select a suitcase.

'Take a leather one.'

They could have been a couple shopping.

'Have you had many lovers?' he asked idly.

She could see he didn't want her to be a whore so told the truth, which was not many. She omitted Lore.

# 39

Schlegel and Morgen watched as a backward, clumsy man in shackles, surrounded by a dozen armed policemen, led them a merry dance. Lampe was having the time of his life: the nonentity whose every word was now hung on. They accompanied Stoffel and Lampe to the murder sites of Abbas and the still-unidentified woman where Lampe gave accounts that were full of holes and yet eerily accurate. When challenged by Schlegel or Morgen he accused them of trying to take his story away.

Any mention of Russian being heard on the night of the Abbas murder was attributed to the neighbouring woman's fantasy. Using a uniformed policeman, Lampe demonstrated how easily capable he was of carrying a body on his own.

'A strong brute,' said Stoffel in approval.

For the location of the murder – as opposed to where he had dumped the body – he never came up with a satisfactory answer and resorted to one of his black states of forgetting, wrestling with himself and banging his forehead with his handcuffed hands.

He denied meeting the woman in the dancehall until Morgen said they had witnesses, then he backtracked and asked to be taken there.

'Yes, it could have been here,' became, 'I can see myself standing outside now I am here,' then, 'Yes, I remember now.'

Morgen said *sotto voce* to Schlegel he was sure Lampe hadn't been in on either night, but no one was going to stop the canary singing. Feeble-minded and fitted up was his verdict and Schlegel found it impossible not to agree.

Stoffel's professional stance, that he was compiling a lexicon to decipher the dark text of Lampe's murderous mind, made it all the more dispiriting. Only occasionally did he have to raise his voice when Lampe threatened to make a nonsense of everything by trying to retract his confessions.

They ended up at Guenstiger's, a small printing press which leased space in the huge AEG Montagehalle complex in Gesundbrunnen, north of where Schlegel lived. This being a Saturday afternoon, the place was closed and they had to get the watchman out.

This, Lampe proudly announced, was where he and an army pal, with the helpful name of Mueller, carried out a robbery the year before. Mueller's current whereabouts were unknown to Lampe.

In a twist Schlegel could only admire, Abbas was turned from chance acquaintance into a long-term pal of Mueller. Abbas, furthermore, generously shared his knowledge of a considerable sum of forged money being produced and stored there. As no one would dare report the theft of illegal money they decided to break in.

Stoffel said he had expected Schlegel and Morgen to be more grateful. He had solved the case of the counterfeit money for them.

'He stole it and left it on the bodies of his victims.'

'It doesn't explain Metzler having it,' said Morgen.

'Come on, man, Abbas was bent. Whatever the Jews were up to stopped when the Austrians came. The money was lying around. Abbas knew about it and he and his two cronies took advantage.'

Stoffel prodded Schlegel in the chest. 'Enough of the long face. Live on easy street for a change.'

\*     \*     \*

Back at headquarters Schlegel and Morgen checked the crime sheet for the Guenstiger break-in. A small amount of cash was reported stolen. The incident was described as a routine robbery. The paperwork was scrappy and barely literate.

The October date coincided with the arrival of the Austrians; at least that part of the story stood up.

Morgen said, 'I had three names for the possible forger, remember. The third was a fellow called Plotkin whom I discounted because he was dead.'

'Jumped off a roof.'

'More precisely, off the roof of Guenstiger's the same day the robbery was reported.'

'And if Plotkin was responsible for producing the money . . .'

'He either threw himself off because he was scared of the consequences or a third party assisted, when it found the money gone and suspected him of having a hand.'

Morgen sat back. 'Nebe can be very pleased with Stoffel's efforts. Everything is answered in one go. It would be headline news if such matters could be reported. Stoffel will retire promoted and Nebe will probably get a push up the ladder too. There still remains one big problem.'

'Which is that?'

'Someone may yet take the basic facts and distort them to their own ends. I now suspect Lazarenko could be right. There may be a dimension of internal feuding. It's why I think we should go to this party of Gersten's, though I personally cannot stand the accordion, outside the context of Texas border music, which I doubt will be entertaining us this evening.'

The barracks was so crowded it was almost impossible to move. With all the smoke the upper half of the room was invisible. Whatever they were drinking was raw, extremely powerful and quickly induced double vision. One reeling couple delivered slow-motion punches as they tried to hit each other as the result of a row. People lay passed out. Maudlin ballads that could have made a dog cry gave way to raucous foot-stompers.

Isolated islands within the room were dedicated to intense games of cards where the players ignored everything around them. One man near Schlegel, unable to stand, keeled over and forced enough space to lie down, where he lay drumming his heels. Morgen made no concessions to the music while appearing to regard the surroundings with intense fascination.

Such wild revelry and colossal drunkenness, even by the standard of office leaving parties, was unlike anything Schlegel had seen before. The top of Gersten's head bobbed in time to the music. The fiddler scraped away so fast he expected to see sparks. The room was like a pressure cooker about to explode. And all on the junction of Ostseestrasse and Goethe, in one of those huge compounds of temporary barracks that had sprung in the last years. No one paid Schlegel any attention, being too caught up with getting plastered or winning and losing hypothetical fortunes in cards. It was the Russians' one night off and they had the whole of the next day to recover. A contingent of German workers seemed to have found their way there too – money was being taken on the door – for the obvious reason that Russian music was more full-blooded and raucous than the usual oom-pah-pah. When the band embarked on a Polonaise the audience, lurching and crashing around, refused to let it end, applauding for encores as soon as the music showed signs of flagging. It was far too noisy to speak. From time to time one of the card tables came to blows and the fights resembled violent dancing.

Inviting Gersten to play there looked like sound Russian strategy. Otherwise the local cops would have been round to put an immediate stop to it.

The band finally took a break. Gersten came and found them. He wore a white Russian-style shirt, drenched in sweat. He was grinning and exhilarated.

'Come and meet Josef. We have about twenty minutes before the next set.'

Josef sat in a back room away from the rest, playing a lazy game of cards, surrounded by bodyguards. He was baby-faced and mean, no more than thirty, younger than Schlegel expected for a barracks leader. He inspected Schlegel with uncurious eyes. He did not offer to shake hands, though he had Gersten's. Schlegel stood with his behind his back, not wishing to anyway.

Josef gave his cards to a bodyguard and suggested they step outside. It was breathtakingly cold. Josef told Schlegel it was the one time in the week the huts warmed up. His English was fair. Schlegel asked where he had learned it. Josef appeared unwilling to answer, not being the type for pleasantries, then said he had attended the School of Oriental and African Studies in London for two years.

Morgen wandered off into the night, looking like he wouldn't bother to come back, leaving Schlegel to arbitrate what he could only suppose was the trap being set for Lazarenko. Negotiations were lubricated with the passing of a bottle, which Josef told Schlegel was better than what the rest drank, which would turn them blind.

Gersten appeared intent and businesslike, studying Josef as he spoke English to Schlegel.

Josef said, 'I will only say this once. Translate it the way I say it. No interpreter's gloss.'

He spoke rapidly, forcing Schlegel to absorb what was said, rather than translate as they went along. It took all his concentration. His world was spinning and unless he shut one eye he saw everything double.

Josef didn't appear at all drunk although he had knocked back two enormous swigs.

Schlegel addressed Gersten. 'He says the three men dying in the paint vat was Lazarenko's work, and Lazarenko is a cruel man with a habit of weeding out Russians. More to the point, he is not Ukrainian as he pretends but former secret police GPU. One of the dead men recognised him from the time when he committed many atrocities around Zwiahel in northern Ukraine. He murdered hundreds of Germans and collaborators too. His expertise on the subject is based on his own crimes. He used a slaughterhouse hammer and knives to dispatch his victims. He is, furthermore, really a Bolshevik spy operating with a false passport. Such passports are easily obtained from the émigré office by going along at lunchtime when they are handed out for cash. He says that while Lazarenko's passport is a proper one all the information on the paperwork is false.'

Josef took another huge pull. Between the three of them they had almost finished the bottle in ten minutes.

Gersten appeared in a state of shock.

'Can this be true? I thought Lazarenko was suspect, but this?'

'It's what the man said.'

Someone came out and told Gersten the next set was about to start. He went inside without another word. Josef stuck his fingers down his throat, threw up copious amounts of liquid, straightened up and held out the last of the bottle for Schlegel. Seeing he had little choice, he downed it in one go, the searing liquid burning his throat. He wanted only to stagger off after Morgen but Josef said, 'As our guest it is rude to leave before the end.'

The music went on and on. Schlegel found himself a corner, where he managed to prop himself and more or less pass out, coming to from time to time, when the stamping reached a crescendo. There was no sign of Morgen, which didn't surprise him.

It was the only time he experienced drunkenness and the hangover to be simultaneous. He was too far gone to leave and supposed he would have to throw himself at Gersten's mercy for a ride home.

At last the evening broke up, though the card games showed every sign of carrying on. Schlegel found himself staring at a dark, gaunt man sitting at one of the tables. The room was still reeling. The man came briefly into focus. Grigor! Schlegel wondered what on earth the Jewish hearse driver was doing playing cards in that crowded and deafening, smoke-filled room. A look passed, perhaps one of sardonic amusement on the other man's part, except Schlegel was too drunk to tell.

When he looked again the man was gone. Schlegel shook his head and wrote it off to drunken hallucination. The room was full of dark, gaunt men as it was.

Gersten had a driver waiting. Schlegel collapsed in the back failing to make sense of what he had translated. Gersten was still high, going on to the driver about what a great time had been had by all.

They dropped Schlegel off outside his house because Gersten wanted to go around the corner to Grosse Hamburger Strasse.

Sybil was asleep and gasped when she woke to find Gersten sitting on the end of her bed. She presumed he had come to extract his price.

Seeing her fright he said she was quite safe.

'Look, I didn't shut the door and the light in the corridor is still on.'

He told her about playing music with a band of Russians, 'As unbelievable as that sounds.'

He said what a strange and sentimental people they were, so long as you didn't cross them.

'I wanted to see how you were settling in. I can't sleep. I sometimes stay downstairs. Don't worry, I won't make a habit of this.'

Sybil prayed for him to go away. She supposed such men helped themselves as and when. But he made no move other than to say to give him her arm.

'Not your hand. Pull up your sleeve.'

He cut her across the inside of the arm, just a shallow cut, whether with a scalpel or a knife she was too astonished to tell. It didn't hurt as such. The action struck her as more mundane than cruel, although she was reminded of her previous observation.

He bandaged the cut using a clean handkerchief, pulling it tight and making a knot, reciting, 'Left over right, right over left.'

He went to the door.

'There, you carry my mark. Happy hunting. Take tomorrow to acquaint yourself with your new role. Think of strategies. We will meet again on Monday and begin in earnest. In the meantime, enjoy your day off.'

# 40

The back exit of the holding centre took Sybil out into Sophienstrasse. She was still in a state of disbelief at the events of the last thirty-six hours.

She had walked in the same way on first being taken there, through a garden gate next door to the Evangelical church. The gate was locked. The guard told her she would be given her own key, which she used to let herself out into the street that Sunday morning. She supposed it was like checking in and out of a hotel, not that she ever had, all very civilised and polite. On arrival her papers had been checked by a concierge, who showed her the register which needed signing every time she left and returned. The place was in noted contrast to the block where she had lived with her mother: clean-smelling, uncrowded, silent and still. The privilege of space, she thought.

Her single room was basically furnished but clean, with proper sheets. The first-floor common room was where meals were taken. Her companions were nine young men and three women. Everyone tried very hard to behave as though their unique situation was ordinary, but the atmosphere was brittle and Sybil supposed this was how a laboratory rat must feel: cared for, caged and inspected. People were friendly and polite in a robotic way. They said little, flicking through magazines and playing table tennis. Some were still out working. The name Stella came up and Sybil wondered if it was the dangerously beautiful Stella from fashion school.

As Sybil walked out that crisp dawn, taking her first uncertain steps down the empty street, the same question drummed in her head: how realistic was the task she had been set of trying to lure this killer? Not at all. It would be only a matter of days before Gersten made her hunt down other fugitives like the rest of them.

At the same time she felt giddy at the prospect of seeing Lore.

As she walked on, gaining confidence, seeing everything with fresh eyes, a part of her she didn't much like told her the whole thing could be seen as an unexpected relief in a horrible way. The pressure of survival had been removed. She could move freely. She could still see Lore, if they were careful. She didn't have to fear patrols.

They were bound to pack her off in the end along with the rest, she was under no illusion about that. But in the meantime, because of her specific task, the question of betrayal was neither here nor there.

She had wanted to ask whether any of the catchers didn't come back at night, whether they jumped off bridges or drowned themselves in lakes or just started running and didn't stop until they died from exhaustion. But she could answer the question herself. Only those with a taste for compromise had been chosen.

Gersten had said to her, not unkindly, 'It's you and me now.'

After Torstrasse, Invalidenstrasse and Alt Moabit, over the river and down Franklinstrasse and across the canal and down to Hardenbergstrasse, past old haunts from student days; some of the cafés gone, some still there. She thought of

Kranzler's white chairs and summer drinks. In the window of a closed restaurant she read an ominous sign: 'I charged extortionate prices which is why I am in a concentration camp now.'

The sight of her reflection in shop windows made her wish she were someone else. She had never done that before, not even at her lowest. Turn right down the Ku'damm and she could be with Lore in twenty minutes. Instead she turned left, back through the Tiergarten. The bare branches of the few trees left reminded her of lung diagrams in biology classes. She tried to imagine her breathing stopped. Seeing how most things broke down, it seemed a miracle the heart lasted as long as it did.

Would she remain Sybil Todermann until the moment of extinction, or become lost in the larger universal pain?

Men in wheelchairs were being pushed with a mournful air. No one looked happy. There were fewer dogs and kids. She talked briefly with one dog owner, an old woman standing idle while the dog rooted around pointlessly. It was the first time she had talked to anyone in her new role.

She rode trams, standing on the cold, open platform, watching the receding street. She took buses. She got on trains at random, making an effort to run up the stairs, despite her aching legs. She stared blatantly, hoping to be denounced, so she could show her new card, with a frozen smile. Before she had always felt horribly conspicuous. Protected now, she may as well have been invisible.

Somewhere along the way she became aware of the tall young man behind her. Was she being followed? She saw him again at Bahnhof Zoo in the arcade, a space mainly given over to limbless veterans, who weren't supposed to beg but no one stopped them. A patrol passed and Sybil instinctively held her breath before remembering the card in her pocket. Outside she did a swift U-turn, as if she had forgotten something, and nearly bumped into him. His hat hid most of the white hair.

Her first reaction was anger that Gersten thought she could not be trusted. She realised she had seen the young man before, standing in the crowd in Rosenstrasse, as it was getting dark, before her arrest.

He knew he had been spotted but continued to tail her, looking sheepish. She was reminded of times when men had followed her in the street, plucking up the courage to approach.

They were spared the embarrassment of standing next to each other at tram stops because the streets had become crowded with workers returning from night shifts. At one point Sybil thought she had lost him when he failed to get on because of the squash. She loitered in Nollendorfplatz to see if he turned up. Sure enough, he stepped down from the next tram as the clock struck. Sybil wondered how she would get through the rest of the day.

At the Bollenmüller she was served by the same waitress with greasy hair and had to send back her omelette because the white was uncooked. Like a thrifty little hausfrau she paid out of her per diem, collected and signed for that morning in the cubbyhole by the back door where she checked in and out.

Sybil entertained the ridiculous notion of summoning the young man loitering outside and offering him a cup of tea and a truce for the day, so they would spend the afternoon as if life were ordinary, before formally shaking hands and departing.

At Brunnenstrasse she got on a train and got off as the doors closed, crossed the platform and jumped on one as it left in the opposite direction. She saw the man stranded on the platform. Feeling a rush of excitement, she resisted the temptation to wave.

After one stop she turned round and returned to Brunnenstrasse and walked to the Jewish hospital, where she found Franz in the day room. She knew he hung out there when off duty because he didn't like where he lived. He had told her pointedly it was usually possible to find a bed with one of the nurses, and the kitchen was generous with its handouts.

He gave her a crooked smile.

She had come to see if he was safe after not turning up the other day. She could tell he was hoping she had really come back because she wanted to resume their relationship.

She said nothing of Gersten, made out she was still underground and was desperate for papers. It was impossible for her to stay where she was.

Playing along, he said he would see what he could do.

'Can you protect me? I can't afford to wait.' Suppressing a spasm of revulsion, she forced herself to put her hand on his arm and say, 'Whatever it takes. I see that now.'

Part of her was thinking if Gersten ever made her a catcher she would settle the score by turning in Franz. Another part of her said Franz was her likeliest lead to the man she was looking for. She was sure he knew much more than he let on.

She had no clues to the identity of her quarry or his whereabouts. He could be underground or he could be sitting in the next room at the hospital. He seemed to have a freedom of movement. Gersten said he liked dancing and had been to the place on Auguststrasse. What was she supposed to do? Get a job as a waitress? Enrol for dancing lessons? On the other hand, it was a shrinking world. He liked girls. He liked dancing. The chances were he was the same age as her or not much older. Perhaps she had known him through college, as part of that large, party crowd. They'd stuck together. She had the strongest image of sitting with Franz in a café and the same way they had of warming their hands on their tea mugs. It even crossed her mind the person she had been sent to find was in fact Franz.

After the hospital she didn't spot the young man and took the train back to Charlottenburg and went to the Ufa-Palast in Hardenbergstrasse, not bothering to check what she was going to see.

Schlegel watched her go into the crowded cinema for the matinee of the big new colour film that had opened that week, which Otto Keleman had missed the press show for because they were getting drunk. Schlegel thought about going in but fantasy was not to his taste. He asked the cashier when the programme finished. It sounded improbably long, with well over two hours still to go. Maybe he would come back and see what Sybil did after the film. His feet ached. With nothing better to do, he went to a café over the road and sat reading a newspaper and watching the sparse Sunday traffic.

It had been easy enough to track Sybil's whereabouts as it was known that Gersten's catchers all lodged in the same building, around the corner from where Schlegel lived. That was Morgen's idea.

He had cursed himself for losing her in Brunnenstrasse, hung around on the platform not knowing what to do, then spotted her ten minutes later when she came back and didn't see him. After that he had hung back and got better. Neither of them was a professional. She didn't look around any more, thinking she had lost him. After waiting at the hospital, he followed her back, taking the precaution of not getting in the same carriage.

He was starting to doze when he saw Sybil walk briskly out of the cinema with a young woman. He hurriedly paid and followed. The light was going. They seemed tense. Schlegel didn't know the companion. He could just make them out as they walked arm-in-arm, their strides matching, heads close.

They kissed when they thought no one was looking. From the way Sybil cupped the back of her companion's head it had to be proper open-mouthed kissing. They acted more like a real couple than many ordinary ones.

The cinema must have been a fallback arrangement in case they became separated, Schlegel told himself, staring, not wishing to but incapable of averting his eyes. When they went into one of the few cafés still open he took up a position in a doorway across the road and watched them holding hands in a way that didn't draw attention. When the companion seemed to look straight at him he stood very still and thought about the distance between them, the traffic and the fading light.

They weren't hard to keep up with as he followed them to the Ku'damm and down a long, straight street to the left with no turnings, past a big church, and down to Hochmeisterplatz where they entered a building that Schlegel recognised as the block where Francis Alwynd lived, and realised they must be his stowaways.

'This is my friend August. He's a policeman,' said Alwynd with typical tactlessness.

Schlegel thought the two women put on a brave show, considering.

They made excruciatingly awkward conversation while Alwynd fiddled in the kitchen making tea. As was the way now, neither woman was introduced nor volunteered her name. Schlegel asked what they did. Sybil's companion said she was a translator and photographer. Sybil said she was a clothes designer.

Schlegel thought carefully before he said, 'I know, I have seen some.'

When Sybil paled visibly he wanted to say he was trying to

show he was not hostile and she was wrong to assume otherwise.

The two women prattled on about the film they had just seen, talking to each other rather than him. What a spectacle! Such fantastic colour!

Schlegel realised she must think he had been sent by Gersten.

Sybil said, 'We haven't seen you here before.'

'In fact I was last week. We had hoped you might join us.'

'Well, here we are,' said the companion facetiously.

Alwynd walked into the room with a tray, saying, 'Tea and sudden death.'

He turned to Sybil and asked in his appalling German if she would be mother.

Alwynd sat back, beamed and said, '*Mea culpa*,' looking not in the slightest remorseful.

Schlegel suspected Alwynd enjoyed making drama from other people's lives.

Alwynd finally said, 'Francis may have dropped a bit of a clanger. I was in my cups the other night and told August I might be harbouring a couple of runaways.'

Sybil didn't understand as they were speaking English. Her companion looked shocked. Schlegel told Sybil what Alwynd had said and she gave a small scream and ran from the room, followed by the other woman.

'It makes no difference to me,' said Alwynd airily. 'They should know that, but at the same time it's not safe here in the long run because the Foreign Office is always sticking its nose in my affairs.'

He stood up. 'Better go and make my peace.'

He strolled off towards the back of the apartment, apparently unconcerned about the damage he could cause, calling over his shoulder, 'I presume you aren't here to arrest them.'

Schlegel felt a fool for compromising everyone. Alwynd

always pleaded exemption through ignorance. Schlegel could see him announcing in his faux naive way he thought everything was above board because he had a friend who was a policeman.

They trooped back in. Sybil looked miserable. Her companion gave Schlegel looks of varying hostility. Schlegel steepled his fingers and tried to appear lost in significant thought. Morgen would know how to handle the situation.

Schlegel asked to speak to Sybil in private. Alwynd was immediately interested. For her the whole thing must be like being stuck in some ghastly play. Schlegel knew she was working for the Gestapo, but Alwynd didn't. It was possible she hadn't got around to telling her companion. And she could of course report Alwynd, if she believed it was to her advantage.

Sybil blew her nose and stood up. Schlegel excused himself awkwardly.

They stood in the corridor. She did not wish to extend the courtesy of taking him into a room. He saw quite another side of her. Her eyes were hard with anger. At the same time she was shivering.

His rehearsed little speech vanished. When he tried to reach out to reassure she flinched. He let his hand drop.

Making an effort to overcome his hopelessness, he said, 'I know Gersten is using you. I think you and I are looking for the same man. He is known as Grigor. His real name is Yakov Zorin.'

Seeing her reaction, he asked if she knew him. She said no but he could tell she was lying. Now was not the moment to pursue the point. First he had to try to win her trust.

'I may be able to try to help you.'

'May be able?'

'Can try to help you.'

'You have to help my friend too,' she said quickly.

'Of course,' he said, knowing it was a promise he couldn't keep. 'What's her name?'

Seeing her hesitate, he said it could wait.

'Lore,' she said.

He asked hers although he knew it.

'Sybil,' she said.

Was he using her as a way of getting to Grigor or did he really want to help? He was still confused by the sight of them kissing.

Alwynd, who enjoyed being crass, said, 'Ah, the lovebirds are back. Secret or share?'

'Oh, share,' said Sybil. 'Our friend here thinks he might be able to introduce me to clients who need tailoring done, which is very generous.'

Schlegel observed Lore. She must have worked out something was going on, if Sybil had failed to come home for the last two nights. She made a point of announcing she was going to rest.

Sybil left too without saying anything.

'A bit sticky that,' said Alwynd. 'Of course the one is a hardened lesbian. It's a pity about the other because I suspect her tastes are broader, but she seems quite besotted for the moment. How's your sex life?'

'Not as busy as yours I would imagine.'

'Seek the wildness, dear boy! The men are all gone. Time to play.' He giggled and proceeded to regale him with the ins and outs of his affairs for the next half-hour before Schlegel made his excuses and left, more confused than ever.

# 41

Nebe arrived five minutes early for Monday lunch at Dr Goebbels' official residence in Hermann Goering Strasse, now stripped of much of its ornament to reflect the gravity of the situation. This was not easy as the size of the place indicated nothing but self-aggrandisement. Oriental rugs and light bulbs had been removed from corridors. Rooms were closed off to create the appropriate sense of economy. The tightened belt was Goebbels' latest catchphrase. A modest lunch would be served. No alcohol to be offered beforehand.

It had occurred to Nebe that Goebbels was strangely powerless, although branding himself the total war man, and going to enormous lengths to get the message across to the public, whose saviour he believed he would be in the end. Nebe suspected it was smoke and mirrors. Dr Goebbels was in the business of massaging public opinion yet there was nothing he could do, even with a muzzled press, to make himself more popular, however charming his personal company.

Known as Popeye because of his taste for spinach, he was also referred to as the Lenten Dr Goebbels. Abstemiousness disguised many indulgences. A fortune was spent on clothes, the same suit never worn twice running, and a supply of hand-made shirts that kept an exclusive outfitter in business for a year. Nebe knew because he used the same tailor and often had to wait because a rush job was on for the minister.

Goebbels made a point of arriving five minutes late. The journey from his office took two, for which he travelled with an armed guard in a chauffeur-driven armour-plated Mercedes.

He swept in alone, the retinue dismissed. Servants had been trained not to attend to his homecoming. He hung up his coat and hat in the boot room and put the umbrella in its rack. Only when he emerged again and placed his briefcase on the hall table did Nebe deem it safe to approach.

Goebbels clapped his hands and said, 'Excellent, Nebe, excellent! What would I do without you?'

Any mention of indispensability needed to be regarded with the greatest heed, Nebe knew, from the fate of others.

Just the two of them sat for lunch. Wine was offered in the expectation of it being refused. Nebe reported on Stoffel's success. Goebbels pulled a long face and said better than a Jewish maniac but it rather endorsed the government attitude towards mental sickness.

'I feel an editorial coming on. Given the greater conflict, we don't bother with domestic crime, but in this case I might make an exception and put one of our top reporters on it.'

He made a note on the pad he kept constantly by his side.

Nebe was hopeful that the rest of the lunch would pass without incident. A solo meal with Goebbels was never a comfortable experience. The man picked at his food and was impatient with the ritual of dining. Conversation proceeded along set lines. First there was the racy political gossip.

'We're kissing on the lips now, Speer and I. No tongues yet but that will come.'

Goebbels regaled Nebe with such indiscreet details of his sex life that Nebe wondered if the recital wasn't relished more than the possession. 'A magnificent flaming red bush.' 'Her orgasm left her squeaking in the most disconcerting manner.'

There was something intrinsically grubby about the man, however discreetly perfumed, and his tedious one-upmanship.

There was his other great love, cinema. He confessed his frustration that films could not be as broad in their taste as he would like. For that reason he closely monitored the latest product from Hollywood and boasted his private screenings were the hottest tickets in town. He was especially keen to see RKO's forthcoming *I Walked with a Zombie*, directed by Jacques Tourneur and written by Curt Siodmak, a defector whose talents he could have put to better use. Goebbels was a huge fan of Tourneur's previous film, *Cat People*, flown in by diplomatic bag from the Republic of Ireland.

'Too risqué to screen for all but the most sophisticated, with Simone Simon, Jewish alas, descended from people who turn into cats when sexually aroused. Deliciously corrupt. Exactly the kind of decadent nonsense our people must be protected from.'

Goebbels made a throaty purring noise, followed by his blankest expression. 'And what of these flayed bodies?'

Nebe badly wanted to relieve himself, faced with what was known as the Goebbels trapdoor moment.

He was let off. Goebbels wagged his finger reprovingly. 'You are lucky I am in a good mood. The Gestapo has just informed me they were the work of a Bolshevik spy since arrested. It was to be the start of a terror campaign to destabilise the civilian population. An exercise in black propaganda.'

He appeared taken with the idea.

That appeared to be the end of lunch yet Goebbels did not finish it by standing first, as protocol demanded. Instead he sat there, making Nebe more nervous.

'We are moving into difficult times,' he eventually said. 'We face our sternest test.'

Toughness, compassion and resolve were the qualities that would see them through. He harangued Nebe for five minutes before getting to the point. Corruption was no longer an option.

'Those previously lining their pockets must be brought to book.'

Nebe wondered if it was some kind of personal message.

'And we are talking about corruption top to bottom. The golden pheasants. The fat cats. The pigs with their snouts in the trough. Our needs require radical reforms. A clean sweep. Showing the people we care. Are you with me on this?'

Nebe could say nothing except of course.

He was sufficiently practised at reading between the lines to understand any clearout would be selective according to Goebbels' requirements.

'We need our own secret agent. Someone who can go hither and thither, like the wind, who appears to operate on his own initiative, acting on the letter of the law, which may be our greatest ally, who of course has no orders, so nothing can be attributed.'

How uncanny, Nebe thought. It was as though his own premonition had anticipated Goebbels' plan. He made a point of pausing for thought before announcing he might have just the man.

'A Scarlet Pimpernel,' purred Goebbels, clapping his hands.

# 42

At the Kripo the day was spent preparing for the big party, which was a combination of a pre-retirement bash for Stoffel and to celebrate his nailing what was being called the biggest murder case in years.

Schlegel and Morgen were required to witness Lampe's signed confession to three murders and the theft at the printers. This was recited by a junior officer as Lampe was barely literate.

He read: '*I, Axel Lampe, for the purposes of this confession admit as a born criminal to the strangulation of Frieda Rosner (29/1/43), Bruno Abbas (28/2/43) and an unidentified woman (1/3/43). The widow Rosner was killed for sexual satisfaction. The Jewish gangster Abbas was an acquaintance. We had previously robbed the Guenstiger printing press (23/10/42) where Abbas knew of a supply of forged money. On 28/2/43 we spent the day drunk together, with a woman (name unknown). A quarrel between Abbas and the woman occurred over the cost of her. As a result of this I killed Abbas in a rage because I had not known he was a Jew. I cut off his penis because he was circumcised. I carried on drinking until the next day when I argued with a woman (name unknown) about the cost of her. We agreed a price, then she resisted intercourse. I took her and left about her person the sum of money agreed. I have no recollection of strangulation but accept it as a repeat of previous behaviour. She told me she was Jewish which may have had something to do with it.*'

Lampe had to mark his confession with the combination of a cross and a thumbprint. Schlegel was both impressed and shocked by how it had been turned into such a plausible and more or less coherent document, with most loose ends tied up. How effectively Lampe had become Stoffel's creature. It had required only a couple of interviews between broaching any given subject and a full confession. Any evidence missing or unclear, Stoffel made up for the sake of his final report, as was standard. One story going the rounds was that a team of screenwriters from Babelsberg studios had been brought in to work round the clock, polishing up the confessions.

That afternoon Nebe summoned everyone to an impromptu meeting to announce the closure of the flayed-body murders. He said, 'Grudging respect where respect is due to our colleagues in the Gestapo. I have a statement here made by a Bolshevik agent found masquerading as a Ukrainian interpreter.'

He read out: '*I, Aleksander Lazarenko, confess to the killing of two unidentified Jews (female) on 26/2/43 and on the night of 1/3/43 towards establishing a black propaganda campaign on behalf of my Soviet masters whose agent I am. The strategy behind these acts, of which there were intended to be many, was to destabilise and spread fear among the local population that a deranged Judeo-Bolshevik slayer was operating. The first body was dismembered in the pig house near Landsberger Allee, Berlin, and to this end a Jewish site was erected. The second was killed in a location near Treptower Park, Berlin, where the remains were left. In this work I was assisted by three Russian forced workers (since deceased) and a Russian Jew, name unknown. I was elected for this task because of experience in eliminating local insurrection in the Ukraine town of Lemberg (25/6/41), involving bestial mutilation and dismemberment (20,000 dead). This was possible because of my previous career as a butcher. On occasion, human remains were sold at market for consumption. I was also responsible for similar crimes committed in the cellars of the law courts at Tarnopol where 2,000 prisoners of the Alpine chasseurs, the*

*Luftwaffe, Ukrainians and ethnic Germans had their ears, noses, tongues and genitals removed.'*

Morgen rocked on his heels. Schlegel thought how hard it was to argue with these official truths. In the end both versions were as convincing as the real thing – whatever that was – in fact more so because they supplanted and erased it.

Nebe underscored the point, saying, 'My official congratulations.'

Morgen said nothing afterwards upstairs in the office. Schlegel wanted to talk, complain, try to work out where it left them, but Morgen sat mute until Schlegel's questions drove him out of the room. He paused only to say, 'I told you before, the lie is the cornerstone of the edifice. Our job if we are to do it properly is to learn to lie better.'

Morgen arrived at the party drunk. He told Stoffel, who had been drinking since Lampe's confession, that the business made a mockery of the law and was a travesty of justice.

Stoffel said, 'A confession is a confession. You heard him.'

The party turned into a circus when Lampe was brought up from the cells, given a drink, and paraded around. A man to whom no one had ever paid the slightest attention now found himself the centre of enormous interest. Lampe rewarded Schlegel with a sly look that said he was nobody's fool. He told him he and Stoffel were scheduled to go on a road tour to talk to a lot of people and be photographed. He made it sound like a public event.

He grinned at Schlegel and said, 'You can't hang me now.'

Lampe had been given a mug of beer, which he drank with both hands, being handcuffed.

Schlegel saw how all Lampe had to do to continue this wonderful situation was to keep confessing.

He questioned the wisdom of parading Lampe like a side-show freak. Whether Lampe read his thoughts, he took exception and tried to swing his empty beer glass at Schlegel's head, which led to a scuffle and Lampe bellowing for all he was worth before being dragged off.

The incident galvanised the party rather than killing it dead. Suddenly everyone was roaring drunk. The women were frisky. One went down like she had been poleaxed and lay on the floor with her eyes fluttering. A member of the homicide crew threw himself on top of her in a lewd pantomime of fucking while a crowd stood around and jeered.

Nebe made a speech to applause and ironic cheers when Stoffel stepped forward, hands clasped above his head like a boxing champ.

Gersten put in an appearance. He was wearing Lazarenko's whipcord coat with the fur collar. Morgen fingered it and said nothing. Gersten had brought his accordion. The reason became apparent when four men came in carrying a large crate which they placed on a table and Gersten played a riff to quieten the crowd and announced he had a gift for his esteemed colleagues.

A stripper stepped out of the crate to whistles and cheers and went into her routine. She looked like she hadn't done the act in a long time. Gersten's accompaniment could hardly be heard for the din. Even Nebe was wolf-whistling. The show ended with her rotating tassels attached to her nipples. Gersten apologised afterwards for her being a bit of a dog but it was the thought that counted. Schlegel wondered where the woman would be spending the night. Gersten said she would be downstairs; she was a social undesirable that had been lent by one of the camps and was being sent back in the morning.

The party spread and drifted as more and more people turned up, few that Schlegel recognised, gatecrashers from other precincts. Nobody seemed to mind as a lot of available women came.

Schlegel found Morgen in a side room listening to a vibrantly drunk Stoffel discourse with several shrinks and scientific experts who were due to pick Lampe's brains. Stoffel emphasised the killer's lack of signature, holding forth on how this apparent simpleton might – because of a different wiring of the brain – represent a jump in the psychopathy of murder. All cases showed different facts, different ways of killing and different motives. At none of the murder scenes did the police manage to find useful fingerprints. This was turned by Stoffel into evidence of new, advanced ways of killing, where the killer in effect suppressed the memory of all previous crimes, approaching each new murder as a *tabula rasa*.

Morgen said Stoffel would soon be on the lecture circuit and no doubt the recipient of a lucrative consultancy from the Ahnenerbe, an organisation ostensibly dedicated to ancestral heritage, with all sorts of strange offshoots.

'The size and weight of Lampe's brain will become the subject of great debate, after which his days will almost certainly be numbered.'

People reached the stage of passing out. Schlegel decided he was drinking to get smashed then realised the decision had been made long ago. There was talk of moving on somewhere else. The evening reached a stage of enjoyable incoherence. Morgen didn't say much to Schlegel and spent time chatting up a woman, which somehow seemed wrong, however much she appeared to enjoy herself, laughing at everything said.

Nebe was standing around with his jacket undone when Schlegel saw Morgen make a beeline for him. Schlegel joined them, trying to look casual. Morgen was offering insincere congratulations on Stoffel's triumph. Nebe, a man without humour, took him at his word.

They had been very lucky, he said.

'What will happen when there is another killing in the same vein, as there is bound to be?'

Nebe gave him a blank look and a fast reply.

'Then it will be your job to make sure no one hears about it.'

'So we will be in the business of cover-up?' enquired Morgen innocently.

Nebe took a step towards Morgen and leaned in. 'There will be no rumour machine. No investigation. It will be your job to make sure it never happened.'

He stepped back, genial again. Schlegel had thought Nebe was joking at first. The three of them were so drunk it hardly mattered. They would all have difficulty remembering.

Nebe made a show of coming clean. 'I'll let you in. I was under tremendous pressure from Heine himself.'

Himmler was always referred to as Heine. He never took much interest in them despite being their overall boss.

'Stoffel's suspect was a gift from heaven because we are able to make a present of him to Heine. As Lampe is an idiot he will be sent to a special SS clinic for further research into the mind of a killer. Heine is delighted, absolutely crowing to have such a prime specimen when so few are left.'

Nebe beamed. Someone found a hunting horn and blew it. A great cheer went up from the other side of the room as a group threw Stoffel in the air and caught him in a blanket.

Morgen drained his glass and handed it to Nebe as though he were a waiter. He took it in good grace, and announced lightly, 'Anything goes wrong, I will say it was your idea to offload everything on Lampe.'

Morgen said that went without saying.

For some reason they were all in a bus. The party was still on, with a singsong at the back, and Stoffel driving, hands clamped to the wheel, drunk and incapable of seeing where he was going.

When he swerved to avoid something he threw half of them into the aisle, to widespread screams of delight. Schlegel saw Morgen on the bus but not Gersten or Nebe. Someone shouted they were all in a handcart to hell and shrieked with laughter. Someone else was being sick in a bag. Schlegel was aware he had been smooching with the woman sitting next to him. He had no idea who she was. Where were they going, he asked. Another party, she said. She thrust her arm at him and said to pinch her. Schlegel didn't want to. They nearly had an argument and in the end he did, so hard she cried out and he wondered what her orgasms sounded like. Only when she explained she had wanted to be sure she wasn't dreaming did he understand, just as Stoffel brought the bus to a shuddering halt and shouted, 'Everyone out!'

Schlegel stood staring in disbelief and asked Morgen what they were doing back at the slaughterhouse.

Morgen shrugged, amused, and said it seemed a good idea at the time. Schlegel thought he had better laugh. He asked Morgen if he could hear a tuba or whether it was his imagination.

'No,' said Morgen. 'Tuba, tambourine and a drum.'

'What on earth is that about?'

They followed the sound until they found the building. Schlegel heard cheering and whooping.

The woman from the bus was dragging on his arm, and they were bumping around like a couple of dodgem cars. She got into the spirit of it, deliberately crashing them into things. The tuba did its oom-pah-pah. The tambourine was being bashed in a frenzy and the drum being thrashed. The cheering went whoo! whoo! whoooah!

A crowd of perhaps thirty stood in the middle of the room. 'Not more fucking boxing!' Schlegel shouted to the woman. 'Hit him! Hit him!' she screamed.

They were chucking something in the air. Schlegel got it muddled with Stoffel back at the party, and decided everything that had happened since was all in his mind. He saw a child being thrown in the air, except it was too big, then a pig, except it was dressed. It seemed the wrong shape for an adult.

He asked the woman to describe what she saw. Her words flew past at great speed so he missed most of them. He made out her saying Hitler Youth and bacchanalia, which took her several goes to get right.

Then he reached a state of temporary lucidity as he watched boys staggering around weirdly dressed. Some wore garlands in their hair. Other were dressed as women. The boy boxer who had won his fight was prancing around with lipstick smeared over his face.

Schlegel saw Morgen tip his hat back, which struck him as the most sensible gesture he'd seen in ages.

He told the woman his life made no sense and she said, 'I know what you mean.'

They should have been fucking, except the moment had passed and they knew it.

The mood remained one of raucous celebration, however sinister the intended outcome.

The woman's mouth opened in an exaggerated 'oh' as she pointed to a hangman's gibbet and dangling noose at the far end of the room. What the boys were throwing in the air was indeed a pig, dressed in human clothes, a man's shirt and trousers with the legs rolled and a woman's bonnet tied to her head.

They carried the pig to the gibbet, still tossing her, whooping all the while as she screamed and the music played on. When they reached the gibbet, the pig was wrestled onto a stool and the rope placed around her neck. The crowd started grunting and oinking and clapping in time to the music, which got faster. It took half a dozen to hold the animal down. Most of the boys were helpless with laughter at the pig wriggling and they carried on laughing after Morgen had fired his pistol in the air, thinking it part of the game.

Morgen fired again and they fell silent. The tracksuited man with the tough face emerged out of the crowd and asked Morgen, 'What makes you think you can walk in here?'

Someone shouted they had been invited.

Morgen asked what was going on.

The tracksuited man played to the crowd, putting his hands on his hips. 'We're hanging a pig.'

A few boys tittered behind their hands. The pig had been let go and was wandering around in a daze, her bonnet crooked and one trouser leg unravelled, which made it hard to walk.

The tracksuited man went on. 'It's what happens to pigs that eat their young. It's what happens to cannibal pigs. It's a time-honoured tradition. So I would ask you to leave so we can proceed.'

'We were invited,' the same voice as before shouted.

The tuba and tambourine had stopped with the gunshots, but the boy on the drum continued a muffled beat. The centrifugal force of the revel had dissipated, leaving everything tattered and dishevelled. The pig stood splay-footed, alone and docile in the middle of the room. The bonnet had slipped under her chin. The trouser legs had unravelled and were spattered with excrement.

Morgen walked out. Schlegel experienced a moment of paralysis that prevented him leaving too.

Stoffel stepped forward and watched Morgen go. He looked like he was swimming in booze. His clothes were awry and he had managed to lose a shoe. No one seemed to know what to do. Stoffel took a while getting his bearings then lumbered towards the pig. Everything appeared to go into slow motion as Stoffel took out a long-barrelled pistol, which snagged in his shoulder holster. Schlegel recognised Metzler's old Mauser. The pig looked at them with trusting eyes as Stoffel stepped forward and fired a bullet behind her ear. The animal convulsed once, made a sound like she was sneezing, rolled over and died without another sound. There was almost no blood.

The woman he had smooched drove them back. It turned out she was in the transport corps. Schlegel dozed in a state of dismay. Stoffel sat behind him and kept punching him on the shoulder. They were going to kill the pig anyway, he said, and not in a nice way.

Back at the Kripo the party was still going on and looked like it would never end. Two o'clock passed. 'I am still able to stagger home. What about you?' Schlegel asked another woman he didn't know. At three they were served sausages. There was no sign of Morgen. The rest of the room was a heaving sea of strange faces. Stoffel reached the sentimental stage, fell on Schlegel and called him his little white-haired freak. Schlegel woke up in the cells with no recollection of how he had got there, with vague memories or dreams of men lining up in the night to take turns with the stripper.

# PART TWO

# 43

Morgen had been gone several days; no sign of him in the office. Schlegel had carried on drinking after the party. They all had. He took to wandering around at night, seeking out dives and the cheapest, roughest bars, looking for what he could not tell. Was it Grigor, or Morgen, or Sybil and her lover he expected to run into, or a combination of all of them? He came to see this nocturnal existence as a submerged world that represented the last traces of everything they wanted rid of. It was thrillingly different, the cheap music with its sentiment, the black marketeers, the deserters and battle-hardened soldiers on leave looking to pick a fight, the racketeers, pimps and their blowsy tarts, all on a private adventure very different from the one prescribed. Some of the habitués of this nether-world looked so rough they could have been clinging to the last of the wreckage, but there were snappy dressers too, well-laundered, middle-aged men in the centre of groups of thuggish youths and insecure young women. Sometimes older, respectable females, who had no place in such dives, came in to sell themselves, a sign of how desperate everything was becoming. Disability was a common sight: a leg stump, a missing arm or hand, an unseeing eye. Schlegel came to recognise the strategic wounds: the limping man who'd shot himself in the foot; the missing fingers that prevented military service. All the men shared the same crafty look of instant calculation.

Twice he heard people say they smelled copper. Often he was asked what he was doing coming to such places, and he lied, saying his wife had been killed in the air raid, which was enough to elicit grunts of sympathy. The act seemed not much different from his usual pretending. When two toughs in a bar wanted to beat him up he surprised everyone by laughing and they left him alone.

He never got really drunk, nor was he ever entirely sober. Loose was the word he used to describe himself; alert but with a pleasant blur around the edges. Sitting in his office, alone and undisturbed, he wondered about the strangely vanished Morgen, and his mysterious disappearance.

He kept returning to how the gun that had shot the pig also put the bullet in Metzler's brain and blown out the eye of the warden, who had made Sybil masturbate him, while she was secretly in love with another woman, who knew Francis Alwynd, who knew his mother and maybe, he decided, had even been her lover. Schlegel felt like his face was pressed against a glass and he was watching all these connections play out on the other side.

Seen one way, the links seemed as improbable as those made up by Stoffel and Lampe, whose version nevertheless acquired a veracity of its own. Sometimes he wondered if he was in the process of reinventing himself in the way Lampe had twisted the facts to suit himself.

He took to staying out all night. One morning, staggering home at first light, he saw written on a wall: *What is authority?* Such graffiti was almost unheard of and rare enough to merit a second visit. He got lost trying to find it again and could not decide whether it was still there and he had misremembered its location; if it had been erased; or if it had been scrawled only in his imagination.

He was stopped by patrols who thought he was a deserter or

a Jew. He found it contemptible the way they were conditioned to look at him like dog shit on the heel of someone's shoe then grew craven when he showed his badge.

Maybe it would be more interesting to leave the badge at home.

# 44

Because of his role in *Emil and the Detectives*, Gersten was a great one for using kids. It was like the murder story where no one spotted the postman. Even when people noticed kids they didn't consider them. The gang he used was paid to skip school; tiny amounts but better than sitting in lessons. They had been issued with laminated cards, which made them feel important.

He called their leader Emil, although his real name was Anton. Emil checked in at the end of each day for what Gersten called a debriefing, which made the kids' days sound more purposeful.

The picture he was putting together of Sybil was not good. She was behaving like a woman on an unhappy holiday, using her privileges, hanging out in cafés hoping for a slice of luck, that she would spot someone or have a brainwave, and otherwise was bunking off with her girlfriend.

Gersten had seen it before. The absence of any real strategy, like a patient with a terminal illness granted an unexpected reprieve. It made him appreciate the Stella Kübler woman all the more. She was his best agent. He could only admire the icy beauty, the nerveless calculation, the appetite and energy for the hunt. He had hoped with Sybil he might have another Kübler. He would dearly like to question Kübler in one of his private sessions, but kept reminding himself she was too good to waste. If the Sybil woman failed and survived to tell the tale he would treat himself to her.

She had gone and visited her mother and stayed half an hour. The mother was posing as a housekeeper for one of the more spectacularly corrupt of the golden pheasants, a former minister, washed up but not without influence, given that he was one of the old guard, and a household name in his time. They were all mad for star gazers and card readers now. They always had been, but not so desperately. Given a leadership based on oracle and interpretation, divination became the obvious way for the second tier to try to get a march on rivals, and so on down to the humble newspaper horoscope.

Sybil had also met with Schlegel, or at least Gersten presumed. There could be only so many white-haired young men in town.

Third, she had visited Schmidt's photography shop, which was interesting, if only because Gersten had been keeping an eye on the man's pornographic activities.

Time to scare the wits out of her.

He had her picked up and taken to the huge, cavernous morgue that lay below ground in the centre of the city. The Gestapo had its own section. Often those that had died under interrogation were withheld from cremation to be displayed to other prisoners as examples of what they would next look like unless they co-operated.

The morgue was damp, more mildewed Gothic crypt than the usual antiseptic, modern space, but it created the right atmosphere of gloom and horror. If the space was medieval, the equipment was spot-on: stainless-steel drawers on smooth-gliding rollers to hold the stacked bodies.

Sybil looked tiny and pale as she approached between two much taller men. Gersten waited until she was positioned before sliding open the drawer.

He saw her gasp. It was an intimate moment. She swayed from shock and Gersten thought her legs would crumple. He pictured her lying on the ground in a dead faint.

'Let's hope this is not you some day soon.'

Sybil's throat made a strange clicking noise. Gersten told one of the men to fetch a chair and a glass of water.

'This is an example of work by the man you are looking for.'

Sybil sat, eyes wide, mouth open, rigid.

'We think this may be a German woman. There is nothing left so you can tell, any more than if it were a lump of beef. But we found one pubic hair that had stuck to the flesh; very, very pale. We think he is shifting and starting to kill indiscriminately, so driven by his loathing that he wishes only to obliterate.'

He told the men to take Sybil upstairs. It was reached by a complex series of tunnels, which led directly to the Gestapo building and by themselves were enough to thoroughly unnerve.

Gersten took his time joining her in the room with the usual river view. A long barge hauling coal was making its slow way downriver, under rain-laden skies.

'Did we give you an umbrella?' he asked when he knew perfectly well he had chosen one, with a malacca cane handle.

He made a helpless gesture and said what he was telling her was in confidence. 'I thought it was over. The butchered bodies were the work of a Bolshevik agent, but we are now hearing through the grapevine more than one killer is at work.'

Gersten paused, pondering the enormity of what they faced.

'The man I need you to hunt is a confirmed murderer, with at least two scalps. Now it seems he is working for this campaign of terror, flaying victims like they were animals, then skinning them alive.'

They were dealing with a killing virus which must be stopped before it spread.

\*　　\*　　\*

Schlegel was dozing in his office when Frau Pelz rang through to say a woman was asking to speak to him and wouldn't give her name.

Schlegel thought Frau Pelz had messed up the connection because no one seemed to be on the line and he was about to hang up when a small, distant voice announced it was Sybil Todermann.

When they met in the Bollenmüller Schlegel worried he still smelled of last night's drink. He was taking Pervitin because he could get by on no sleep. He attributed the sweating and occasional dizzy spells to a chill. No one seemed to notice, the simple reason being – his newly alert state told him – the rest of the department was pilled up too.

Sybil Todermann appeared so withdrawn he insisted she took a pill. She told a rambling story about being threatened by two youths on her way back to Grosse Hamburger Strasse, who accused her of being a Gestapo spy. They were about sixteen, nervous and almost certainly Jewish. One had a hat on and the other a very low, straight hairline. She drew a line with her finger across her forehead to show him. Schlegel, paying more attention to her than to what she was saying, found the gesture touching.

The incident had left her shaken. All she wanted to do now was stay in bed. She was too depressed to go out and hid in her room.

Schlegel threw out suggestions. It could be shown that Grigor had been deported. She could offer that to Gersten.

Sybil looked doubtful. Schlegel immediately revised that to say it was almost certainly a ruse.

Sybil, not listening, said, 'Gersten showed me this . . .' She stopped, lost for words. 'You could hardly call it a body.'

'He said Grigor did that?' asked Schlegel in surprise.

'Gersten says there's more than a single killer. Grigor is just one.'

Schlegel described the man he had seen driving the hearse.

'That's Grigor.'

Seeing her apathy, he added unless she pulled herself together Gersten would lose patience.

'You are hanging by no more than a thread.'

The waiter at Clärchens was her best lead and he offered to go with her. Sybil said his presence would compromise her if she was being followed.

Schlegel suspected she would retreat back into her funk. He was no leading example. The real reason for offering to accompany her was because he could drink there and stagger upstairs afterwards.

He got her to promise she would go to Clärchens and suggested they meet again the same time tomorrow.

Sybil went back to Grosse Hamburger Strasse to tidy herself before going out but lay down instead. She was surprised she slept at all but she had only to shut her eyes and it was like someone had switched her off, however active her unconscious brain, for she always woke exhausted. On that occasion she failed to sleep. She supposed it was the pill. It failed to make her think any more clearly and she lay unable to move.

The following morning she was pulled from her bed by two of Gersten's men and taken to Gestapo headquarters. Schlegel must be right; she had used up the man's patience. He would deport her.

She was left on her own for several hours to fight her rising panic. She knew waiting was part of the torture. Eventually she was taken back into the space with the two-way mirror.

The room was lit up and empty. Sybil didn't know what to expect. Her mother again, she supposed. She would have no choice but to do as they ordered. Her reflection off the glass showed her looking eaten up and older. Whoever she was expecting to be brought in, it wasn't Schmidt, the photographer, beaten up and very afraid.

While Schlegel waited for Sybil at the Bollenmüller two Gestapo men swept in checking papers. He stared, daring them to challenge him.

He couldn't decide about Sybil. He wanted to help but he was feeling little more than drunkenly philosophical.

He stuck his foot out as the Gestapo men passed and one had to grab the back of a chair to stop himself from falling. Schlegel held his hands up in mock surrender. The man glared and told him to watch what he was doing. Schlegel shrugged and said he was waiting for a friend. When Sybil didn't show up, Schlegel decided he wasn't surprised and put her down as unreliable.

Sybil jumped at the sight of Gersten's reflection. He was standing behind her with a manila folder.

'Quite sweet,' he said, showing the photographs of her posing in the nude in Alwynd's apartment, as well as kissing Lore.

'I am not so sure about these.'

It was the contact sheet taken by Schmidt. Sybil stared, ashamed not of their nudity but her brassy calculation.

'Like a fallen angel with a nasty look in her eye,' said Gersten. 'Such a fine line between survival and corruption, I find. It interests me. I had expected more of you, in terms of talent and honesty, not this inertia and lack of will.'

How had he found out about the photographs was all she could think to ask.

'We have been watching Schmidt for weeks. He'll be lucky to escape with his neck.'

Gersten had been surprised when he saw the stake-out photographs of Sybil going in and out.

'To be honest, I wasn't expecting that. Schmidt tells me he was quite friendly with your girlfriend when she was younger and it crossed my mind she might have sent you, rather than go herself, because she knew the shop was being watched. Not that I am trying to mark your card. You can ask her.'

He gestured with his head for Sybil to look behind her. Schmidt was gone and in his place sat the hunched and stricken figure of Lore.

Sybil was aware of her cry reflected back at her.

'She wouldn't be here if you were doing your job.'

Sybil pleaded for another chance, daring to clutch at Gersten's sleeve, begging him to release Lore. She had a good lead now.

'From that idiot with the white hair?'

'How did you know where Lore lived?'

Sybil feared she already had the answer.

'You, precious. Spot checks to see what you got up to until we could trust you. You went home once too often.'

Had Schlegel reported her?

'I must say, Francis Alwynd is an irresponsible man. He was looking for an abortionist recently. Not you, I hope.'

Gersten told Sybil he liked her. He had cut her a lot of slack as a result.

'You don't want to know about the ones I don't like. But now this – pornographic photographs, a lesbian lover. The way I look at it, we're no further forward. You don't do enough. I want your girlfriend on the case as part of the team, working as a regular catcher. Same terms apply, but she now has to work for her papers. Do your job properly and I will let you both go. As an example of my good faith – and do not tax my patience further – you can share a room. Now you can watch while I cut her.'

Lore, perhaps sensing Sybil's presence, seemed to be staring right at her, though she could not see through the glass. Sybil suspected Gersten would try to split them, out of spite or idle amusement. Lore struggled when Gersten produced a scalpel. One of the thugs standing back stepped forward and grabbed her, then a quick slash and the clean handkerchief applied. Sybil saw in Lore's face the same disbelief as when he had done it to her.

They were driven back to Grosse Hamburger Strasse. Sybil tried surreptitiously to reach for Lore's hand and sensed her withdrawing it.

An extra bed had already been put in the room. Sybil didn't know what to say now they were alone. Lore sat mute and flinched as Sybil reached out.

They still had each other, Sybil said.

Lore, eyes downcast, searched for her words. 'My love for you knows no bounds but I feel my soul has been cast into a darkness where no contact or reassurance is possible.'

Sybil was taken aback by her strange, biblical language, but saw how what once was whole had been split asunder. They had been transformed into damned monsters out of all proportion to what they really were.

The heat of the moment that had sustained them melted away, passion reduced to clumsy embrace, as if some malignant presence clung to them. They created falsely cheerful cutouts of themselves, playing table tennis in the day room, laughing self-consciously and making a show of being entertained, under the watchful eye of Stella Kübler, queen of the catchers, whose friendship was like being brushed by death. Stella made a point of recruiting them into her social circle. Lore told Sybil that the brightness of Stella's eyes and film-star smile eclipsed everything around her until she wore a halo of darkness.

Stella was quick to remind Sybil they in fact knew each other quite well from the Feige-Strassburger school of design. She told them she was first arrested in the same café where Sybil and Lore had nearly got caught. She had lived a life of adventure. Brutal beatings, escape, recapture. Her parents were being held as hostages in the same building, on the other side of the dividing wall. She sounded quite resigned about it.

Stella insisted Lore come and work with her. She talked of the sexual thrill of catching and how she often needed a man afterwards and being taken from behind was best because it turned fucking into pure sensation, with none of the usual bother of address. Stella seemed utterly without illusion, saying they were all running scared but why pretend.

Sometimes Sybil looked at Stella in awe.

Lore's mouth turned into the memory of her mouth, even as they kissed. Blood no longer coursed through them as it once had. They stored their love for whatever fragile future they might have. They would escape. They would survive. Delivering Lore to Sybil, Gersten had returned the one person he could have held and used against her.

They talked about Grigor. Sybil remembered him, which she had not let on to Schlegel.

Grigor had been older, one of the aloof, arrogant ones, able to take his pick. He had a temper and used his fists. Their only acquaintance had been in a kitchen five years before, after Grigor had been street fighting during the November pogrom. Sybil remembered days of shock and high drama, of nervous gatherings, and on that occasion the smell of witch-hazel as Grigor's wounds were treated by a beautiful young woman who dabbed uselessly at a graze.

Grigor cultivated a look of the French anarchist actor Artaud, a big rebel star for the students. The girl with the witch-hazel looked helpless and Sybil took over. She at least had some first aid. Grigor complained of his hand hurting. She made him move his fingers and said no bones were broken, which was about the extent of their exchange. He asked her name and said in an ominous way he'd heard of her. He didn't thank her afterwards, only looked at her in a smouldering fashion that she remembered and thought he would instantly forget. Afterwards it was said Grigor had killed one if not two brownshirts and had been forced into hiding.

Based on what Gersten had told her, and her single observation, Sybil supposed Grigor could have become transformed into this dramatic killer. There always had been something uncontrolled about him. One or two each year used the persecution to fuel delinquent fantasies. Normally it was a pose; with Grigor she was not sure. Perhaps he had become tempered since by all the cruelty. Sybil had witnessed enough unthinkable change for Gersten's theory to hold.

She'd heard how Grigor used and discarded women in an animal way that made Alwynd appear sophisticated. Franz had known him slightly and aspired to the same pose. Much late-night discussion took place, with candles stuck in empty bottles, about the validity of the anarchist soul versus the sterile regimentation of the new order. Sybil noted such talk was always about the men.

Lore fell into Stella's bright and amoral orbit, leaving Sybil jealous. Stella had highly developed antennae to anything hidden. Other girls shared rooms but Lore suspected Stella guessed their secret. Stella encouraged Lore to become more feminine, forcing her to dress in a way Sybil hated.

During the day Stella and her catchers swept through the city, with a checklist of addresses. They hung around cafés, parks, theatres, embassies and cinemas. Stella's beat was around the Kurfürstendamm, with its once smart shops. She had the authority to check the papers of anyone she thought Jewish.

She taught Lore what telltale signs to look for. Any suspect should be treated to a friendly approach with an offer to help and given a rendezvous, where police would be waiting. Stella said it was OK to line their pockets with the possessions of anyone they found hiding.

One night they trooped off to the theatre where Stella spotted people in the audience and made the necessary telephone call during the interval, and afterwards they were arrested. When one tried to run away Stella shouted at the top of her voice, 'Stop him! Jew!' They all travelled back in one of the Gestapo removal vans, catchers and caught alike, and Lore burned with shame under the fright and contempt of those they had snatched. Stella was chatty and cheerful, saying she thought the play quite good.

On the first day Lore was out with Stella, Sybil had nothing to do until the evening. She tried to sleep. She visited her mother again and asked her to do a reading. Her mother refused, saying it was all nonsense. She wore a housekeeper's coat. She said she was well looked after, all things considered, although her host made physical demands.

Perhaps her mother was smarter than she thought, selling her placebo to gullible power brokers. They sat undisturbed in a comfortable kitchen in Dahlem where the bigwigs lived. She was touched and surprised when her mother took her hand and asked if she was all right. They had never been close. Yes, she said, not meaning it any more than the insincerity of the question. It was just another rehearsed gesture. Sybil said nothing of Gersten.

Sybil wanted only to be honest but lacked Stella's forthrightness and said nothing about her and Lore and love and what she thought about life and all the things people were supposed to discuss. She decided she probably would be capable of betraying her mother after all, for the sake of Lore. It would take perhaps as little as a few weeks to become as hardened and polished as Stella. Sybil recoiled from Stella's naked gaze, knowing it was only a matter of time before she acquired that look.

Sybil introduced herself to Herr Valentine, the manager at Clärchens, as told to by Schlegel. The waiter didn't show. She waited two hours, refused invitations to dance and went home, a short walk of a few minutes. Lore appeared to be asleep. Sybil told her to stop pretending but Lore refused to budge. It was barely nine. She was too tense to go to bed but could not face the Kübler woman downstairs. She lay down and the night stretched ahead, her world closing down.

Gersten had talked of the killings as a virus. Equally, he had infected them by the act of cutting them, turning them into his contaminated creatures.

The next night the waiter was at Clärchens. The man clearly expected a favour for his information. Sybil felt good and bad showing her card that said she worked for the Gestapo. It was pitiful. Flash a card and they backed down. She experienced some of the Kübler woman's contempt: honour and loyalty were indulgences; animals took evasive action to survive and morality had nothing to do with it.

Her dislike of the waiter grew so she could barely question him. Was the information she came away with any use? Grigor worked part-time as a cinema projectionist. Sybil thought it pathetic, the great rebel reduced to showing phantom images.

Lore didn't come back until late. This time Sybil was the one pretending to be asleep even as she lay awake listening to Lore's near silent crying.

# 45

Otto Keleman telephoned Schlegel in the office for an apparently inconsequential chat until, sounding scared, he hinted at information that made what they were talking about last time look like child's play.

They met, both already drunk, at the bar with the green door, where, in a hoarse whisper, Keleman told such an outlandish story of bribery and corruption that Schlegel told him to ignore it.

Too late, he said. Someone had already tried to push him under a train.

Schlegel wasn't sure whether to believe that either. It sounded more like being jostled on a crowded platform, which happened every day.

Keleman's extraordinary claim was almost every single Party member of consequence was paid a monthly tax-free bribe out of a slush fund. This extended to top military as well. The size of the bribe depended on seniority. Minister of Propaganda Goebbels received 7,500 marks a month.

'No fucking around with the revenue. Now someone is saying every single one of these cases should be investigated for unpaid back taxes!' Keleman gave a sharp bark of disbelief. 'It is impossible to say whether this is mischief on the part of the paymaster, to embarrass those taking the bribe, or a campaign against those making the payments.'

'Who is pushing you?'

'I don't know! And equally someone seems to want me dead for even knowing.'

'How is the information being fed to you?'

'A combination of letter and telephone calls in the middle of the night.'

'What is your reading?'

'As before. Power struggle at the top.'

Schlegel asked whether Keleman was saying they both knew who was responsible but it was in their interests not to. Keleman nodded. Neither Bormann nor his paymaster, Lammers, were among those being bribed.

Then it had to be Chancellery, said Schlegel. No one else was in a position to make such payments.

'That's the last we say about it. Apply for leave and make yourself scarce.'

'It's too late for that.'

'What do you mean?'

'That fancy grocer Nöthling and the ration card scandal.'

'What about him?'

Keleman had been told if he provided evidence of his corruption the rest would take care of itself. Nöthling was on the list. He received a monthly payment to subsidise his supplies.

'What's your point?'

'Nöthling has an illegal supply of pigs coming in tonight.'

'Where?'

'The Landsberger Allee marshalling yard.'

Where the first flayed body had been found. Again, Schlegel thought. He should have seen it coming that Keleman was bound to ask for help.

Keleman said he could still just about drive if Schlegel got a car. Schlegel thought, Stoffel's Opel again, and sighed.

*       *       *

Schlegel, sobering up fast, was running on Pervitin, which Keleman was shovelling down too.

'Been taking them for years. Dutch courage.'

A night mist reduced visibility more than usual, which, combined with Keleman's drunk driving, made Schlegel a nervous passenger. The car's cowled headlights showed nothing but white.

He yawned, exhausted yet wide awake.

They parked away from the siding. Mist turned to fog. Any worse and they wouldn't be able to see. From up ahead came the clank of shunted wagons, shouted orders, the panicky clatter of animal hooves and occasional squeal as one fell off the unloading ramps. They passed the stationary silhouette of a parked van. Keleman pointed to Nöthling's name, just discernible on the side.

Schlegel groped his way forward until he reached a fence. The pigs passed beneath, barely visible. He moved on, startled by a figure coming out of the mist, who seemed not to see him.

He came to what felt like a larger area, presumably pens, where the animals' confusion was evident, and realised he had lost Keleman.

A lorry pulled up further down the track, followed by more shouted orders. Keleman swam back into view. Schlegel suggested they investigate. Keleman nodded uncertainly as two Hitler Youths marched past with antiquated rifles.

Taking his bearings from the train, he walked towards where he had heard the truck. The mist rolled in thicker until he could barely see his hand. Keleman was gone again.

A bolt slid on the other side of the truck he was next to. Crouching down, he could see nothing and felt his way between the wheels. A succession of handlers' boots clumped on the wagon floor above, then down the ramp. He heard whatever they were carrying being flung onto the lorry.

They worked in silence, as though not wishing to draw attention.

Approaching footsteps crunched on aggregate. Something was put down. Schlegel crawled forward, trying to see. He could make no sense of the blurred image that looked like an enormous white worm or larvae, or even the remains of a snowdrift.

Whatever it was groaned and he realised the cargo must be human. The train shifted forward and stopped. Time to get out. Keleman was probably a liability wandering around on his own.

Conditions made distance impossible to judge. The scrape of a match sounded like it was being struck in Schlegel's ear, yet when he called Keleman's name it died in the air.

A figure loomed and ran past, leaving Schlegel with the impression of a toothless, gaping mouth, and a reek of paraffin. He was contemplating the unsettling combination of fog and Pervitin when a man shouted. There was the noise of a scuffle. Someone called for help, followed by a report, more a dry mechanical cough than gunshot, then running footsteps.

Schlegel charged after. The footsteps stopped. Schlegel saw a yellow flash, and another. Only when the bullets sang past did he understand they were meant for him. The shooter ran off. Schlegel chased on, the pill giving him a wild determination.

The man ahead entered a building. Schlegel followed, skidding through the doorway. The train started to move out, the engine and the grind of the wagons drowning everything. Schlegel hit his shin against something hard and cried out. He was being reckless. He wasn't carrying a gun. Adrenalin and panic overrode caution.

The other man seemed unbothered about making a noise now.

Schlegel reached the end of the building. A door was open.

The smell said he was at the entrance of the pig shed. The pill told him he was invincible, however much the counterargument in his head warned that jittery alertness was no substitute for stealth.

He stood in the middle of the shed, hearing only pigs. He hurried on, afraid of losing his quarry.

He came to, aware of the pungent smell of shit filling his nostrils. He was lying face down in the stuff while being pressed and prodded from above. A light was on that hadn't been before. He decided he must have been drinking and the hangover accounted for his head feeling split open, and the smell was some terrible practical joke perpetrated by Stoffel after another staff binge.

He couldn't breathe. He was aware of being walked over and something sharp nipping at him. Teeth; he was being bitten and tried calling out. He was too weak to stand. He struggled to gain his breath. He made it to his hands and knees and found himself face to face with a pair of pale blue eyes that stared back implacably.

He understood. He had been chucked unconscious into a pen, and had he not regained his senses the pigs would have eaten him in their prosaic thorough way, simply because he was there.

Keleman was so covered in muck he was barely recognisable. Schlegel saw the man's dead eyes, open in terror and surprise, as though the last thing he had been conscious of was the bolt of the animal gun driving its way into his brain.

The pigs had already made a meal of him. A shoe lay discarded. His foot and his cheek had been chewed to the bone.

He dragged Keleman's body away from the pens and left it on the concrete.

It took ages to find the night watchman, who looked at

him in disbelief. Schlegel told him to call the police and get Stoffel.

He cleaned himself up as best he could in the slaughterhouse washrooms. He showered in cold water. His coat was beyond saving, the trousers too, but the rest was just salvageable. He got the worst of the shit off his shoes using the tap. He found a workman's boiler suit hanging on a peg and took that. He thought he had lost his hat again.

Stoffel arrived, grumbling at having been dragged out, annoyed that Schlegel had taken his car yet again and even more furious to discover it had been driven by an uninsured civilian.

'A dead uninsured civilian,' said Schlegel wildly.

A carload of uniformed cops turned up and muttered about flayed bodies and cannibal pigs. Keleman wasn't where Schlegel had left him. Stoffel's scepticism shone like a searchlight.

'Get this straight for me, son. You woke up to find yourself being eaten by pigs, and the other fellow was lying half-eaten after a bolt had been put through his head.'

Of his own survival all Schlegel could think was even death had washed its hands of him.

'Then where is he now?'

'Ask Haager who kills the animals. He once snuck up behind me with a stun gun.'

Haager lived only a street away and came to the door in his pyjamas, with his hair sticking up. He said he had been home all evening and had family to prove it.

Afterwards Stoffel said, 'Give me one good reason why I should give you a lift home.'

Schlegel protested that a man was dead. They should be making a proper search. Stoffel sighed and asked if Schlegel was taking pills.

'You're staring like a madman. Psychotic episode, bad hallucination. It happens a lot. Gets harder to sleep. Gets harder to catch up, and you end up seeing all sorts of things. Don't deny it.'

Stoffel said his story made sense, up to the point where Keleman got lost in the fog.

'I'm not saying you didn't roll around in shit, son, but why would anyone want to kill a fucking accountant?'

# 46

Lore didn't come back that night. Stella Kübler, flicking through a magazine in the common room, cheerfully said she hadn't seen her.

'It happens quite a lot in the early stages. They wander off, usually only for a few days, then come back with their heads straight. One or two jump, but I wouldn't say yours was one of those.'

Sybil walked out. Stella caught up with her in the corridor, grabbed her arm, spun her round and kissed her on the lips.

'I made your little friend so hot and wet she was sobbing for it. She said you need to be more adventurous.'

Sybil slapped her. Stella put her hand up to the red mark on her cheek and laughed.

'Darling, so jealous. Don't be so possessive.'

Sybil got through the next day by working herself to distraction, using newspapers in cafés to make a list of cinemas and going to speak to the managers, with a story about wanting to contact her brother-in-law who was working as a projectionist. In the big cinemas she found staff were fairly permanent; the waiter had said Grigor was part time.

She trawled suburbs, visiting rundown picture houses. One venue was reduced to a bomb site and she thought it was just her luck if he had worked there.

At night she concentrated on the city centre. Some late-night joints were free for troops. The flea-pits showed more or less anything. There were newsreel theatres and a couple that ran only cartoons. The picture palaces and the dives all smelled the same, of stale smoke and dirty bodies.

She walked miles. She knew she wasn't even close. It wouldn't have been beyond the waiter to have made it up.

Lore didn't return that night either.

Stella came to Sybil's room with a contrite face. 'Sorry, darling, I am such a bitch. Don't believe anything I say.'

She was so insincere Sybil decided she was only there to churn up more doubt.

'Take my hand and say you forgive me.'

When Sybil cried Stella insisted on holding her. Sybil weakened in spite of herself, thinking any embrace was better than none, her mind in utter confusion.

'She'll come back. I am so sorry. Are we friends again? Kiss me like we are sisters and I will say goodnight.'

Sybil couldn't bring herself to and saw the blazing hatred in Stella's eyes.

The next morning Gersten talked of the war against the forgers and how good Stella Kübler was and how delighted he would be if Sybil became half as accomplished, which was when Sybil realised he never meant to let her go.

'Mikki Hellman's gone. Schönhaus can't last much longer. These are all names familiar to you.'

They had all been part of the same student scene.

'There's even a Chinese forger. He must be the last Chink in Berlin, so if you see him . . .'

Gersten laughed. The few Chinese restaurants left were run by Germans. Everyone said the one in Schmargendorf served dog.

'How's your friend adjusting?'

'She'll be fine,' said Sybil, saying nothing of Lore's vanishing.

He probably knew already from the Kübler woman, who would have boasted of her conquest, true or not.

'And Grigor?'

She hoped one more day would be sufficient.

Life became a series of bets with herself. A train passing overhead when she crossed under the S-Bahn was a sign everything would be all right. The next corner reached in fewer steps than she had guessed meant Lore would be back safe that night. Her fingers ached from keeping them crossed. And all the time pictures like film flickers bombarded her head, showing Lore writhing with the Kübler woman.

Alternately she had the clearest visions of Lore falling to earth. She saw Lore drowned, throwing herself in front of a hurtling train, and broken on the ground after jumping from a high building.

She returned to Alwynd's to see if she had been back. Alwynd was his usual beady self. Unusually, there was no female companion around.

No, he hadn't seen Lore. He had been wondering.

'I haven't seen you in days. Are you still staying here?'

He said she looked tired and they could always go and lie down.

'I don't have any classes until this afternoon. It will relax you.' Sybil ignored him. 'I promise not to mention your Jewishness to anyone.'

She couldn't tell if this was a threat or more drollery. She said she had to go when what she really wanted was to be held, and left at that.

In desperation, she called Franz, who sounded surprised. She told him she was at her wits' end and badly needed to reach Grigor. She listened to his long silence before she said she was desperate to know how to find out if Lore was still alive.

Franz said it was easier to check if she were dead. He spoke

in a tough way, as if even the idea of a single death was sentimental. He suggested she try the hearse drivers.

The hearse driver she spoke to had picked up no one of
Lore's description but he couldn't speak for the others.

Sybil asked, 'Do you know Grigor? He used to be one of the
drivers.'

There had been a lot of changes. The man looked like he
couldn't care less about her plight.

'If you see him, tell him I am looking for him.'

She might as well put a message in a bottle and chuck it in
the river.

The driver decided to be helpful after all and produced a
tatty exercise book which listed those they had fetched. Twelve
dead were down for the last two days.

Sybil read down the entries, written in several hands.

*Couple, middle-aged, presumed Veronal poisoning, Frankfurter Allee.*

*Female, approx. 40, drowned Gross Glienicke See.*

*Male, 50s, jumped Damaschkestrasse.*

*Female, 30s, slit wrists, Steglitzer Damm.*

*Male, 40s, gassed, head in oven. Orber Strasse.*

*Mother and child, approx. 30 and 5 or 6, Veronal poisoning, Alt Moabit.*

*Child, approx. 15, natural causes [?], Reinickendorfer Strasse.*

*Couple, 70s, Veronal, Brunnenstrasse.*

*Female, 50s, drowned, Halensee.*

That night she avoided Stella and lay in her room, hoping by
sheer willpower she could conjure Lore back. No one came,
except Gersten, standing in her doorway, watching as she
pretended to be asleep.

The following morning a mist hung in the air. She was shut-
ting the gate to the garden when a ghostly figure approached.

It had to be chance, was her first thought; then she realised he must be looking for her too. He looked older, with deep lines down the side of his face, but had lost none of his aura. The easy way he moved on the balls of his feet was like a big cat, alert and self-contained in a way Franz could only dream of. Sybil wondered if Franz had done her the favour after all.

But if he knew where she lived he would also know what that meant.

'Sybil,' he said.

# 47

Schlegel wandered drunk, from bar to bar, taking too many pills, as if he could hallucinate reality away.

As long as Keleman's body was missing there was no case.

He had gone back with Stoffel's crew, minus Stoffel, to the slaughterhouse. Baumgarten professed ignorance of everything. Schlegel stumbled around to little purpose. He remembered to return the boiler suit. He knew he had lost his hat but couldn't think where. He confiscated the slaughterhouse stun gun, suspecting it was a waste of time because if it had been used on Keleman it would have been steam-cleaned so no trace was left.

Schlegel did his best to persuade himself that Keleman had made himself scarce after all. There was no sign of Morgen. He forgot to send the stun gun on to forensics. His thinking was all over the shop.

He spent a long time nursing a drink in a bar, developing a theory of parallel memory. He had always thought of the past as something to be moved on from, the way something chucked from a speeding boat receded and became absorbed. He had imagined the ditch shootings would grow similarly distant. Most of the time he didn't think about them; it belonged to a time known as then that had nothing to do with now. But since Morgen's disappearance he started to accept the past as an adjacent space, like a room into which one could step.

He was in a bar in Mitte, probably talking to himself. Then

he was wandering around Alexanderplatz, thinking about Lampe and his dark fantasy world, which was maybe preferable to the state of denial the rest of them lived in. He supposed he was going through a crack-up brought on by a combination of catharsis and disgust. Enough was enough; one more drink then go home and dry out, before dedicating himself properly, to what? Was there any point in trying to track down Grigor, who would be crushed by the machine sooner or later? They all would. Even if a fraction of what Keleman had been saying was true, Schlegel couldn't see how he could begin to make a dent in it.

He spotted a couple of underground Jews. He was getting good at picking them out. He tried talking to them. They didn't want to. He supposed they were worried his being drunk would attract attention. Then he didn't know what was going on because two men were addressing him and it seemed to be his turn to be the U-boat. They were asking for his papers. That was easy enough. He stayed them with a raised finger and reached in his jacket, except his papers weren't there. He patted other pockets in desperation. When he said he was a policemen they laughed in his face, punched him in the stomach and made him show his cock.

'Come on, Jew boy, under arrest.'

# 48

Sybil sat in the cinema. It was in a bad part of town, much given over to foreign workers' barracks. The cinema showed cheap fodder for sex-starved troops, featuring sturdy, prancing, scantily dressed women. Sybil presumed it was a relic from more permissive times. From what she could tell, everyone else in the cinema was male. Much furtive rustling went on. The place was a free-for-all. She even spotted some noisy boys presumably there for a dare. The only empty seats were all down the front because they were too close to the screen. Sybil had no one on either side and was fairly sure the man two seats away was pleasuring himself under his greatcoat.

She had told Gersten about Grigor, hoping he would intervene.

She was flattered in spite of herself that Grigor had remembered her name, until he said she worked for the other side now.

Gersten asked what she had said to that.

'I told him I was looking to get out.'

'Good. What was his response?'

'He asked if I was another of your traps. I swore I wasn't and he said, "You know what happened to the others who were sent." '

'Did he mention me by name?'

'He just said Gestapo.'

'But he admitted to killing them, so I am right. You have

done well. I expect you can't tell if you are the spider or the fly.'

Gersten unnerved her. Grigor unnerved her. Her response to Grigor unnerved her too. She didn't know if what she was saying was just words or she believed them. Would she throw in her lot with him? What choice she had from what she could see amounted to deciding who between Grigor and Gersten she would elect to kill her. Compared to the artistry of Gersten, who would hide his true face until the last moments, Grigor came over as primitive and unpredictable. His gaze so unsettled her that she considered him quite capable of flaying someone. She could imagine him doing it to the Kübler woman and experienced a perverse thrill. She had heard that beyond extremes of pain lay unsuspected hinterlands that were not unpleasant and even pleasurable.

Grigor had named a cinema, a dive, he said, under railway arches that ran late-night sessions. She wouldn't find it listed in any of the papers, he added, as though he knew what she had been up to. He gave her a time and told her to sit down at the front, as far to the left facing the screen as she could.

She had asked Gersten to intervene, but he only said it was too early.

'I want to know more now you are close enough to smell him. I need evidence that he is the flayer.'

She had looked in vain for Schlegel and left a string of desperate messages, hoping he might materialise and afford some protection.

The film was terrible. It was old and scratched, with chunks missing, because of the censor or projectionists hacking bits out for private enjoyment. She tried hard to follow it, in an effort to blot out everything else. Time seemed to be accelerating. Events of only a few days past – that first gut-churning glimpse of Lore as Gersten's captive – seemed half a lifetime ago. The man two seats away had his cock out, his hand a blur as he worked away, spine arched, head tilted back over the edge of the seat, and groaning like a dying man. The boys sniggered and pointed. On the screen two buxom flaxen-haired maidens in bathing costumes threw a beach ball at each other.

Something prodded her in the back. Before she had time to be surprised a voice whispered, 'Follow me.'

The auditorium was almost pitch-black because the screen had gone to a night scene. Sybil had to feel her way down the aisle, vaguely aware of the shape of Grigor's long army surplus coat ahead of her. He took her out not by the front, as she was expecting, but through the fire exit, which took them into a back yard, and from there up an outside staircase to a gantry where the projection booth was housed in a wooden hut. The projector ground away unattended.

Grigor turned and slapped her so fast that Sybil had no time to protect herself. She fell in a heap, her head ringing, seeing stars. She supposed this was the start of what he did. The strange hiccoughing must be her, she decided, a sound unlike anything her body had ever produced before.

Grigor wanted to know who the white-haired young man was he had seen hanging around outside the back of her lodgings.

She was about to deny everything but Grigor's murderous tone made her say, 'He's police. He's harmless.'

He bent down, too fast for her again, and picked her up by the front of her coat so she was lifted off the ground, feet dangling. His strength was evident in the way he held her one-handed. In the other was a knife whose sharp point he stuck into the soft skin under her jaw.

'Why is he following you?'

'Because he is looking for you.'

The knife pierced her skin. Her whining sounded despicable. Snot ran down her face. Her bladder was about to burst. Rain fell outside, a sudden, sharp squall. There was no shame in losing control. She was tired of trying to hold it all together.

The room went suddenly bright, followed by slow handclapping and wolf whistles. For a moment Sybil thought the audience must be watching them on a stage, but Grigor had missed his reel change. The projector had run out of film.

He worked fast and professionally as though a few seconds ago had never happened. Sybil considered running but her legs were like feathers. No one had ever hit her that hard before. All her scrambled brain could think was Grigor would be led as much by his cock as the masturbating man downstairs.

Grigor might toy with her for a while but he would kill her unless she could offer something. She'd heard of double agents, people who worked for opposite sides at the same time. She supposed that was what she was about to become, pretending to work for both men in the desperate hope that she could play off one against the other.

Grigor appeared embarrassed by his earlier violence. Sybil took her chance, asking if he had a cigarette. Grigor said it was forbidden in the booth. Sybil laughed at that, thinking he mustn't see her fear. She scoffed at being told she couldn't smoke.

She didn't want the cigarette but took it anyway. She made it clear she expected him to light it for her, and sucked greedily at the flame.

'So we have an interesting situation,' she said as coolly as she could manage, wriggling for the slightest chance of survival.

'Let's say I deliver the Kübler bitch to you, so we can take care of her the same way as the others.'

She now considered him easily capable of flaying Kübler alive, and experienced the same spurt of nasty pleasure as before.

'The white-haired one is harmless. He's only interested in you because of some forgeries. He's easily taken care of.'

The knife was in Grigor's hand again, pressed against her belly. The other one lay splayed on her breast. The threat was still there but not as strong. Sybil sighed inwardly. She would have to fuck him in the end, however hard she tried to string him along.

'I have nothing clever to say. You want the Kübler woman or you don't. I am going now. As for meeting again, I could name a place and turn up with Gersten, so what do we do?'

'You come here, to this booth, any time after dark. Bring anyone and there's enough flammable materials to blow the roof off the cinema.'

Sybil saw herself out, climbed downstairs and paused in the alleyway to spew up the contents of her stomach. The cobblestones were slick from the rain she had listened to drumming on the booth while thinking she might not be alive to hear it stop.

Gersten came on what Schlegel reckoned was the third day.

He was alone and said, 'You look awful.'

'What took you so long?'

Schlegel was in a cell on his own, not much bigger than a tomb, that felt deep underground. He had a wooden bunk, one grimy blanket and a bucket. He slept curled in a ball, sweating from withdrawal, so exhausted he didn't care about his plight or that no one came. The thin gruel always delivered while he slept was stone cold when it came to eating and scarcely alleviated his hunger. The last thing he remembered were sausages at Stoffel's party.

Gersten looked suave, wearing the whipcord coat, his hair silky, freshly washed.

'You needed the rest to judge by the state of you.'

He took them via a series of complicated tunnels to a huge vaulted space like a crypt, full of stainless-steel containers.

'It's a morgue. In case you are still having trouble thinking.'

He slid open a drawer and Schlegel was presented with the sight of flayed meat.

'Another torso. Fresh. What do we make of that?'

It was like the first body. Butchered, rendered inhuman. Schlegel stared, thinking how Morgen had predicted the killings would carry on.

'Where was it found?'

'In the middle of Alexanderplatz, if you please, in a sack, by a Polish street cleaner, at six in the morning. Three days ago. In the rain.'

Schlegel looked at Gersten. 'Meaning it was someone other than Lazarenko.'

'I was talking to the Todermann woman the other day, saying I thought it was turning into a killing virus. It could be a copycat.'

'Do you have any idea who?'

'I have my theory.'

'Boot's on the other foot now,' said Gersten. 'You're the one answering.'

They were in the usual room above the river. Gersten picked up a file and waved it.

'Interesting reading.'

What little was left of Schlegel's spirits sank.

'Heady days. Summer of '41. Bezirk Bialystok. Everyone on the charge. Gateway to the east. Big skies, golden corn, enemy on the run. From what I understand your boss Nebe, who commanded your brigade, was a bit of a slacker when it came to anti-partisan duties. And so it seems were you. A bit of a Pinko even. Refused to roll up your sleeves and get your hands dirty. Conscientious objector?'

'Such operations were on a voluntary basis.'

'And there were more than enough volunteers?'

'There seemed to be.'

'And what did anti-partisan duties consist of?'

'Mopping-up operations behind the front line.'

'In detail.'

'We liaised with military intelligence in pinpointing areas of resistance.'

'You took the war to the civilian population.'

'Only when it was shown to have been penetrated by the resistance.'

'How long did you last?'

'I was sent home after a couple of months.'

'Any particular reason?'

'I believe mental fatigue was what the record stated.'

'Again, any particular reason?'

He had been a staff officer working for Nebe. From a distance, the operations had sounded as plausible as he had described to Gersten. Covering ground, venturing into the badlands to engage with partisans in the heady days of the big eastern expansion. Many of the brigade were police reservists, older men, not kids, ordinary. He wrote up the operational reports, making them sound like military duties undertaken in response to resistance atrocity. The partisans were compared to Red Indians because of the same crude practice of mutilation, including scalping. Schlegel remembered many accounts similar to ones cited by Lazarenko. Partisans took no

prisoners and anyone who fell into their hands died a grue-
some death. The first corpses he saw were the charred bodies
of three airmen who had been caught and barbecued alive.
They were shown filmed evidence of atrocities by an enemy
considered endlessly cunning, relentless and unguessable.
Children and old women were just as likely to carry grenades.
Children were initiated to kill from as young as ten or eleven.
During periods of famine they resorted to eating each other,
and any enemy regularly had his liver cut out and eaten as a
way of stealing his soul.

It was impossible to describe the sense of bewitched trepidation that lay over them.

Schlegel suspected he was a coward. Nebe had encouraged
him to go. He was putting together a police force to keep
order behind the lines in what was called bandit country. It
would be designated as active duty and they would all get a
pay hike.

The thought of anything resembling military duty and the
possibility of shooting and being shot at appalled Schlegel. He
squared with his conscience by telling himself they were going
as a policing force, operating in conquered territory and little
active work would be required. Everyone said it would be like
Poland, a known slacker's posting.

He wangled a staff job.

Then the reports started coming in of men cracking up.

A team of shrinks turned up.

Schlegel talked to a smooth, dark-haired one called Krick.
Afterwards Schlegel decided Krick must have confused him
with someone else. Talks between staff and shrinks were always
informal, usually done over a drink. Krick, sympathetic and off
the record after many beers, said to Schlegel, 'You have a bitch
of a job. First, don't order anyone to do it. Ask for volunteers
and if anyone has a problem send them to me. The trick is to

normalise the process. Weed out the thugs and sadists and make it scientific and technical, and don't discriminate against or punish those who say they have no stomach for the job. Plenty will.'

Schlegel was accused by a sergeant of being a shirker. They were both wildly drunk, as was the norm. Schlegel was within his rights to have the man cashiered. The sergeant couldn't care less. He said he could hit Schlegel and have done with it. Eighteen months in a penal colony would be a holiday by comparison.

The facts were cleaned up in the paperwork. A bureaucratic structure was created, with official notations, workshops, directives and mandated progress reports ('Such and such an area cleared of partisan activities'). Civilian consultants came in, bringing a pretence of management, and the shrinks' gloss provided earnest exhortation of the dire necessity of the task.

Order did not extend to the field. The drunken sergeant challenged Schlegel to accompany them instead of hiding behind his desk.

Schlegel remembered the journey, a two-hour drive, sitting in the front of the Kübelwagen, wearing goggles because of the dust, the landscape ahead like a child's drawing of a huge cloudless sky bisecting endless plain, and them racing unchallenged down open roads. He was there as an observer, and that made him unpopular, being there to watch others do the dirty work.

They rounded up an entire village, made some dig an enormous ditch while the rest waited, forced them all to undress, then shot the lot, carefully positioned on the lip of the ditch so their bodies tumbled into the vast makeshift grave.

Officers were not present.

'You will drink a lot of schnapps tonight,' said the sergeant.

A regular round of gunfire came from the site, two hundred metres away.

'You will have to take a closer inspection for your report,' the sergeant said.

They went down at the end. Schlegel had expected to be faced with something finished and somehow orderly, the neat result of a job properly done. The swarm of flies that had gathered above the pit was dispersed by a sudden geyser of blood spraying like a hydrant. Although he had heard shooting all afternoon he was still shocked by the extent of the sea of bodies, like marble streaked with dirt, the flesh unnaturally white against tanned necks and hands. Some remained alive, writhing.

Stunned, he clambered down the side of the ditch, falling and landing among the bodies. He struggled to stand, knee-deep in viscera, thinking of himself as finishing the job – pistol to neck, eyes shut, pull trigger – walking on corpses, standing in pools of blood, reloading with shaking hands. After a beseeching look from a woman who raised both hands, he turned away and fired, hoping he had put her out of her misery. There was just him in the pit and no one watching. Later he tried to remember how many magazines. The sergeant told him four. More than thirty rounds. No one helped him out and several times he slid back down. What he had done would turn him into some mad dog or pariah. Such a hot day. He smelled his bitter sweat, cordite, shit and vomit, the waft of cigarettes on the breeze, a metal taste in his mouth, like he had been sucking coins. Then came a sudden rainstorm, what the tough sergeant surprisingly called the heavens weeping. The men filled in the ditch and they drove home drinking beer, brought with them for the occasion. They got Schlegel legless that night and from then on he counted as one of them.

\*  \*  \*

He reasoned he had acted in the most humane way in an impossible situation. His body told him otherwise. His hair went white in the time it took to send him home, bleached by the sun he thought, until he saw himself properly in a mirror, which was not a feature of life in the field.

He attended his desk. He knew he was cracking up. He attacked a fellow officer in the mess with a brass candlestick. He spent a deranged week where he insisted on attaching himself to a mobile shooting unit and watched everything. He lay in bed for a week in a trance until sent home for psychiatric observation. Knowing that Nebe was less than keen in his pursuit of their orders, and they had managed to save thousands of civilians from execution by falsifying figures and claiming credit for shootings that had never been carried out counted for nothing in Schlegel's mind.

'Torture is a strangely intimate business,' observed Gersten, then hurried to reassure Schlegel. 'Oh, don't worry, I don't have that in mind for you.'

The room to which he was now taken was almost a mirror of his office, with a blank wall outside and crack of sunlight that lasted twenty minutes as it moved across. After their third or fourth session, as Gersten liked to call them, Schlegel noticed he seemed to be brought there to coincide with the brief passage of light.

Sometimes they appeared to talk about nothing of consequence although Schlegel supposed what passed for gossip on a variety of subjects such as Stoffel and Nebe and the quality of canteen food came down to information gathering.

'These bodies,' said Gersten. 'How do you see them?'

'Which specifically?'

'Let's start with the old woman who was murdered for the princely sum of one mark.'

'Lampe confessed to that.'

'Who confesses and who commits is not necessarily the same thing.'

'I don't know.'

'Fine detective you are.'

'I work in the financial division.'

'Ah, yes, forged money. Who in your opinion killed Abbas?'

'Whoever Abbas as your agent was meant to betray.'

'And who was that, in your opinion?'

'A man who calls himself Grigor whose real name is Yakov Zorin.'

'A Jew?'

'A forger.'

'You know more than I do. Go on.'

'He appears to have been sent away. Or perhaps he faked it to look that way.'

'And the woman with money stuffed up her hole?'

'Zorin or Grigor, or whatever you like to call him, posed as a waiter to pick her up.'

'Call him Grigor. It has a ring of Dostoyevsky. Have you identified the dead woman?'

'No, but if she was your agent we were negligent not to check with you.'

'The thing is, I have no idea who she was.'

He showed his open hand to say he had nothing to hide. Schlegel thought it sounded believable, although Sybil was being used for an identical entrapment.

Gersten made light of that, saying the arrangement was nothing unusual.

'You seem quite pally with her. I am bound to ask whether you are a Jew lover on the quiet.'

'She witnessed the Metzler shooting.'

Gersten sighed. 'Let's not get lost in that particular thicket.

What I can't decide is whether Grigor is responsible for the butcher murders.'

'You wrote those off to Lazarenko.'

'I mean in cahoots, as part of some ghastly tandem cooked up by the Jewish Grigor – who from his name must have Russian connections – and the Bolshevik Lazarenko. We assume a man who cuts off another's cock is capable of anything. What do you think?'

'What I think is not important.'

'What would Morgen say? Where is Morgen, by the way?'

'Gone.'

'I must say I found him a terrifying combination of dark horse and fierce dog. How do you find him?'

'All I can say for certain is he smoked a lot and has been to Russia.'

'And Morgen on the killings?'

'I don't know.'

'There's a lot of not knowing with you.'

'He would say something metaphysical, such as the murders forming part of the same volcanic upheaval, whether physically related or not.'

'A bit deep for me, but with Lazarenko gone who are we naming for this latest butcher's murder?'

'Grigor must be part of the network. If there is a counter-propaganda element it's important they carry on.'

'Are you saying the killings themselves are more the point than the identity of the killer?'

'It seems.'

Gersten smiled and said, 'To get metaphysical for a moment, then it doesn't matter who the actual killer is. He can be whoever we say he is.'

'Didn't that happen already?'

'*Touché*. Except the urgency is becoming overstretched in

terms of a solution. We live in a world of results. Two years ago no one would have cared about some shitty little terror campaign, but with the army not chalking up victories, this takes us into another dimension. Ministers are starting to jump. Everyone is terrified Adolf will get to hear.'

Gersten studied his hand and said in the absence of Grigor he would have to come up with someone else.

'It's a hungry monster we feed. I abhor this new fashion for the quick fix, but let's say we set you up in a soft camp, on the quiet. You can be a librarian. I could arrange to have you driven there, save you that degrading business of going by train.'

Schlegel was left struggling to absorb that Gersten was about not only write off the new flayed body to him, he was about make him disappear altogether.

Gersten held up his hand, amused. 'I know. A lot to take in.'

Schlegel saw how much he had brought to the table in terms of framing himself. A history of delinquency and recidivism. The disturbed background. Evidence of participation in traumatic shootings that Gersten would claim had messed up his head. Psychiatric reports. Lack of spine. The fugue state of the last days. He was being fitted up as effectively as Lampe and Lazarenko.

'Your motive is the only thing that worries me.'

When Schlegel angrily responded there was none, Gersten lazily pointed out he was bound to say that.

'I think you buckled under pressure.' He rubbed his thumb and forefinger. 'That crack or fissure in the brain, working away, turning to self-loathing, until you cannot live with yourself, so you find a substitute that lets you both relive and exorcise the trauma. I am starting to sound quite philosophical.'

He reached into a drawer.

345

'I have forgers too. Jewish ones who work for me. Good, but not as good as Grigor. I had these done for my amusement.'

It was a Jewish identity card for Abbas, except instead of Abbas's photograph was the mugshot they had taken of Schlegel.

'As I say, done as a stunt, until I thought . . .' He reached into the drawer again. 'We could turn you into Grigor.'

Schlegel's face was now on a Jewish card that stated he was Yakov Zorin.

He realised Gersten had known all along about Zorin.

'Profession, butcher. I rather like that touch.'

Gersten leaned forward, his contempt clear. 'I don't give a fuck what profession Grigor really has, he is what I say he is and so are you. The person known as August Schlegel will quite disappear. Soon there will be nothing to say you aren't Grigor or Abbas, or whatever wretched part I decide you should play. Nothing like this had crossed my mind until they brought you in, paperless and out of your head. Your office was about to report you missing. Do you see what I am saying?' He snapped his fingers. 'The thing about you, Schlegel, is you are a classic victim. Maybe because you shot Jews and felt bad you thought you had to become like one, which was why you took to wandering around with no papers, asking to get caught.' Gersten snorted. 'Your circumcision doesn't help. Why on earth take a knife to a kid's cock, what's that about? The shockingness of your condition when they brought you in made me embarrassed for you. You stank so much we had to hose you down. Don't you remember?'

Schlegel shook his head.

'Anyway, you kept asking for me; not wise under the circumstances. And anyway again, be grateful we cleaned you up rather than let you live with your depravity. Do you see what I am saying? I would have been professionally negligent had I not made the observation that here was a man capable of anything.'

'This is ridiculous. I want to talk to Nebe.'

'Why should he care? Camps are full of people who thought they would never disappear. Statistically those at the top of the alphabet have a better chance of survival. Less standing around in the freezing cold waiting for your name to be called. As Zorin you would fare less well than Abbas.'

'In a soft camp?'

'There are no soft camps. Not really.'

# 49

Sybil still had the key to the back stairs up to Alwynd's apartment. She knew which days he left around ten and didn't come back for lunch. She would tell Stella about a place where Jews were hiding, luring her to where Grigor would be waiting.

In trying to match Stella's understanding of everything as power and control, Sybil knew she risked being trapped between her, Gersten and Grigor, all of them predators. She had loitered around Stella for the best part of an evening, waiting for her to pick up the scent. In the women's washroom Sybil told her story breathlessly, sounding excited at the prospect of the trap while trying to create the right atmosphere of intimacy.

'You have such beautiful clothes.'

She played the same game with Grigor, letting him kiss her, saying they had to be prepared like hardened professionals. 'Later,' she promised.

In a world of such shifting alliances, she sided with whomever she was with. She suspected Gersten would kill her if he learned she was about to betray Stella. She suspected Gersten would kill her anyway, given half a chance. She was smart enough to see she was offering Stella to Grigor as a substitute for herself. Stella she had to pretend to fall a little bit in love with, blanking Lore from her mind.

Gersten was hardest. She told him Grigor was susceptible.

'Let's play the long game. I am rather enjoying the idea of my little agent in an act of deep penetration.'

The occasion was another of Gersten's nocturnal visits. Gersten sat on the end of her bed, making a show of keeping his hands to himself. She suspected he was about to make his move, but he stood up and said, 'Side with him all you like but remember you have to deliver to me. Don't get out of your depth or I will push you under.'

He leaned down and pressed his palm hard against Sybil's forehead, held it there for long enough for her to see his intent, then stopped as suddenly as he had begun.

'No news of your beloved?' he asked as he strolled out.


Sybil told Stella there was a back entrance and the elderly couple upstairs were too frightened to go out much, and the wife was ill anyway.

'It's not very glamorous but they're an easy catch,' Sybil said, trying to sound casual. 'We could meet afterwards for lunch. I'm told twelve is the best time for them.'

'Who told?'

Sybil was ready for that. 'My mother. She's a fortune teller.' She gave a brittle laugh, in imitation of Stella.

'Copy me any more, darling, and you will become me.'

It was said so lightly Sybil could not tell if malice was intended.

'My mother knew these people.'

'Stop trying so hard. It will all be fine. Yes, let's meet for lunch. I'll check them out.'

They were alone in the day room. Stella was immaculately turned out as always, with hat and kid gloves. She said, 'Have you noticed how women are wearing hats less? All those terrible scarves. So unflattering.'

She checked her handbag. 'I have a better idea. Why don't

we meet at twelve and go up together. It's your catch as much as mine.'

Sybil supposed she would go early and warn Grigor to make himself scarce. Would Stella suspect?

'Better still, come with me now. Let's go window shopping. I feel we have missed out on knowing each other. We will make up for lost time. It would brighten my day to spend it together.'

Sybil had to spend the morning being chatty and vivacious as they strolled down the Ku'damm arm in arm.

Stella said, 'There's a bittersweetness to everything, don't you find, in our situation?'

Sybil agreed it could hardly be otherwise.

'Appetite for life counts, I believe. It stands to reason. We only get one chance. I am not responsible for the situation we're in but I am damned if I am going to give up on their terms. They're such monsters, some of it is bound to rub off.'

She laughed her trilling laugh, to Sybil's ears the most heartless in the world. Would she watch as Grigor flayed her? Sybil was in no doubt Stella would watch Grigor do it to her, given the chance, transmitting her sexual charge.

'What's the matter, darling? You look nervous.'

It was five to twelve. They were downstairs in the yard of Alwynd's block. Sybil pictured Grigor standing behind the door, knife ready.

Sybil said it was her first time.

'A virgin! You must go first, I insist.'

She suspected Stella had known all along. It was why she had not let her out of her sight.

'Darling, do go in first. Take my coat. It will bring you luck. And my hat. Now give me yours.'

Sybil protested it was a silly game. Stella stopped pretending, sniffing the air.

'Is that a rat I am smelling? If you don't do it, darling, I will know something is wrong.'

She still contrived to sound coquettish and beguiling.

Sybil put on the coat and hat and feared Grigor would be too fast for her to warn him. She would lie on Alwynd's floor watching her blood pool, thinking her last thoughts of Lore.

Stella pushed Sybil into leading.

She reached the first landing and turned back to see Stella's eyes glisten with excitement, willing Sybil up into the trap.

Stella followed, always waiting behind Sybil, whose messy thoughts revolved around naked survival and reluctant admiration for the simplicity and elegance of Stella's trap.

Sybil reached the top of the stairs. She turned back and looked at Stella, who said, 'Go on. Knock on the door and when there is no answer, which there won't be, try the handle because it won't be locked.'

Sybil faced the door, with her hand raised. She froze. She listened to Stella's light footsteps, was briefly aware of Stella turning the handle, followed by the force of her own weight throwing the door open as Stella pushed her in, turned and scampered downstairs laughing. She saw Grigor facing her, his arms raised. She supposed a split second of recognition stopped him from pulling the trigger. She hadn't imagined a gun or silencer.

She felt foolish and afraid, dressed in Stella's coat and hat. She sank to the floor weeping. She would have to go back to Grosse Hamburger Strasse and brazen it out with Stella, who would inform Gersten, who would throw her to the wolves. And Grigor would suspect her of double-crossing him, however much she might protest.

Grigor meanwhile was putting himself in a position to console her, taking her in his arms, faking concern, using the fact of near death to turn one thing into another. Sybil went limp, too defeated to resist. He surprised her by taking her more tenderly than she was expecting. It was just fucking, she told herself, that old animal instinct to preserve life. She stared at the ceiling, imaging herself looking down on the unfortunate wretch lying like dead meat under the thrusting man.

# 50

Schlegel, abruptly woken in the middle of the night, groggily tried to put his shoes on and was ordered not to by two guards shouting, 'Get up! Quick!' They frog-marched him down the corridor. Everything done at the double, being made to go shoeless – it could only end with being hustled onto the hanging trapdoor, the noose slid over his neck and the lever pulled, all within seconds, and being conscious still, after hearing the terrible snap of his neck, as his legs bicycled uselessly in the air. They marched him down endless flights of stairs until deep underground and shoved him through a door, which shut behind him.

It was dark in the space. He couldn't tell how large. He sensed another presence. He stood still, trying to breathe silently.

'There is something you should see.'

Gersten's voice came out of the dark. He flipped a switch and in front of them lit up. They were in a viewing gallery like a trench and beyond the glass screen was what looked like a huge, empty aquarium, harshly lit. Sand on the floor contributed to the impression of a fish tank. The far end was covered with old doors, much splintered. Sandbags covered the sides of the space. A narrow set of rails ran down one edge, at the end of which stood a large trolley. Schlegel supposed they were in a deep pocket of silence where all noise went unheard.

He didn't notice a functioning door to one side until it opened. After a long pause a spindly, broken figure, wearing only a tatty vest with long johns, his face horribly smashed, was thrust blinking into the light. He cowered where he stood, staring myopically and wringing his handcuffed hands. That he was barefoot alarmed Schlegel, making him think he must be next.

It was Lazarenko, almost unrecognisable without his glasses and for being so beaten.

Gersten wore Lazarenko's coat like a trophy.

Lazarenko opened his mouth to let out a wail or shout in defiance – it was impossible to tell as the range was sound-proofed – then the force of the bullets spun him round and the shooting seemed to go on and on, its sound carrying only as a vibration. Lazarenko stood pinned against the splintering doors, twitching and jerking like a man with St Vitus's dance his underwear soaked red, a broken artery in his arm pumping like a hose to form a clotted puddle in the sand, and all the while the head jumped up and down in what looked like vigorous agreement.

They were machine-gunning him. As his remains slid down the wall, the gunner stitched a line up his torso, reaching the head, which exploded. Lazarenko pitched forward, rolled over, gave a huge convulsion, then abruptly sat up as if levered on a hinge, until another round of bullets hammered him back down.

Gersten said, 'You can go now.'

Again Schlegel was woken from the bleak sleep of defeat by the same guards. This time he was allowed to put on his shoes and he was taken without handcuffs. He decided his turn must have come. Gersten had laid down his cards. Nothing was left, other than for Gersten to enjoy his moment.

Instead Schlegel found himself being taken up and led down normal corridors which ended in the building's reception area.

The pillared marble hall was a quiet empty space with smart men standing around. Schlegel was astonished to see Morgen among them, next to a scowling Gersten. Morgen was back in uniform, accompanied by two young equally impassive men, also in black. He looked older and severer, his face a mask of haughty authority.

Gersten, protesting, said, 'He's mine.'

Morgen said, 'I have the wherewithal to re-arrest this man.'

'On what charges?'

'Corruption. Selling confiscated property for personal gain.'

'The lesser charge, you will find.'

Morgen produced an order and presented it peremptorily to Gersten, who flicked it back and walked off.

Morgen appeared no friendlier with Gersten gone. He nodded at one of the underlings, who stepped forward and snapped a handcuff on Schlegel's wrist.

The angry march of Gersten's departure rang down the corridor.

Outside a car was waiting, with a driver. Morgen sat in front, saying nothing and lighting up. Schlegel sat squashed between the two men, who were not generous with their space.

Schlegel watched the passing city and craved ice cream of all things. How depressed everything looked, as though he was seeing it with other eyes for the first time. He supposed he was facing three years' hard labour. Stoffel had been right. Morgen was not to be trusted.

Ten minutes later, Gersten was fucking Stella Kübler, hard from behind. As he did, he was as admiring of Lazarenko's coat, which he kept on, as he was of her magnificent arse. Stella was spread face down across his desk, gripping its edges. Her hot breath misted the brass inkstand in front of her. Gersten liked that detail and filed it for later. His mood improved. He had wanted to hike up her skirt but she didn't let him, saying it would crease, and had taken it off instead, then performed a slow striptease of rolling down her stockings while feeling him up. He couldn't be bothered to argue, just as he didn't care if she was faking her orgasm, wanting only his own immediate relief. He stared at the fleshy whiteness of her hips as she ground them faster, and started to buck under him, moaning. He kept up the scything motion as he came, gripping her neck, calling her a Jewish cunt, which she responded to with a throaty laugh, whether in accord or at him he could not tell. She hadn't let him kiss her, in order not to spoil her make-up. The last time he had squashed her face in one hand and smeared off the lipstick with the thumb of his other and made her suck him, for the only time because he was nervous she would bite off his cock. He told Stella how he had once stuck a gun up a woman's arse as he fucked her and pulled the trigger and the convulsion gave him the most spectacular orgasm of his life. She didn't believe him but made a show of enjoying his stories, running her tongue round her lips. Gersten suspected such lascivious depravity was her way of keeping him interested and herself alive. She was never wet when he started fucking her.

Afterwards they sat in opposite armchairs and Stella told him about Sybil's deception.

'Have her beaten up. Join in yourself. You'll enjoy it. She won't hang around. It will set her off running back to Grigor. If she turns up in a bad way he will be more inclined to believe her.'

The car came to a stop. Morgen told the men to take off Schlegel's handcuff. The one on the pavement side took his time getting out and gave Schlegel a look of amused contempt.

Morgen said, 'Thanks, boys,' then addressed Schlegel. 'Not easy to get you out of the holes you dig yourself into.'

Schlegel never could have guessed their destination. They were at the bar with the green door.

Another surprise inside; Morgen said to the barman, 'Give the man back his hat.'

It was produced from under the counter. Morgen said nothing. Schlegel fingered the brim, feeling careless and ashamed. He hoped Morgen would not lecture him about taking responsibility.

Morgen wasn't drinking and asked for tonic water with Angostura bitters.

The barman observed there was alcohol in the bitters. Morgen said, 'You can't call that drinking, not really. Give our friend a beer. He's allowed only the one as he has been ill.'

Morgen never said where he had been. When Schlegel had failed to show for the third day, Morgen said, 'I even asked your mother.'

Not him too, thought Schlegel, added to her conquests.

'Day four, it was clear you were dead or arrested. You weren't among the dead but you turned up on the Gestapo arrest list as Unidentified Man, Paperless.'

Morgen drained his bitters. 'Next time hold on to your hat, Schlegel.'

Everyone ignored Sybil being beaten up in the common room of Grosse Hamburger Strasse, to the extent of a foursome continuing to play the table-tennis game known as Around the World, which required them to run from end to end.

They had set into her without warning. She was sitting reading a magazine, hoping to bluff it out, when Stella breezed in, waved cheerfully, and looked on in thrilled expectation as Sybil was pulled to her feet by a thin man with a wiry frame, much stronger than he looked, and reputed to be one of Stella's lovers.

He held Sybil at arm's length and drove his fist into her solar plexus. As she lay doubled-up on the floor, Stella kicked her winded stomach. When Sybil tried assuming a foetal position they attacked her back and kidneys, which became the focus of even more intense pain. Sybil couldn't tell which of them was dishing it out. She suspected Stella mostly, with the occasional sharper, harder blow from the man. And all the while the clack-clack of the table-tennis ball back and forth.

They prised her apart. Her legs were held so Stella could straddle her, pinning her down, and beat her around the head. She took off her shoe and grunted with satisfaction as she landed each blow. Sybil refused to give the woman the pleasure of seeing her terror. Her eye started to close. Stella called her a cunt, over and over, and ordered her to look at her. Sybil refused and told her instead that she stank of sex. This set Stella into a greater frenzy until the man had to pull her off.

Stella paused to lean down to spit in Sybil's face, and hiss spitefully, 'Your bitch is dead!'

After they left, Sybil lay listening to them continuing to play Around the World. No one came to help. Stella's authority prevailed. Sybil guessed she had a spy in the room. She heard the rustle of a page of a magazine being turned. Her head hurt unspeakably, as though her brain had been knocked loose.

With nowhere else to go, she returned to Grigor's cinema, and sat down at the front again where it was less crowded. The same bathing-costumed young women frolicked in the sand. Sybil supposed she passed out rather than fell asleep. She was woken by a man groping her and snapped that she had syphilis, but please carry on. The man jumped up and was gone.

She struggled to the back of the cinema and using up the last of her strength hauled herself up the outside staircase to the projection booth. She was rehearsing how to present herself to Grigor when she was shocked to find another man in the booth, much older, and worldly enough to accept her appearance without comment.

He pointed to a chair and silently went about rewinding the reels, then dressed her wounds with alcohol, which stung, continuing to say nothing. When he was finished he told her she didn't need a hospital.

Sybil asked if she could stay, she had nowhere else. The man said he would have to lock her in. The cinema closed at two and reopened the next day at ten.

She suspected he knew she was there for Grigor.

The next morning Grigor came and asked why had she come back.

Because she had nowhere else.

He didn't seem surprised by the state of her, except to ask what had happened.

Sybil said it only made her want to kill Stella more.

'What else can I say? That it's me that wants to be killed and would you please be quick about it?'

He took an aggressive step forward, as though she were undermining him.

'My survival no longer matters. The person I love is gone. I wish only to get even with Kübler and deny Gersten the pleasure of killing me. After that you can do what you want.'

Grigor kept her in a dark bare lockup garage under railway arches, with only a mattress. He came and went as he pleased. He tied her up, either before he left or when he came back, and it seemed more to do with mind games than security. Sometimes he kept her bound while they ate and spooned food into her mouth. Sometimes he gagged her. More often he used a blindfold, even though he left her in the dark. He told her she could scream as much as she liked. No one would hear.

On the third day he let her out to hunt Stella Kübler, first bandaging her head so she couldn't see where he was taking her. He escorted her through the streets, guiding her with solicitous concern, a companion to her blindness.

The first day she missed her footing, causing her to cry out. From the sound alone, crossing big streets became terrifying. At last he told her she could sit and guided her onto a bench. She supposed they were in a park. The city noises had receded.

'Count slowly to five hundred before taking off the bandage. Memorise where you are and return to this exact spot by five. You have eight hours. If you don't come back I will hunt you down.'

She loitered in the part of town where Stella operated and went to the same cafés. The Richler. The Wintergarten. Café Möhring. Stella passed through them all at least once a day.

She found her in the Richler having tea with the man who had helped beat her up. Stella's eyes involuntarily lit up on seeing her before showing their hatred. Sybil kept up the pretence, like they were friends from the old days, saying they must all get together. She enjoyed watching Stella unnerved, confronted with her own method. It was how she did her catching, always using the softest friendly approach.

Stella appeared mortified that anyone would dare challenge her. The man frowned, embarrassed, as Sybil pointed to her bruises.

Sybil addressed the room and said, 'You better watch out. This bit of blonde poison is a Jew, so is her friend.'

She turned and marched out.

Sybil so relished Stella's recoil she continued to stalk her and that afternoon confronted her again, this time in Kranzler's where she was alone.

Sybil sat down at the same table and ordered tea. Stella didn't leave, unwilling to cause a scene, and Sybil saw what a scuttling, shifty little figure she really was.

She sat staring at Stella, saying nothing, other than she was next, which was the sort of thing girls said to each other in school, but it seemed to have the desired effect. She said Grigor was coming to flay her and enjoyed her moment as Stella fled to the toilet.

After her day out, and swearing she would never go back, Sybil returned to the bench in Treptower Park because she could see no other way of keeping Grigor within reach.

Grigor came after half an hour and made her put the bandage back on.

In her endless hours alone, Sybil spent a long time thinking about Grigor's perceived power and her weakness, and decided she might yet gain the upper hand. She wheedled and cajoled him into using his forgery skills to prepare a death sentence for Stella in the name of the German people. She suggested using an official form from a district court. She could see such a campaign of terror appealed to him.

Sybil came to luxuriate in the possibility of revenge. It was all she had left.

Copies of the death sentence were sent by registered post to Stella at Grosse Hamburger Strasse and Gersten at Gestapo headquarters. Part of her knew this persecution made her like them, driven by irrational hatred, but she didn't care and would not relent, however much Stella's boasting about Lore now sounded like a shoddy fantasy.

Grigor told her Gersten had confined everyone to quarters,

for fear of losing his agents. It was the only piece of information he volunteered. Sometimes in the night Sybil woke to find him on top of her, a process so impersonal it might well not be happening.

'I could beat your pretty little face even more black and blue,' Gersten said.

He chucked Sybil under the chin, then leaned in as if to kiss.

'The trouble you cause. Kübler is up in arms. Was that death threat your business?'

Sybil smiled for an answer.

'Do you know what I think? It's a power struggle. You want to take over Stella's role, be queen bee. And you can, with my complete backing.'

Not true, but clever of him to point it out.

'I am your best bet. But time is running out, so make up your mind. You're thinking: him or the other one. And can I fix that bitch too. She told me how turned on she got beating you up. As it is, you are walking the plank. Jump with Grigor or come back to me? My offer stands. Give me Grigor and my largesse knows no bounds.'

'He fetches me from a bench in Treptower Park.'

Except that evening he didn't.

Sybil sensed Gersten's people lurking in bushes and behind trees, growing bored and giving up.

She supposed they waited until the park closed then all trooped out.

Left with nowhere to go herself, she followed the path of the railway to try to work out where Grigor was keeping her.

She walked until she was grabbed from behind. She knew him by his smell.

He didn't kill her for her betrayal, as seemed inevitable, but savagely blindfolded her and dragged her back to the lockup.

He cross-examined her about where she had been and so on, roughed her up, trying to force her to say.

Sybil refused and said, 'Do what you like. I don't care. Just get on with it.'

Grigor stopped and she realised he wasn't going to kill her after all, because he had grown dependent on her in some sick way.

# 51

Morgen worked at a whirlwind pace, twice as fast as if he had still been on Pervitin. They drove out to the SS Ahnenerbe scientific research centre in Dahlem where Lampe was being held for what was quaintly called observation. Morgen explained on the way that he had fixed the trip on the quiet through his brother Theodore, who worked there.

'We don't really get on, though I should be more grateful, because Theo fixed my membership with the Foreign Press Club.'

Theodore Morgen turned out to be a more compact version of his brother, so much so that Schlegel couldn't resist asking were they twins, to which they snapped in unison, certainly not. Theodore was quick to add he was the elder.

He wore a double-breasted waistcoat with mother-of-pearl buttons and smoked as much as his brother, with the same habit of switching sides with each drag. He took them to his office with a library of rare and exotic books. He told Schlegel he was employed as a Tibetan scholar but the place was like working in a mausoleum.

'Are you the young man who loses his hat? Ever been to Tibet?'

He made it sound as commonplace as Hamburg or Kiel.

'Your man is being brought downstairs now. It'll be about five minutes. They're tickled pink to have him.'

Schlegel found the brothers like a warped adult version of the Max and Moritz cartoon.

Morgen smoked by the window while his brother proceeded to lecture Schlegel.

'I do have scholastic training, but the institution is interested only in a combination of new-age rubbish, historical fantasy, bogus science, pseudo-research and neo-paganism. The place is staffed with opportunists—'

Morgen interrupted to ask if Theo was talking about himself again.

Theo hissed at Schlegel, 'Tell him to do something useful with his judicial powers, like sending himself to prison.'

The brothers' rivalry was like static. God only knew what their childhood had been like, thought Schlegel.

Theo went on, 'We have progressed from dotty scholarship and exotic field trips to conducting freezing tests to see how much cold the body can endure, using humans as guinea pigs, where revival methods include coital tests done to flatter Himmler's belief in the magical powers of body heat, and his theory that contact between the sexes provides the transmission of a vital force from the stronger to the weaker.'

'Does it work?' asked Morgen.

Theo snapped, 'See what I mean? The flippancy. No, it doesn't. Obviously.'

'Come on,' said Morgen, tetchy. 'We don't have time to stand around all day.'

Axel Lampe was heavily sedated, to the point of drooling. Any previous talkative self was replaced by muteness. The pudding-basin haircut had gone, his skull shaved to the bone.

'It must be pretty dim in there, Axel,' Morgen said. 'Let's play a game my way. I ask the question. You don't have to answer. Instead I hold up a finger. One finger for yes and two for no. Just nod or shake your head. First question, is Stoffel an arsehole?'

Lampe looked uninterested but eventually nodded at the single finger.

'A yes. Next question, did you kill those people Stoffel said you did?'

Lampe stared at the single digit, looking stupid. Morgen held up two fingers and Lampe immediately nodded. A no.

'And did you steal the money from the printers?'

Lampe hadn't the faintest idea what they were talking about, even when they explained to the point of exhaustion.

Morgen stood up and said, 'It's important to remind ourselves of what the system is capable.'

They discovered the first flayed body in the cattle wagon had in fact been referred on from the city pathology department to the Jewish hospital at Iranische Strasse, on grounds of backlog and lack of staff.

The arrangement was quite common, according to Lipchitz, the Jewish pathologist they talked to. He implied most unidentified bodies ended up with him because the city department was lazy.

'Even with a case of homicide?' asked Morgen.

'Someone must have made the decision the flayed bodies were Jewish, though how he could tell I have no idea.'

Schlegel could not identify the guttural accent. Lipchitz was a careworn, elderly man, who wore pince-nez and a grubby white coat. He was grateful for Morgen's offer of a cigarette, taken with unsteady hands. His office was like a laboratory, half-tiled and with gas jets, but so cold he wore an overcoat under his overall.

Personal curiosity had led him to conduct a proper autopsy. No one had been chasing for the report.

'Don't you always?' asked Morgen. 'Aren't there professional standards?'

'I can conclude what I like, for all anyone cares in this king-dom of death.' He studied Morgen, calculating. 'You look all right to me, so I will tell you that your lot are obsessed with paperwork that no one reads. I did both bodies, for what it's worth.'

'Would you say they were the work of a single hand?'

'I would say.'

'Based on what?'

'For all the show of artistry, I would venture the man isn't a very good butcher.'

'And?'

'The first showed signs of having been kept on ice, by the way. The other not.'

'As in frozen?'

'Yes, kept on ice.'

'What's the sense in that?'

Lipchitz shrugged. 'What's the sense in anything? I don't mean to be facetious.'

The man's skin was grey from exhaustion. Rings of tiredness under his eyes looked like bruises.

'Was it the flaying that killed them?' asked Morgen.

'I can't say. As a victim you would rather be dead first, because death can last hours, even days, in cases of being flayed alive.'

He knew of no modern examples but there were historical precedents. The Neo-Assyrian tradition was for flaying alive. The Aztecs skinned victims of human sacrifice after death.

'Yes,' said Morgen. 'I have been somewhere recently where there was talk of human lampshades.'

Schlegel looked at the man. What could he mean? It was the closest Morgen had come to admitting his recent absence was another assignment.

Lipchitz had also done the autopsies on Abbas and the unidentified woman.

'Where are the reports on those?' asked Morgen.

Lipchitz said he had been asked to forward them to the city pathology department.

'Though they were Jews?'

'No rhyme or reason.'

Morgen asked for Lipchitz's report copies. The man was organised and had them to hand. Morgen studied them and looked up, puzzled.

'The report says the autopsies were conducted by the city department. It's even written on their forms.'

Lipchitz said quietly, 'That's the way they like it.'

'So they subcontract to you and you make it look like it was done by them.'

'It's about quotas and bonuses.'

'They pad their figures with your numbers?' asked Morgen, astonished.

'When they can make our dead count for something.' He smiled coldly. 'We are more valuable to them that way.'

Morgen asked if there was a possible connection between the two types of killing.

'Show versus obliteration. Part of the same coin. Both obviously forms of display. As polar opposites they ought to be the work of different twisted minds, but these days . . . they could be the product of a schizophrenia.'

A killer driven to extremes, thought Schlegel, both forms involving exhibition.

Lipchitz looked at what was left of his cigarette, which he had managed to keep going by letting it burn out and relighting.

'The hour is getting late. I don't care any longer, but do you mind if I ask if you do?'

Morgen said, 'We wouldn't be here if we didn't.'

Lipchitz asked if he had been educated by Jesuits. No, said Morgen.

'Such casuistry,' murmured Lipchitz. 'I was interested in the insistence on utter erasure, beyond anything that would render the flayed corpse identifiable. I'd never heard of such a thing in a so-called civilised society and with this flaying I wonder if we haven't arrived at something where what's done to the body is more important than the actual killing.'

'You mean like dead meat?' asked Schlegel.

Lipchitz looked at him properly for the first time and said yes, exactly.

'I presume the preparation of the bodies in this manner is for symbolic reasons rather than actual consumption, but among natives in Brazil eating your enemy becomes part of a cycle of vengeance. In this cycle one consumes the enemy, and is later consumed by the enemy, dying at his hands, precisely to bring vengeance into being, and so bring about a future.'

'What does that tell us, other than about future vengeance?' asked Morgen, interested.

The man looked desolate. 'You ask me? There are so many things that are in the process of being obliterated. All I can suppose is it is a reflection of the larger viciousness.'

Morgen clicked his heels and formally addressed the man. 'My dear doctor, our appetite for the epic and the trite knows no bounds. Those in thrall – and I include myself up to a point – fooled ourselves we were being offered a narcotic sense of historical destiny, absolved of all responsibility.'

'No,' said Lipchitz. 'Any Jew will tell you there is always a price to pay.'

Gersten, they discovered, was no longer available for questioning, being away on a course in Baden-Baden.

They wasted the best part of a day looking for a freezer in the slaughterhouse. They dismissed the huge ice factory as too public and conspicuous. Compared to the rest of the site, it appeared as busy as a stock exchange.

Otherwise each animal section had its own cold-storage facilities, but the freezer sections had been decommissioned. They were told this by Baumgarten, whose slow and uncomprehending manner became more questionable with each acquaintance.

With such widespread meat shortages there was no reserve to freeze, certainly not in the case of the pig section. Only one cool room remained in use, located next to the slaughterhouse, by the railway siding. Entrance was by enormous thick steel doors. Inside was a gigantic vault, cold enough to make their breath visible.

The state of supply was evident from the empty hooks and only a handful of carcasses hanging.

Morgen asked, 'What of Nöthling's pigs?'

'We didn't deal with them,' said Baumgarten.

'Not what I asked.'

Nöthling had brought in his own team.

As to where a frozen body might have been kept – or the existence of any temporary morgue – Baumgarten made a good show of being clueless. He emphasised the enormity of the area. Only about a quarter was currently in use.

Schlegel wondered if Baumgarten's huge hands had been responsible for Keleman's murder, but there was no motive or evidence, other than the man living with death every day.

Morgen asked to be shown the freezer room. The supply was switched off, as Baumgarten had said. The trenches were empty and unfrozen.

Morgen decided they should go and talk to Herr Nöthling about his pigs. Schlegel wondered if his mother still kept an account, and how toward was her use of ration cards.

Baumgarten seemed pleased by their wasted effort.

\*     \*     \*

Schlegel expected them to go back to headquarters and take Stoffel's Opel as usual. Morgen said he couldn't be bothered.

They passed above the chambers and paths of the slaughter yards, along the seemingly endless pedestrian bridge, a windowless passageway known as the Long Sorrow that carried them over to Zentralviehhof station. There they caught the S-Bahn, skirting the south-east of the city, past Treptower Park. Another day of overcast skies, the belching smoke of factory chimneys practically indistinguishable.

What was this talk of lampshades? Schlegel asked.

Morgen stared for a long time before saying instead, 'Maybe the bodies were frozen elsewhere.'

After Schöneberg they had the carriage to themselves and Morgen came closest to admitting what had been preoccupying him.

'I joined the SS Judiciary partly because it offered a swifter rate of advance than its civilian counterpart. I thought stability and order would lead us out of the mire of the twenties. But what I feared about too much power becoming invested in one man has come to pass. He has no military experience, apart from his time as a corporal runner in the war, and at the last count monopolises no fewer than seventy state functions. No wonder we are paralysed.'

Schlossstrasse was a major shopping area in the affluent suburb of Steglitz, catering for the wealthy neighbourhoods of Lichterfelde and Dahlem, a boulevard with trams and broad pavements. Substantial Wilhelmine buildings, castle-like apartments and public halls with imposing facades of rusticated stone, spoke of unassailable prosperity. It was a street down which uniformed nannies still pushed prams and leisured women met in tea rooms.

Nöthling's store had an impressive double frontage, with his name written in enormous letters above. The old pillared entrance was flanked by two large modern picture windows, filled with an artful display of harvest baskets and produce boxes, which Schlegel suspected were empty.

Morgen asked, 'How would you describe this place?'

'A delicatessen, I suppose.'

'Is that enough? I am sure Nöthling considers it an emporium and himself a purveyor of fine goods. I feel hungry just looking.'

Schlegel couldn't remember when he had last eaten a decent meal, other than at his mother's, and even she complained. Whatever she lacked, there was little shortage of meat, and he wondered about her supplier. Pork, beef, chicken, game. Once she had put her knife and fork down and announced, 'This meat tastes like horse,' to which he asked, 'How do you know what horse tastes like?' which shut her up.

The shop was large, clean and well-presented, presided over by female assistants, young and elderly, neat in white grocers' coats and caps. The cashier sat in a booth of her own. Marble countertops matched the floor, and looked expensive, as did the fearsome meat slicer. Nothing had been spared to convey an atmosphere of quiet ostentation, but in keeping with the times the shelves were understocked. Homemade jam was for sale. Morgen whistled at the price.

He asked for ham. They had run out. More would be in tomorrow, they hoped. The same with everything. The daily supply sold out early.

Morgen asked for Nöthling. He gave his name and rank. One of the counter girls addressed the cashier, who spoke to Nöthling on an intercom and a minute later the man emerged, preceded by the smell of expensive aftershave, rubbing his hands with bonhomie and professional concern.

He bore little resemblance to the traditional shopkeeper. His clean looks and antiseptic air made him appear more like a scientist, as though shopping were a modern discipline. Unlike the women in their white coats his was blue, under which he wore an expensive suit. His shoes were well-heeled. Schlegel thought them handmade.

Nöthling was manners itself, leading them into a back office, done out as smartly as the front, with armchairs, an Oriental rug and a huge rosewood desk whose size reminded Schlegel of criminal masterminds in old films, unlike the man, who sounded about as engaged as a speak-your-weight machine.

Nöthling's brown hair was brilliantined, parted, worn short at the back and sides, with a cowlick at the front. His expression was guileless. Schlegel wondered how he had avoided the army.

He denied knowing anyone from the tax office called Keleman; his books were in order.

'Tell us about your pigs,' said Morgen.

Nöthling pointed to himself and assumed an expression of surprise.

Morgen said, 'We are bound to ask whether the import of pigs is a criminal business.'

'Of course not! I have the paperwork.'

'We would expect nothing less.'

'They come from Sweden. Keleman, you say?' He shook his head again.

'Can we import from neutral countries?'

'There's nothing illegal about it.'

'Swedish pigs?' asked Morgen as though he didn't quite believe it.

Schlegel asked if Nöthling had unloaded anything else from the train.

'Human cargo?' he prompted.

Nöthling blustered.

Morgen said, 'A grocer with fingers in a lot of pies.'

He stood with his hands thrust in his pockets, looking suddenly miserable. Pigs were the bane of his life, he confessed. Food in general, but pigs in particular, as he was expected to provide according to previous standards.

'How much do you know about pigs?'

Morgen said he knew about dead ones, having eaten them, not so much about when they were alive, except they were not stupid.

'They're not unlike us. They eat the same. They are not a grazing animal, like cattle and sheep, which means they compete with us in the food chain. Two years ago, the cereal crop that was their staple diet failed. So they had to be fed potatoes, which in a wartime economy is our standard diet. It caused rationing to be introduced, to allow enough for the pigs.'

'And after that the market became harder,' suggested Morgen.

'For some. I had an employee transferred to the catering corps who was able to arrange regular transports of livestock from the Ukraine.'

He also had a brother who was a pig breeder in East Prussia.

'Fat, healthy stock and no complaints until the herd was decimated by swine fever.'

'And beef and mutton?' asked Morgen.

'The same shortages, though pork is more of a national dish.'

'Yes, I suppose. A civilised animal, not nomadic. Principles of husbandry and tenure.'

'You are right!' replied Nöthling, apparently enthused. 'As the British have their roast beef, we expect pork. Even the humble *Schnellimbiss* requires its bratwurst. I wonder if the basis of our argument with the Jew isn't that he regards such an upstanding animal unclean. One can have a relationship with a pig in a way one never can with a cow or a sheep. Some say they are as intelligent as small children.'

Schlegel had once made the mistake of ordering chicken bratwurst from a food stand. He complained. The stall owner agreed not only was it unpopular because tasteless, it was seen as a sign of a fundamental right being taken away.

Morgen said, 'About your Swedish pigs.'

Nöthling pulled a long face. 'My wife is Swedish. Her brother sends them from his farm in Ystad. He started breeding them upon my recommendation.'

'Not happy pigs from what I am told.'

'My brother-in-law blames shortages but the truth is he is a careless farmer and he drinks from early in the morning.'

Schlegel found Nöthling slippery and impressive – the cool demeanour, the appearance of openness, his answering in an apparently honest way. The real expertise probably lay in what he chose not to reveal.

'So your clientele is eating inferior pig,' said Morgen.

'My clientele is lucky to get what it has,' answered Nöthling, showing a flash of anger that was the first sign of the pressure he might be under.

As they passed back through the shop, he asked them to wait and returned with a brown paper bag and handed it to Morgen, saying, 'Wild boar sausage. Not a bribe, gentlemen, but I would like you to appreciate the efforts to which we still go to satisfy our customers. It is hard these days to bring enjoyment into the world, but . . .'

He gave them a charming, boyish smile of embarrassment and dismissal.

The sausage came wrapped in greaseproof paper and had been sliced. They demolished it at a sitting on a bench down from the shop.

Morgen said, 'The man most likely believes he will be protected by those he serves, instead of being hung out to dry. Still, he makes an excellent sausage.'

Over the road the local branch of the Commerzbank was closing for the day.

'Come on, quick,' said Morgen, wiping greasy fingers on his trousers.

The banking hall was the usual well-appointed temple to security. Morgen was betting Nöthling banked there.

The manager appeared huffy, unused to being summoned. He was formally attired in a wing collar and morning jacket. They were closing, he said. Business was terminated for the day.

Morgen insisted they speak in private. The manager reluctantly took them to his capacious office. Morgen said they were there to inspect a client's accounts. The manager protested until Morgen threatened him.

'But I have done nothing!' he exclaimed.

'Exactly. When I asked you to do something.'

The manager pleaded client confidentiality until Morgen offered to arrest him on the spot. Schlegel knew a warrant was required but the manager conceded, inclining his head stiffly, in the way of minor authority bested.

While the manager was fetching the files, Morgen inspected the furnishings and pictures on the walls.

'Look at this.'

It was a formal group photograph of men in uniform. They wore old-fashioned spiked helmets. It was dated 1917 and identified as part of a local regiment.

'Look at the names,' said Morgen.

Schlegel read along the list until he came to 'Metzler'.

Standing on the right, one in from the end.

'Can that be him?' asked Morgen.

'Hard to say with that helmet and size of the photo.'

The manager returned with an armful of ledgers. His absence made him mindful of his authority.

'I will have to make a report on this. It is not regular.'

'As you wish,' said Morgen. The man appeared thrown.

'Metzler,' said Schlegel.

He had to be reminded.

'That was years ago. What about him?'

'He put a bullet in his head recently.'

'Why?'

They said nothing, waiting.

'Oh, I see,' the manager eventually managed.

'Did being a Jew make a difference? In the good old days,' asked Morgen.

'All that mattered was whether you were a good soldier.'

Morgen was curious. 'Was he?'

'Drilled. Disciplined. Brave.'

Schlegel produced Metzler's medal, surprised he was still carrying it. The manager inspected it as if he couldn't quite believe what he was looking at. Morgen studied the photograph again and pointed out that the manager was an officer.

'Metzler wasn't?'

'Later. He worked his way through the ranks.'

Metzler was the best shot in the regiment.

'He won many shooting competitions. He was a sniper. He would spend days in the field alone. Usually they worked in pairs.'

'Because he couldn't find a partner?' asked Morgen.

'He preferred it that way. I used to see him go off at dusk. He could be gone three or four days then I would see him return at first light.'

The manager stopped, confused. Schlegel suspected that for a man of such professional impartiality any personal observation was almost never ventured.

'Did you know him after the war?'

'Only through regimental dinners. The regiment was disbanded but they kept the dinners going for ten years. Metzler came for a while, then stopped from what I remember. He was known as Dead-eye.'

'Because of what he could hit?'

'One day in the trenches he was using the periscope to scan enemy lines. It was sweltering and we were in shirtsleeves. He was smoking a cigarette and said to me, "Hold that," picked up his rifle, stood on the platform, stuck his head above the trench – which was dangerous because you could get shot back – lined up his sights, fired, stood down, placed his rifle, asked for his cigarette and said that had put Tommy's lights out. The whole episode took perhaps three seconds. I asked where he had hit the man. He smiled and pointed to the bridge of his nose. I congratulated him and he looked annoyed and said he had been aiming for the eye.'

The manager seemed no longer sure who he was. The pedantic figure of authority had briefly revealed himself, before reverting to type by insisting as the bank's custodian he was bound to state what they were doing was highly irregular.

Schlegel said, 'Metzler didn't miss when it came to shooting the warden through the eye.'

The manager looked uncomprehending.

'He must have had good reason,' he said after Schlegel explained.

'What do you mean?'

'In spite of what I have told you, he was reluctant to take up arms. The only time I heard him offer anything close to a confidence, he said, "The rifle makes me." I asked what that meant and he said he didn't like what guns did to him, but a gun in his hand became the perfect extension of himself. Metzler always was complicated. The rest of us were simple soldiers. We obeyed orders and complained about the command and the food and just about everything else.'

They inspected the ledgers. Nöthling's staff wages were paid in cash, drawn on a Friday. Cheques were paid to suppliers and received from clients.

'An impressive clientele,' said Morgen. He asked if the manager had an account with Nöthling. Seeing where that might be going, he replied that all such business was left to his wife.

Morgen finally shut the ledger and said, 'The marching columns of numbers broadly confirm what we know. Herr Nöthling appears transparent in banking terms. We suspect anyway his misdemeanours take place off the books.'

Schlegel was inspecting a different ledger with each entry handwritten in formal script, with black and red ink. So many figures made him dizzy.

'There's a payment in on the fifth of every month.'

Always for 5,000 marks. The ledger listed the payer on each occasion as 'Konto 5', and the amount as recompense for expenses.

'What expenses?' asked Morgen, adjusting his spectacles. 'Nöthling is the trader. You would expect him to be the one paying out.'

The manager had gone very quiet.

'Will you tell us what Konto five is?'

The man visibly shrank. 'I couldn't possibly say.'

'Not even if we offered you boarding arrangements at head-quarters for the foreseeable future?'

He still refused.

Morgen appeared unbothered. He would ask Nöthling instead. The manager let out a wail and said Morgen had promised.

Morgen replied he had decided he wasn't so principled after all.

They found Nöthling still in the shop, now serving behind the counter.

Morgen walked straight through to the back telling him to follow.

Nöthling was outraged when they told him about inspecting his statements. He invoked the law and Morgen shouted, 'I am the law!'

Undeterred, Nöthling threatened them with the top end of his client list.

Morgen said he could call whomever he liked, after he told them what Konto five was.

Nöthling paled at its mention, more nervous than the bank manager. They would get nowhere by asking.

'Are you telling us you don't know?' asked Morgen.

'It is not for me to say, and if you find the right people with whom to take up the matter you will be out of your depth.'

The smooth manner was gone. Nöthling's lips were flecked with spittle.

Morgen said, 'Five thousand a month is a lot of money when you think of what a regular fighting soldier gets.'

Schlegel thought about the world getting smaller. Its daily unfolding now seemed to depend on unsuspected connections, as though ruled by deeper assignment rather than chance.

At headquarters they found several messages from Nebe, demanding an immediate appearance. They were shown straight into his office, where he was pacing.

Another flayed body had been found, on the banks of the Spree. The area had been cordoned off and a guard mounted.

'Get down there now and sort it out. No doctor. No photographer. No autopsy. Get rid of it.'

The body was to be delivered not to the hospital but straight to a local animal crematorium and Morgen and Schlegel were responsible for co-ordinating its collection for delivery to its incinerators.

'And any future ones,' Nebe added ominously before proceeding to address them in the manner of the newly converted, subscribing to what had previously been dismissed. Lazarenko's theory had been absorbed and endorsed, and Nebe regurgitated the latest version as if it were his own.

Fear was being expressed of a persistent Judeo-Bolshevik link operating in the heart of the city, as a result of contamination from the east. Malignant elements were operating within the huge underclass of zombie slaves that now inhabited Berlin.

Since Goebbels' screening of *I Walked with a Zombie* it had become the latest watchword among the upper echelons.

Morgen took a photographer anyway. A tent had been erected around the body. At the top of the bank, the incinerator company's van waited rather than the usual ambulance. Nebe had insisted on no paperwork.

Morgen did little more than glance at the body, and left Schlegel with the option of not looking. Schlegel stared at the black river gleaming, thinking how these killings had become their own dirty secret. No Stoffel. No Gersten or Lazarenko now. Just a nervous patrol of junior police who had been ordered to keep their traps shut.

Morgen appeared like a man in a trance, mumbling to himself, smoking furiously. He reminded Schlegel of people talking in strange tongues.

The corpse was taken away covered with a tarpaulin. The tent went. The photographer came over and Morgen became normal, asking if he had his own darkroom.

'Don't put them through the police lab, and give them to me in person afterwards, with the negatives.'

Morgen dismissed him and said to Schlegel, 'Walk with me.'

It was just light enough to see. Morgen talked at such speed that he appeared barely in control of his thoughts. Most of his fizzing monologue went straight over Schlegel's head.

Morgen seemed to understand as much himself. He stopped suddenly and said they should climb the bank and walk back along the road.

Once on even ground he said, 'The dog eats its own tail in the system we have created. A state of super-vigilance has to be maintained. With the Jews nearly gone that fear has to relocate.'

He pointed to the last of the city skyline and said nearly all the men are away now, leaving the bulk of the male population consisting of aliens.

Nebe had said as much.

'It is what we always feared. The foreign presence. The racial virus. The Russians are a sullen, grumbling attendance in our midst, cowed for the moment but the beast will awake. We've had our time in the sun as divine monsters. All that's left now is this mutating state, a side effect of the war machine, which is technical, rational and scientific, in contrast to the irrationality given to inventing improbable grandiose enemies. The insecure hysteria that swept us into power was bound to reveal its dark Wagnerian heart and that implosion is starting to happen.'

He surprised Schlegel by collapsing with laughter.

'Of course, it's all true. That's the irony. The paranoia is justified for the wrong reasons. It isn't the avarice and mind games of the Jews that is our greatest threat, as they insist, but the Ivan peasant with his strapping hard-on, which he will stick up our womanhood. They were right all along, but not in the way they thought, and now they invite it on themselves because what is most feared is what is secretly desired. Their darkest fantasy is to be spread-eagled and fucked up the arse by the Ivans rather than watch them do it to our women. You may think it a matter of simple hydraulics, but never underestimate the complexity of male desire, Schlegel.'

Sybil watched Grigor watch her, seeing he suspected or could not trust her, any more than she could him. Suspicion festered. Grigor was right to be wary, because Sybil still could not decide which way to jump.

Grigor accused her of being in cahoots with the Kübler woman, however much she insisted otherwise. He accused her of working with Gersten to trap him, in which case he would have to kill her. He asked if she was Gersten's lover and didn't believe her denial. What excited Grigor most was sexual jealousy. It led her to make up stories, taunt him with suggestions of betrayal. His rages grew ecstatic. The hardening core inside her learned to interpret his beatings as loss of control and therefore weakness.

He pulled her out of the lockup, saying it was no longer safe, and forced her to come up with somewhere else. Sybil didn't know anywhere. Grigor put his hands round her throat. She hoped the act was less homicidal than an expression of deep frustration.

She knew somewhere, she said, when he relented.

The condemned house near Francis Alwynd's was still accessible, with a bit of ingenuity and from the back.

Grigor was unappreciative of the library, which was when Sybil lost all patience.

The rules changed. Grigor was gone more often than not, coming whenever he needed her. There was no question of leaving her tied up in such a place. The days offered some small respite. She finished the story about Franz Biberkopf.

Grigor always failed to make her reach her climax, which offended his vanity.

He boasted about his skills as a forger yet there was a tremor to his hands.

Sybil got him to talk about Metzler, enticing him by telling her how she spent Metzler's last night in his company.

Grigor started to talk.

Sybil repeated until it became her mantra: what you don't possess you can't destroy.

The next day she went to Gersten with the intention of telling him she wanted to be followed and the rest was up to him. But he wasn't there. They said he had gone away.

She made what she considered a rather exquisite deal with Stella Kübler, saying where Grigor could be found if she wanted to catch him. She enjoyed the resulting confusion. Maybe Stella would act but she doubted it. She appeared unsure and withdrawn.

In Gersten's absence, she phoned Schlegel. He wasn't in and she spoke to a secretary and left the address of Frau Zwicker, hoping he would work out she meant the attic.

She told Grigor the condemned house was no longer safe. Police had been sniffing around and it was time to leave. The only place left she knew of would not be secure for long, but was better than nothing. People worked downstairs so they would have to be as quiet as church mice.

The real reason to go there was because it brought her closer to the memory of Lore.

It also took Grigor into her world and nearer the surface.

They were entering the final run.

# 52

Until then Schlegel had not really considered himself part of an investigation. Rather, a series of events had resulted in dead ends. The flayed body murders were formally closed even as they went on, with he and Morgen now assigned as unofficial undertakers. Whatever the truth, it was variable. Morgen was right. The lie was the cornerstone of the edifice. Either there was no truth or it was meaningless.

He started to consider how the puzzle of Metzler might be answered not by uncovering his motives but through Sybil, the fleeing witness.

At another of his mother's Sunday parties, with an apparent sense of equilibrium restored, he told her and Nebe the story of the coincidence of finding an old photograph of Metzler in a bank manager's office of all places.

His relationship with Nebe now ran silent and deep, with no aside that afternoon of anything passing below the surface. This latest secret disposal of bodies seemed to have initiated him into a world where things were taken care of without further reference, on personal initiative, where situations could develop which Nebe could pretend to ignore while viewing Schlegel with the same free-floating anxiety with which he regarded Morgen. In other words, Nebe would make something of Schlegel then grow suspicious of his creation.

Later that afternoon his mother mentioned casually about seeming to remember quite a good painter named Metzler, and

Schlegel, thinking it a coincidence, refused to take the clue seriously.

'How were the flayed bodies selected?' asked Morgen. 'If we knew that we would have a clearer idea of what went on.'

Schlegel suggested they question the Russian who had fingered Lazarenko for Gersten.

'Shipped east.'

'By whom?'

'The paper trail starts and stops with the Department of Labour. There's an official stamp and a clerical signature by a pen pusher with no memory of signing it because that's all he does all day.'

Morgen threw up his hands. Like Schlegel he thought what they were looking for wasn't the obvious, or so obvious it was staring them in the face.

Morgen asked, 'What was it the Jewish pathologist said about paperwork?'

'That we were obsessed with it and no one read it. Metzler may have been a painter, by the way.'

'What, a house painter like Adolf?'

'A picture painter.'

'Like Adolf?'

'Better. Even my mother has heard of him.'

He was being unfair. His mother was more cultured than he was.

Morgen said, 'The record always tells, if you know where to look.'

They spent an intense period sifting through stack rooms, archives and storage warehouses on industrial estates given over to old records. They became acquainted with the General Archive for German Jews, housed next to the synagogue on

Oranienburger Strasse. They visited the Jewish picture library on Schiffbauerdamm, where Abbas had worked. There they found a small collection of photographs preserved, detailing the histories of the Jewish art school on Nürnburger Strasse and the Feige-Strassburger college of fashion and design on the Kurfürstendamm, both since closed.

Harder to find were records of admission and graduation for both. At first they were told they were lost, until one of the more helpful archivists working in Oranienburger Strasse, where the Office of Genealogical Research kept a room, told them that just because the files were missing did not mean they were lost. She came back a few hours later, in triumph, saying she had located them as being held in the stack rooms of the Gestapo office in the same street as the Jewish hospital. Schlegel elected to go, grateful for the fresh air after hours of musty rows of files and the dry smell of paper.

He was helped by a redhead with a beguiling smile, a sly way of looking up and full breasts beneath a tight woollen sweater. She led him down to the basement which contained a desk area and miles of shelves behind. He watched her ask for the files, thinking of the erotic combination of her white thighs surrounded by all that knowledge. He could reach out and touch her and knew she wouldn't mind, even with others watching. She smelled a little of sweat.

'Can I buy you a drink?' he asked later.

'I'm engaged.' She didn't sound serious about it.

They shared the laugh. She would be easy, he thought, and nice too.

Her arm tightened as she mimeographed the pages, casting her eyes upwards with her supplicant's look. She smiled as she gave him the pages. An attractively crooked tooth only added to the perfection.

*　　*　　*

Back in the office, a shroud of smoke hung in the air. Morgen was in shirtsleeves, braces loosened. He had found a black-board and easel from somewhere, as well as chalk. His diagrams and scribbling looked like a combination of cartography and higher theory.

'Paperwork returns to haunt. Everyone has a link, starting with Metzler.'

He pointed to his hieroglyphics and talked Schlegel through them.

'Metzler was a soldier and war hero, who went on to become a considerable artist. Before the last war he studied at the Berlin College of Arts and Crafts under Emil Orlik where one of his fellow students was George Grosz. Metzler's paintings were represented in the 1937 exhibition of Degenerate Art by three works, the first filed under *Revelation of the Jewish racial soul*; followed by an abstract nude in the section *Insult to German womanhood*; and a blasted wartime landscape listed among *Nature as seen by sick minds*. By such a reckoning, Metzler was lucky to have hung on to his teaching post at the Jewish school of art.'

Metzler's former profession had been listed as a teacher, but what kind of teacher it hadn't said.

'We now know among his pupils was Yakov Zorin a.k.a. Grigor and Franz Leibermann. When it came to forging money, which seems to have been Metzler's brainchild, he turned to his old students, who had already made a reputation providing false papers. I can't prove it but suspect at least three of his former students, since deported, worked in this field. There's another connection: the printer Plotkin who jumped or was pushed off the roof of the printing works from which Lampe and Abbas were supposed to have stolen the forged money. He and Metzler had previously published an avant-garde magazine.'

'How do you know?'

'There are still books that list Metzler's work. As Lipchitz said, no one bothers to read any more. Paperwork becomes a monument to itself. *Blitzen* magazine ran for two issues only, in deliberate imitation of the earlier Vorticist *Blast* magazine.'

Morgen said Schlegel's guess was as good as his. Progressive art was not something he gave any thought to.

In more practical terms, he had found several connections like railway points between the different tracks. Of these Sybil Todermann was the most important. She knew Metzler's former students; knew Metzler, although the precise nature of the relationship remained unclear; knew the man Metzler had shot; and she knew Gersten. And Sybil's lover Lore had been a student of the Irishman Alwynd, who was known to, if not acquainted with, Gersten.

Morgen turned back to the board and Metzler's other salient point, a professional one connected to the slaughterhouse.

'We presume he was known to Baumgarten. He was certainly familiar to Sepp in the steam room. He knew Gersten, of course. We move into difficult territory here.'

Schlegel sensed where they were going. Everything collided in the end.

Morgen hesitated. 'I have known about your background from the beginning. Of course I read your file. I should have said when you told me about you and Gersten.'

The man was trying to apologise and was so hopeless at it that Schlegel wished he wouldn't.

'I have no judgement to make, otherwise I would have said something sooner,' Morgen mumbled.

'Well, now I know,' mumbled Schlegel in return.

'The point is they were all there in the east at the same time. Baumgarten and the rest. Alternating between Belarus and Ukraine. The tracksuited leader of the Hitler Youth, whose name is Reitner. Sepp in the steam room. Haager who does the stunning. Even Lazarenko. The dead warden too.'

'Gersten?'

'Gersten above all. Summer of 1941, described as liaising with military intelligence; in fact, attached to a special anti-partisan unit that answered directly to Himmler.'

How did he know this, Schlegel asked.

'Paperwork.'

For all the secrecy, there was endless analysis and report, prefaced by a considerable library of military theory. Theoretical experts in counter-insurgency vied to have papers adopted; the more radical the better.

'The most extreme advocated rogue units posing as partisans to undertake what were called pseudo-atrocities.'

'To what end?'

'To justify reprisals.'

For all the roundups and shootings, Schlegel had naively believed the field intelligence was accurate. Now Morgen seemed to be saying they had been responsible for everything. He was shocked.

Morgen said yes, they created the situation that invited the response. 'Rather than sitting around waiting for it to happen.'

He knew all about it because in Lublin in 1941 he had investigated the activities of a brigade commander whose men continued to murder, rape and pillage as part of their leave activities.

'I would like to be able to say it was Gersten, but unfortunately life is not that neat.'

The commander was a convicted rapist. No one told Morgen it was a protected unit until his investigation was almost done, whereupon it was quashed. Nor had he known it consisted only of reprieved criminals who were known as the Poachers, because of the original stipulation for eligibility.

'There were several such roaming gangs.'

'Including Gersten's?'

'Including Gersten's. They had *carte blanche*.'

In spite of the gangs' autonomy, considerable thought lay behind the whole enterprise. One theory Morgen had read talked of creating states of applied lawlessness, to be seen as extensions of the primordial struggle.

'Are they secret papers?'

'No. They were openly published in military and academic journals.'

They were written with much appeal to and exploitation of myth. One spoke of the need for cruel hunters, like berserkers and werewolves of old. The strategy was to create a mental landscape conducive to rage, cruelty, courage, possession, punishment and alcohol, in order to create the most potent and destructive force.

Morgen gestured in disbelief.

'The surprise is how much thought went into everything, especially what lay beyond the pale.'

'Did the authors believe these myths or was it a way of dressing up the extreme edges?'

'I suspect the beauty was both theorists and executors came to inhabit the myth. The founding of such hunting units venturing deep into the forests of the east draws on ancient folklore, and the collective imagination – which is formed from dread – created the conditions that made such paroxysms of violence possible. Do you see where we are going with this?'

'That the flayed killings might be another unofficial version of the same imagination.'

'What if Gersten's old unit is being used again in some way we don't understand, or simply has gone rogue?'

'Operating here as though it were still there.'

'Gersten's lot were known as the Butchers, by the way.'

\*　　\*　　\*

Upon trying to visit Gersten in Baden-Baden they were told the Gestapo ran no courses in that tranquil and picturesque spa town. Morgen understood this to mean Gersten had a level of protection. Schlegel asked what they should do now.

Morgen said, 'Go back to the beginning.'

The block warden's widow was no longer orange. From the little that showed under her neat hat, her hair was now dyed a present-able colour. She looked altogether different, the slattern wife gone, her manner reformed. When Schlegel had telephoned to say they needed another statement about her husband's death she surprised him by volunteering to come to headquarters.

'As long as I don't have to see those terrible photographs of the drowned.'

Schlegel said he could meet her at the back.

He didn't recognise her at first in her hat and brown over-coat, carrying a handbag and wearing proper shoes.

Morgen was waiting upstairs. He addressed the woman formally, calling her Frau Schmeisser. She said she preferred now to be addressed by her unmarried name.

'Frau Weiss it is then,' said Morgen, all manners and holding the chair for her.

Schlegel found Morgen's manner sinisterly avuncular but the woman appeared to lap it up.

'Perhaps I can start,' Morgen prompted, 'by asking if you are anyone's informer.'

The woman laughed and said, of course, it went with the job. She looked like she hadn't enjoyed herself so much in years.

'Can I ask whose?'

'I am not supposed to say but I don't think it's terribly important.'

'Let's leave that for the moment,' said Morgen equably. 'Who were you informing on?'

'My husband mainly.'

The woman gave a shriek of laughter.

'And who did your husband inform to?'

'That flashy, long-haired cop.'

'Your husband spent time in the east, did he not, with Gersten?'

'He was a reservist policeman.'

'Why did he leave?'

'Court martial for theft.' The woman snorted. 'He was lucky to find work as a janitor after that.'

Half an hour later she reviewed her statement and said, 'That sounds right.'

The signature was surprisingly elegant.

She admitted she had been informing to the Austrian Commission, which was investigating Gersten, aware of his connection to her husband.

'They paid quite well actually.'

But that dried up when the Austrians moved on before anything of consequence happened.

The meat of her statement concentrated on the night before the roundup, starting with an argument overheard between her husband and Metzler.

'More of a blazing row really.'

She was in the kitchen when the voices next door became raised.

They were quarrelling over the warden's sexual abuse of Sybil and the warden bragged how he was going to pass her on to Gersten. The row developed a tangent when he boasted how, some nights before, he had been out all night on secret business, which he told Metzler would 'settle the hash of your Jews'.

The argument then turned to what was referred to as the accident and what the warden sneeringly referred to as other kinds of trains.

It was the first they'd heard of any accident. The widow didn't know what it meant either.

As for other trains, from what they understood, the smuggling stopped when the Austrians came, and after that Metzler was transferred, through Gersten's intervention, to a cushy job at the slaughterhouse goods yards.

Morgen said to Schlegel, 'Let's be clear. This is no time for faint-hearted speculation. In every case reality has turned out more extreme than any speculation.'

'What if Metzler transferred to his new job to replace one escape line with another?'

Morgen smoked another cigarette. They were back upstairs.

He finally said, 'We have to presume Metzler was working for Gersten.'

'As in using him?'

'Perhaps not running rings but playing him well enough.'

Morgen went to the blackboard. 'Say, for argument's sake . . .'

He wrote: *1) Gersten was persuaded or fooled by Metzler into continuing the arrangement.*

'For whatever reason,' Morgen said, chalk poised, then added: *2) Something went wrong.* 'We don't know what.'

He turned back to the board. Schlegel couldn't see what he was writing until he had finished. He read: *3) What if Metzler's transfer to the pig room was to do with whatever went wrong?*

'What if. Whatever.' Morgen threw down the chalk. 'I can tell you what I see but it doesn't answer anything!'

'What exactly do you see?'

'It's obvious, man! You don't need a crystal ball. Seismic tremors in the east. A change in historical weather. Our glorious summer of 1940 replaced by the endless winter of discontent. Austerity. A brooding city full of foreign men and too many lonely women. And now these bodies, where we have two conditions. Are you with me?'

'The conditions being?'

'Intense agitation and glee of killing.'

What was the difference in the end, Schlegel asked.

'Skinning someone alive, I would venture, comes from living with lots of bodies. What was your main impression of your time in the east?'

'Everyone's fear of what was out there. Figures lurking in empty landscapes.'

'Figments of the imagination. Exactly! Superstition. Agitation is cutting off a man's penis and dressing the corpse with money. Flaying something beyond recognition is about the pleasure of killing. I doubt if you will find Grigor is the flayer. His killings seem too directed as messages to Gersten.'

'Is the flayer one of Gersten's crew, or even Gersten himself?'

'Maybe Gersten knows. Maybe he doesn't. Maybe it is more than one of his men. From my experience of the east, they like to watch. For all that, you could argue the desire to strip the victim of all identity is a secret wish on the part of the perpetrator to embrace what he fears most.'

Schlegel wondered what Morgen feared most.

'The fear without reflects the fear within,' Morgen went on. 'Which means he will give himself away in the end. Anyway, it's very different from Metzler's day of sticking your head over the parapet for three seconds and nailing someone six hundred metres away. Simpler times.'

'And until then?'

'Nothing probably. No proof, no evidence or hope of a confession. For Gersten's lot it would be a mark of toughness and honour not to tell. Gersten is probably arranging to have himself moved on. Nebe is covering up. There's no body for Keleman. I would say the situation we are dealing with is amoebic, involving a series of splittings and doublings. We may be witnesses but it would be wrong to think we can solve anything or bring anyone to book.'

Schlegel thought of something else and paled. 'How many flayed bodies have there been?'

Morgen looked at him with incredulity. 'Come on. Three!'

'Yes, first the railway wagon, number two in Treptower Park and the third just now on the banks of the Spree. But Gersten showed me another which he said had been found in Alexanderplatz by a Polish cleaner.'

The flayed body shown by Gersten to Schlegel was no longer in the Gestapo morgue. The search warrant – a waste of time given how long it took to get – was to no avail. Morgen brought several men and they clattered about and found nothing.

A frustrated Morgen lit up in defiance of no-smoking signs. Schlegel recognised Gersten's hatchet-faced, tubercular-looking assistant when he came down to see what the fuss was about. He was expert at what was commonly known as the bureaucrat's shrug.

Nebe, Schlegel suddenly thought. What if Nebe knew what was going on and had been dragged into the cover-up? He had much to hide. His name was on Keleman's bribe list. Those charges alone would be enough to destroy him.

Was Nebe being squeezed or squeezing? Covering up on his own initiative or for someone else? Did it explain why he was so disturbed by Morgen? Schlegel now understood Keleman's fear. It was like facing a giant tidal wave about to crash down. His hands were clammy. He wished he could sit in the bar with the green door with Keleman and be a better friend.

He felt compelled to explore, to see if the place was as frightening as before. Once he had been taken to a theatrical green room as a boy, where the makeshift warrens backstage and the unpainted reverses of scenery flats reminded him of where he was now, the secret runs in marked contrast to the building's public facade. As with backstage, the illusion was threadbare, however palpable the menace. The pain in the building was the realest thing about it.

Five minutes later he might as well have been wandering in a forest for all the sense of direction he had, yet he was more fascinated than afraid, drawn by a strange buzzing which made him wonder why there should be flies in winter. He found himself thinking about Sybil. He worried he had been remiss. All the messages she left when he was with Gersten she must have thought he had ignored. He should have protected her more, even in the knowledge that his motives were conflicted. She was haunted and beautiful, all the more for being forbidden.

The buzzing sounded electrical. The building was a monument to bad wiring. Many corridor lights, hanging on exposed cables, didn't work. Others flickered and hissed as the buzzing grew closer.

He was aware of a residual aroma. He couldn't think what he was reminded of, then identified it as the same sticky smell as butchers' shops. He came to an open door. The lights inside were off. He put his hand round the frame, feeling for the switch.

The flickering neon hurt his eyes. Blinking, he was confronted by a near replica of the slaughterhouse murder room. The only difference was it was quite stripped and appeared recently tidied and cleared. It was a common utility space, ubiquitous even, but the similarity struck him as uncanny.

The humming was coming from next door.

Schlegel paused outside. The light was on.

Several sets of naked feet were laid out in rows on the floor. He stepped into what more resembled a stack room for the dead than an official morgue. A dozen and more corpses were stretched out on the tiles, covered except for bare feet. Schlegel forced himself to look under each cover. None was flayed.

One he was sure was the still-bandaged man he had seen unloaded from the train in the fog.

The generator whose noise had drawn him there was powering a freezer trench of ice. In it Schlegel found a severed hand in a transparent envelope, then a foot and a thigh bone in their own see-through bags. The round object he supposed was a head, flayed or boiled, as were the other parts, reduced to musculature and bone, stripped to their essence.

Schlegel forced himself to look at the head. It was intact; no hole in the forehead, so not Keleman. Its size suggested a woman. He feared for Sybil.

Metal heel-tips rang down the corridor. Footsteps approaching; Schlegel couldn't tell how many. A sound of squeaky wheels. Step into the corridor and they would see him. He could hide behind the door and use his pistol to club anyone, but the prospect of behaving like a tough guy was ridiculous. If they were pushing a trolley they were bound to be coming there. He was trapped.

From what he could hear, two men were loading a pair of bodies onto the trolley. They complained of the epic proportions drunk the night before, and the size of their livers.

Schlegel was lying among the corpses, under sacking, hoping he looked dead, praying they would not choose to cart him off. His feet were naked, socks and shoes under his head. He was positioned in the far corner, gripping his pistol.

One of the men farted malodorously. The situation was so close to leaden farce that Schlegel was reminded of bad theatrical turns, at the same time thinking: this is a living morgue, serving a purpose beyond death.

It was a stupid observation. The dead were dead.

He heard his name called from a distance. It sounded like Morgen.

The two men engaged in an urgent exchange, telling each other they should get out.

Schlegel thought one of the voices could belong to Haager, who had snuck up on him with the stun gun.

They hurried off. The wheels didn't squeak with the trolley loaded. Morgen called for them to stop, but he still had too far to catch up.

Schlegel was sitting on the floor putting on his shoes when Morgen came in. It was the first time he had seen him look properly surprised.

Morgen inspected the bodies in turn, as Schlegel had.

'Fourteen, not including the two taken away. Eleven I would say died from wounds sustained in action. The bandaged man is a case of severe burning. Numbers thirteen and fourteen, I can't say. I would hazard these boys are our glorious dead from the east.'

'Do body parts have any intrinsic value?' asked Schlegel.

Morgen looked at him queerly. 'Not these days. Two a penny.'

Schlegel said he had been thinking about grave robbers.

'Now you are clutching at straws.'

They took the parts from the freezer, wrapped in old sacking, and delivered them to Lipchitz at the Jewish hospital, an occasion that caused Lipchitz ghoulish amusement.

'What am I to do with these?'

'Keep them safe,' said Morgen. 'I don't suppose analysis will reveal anything.'

'Not with the equipment they give us,' said Lipchitz.

# 53

On his way home Schlegel stopped off at the back entrance to the Grosse Hamburger Strasse holding centre. He spoke into an electronic grille on the outside gate. A caretaker came out to let him in.

'Warmer weather,' he observed laconically as he led the way. Schlegel couldn't say. He had stopped noticing weather.

Inside, the man made him wait until he was in his hutch-like room and opened the glass divide. He asked Schlegel to state his business. It was all ridiculously formal.

Schlegel said he wanted to speak to someone who had known Sybil. The caretaker referred him to what he called the residents' common room and said he thought Frau Kübler was in. Actually they all were because they were confined to quarters. 'You can't miss her.'

You could not, was Schlegel's first thought. The blonde perm. Bright red nails and lipstick. The coquettish angle of the head. Schlegel had never encountered anyone so aware of being watched, like a spotlight was on her, and she adjusted accordingly. He supposed that was how life was for film stars. Stella made the others in the room look dowdy. She was sitting in a chair reading an out-of-date fashion magazine.

She put it down when Schlegel addressed her, stood up, looked at him ruefully, as an equal, and said, 'No more fashion now. I had to make this skirt myself. Not bad.'

She pouted at the mention of Sybil's name. For all the woman's star quality, she was not a good actress. Perhaps she didn't have to be because she was there only to please herself, leaving others to stand in her reflected glory. She was magnificently superficial.

Schlegel asked if they could speak in private.

Stella suggested they go to her room. Schlegel was aware of blushing. She touched his arm and smiled becomingly.

'Get your coat,' he said, stiffly. 'We can talk in the grounds. I'll wait downstairs.'

The caretaker looked at them askance and told Stella she had to sign out. She called over her shoulder that she wasn't leaving.

It was nearly dark. The garden consisted of unkempt grass, a few laurel bushes and naked flower beds. Stella took her cue from this forlorn sight to talk about her grandparents' summer garden, bursting with blooms.

Everything about the woman was predicated on seduction. She must be very successful, otherwise she would not have lasted so long.

He could see she dismissed him as harmless and only useful as a rehearsal for trickier situations.

'What is your interest in the Todermann woman, if I may be so bold?'

'She was helping us locate someone.' How awkward he sounded.

'Grigor,' she said, contemptuous. 'They deserve each other.'

'Do you know Grigor?'

'Most of the pretty girls made a point of having him once.' Stella pulled a face. 'Less than meets the eye. Insecure, then he would get angry afterwards for being no good and blame the girl. I can see you're dying to ask. Just the once. He came in his trousers.'

Stella wanted a cigarette. When he said he didn't smoke she produced one of her own and lit it.

'He liked beating up, but I wouldn't have said then he was capable of killing. It's cold out here. What do you want?'

'Where are they now?'

'Dead for all I know. The woman was a thorough bitch. She was so jealous she tried to have me killed. Grigor beat one woman so badly she died and he skinned her afterwards.'

'Who told you?'

'Word travels.'

'What about her friend?'

'Lore. She'll be dead too. She had no stomach for the job. We're all trapped. The difference is some fight to survive. Are you a fighter?'

'Do I look like one?'

'I like you. You're confused. You're confused about Jews and even more confused about women. I could eat you for breakfast.'

She laughed, ostentatiously dropped her unfinished cigarette and ground it out with her foot.

'Ah, well, we step back into our lives.'

She brushed his cheek with her hand, the *femme fatale* act back in place. Schlegel felt lonely for both of them.

It was the first night his bed hadn't been cold to get into. Sybil was dead or in danger. From the beginning she had always been just ahead, running away from the Metzler shooting just before he got there. As for her whereabouts, she could be anywhere. Then he thought, no she wasn't. People were creatures of habit, even in extremes.

He took out Metzler's diary again. The man's obsession with Sybil seemed more obvious. He wondered about the razored pages.

He got up and went up on the roof and leaned over, looking down, trying to work out the exact point where night turned to total darkness.

# 54

Schlegel walked into his office, ignored as usual by Frau Pelz in her alcove. His unexpected good mood brought on by the good weather evaporated with her indomitable presence. Outside, the most pleasing feature of a beautiful spring day was the sight of adventurous girls wearing no overcoats.

It sounded like Morgen was already in. As Schlegel entered the room he was stopped short by the sight of Nebe, sitting at his desk, going through its contents, not looking at all put out to be discovered. He subjected Schlegel to his camel-like gaze, then continued to inspect drawers until he came across the animal stun gun, which Schlegel had done nothing about.

'What are we to make of this?'

'Confiscated, sir.'

Nebe sat back and folded his hands. 'Where do we start?'

'I am not sure what you mean, sir.'

'With your arrest, my bribes, flayed bodies, the impossible Morgen or forged money?'

*His bribes?!*

'Do you know what Morgen was up to when he was away?'

'He hasn't said.'

Apart from human lampshades.

Nebe studied his manicured nails. 'I hear he went off to Weimar and was staying in the Elephant Hotel, which you don't do on a budget. Heads previously believed to have been firmly attached to shoulders are starting to roll. These are dangerous times, revolutionary even for the old guard. From what I understand, Gersten could easily have lost you in the system.'

'Who told you, sir?' he asked without meaning to.

'Morgen. Who else?'

Who wasn't in bed with whom? Schlegel experienced that face-pressed-against-the-glass moment and wondered who his bedmate was supposed to be.

'The Italians say keep your friends close and your enemies closer.'

Schlegel felt he had enough leeway, just, to ask which he was. The remark verged on the insubordinate, but he knew Nebe didn't mind because it made him appear tolerant.

'For you to work out, dear boy. In the meantime, watch Morgen. He has a soft spot, but don't be fooled. His behaviour in Weimar was astonishingly ruthless.'

Nebe, usually so smooth, grew awkward. Schlegel presumed he was about to be told something he didn't want to hear.

'I like to think of you as the son I never had.'

Schlegel felt they were all swimming in molasses. The man's eyes were moist. Whatever the emotion, he was sure it wasn't paternal. He was as slippery as they came. Schlegel couldn't believe Nebe had made reference to his own bribes. Was it a brush-off or a dangle he was supposed to pick up on?

Nebe went on, seeming to address himself more than Schlegel. 'These are hard times to read. We did our best to get rid of religion, yet we seem to be entering an age that can only be described as biblical, perhaps even pre-revolutionary.'

Was this seditious talk, or was Nebe trying to trap him by hinting at such matters?

Nebe stood up and again Schlegel wondered if he hadn't been meant to bite. Nebe rested his hand briefly on his shoulder.

'Let's leave it at that.'

Instead of going, he went and looked out of the window, hands stuck in his pockets, a picture of easy authority.

'Spring is in the air but sometimes it is better to stay hibernating,' he said, seeming to imply Schlegel should make himself scarce.

Schlegel had had enough. 'Is there anyone who can tell me what is going on, sir?'

Nebe looked at him sharply. The question was far too direct.

'Your name is starting to come up in the wrong way. Someone mentioned it in connection to Konto five.'

Nebe cocked his head, studying Schlegel's Adam's apple.

'You don't go there, whatever Morgen tells you. The situation is extralegal and I state that categorically. The one that can go is Nöthling. He's a ladies' man. Take care of that. Use a woman.'

'A sex trap, sir?'

Nebe sighed. 'Oh, do grow up. Do it now. The time is right.'

Schlegel was sitting at his desk in uneasy contemplation when Frau Pelz rushed in breathless with excitement to ask if he knew where Morgen was. Schlegel didn't and saw it was her own news Frau Pelz was bursting to share, even with him.

She had spoken to Reichsführer-SS Himmler's personal attaché who wished to speak to Morgen. Never did she believe such a thing would happen in their little outpost. She proffered the telephone number, written in her neatest hand, with double exclamation marks after the caller's name.

After all the flannelling with Nebe, it was a relief just to tell her to go away. She left, resentful and deflated. Another bridge burned, thought Schlegel, another twist. Morgen had given no hint.

Morgen was no more forthcoming when he came in. His mood was foul.

'What are you doing anyway?' he asked, accusatory.

'Thinking about where you were when you were away.'

Morgen gave him a look of warning.

'The Reichsführer's office wishes to speak to you. I have never seen Frau Pelz excited.'

He pointed to her note, supposing Morgen would take the news in his stride.

Instead his hands shook as he reached for the inevitable cigarette. Morgen slowly picked up the receiver and told Frau Pelz to place the call, which had to be the most thrilling moment of her desiccated life.

Morgen announced himself and was told to wait while he was put through. He looked tight and tense. His voice was hoarse when he spoke.

Not only was the call to Himmler's private office, it was to Heine himself. Seeing Schlegel studying him, Morgen stood and turned his back.

Himmler; no wonder Nebe was worried.

Morgen stood for the call, answering in a series of affirmatives. Schlegel counted eight. He had never seen the underling in Morgen before, so clipped and wary.

Morgen hung up and said, 'Fuck.'

He sat down and stared for a long time at the replaced receiver. Frau Pelz came into the room in a dither. Morgen said not now, shooed her out and shut the door. Hanging on the back of it was the reprimanding sight of the yellow suit made by Sybil for Schlegel's mother's friend, which he had failed to deliver.

Schlegel pretended to work, thinking he needed to sort out the suit. It reminded him of the attic above the shop where Sybil had hidden Lore. A place with sentimental associations, worth checking. He could take the suit back as well. He must have been mad to think he would get around to delivering it.

Morgen's apathy lifted and he seemed visibly to shift up several gears.

'I had intended to spend the day taking Haager from the slaughterhouse apart, a pleasure that will have to wait, as I now have to go out. Get him in and sweat him in the cells. Say we have evidence linking him to the death of Keleman.' Morgen nodded at the stun gun on the top of the desk. 'I am sure Lipchitz will oblige us with whatever forensics we need. And while you are about it, issue a warrant for Gersten's arrest, citing financial irregularities.'

'Are you going to tell me what's going on with that business just now?'

'You mean as partners?' Morgen snapped.

'No,' said Schlegel coldly, addressing the papers on his desk. 'You are a temporary associate. Go and attend to whatever you have to.'

Morgen pointed to the telephone as the real object of his anger.

'We are talking about rarefied levels of stupefying intrigue here, and it has to do with us.'

'Us!' exclaimed Schlegel.

Morgen looked around the room and gestured for him to follow. He led the way to the washroom. After checking the cubicles were empty he ran the basin taps.

'Excuse the precaution. I've heard that the whole of the Ministry of Propaganda is bugged, as well as the Foreign Press Club, so one can't be too careful.'

Reichsführer Himmler had a new whim. It had come to his attention that an occasional clandestine smuggling service had been operating whereby a few Jews were allowed to buy their way to safety.

Schlegel presumed Himmler wanted Gersten brought to book, given the arrest warrant.

'Quite the opposite. The Reichsführer wishes privately to sponsor one such train himself.'

Schlegel cast around in disbelief.

'Yes, yes,' said Morgen, as though such a *volte face* was obvious. 'It's called hedging your bets.'

Schlegel continued to flounder.

Morgen said, 'It's astonishing how it all clicks. Gersten will provide the service as usual, in exchange for his slate being wiped clean.' He paused. 'I agree, it is an upside-down world. On the other hand, Gersten will have to resurface. We have maybe forty-eight hours, maybe as little as twenty-four, to get to the bottom of this.'

'Metzler's dead. There's no broker.'

'The money will be paid in US dollars.'

Schlegel could not believe what he was hearing. A grubby deal involving fake money and a venal Gestapo man had been piggybacked by none other than the Reichsführer-SS with US money now being waved around.

'Who's the broker?'

'Not the right question. I am appointing you.'

'The world has gone crazy.'

'Quite some time ago.' Morgen caught Schlegel's eye in the mirror. 'Yes. Lampshades made of human skin. The thought disgusts the Reichsführer. He is a fastidious man. He hates cruelty. When they showed him firing squads in the east he went green and raved. The closed door, Schlegel, the closed door. What exactly goes on behind it we may never know. There is no time to lose.'

He walked out, leaving Schlegel to stare at his reflection and see the dangling man; he was unable to decide whether Morgen was responsible, prior to letting him drop.

The yellow suit hung reprovingly on the back of the door. Schlegel was alone in the office. Morgen had not said where he was. Whatever was going on, it could play out too many ways, none good.

Like a man facing long exile, he decided to put his affairs in order.

He applied for a fortnight's leave.

He ordered the local flatfoots to arrest Haager and hold him until he could send a van from headquarters.

He took pleasure in drawing up the warrant for Gersten's arrest.

He had a brainwave about Nebe's trap for Nöthling.

He decided to take the yellow suit back to Sybil's employer, embarrassing as that was, and see if Sybil had used the attic. He even had the crazy notion of staying there himself until she showed up, as he was sure she would.

First he went to Grosse Hamburger Strasse to speak with Stella Kübler. They talked outside again, sitting on a garden bench in the spring sun. She thought he couldn't get enough of her. When he said he needed someone to set up a trap she didn't look surprised. He told her who the target was and it needed a compromising rendezvous.

'You want it to be a race thing, is that why you are asking?'

Yes, he said a bit desperately. 'He will be charged with protecting you, and the other thing.'

'Carnal relations, darling. Don't be shy. Call a spade a spade. I'm racial defilement.'

'We need proof.'

'A big brute of a photographer kicking down the door?'

The woman was impossible. He was out of his depth.

'No. We have technical people who can rig a room.'

'Whatever you say, darling. It will make a change. I must say, I didn't have you down for a sex intriguer. What's in it for me?'

'You will remain safe of course.' How pompous he sounded.

'I am safe as it is.'

He supposed he could find her something from the contraband deposits.

She asked what was in the bag he was carrying. It was the suit
Sybil had made; Stella was all over it in seconds.

'It's beautiful! Look at the stitching. It must be worth a
fortune.'

Schlegel had never seen anyone covet something so nakedly.

'You can't find anything like this now. Where did you get it?
Who made it?'

He thought it better not to say.

Stella shrugged off her jacket and put the other on.

'I'm an absolute fit.'

Looking around conspiratorially, she reached out for his
hand as she removed her shoes. She took off her skirt so she
was standing in her slip. Schlegel glimpsed white thigh above
stocking top as she changed into the yellow skirt. He experienced a stab of desire and saw it register as she reached for his
hand to slip her shoes back on.

The sad thing was the suit didn't look that good on her. The
yellow was all wrong for her hair, but she twirled for him like a
model.

'Perfect,' she said. 'So clever of you to think of it and know
my size. And so much more tasteful and personal than the
financial transaction, don't you think? We should go on a date
and I'll wear it for you.' She looked at him, all innocence, and
said, 'You are sweet,' as though they had agreed all along the
suit was the price of the transaction.

Sybil lay on her back with Grigor on top, her eyes shut, the
better to transport herself to other places while he poked away.
For all his finesse, she sometimes felt like a field being ploughed.
Her body no longer seemed particularly hers any more,
connected to inner feelings. She thought of it as preparing for a

withdrawal that would end with her leaving; in other words, she was getting ready to die.

She opened her eyes and saw a movement in the skylight above. No more than a bird, she thought. Then it was there again and gone. She covered her eyes with her arm and looked under it. As for the others, Gersten seemed to have disappeared, the Kübler woman wasn't in any of her haunts. She was cut off except for Grigor, insisting on making sad love. His behaviour swung between threats of violence, rage and sex, which seemed only to edge him closer to despair. Seeing the pressure build in him, she supposed that was how he would reach the killing point.

In as much as she thought about it, she had always presumed murderers were murderous all the time rather than dull, ordinary people, difficult to be with, until driven to pointless destruction. Was there any reason to murder? Even Stella Kübler? Her own desire for the woman's obliteration was probably part of a complicated sexual jealousy and perhaps a way of channelling her grief for Lore.

Still looking under her arm, Sybil saw first one face in the skylight then a second: two boys goggle-eyed, popping up and ducking down like pecking birds, growing bolder, nudging and sniggering in awe.

She considered warning Grigor then decided, what if they gawped? It made the whole thing less lonely. She thought of the boys' excitement as they ogled the stark image of their entwined bodies, while knowing nothing about her, or her abstraction as Grigor ground on, leaving her as numb as a patient under anaesthetic.

Schlegel had his eye glued to a tiny crack in the rough, uneven planks of the attic door. He could make out Sybil with her arm over her face and Grigor's naked buttocks pumping.

Schlegel carefully got out his gun. Whatever he had been expecting it wasn't this. He dithered between stealth and charge. If he barged in, Grigor might have a weapon on the floor and get a shot off first.

The door was on a latch. He remembered there was no lock. If it squeaked he would have to take his chances.

He slipped in and took what felt like an age to close the door. He levelled his pistol, as he had been taught in weapons training, gun raised and sighted, drawing a bead on the target, double-handed grip, right elbow out. Point and squeeze, the armoury master said. Schlegel hoped it wouldn't come to shooting. His scores on the range were akin to being unable to hit the barn door.

He crept forward, heel to toe, praying the boards wouldn't creak, gambling on surprise to give him an edge.

Sybil started to turn towards him. Her arm was still over her face but she seemed to be looking under it and straight at him. He thought her about to scream. Grigor stopped thrusting and was about to raise his head. Schlegel could not shoot for fear of hitting her. She stared for a moment before she turned back, dug her nails in Grigor's shoulders and drove her body into his. Schlegel blushed to his roots as he watched the object of his fantasy enacting the primal scene.

He thought she must be using Grigor to show her contempt for him. She had looked at him like he was a Peeping Tom. He wanted to leave and go quietly out. He didn't want to see them uncoupling, didn't want to face her.

Sybil started to moan. Grigor paused again and tried to lift his head. She cradled it with her arm, stopping him, and Schlegel saw she was trying to help after all.

Three or four more paces. He had to get the gun to Grigor's neck, or too much was left to chance. Sybil's moaning turned to rhythmic groaning as Schlegel took another step. He was about to rush, thinking he would club Grigor and stun him, when a loud yell came from above outside, followed by a clattering down the roof, a crash and scream of pain.

Schlegel's pistol automatically went up to the source of the commotion. He saw a shape and his nervous trigger-finger fired off a round, putting a hole in the skylight.

Grigor was already on his feet, holding Sybil in front of him, both hands around her neck, lifting her off the ground. Schlegel couldn't fire. Grigor was using her as a shield. It seemed to take him no effort to hold her in the air at arm's length. Sybil was in danger of being choked as she struggled to loosen his grip. Schlegel was distracted and embarrassed by Sybil's nakedness and Grigor's still half-hard cock.

He traced their progress to the door with his gun, with no way to shoot. Grigor told Schlegel to throw him his clothes. Sybil thrashed for air.

Schlegel shouted for Grigor to put Sybil down. Grigor bared his teeth. Sybil started turning blue. Schlegel fired once, wide, hoping to make Grigor drop her.

An explosion came from above Schlegel's head and a blurred shape crashed through the skylight, landed on the floor, in a shower of broken glass, and propelled itself at Grigor, who let go of Sybil out of surprise. Schlegel fired off two shots as Sybil fell to the floor, gasping.

Grigor roared and began hopping in pain, all the while being pushed, pummelled and kicked by what Schlegel saw was a boy of no more than twelve or thirteen. He fired another shot in the air, which stopped everything, except Sybil's laboured breathing, which turned to screams of terror. Schlegel ordered Grigor to move from the door and lie face down in the middle of the room. Grigor glowered, looking like he would refuse. He would shoot again, Schlegel said, and Grigor could see he meant it and the fight went out of him. The cause of Grigor's agitation, Schlegel saw, was that one of his shots had hit him square in the buttock.

Schlegel laboriously extricated his handcuffs while still holding on to his gun and threw them to the boy, who was caught between excitement and shock. He told him to put them on Grigor, who lay writhing and making growling noises.

He was in the act of covering Sybil's nakedness when he heard footsteps coming up the outside stairs. Sybil was crying, saying she wanted only to be left alone. The door opened and Schlegel saw Frau Zwicker come to see what was going on. She stood there petrified, with a pair of nail scissors in her hand.

Schlegel turned back to attend to Sybil when he felt a fierce pain and looking down he saw Frau Zwicker had stabbed him in the leg with her tiny scissors.

# 55

Schlegel was given a tetanus shot, had his leg bandaged, and told to go home. The wound was superficial. The boy who fell off the roof had broken his leg and was in hospital. Grigor's bullet was extracted and he was downstairs at headquarters, in a cell next to Haager from the slaughterhouse, who had also been brought in.

Morgen had Sybil spirited away, Schlegel wasn't sure where.

The aftermath had offered a tableau of extreme awkwardness. Grigor lay naked and cursing. Sybil retreated to a corner and dressed under a blanket. She avoided looking at Schlegel. Frau Zwicker behaved like a woman trapped on stage and repeated over that she hadn't meant to. The boy went off to call the cops and Morgen and didn't come back. Schlegel told Sybil to get away before anyone came but she refused and sat waiting.

The local police turned up, followed by Morgen, who took charge.

Schlegel, Grigor and the brat were packed off together in an ambulance, Grigor scowling malevolence, the boy whimpering and Schlegel in an unsteady state of adrenalin rush and prurient embarrassment at the memory of Sybil naked.

Morgen appeared most amused that Schlegel had been stabbed in the leg by Frau Zwicker, in fact seemed delighted by the choreography of the entire episode, and was able to report that the youthful voyeurs were part of a band used by Gersten for surveillance, inspired by Gersten's own experience as a young actor in *Emil and the Detectives*. They had followed Sybil to the cinema where Grigor worked and picked them up from there. With Gersten no longer around to report to, they had become distracted by risqué movies and sex snooping.

The boys struck Morgen as feral, uneducated and already delinquent. Soon there would be a generation of soldiers the army could make nothing of.

Frau Zwicker's intemperate moment was attributed to a spasm of blind rage brought about by accumulative frustration, for which Schlegel was to blame, having not delivered the yellow suit as promised, which had led to her being accused of theft by the client. Morgen looked at Schlegel owlishly and asked if any of that made sense. He was merely reporting what he had been told. Schlegel said he would make the necessary recompense. He was too ashamed to say where the suit was now.

Morgen asked if he wished to press charges against Frau Zwicker. Schlegel said it wasn't necessary.

'Perhaps you would like to tell her she is free to go.'

It turned out Morgen also had her locked up downstairs. They went down together. Frau Zwicker scuttled off.

Morgen dealt with Haager next.

'So, friend from the slaughterhouse,' Morgen said, 'I am not asking you to talk, only to listen.'

Haager looked puzzled.

Like a man telling a story to a child, Morgen began with how he had been out of town and just come back. Schlegel sensed the account was as much for his benefit.

'Only for a matter of days. Everything was going according to plan until my star witness mysteriously died. It was a corruption case with a lot at stake.'

Haager asked what did any of this have to do with him.

Morgen ignored him and went on. He suspected an SS doctor

of poisoning his man to stop him testifying but he had no evidence.

'Each of us has his breaking point,' he said, looking at Haager.

He invited the doctor to dine at the officers' mess. Protocol made it impossible for him to refuse as it was a point of honour to accept an invitation by a fellow officer of equal rank or higher.

'I ordered a private dining room and the doctor turned up and went white at the sight of the dead witness on the dining table, opened up for autopsy. The contents of the man's stomach had been transferred to a tureen. There were also three Russian prisoners in the room. And an armed guard. It was all very formal, silver service and so on.'

The doctor was made to watch as the slops were force-fed to the three Russians, who died slow, agonising deaths, proving Morgan's theory.

'You see the doctor in question was lazy. He maintained he had carried out the autopsy and the man died of natural causes, but he hadn't, and he was arrogant and careless to boot. He failed to dispose of the body, which we found waiting for us in the morgue.

'I told the doctor that what was now in the stomachs of the dead Russians would be extracted and fed to him, as a point of curiosity, to see if he survived being poisoned at third-hand by the strychnine he had administered.'

Morgen said, 'Everyone sings in the end.'

Bluffing or not, his capacity for ruthlessness was evident.

'Now, with you, my friend,' Morgen went on quietly, 'I suspect my brutality will have to match behaviour familiar to you from the east. Torture is a search for the truth by other means, eh, Haager? And Schlegel here, who is a sensitive soul, is thinking, "We are becoming like them", to which I am bound to answer you can't cure sickness and not risk infection. Am I to become a brute like you? Here's the story. Of course, you prove as tough as an ox, even after your shoulders dislocate from being strung up with your arms behind your back. You scream in agony, and I sympathise. It's curious how one identifies with pain. And still I ask no questions, which puzzles you to distraction and will break you in the end. Then we chuck you in the slurry pit where your dislocated shoulders make it hard not to drown. With the fumes, you struggle to stay conscious, then decide you weren't born to die swallowing liquid shit. So you tell me everything.'

Haager glowered as if to say mind games would get Morgen nowhere.

'I am going to leave you alone to think about this now. Look at your hands and ask yourself about all the things they did in Russia.'

In the corridor, Schlegel asked if the story about the poisoned Russians was true.

'No love lost between me and Russians, and even less for those who sit at home, pretending to be soldiers, lining their pockets and claiming running a concentration camp is a front-line job because they are fighting the internal war. Hah!'

Grigor was lying on his bunk with his hands behind his head. When he struggled to get up Morgen pushed him back.

He said he wasn't empowered to investigate the murders, he was only interested in Metzler, Gersten, safe trains and fake money.

Grigor, as the forger, seemed in no doubt he was the star.

Schlegel found him vain and insufferable, an appropriate foil to Gersten. With both men everything had to pass through the portals of large and self-regulating egos.

Morgen said, 'I have no wish to listen to you. Just say yes or no. Abbas told Gersten that Metzler was using forged money and Gersten was sufficiently enraged to arrange its confiscation, disguised as robbery, and have Plotkin chucked off the roof. Metzler was about to be packed off when you stepped in and announced you were capable of producing the perfect forged note. Yes or no?'

Grigor looked smug. 'Yes.'

'It only needed Metzler to point out to Gersten the advantages of such a source of untraceable money for him to become greedy and allow the smuggling to resume, now departing from the slaughterhouse yards. Yes or no?'

'Yes.'

'What do you know of the accident?'

Grigor looked blank and said he was just a technician.

He radiated the superiority of the underdog. His contempt for Schlegel was clear. With Morgen he was cannier, suggesting his services might prove useful.

Morgen said, 'I suggest half a deal. We lose you in the ordinary penal system and send you up the road to Moabit where I keep an eye on you. The condition is you have to provide yourself with a false identity card to my satisfaction, which should be easy for a man of your skill. You probably have such a card already.'

Grigor looked at them with tragic eyes and held out quivering hands.

'They have been like this for a month. I can no longer work. I need to see a doctor.'

Morgen said, 'We'll find you one. Tell me where your tools are and I'll have them sent over. I am sure your second best will be good enough. Think of yourself as working for me now but get rid of the shakes because I have exacting standards.'

Morgen had acquired a car with its own driver, the same man who had held the door for Schlegel when getting out at the bar with the green door.

They drove the short distance to Auguststrasse and stopped outside Schlegel's apartment. Schlegel thanked Morgen for the lift. Morgen said they weren't finished and led the way into the dancehall and asked for the manager, Herr Valentine, who took them to his office where Schlegel saw Sybil lain on a chaise longue, passed out from exhaustion. Herr Valentine withdrew discreetly. Sybil flinched when Morgen woke her.

He told her she was safe. Sybil appeared somewhat reassured. Her throat was bruised.

Morgen said she could rest soon. Herr Valentine could provide a room upstairs where she would be safe.

'I need you to tell us about the last night of Metzler's life. I believe you were with him.'

She looked aghast. 'How do you know? I told nobody.'

'Boring detective work. The aspect that puzzled me was the timing of your leaving the building just as the shooting occurred.'

Sybil bowed her head.

'You were going to meet Metzler, to escape the roundup together.'

'But what about your mother?' asked Schlegel.

Sybil had warned her mother, who decided to take her chances and hide in the building.

'Why were you trying to help Metzler?'

He had come to her that last night. Not only had he just learned the warden was blackmailing her, he had been told he was due to be deported, and that was far from the worst of it.

'Why were you being blackmailed?' asked Morgen.

'The warden knew I was having an affair with a woman.'

At the time they only had Sundays together. Lore lived far away and, like a lot of others, they used the boiler room for their trysts.

'He showed me his spy hole in the back of his apartment that let him make note of couples going in and out.'

The warden had told Metzler out of spite, because everyone knew he had a crush.

'What he didn't know was we had known each other since I was a student. Metzler was a real artist. I was young and heartless.' She spoke in an automatic way. 'I didn't realise how serious he was. We all slept around, in reaction to the urgency of the situation, living for the moment. He was older, as you know.'

'What else did he tell you that night?'

'Everything.'

'Did he tell you about the perfect note?'

'Is that what Grigor told you?'

'He said it financed the second phase of the operation.'

'Well, he would, wouldn't he?'

She confirmed Grigor sold the idea of the perfect note to Metzler, who sold it on to Gersten, who bit.

Morgen ventured that Grigor perhaps hadn't been as good a forger as he made out.

Sybil said he had confessed that some tiny flaw or tremor stopped him from achieving perfection.

'By the time I knew him his hands shook quite badly. Metzler said there was nothing resembling a perfect note. Well, there was in that he was using real money to pay Gersten.'

Morgen looked astonished. 'How? There was none left.'

'Through his art. He knew a dealer who could sell in Zurich. He had collectors there, and in America, who paid well though he complained that the dealer charged a terrible fee because the transactions were illegal.'

Sybil started to cry silently, saying it was all too painful. Morgen offered his handkerchief, which she refused, saying that's what Gersten did.

'How many words are we given to speak in a lifetime? I feel I have reached my limit. I have lost everything that ever mattered to me. Metzler was a broken man and I promised I would never repeat what he told me.'

Morgen looked at Schlegel for an answer. Schlegel had none. He felt shamed because if Sybil ever saw the Kübler woman again she would see her yellow suit.

Morgen told Sybil he respected her discretion. He stood up to signal they were done. She looked at him surprised.

Schlegel wondered if Morgen's move was another of his manipulations.

Sybil eventually asked, 'Do you know what the Judas goat is?'

Morgen said yes. It was the creature that led unsuspecting animals to the slaughterhouse, moving aside at the last moment, to let the others go to their death.

'Metzler called himself the Judas goat that night.'

'Because just as the perfect note was a fantasy so were the trains he thought he had arranged?'

The warden had taunted Metzler about the futility of his efforts. On the occasion of the first departure those waiting to leave had been hidden in a decommissioned meat fridge, which was turned on accidentally. Their deaths were hushed up.

After that accident, it became policy to repeat the process. Metzler learned that night all the subsequent escapees had been killed instead.

'Who was responsible? Did he say?' asked Morgen.

'He was too distraught. He held himself responsible, however much I tried to tell him he wasn't.'

Schlegel thought the slaughterhouse was the perfect place to replicate the killing fields of the east.

It still didn't explain why bodies were being shipped in.

Sybil had spent that last night whispering on the stairs outside Metzler's apartment, desperate to persuade him to live.

She thought she had succeeded, offering the attic as a hiding place, even for a day or two. He finally agreed, which was why, as Morgen had surmised, they had got up early, to avoid the roundup.

As for the razored pages in the diary, Sybil said they were now hidden beneath the attic floorboards. They were sketches, made the previous summer by Metzler, of her sunbathing on the block roof where there was a hidden space between the chimneys. He had cut them out that last night and given them to her.

Morgen said to Sybil, 'There is a train out tomorrow or the next night. I could get you on it.'

'And have happen to me what happened to the rest,' she answered, with some of her old spark.

Morgen conceded with a gesture of apology and said this time everyone would be safe.

Sybil said, 'I am not sure I want a future.'

Herr Valentine was fetched to show Sybil to her room. They parted with no farewell. Sybil staggered under her great burden.

Morgen asked Schlegel to step outside and said, 'Be down here at midnight. You have work to do.'

Morgen's car and driver were still waiting.

'Hans will fetch and watch out for you. He knows where to go. Pick up the money and pass it on. You know both parties.'

'Watch out for? As in trouble?'

'No trouble. Don't fall asleep and be here at twelve.'

Not wanting to be alone, Schlegel went back to the dancehall to get a drink and was surprised to see Sybil at a table on her own. He approached uncertainly and asked if she wanted to be alone. She pointed to a spare chair. He asked a waitress for a beer. Sybil didn't want anything.

Small talk was pointless. To explain his presence, he said he lived upstairs and left it at that. He drank his watery beer, wondering what was going through her head. There was a new band, worse than the last. Sybil sat with her hands folded while he tried not to think of her with Grigor. The band played a waltz. Sybil asked if he danced. Hardly ever and badly. It didn't matter, she said, and stood up and walked onto the floor. She said Lore did the man's steps. He took her hands. He worried about his perspiring. He concentrated on the beat, with her lost in a world of her own. He messed up his timing but was less awkward than he expected. When the music ended she broke away and went and sat back down.

'Can you show me where you live?' she asked. 'I need to be by myself but I don't want to be alone.'

He noted Herr Valentine watching them leave together.

They climbed slowly upstairs. Did she need help and should he take her arm, or would that be misinterpreted? He was as tongue-tied as any lovelorn youth.

She looked at his apartment and said, 'You don't get much.'

He agreed it was nothing to write home about. She noted Metzler's diary on the arm of the chair. She asked if she could take a bath.

'I feel unclean.'

He thought there wouldn't be any hot water.

'It's not as though you haven't seen me without my clothes on,' she remarked flatly.

Nothing enticing was meant but the air seemed full of electricity.

He said he could only stay until twelve because he had to work.

'Please take the bed. I can sleep in the chair until then.'

She nodded like someone who had lost the thread. He just needed to get the alarm clock in case he fell asleep, he said, knowing he was fussing too much. Alwynd would play the situation, going to bed with her as a way of obliterating the bad memory of Grigor. And so on, round in circles.

She wandered off dazed into the bedroom and shut the door.

Schlegel sat in a hinterland between sleeping and not sleeping, racked with desire. He heard her weeping and couldn't decide whether to go in. He imagined getting into bed just to hold and be held, imagined the lingering smell of her body on his sheets in the next days, struggled with the impossibility of intimacy, after what she had been through. She didn't like men anyway.

They drove east. For all his anxiety, Schlegel had trouble not falling asleep. He imagined Sybil turning over restlessly in his bed. Once he was jolted awake by the car hitting a pothole. Hans the driver was too controlled to curse.

Eventually they turned off down a dirt track and pulled up on what Schlegel presumed was scrub or wasteland. His impression was of no buildings nearby. He rolled down the window. Wind moved through the trees. The engine settled on its mount and from the distance came the drone of a monoplane.

There was no traffic until a vehicle with a faltering engine turned off the main road. It was a comparatively clear night and Schlegel watched through the rear window as it pulled up. Hans nodded at Schlegel, who saw him loosen his pistol.

Schlegel walked the exposed distance between the cars, taking care not to stumble or make any sudden move. The shape of the vehicle seemed familiar. As he approached he saw it was the Jewish hearse. The passenger door opened and a man with a strange accent told him to get in.

The passenger seat turned out to be an upturned fruit crate. 'Lipchitz. We've met.'

The whole arrangement was so furtive Schlegel was surprised

he hadn't been given half of one ridiculous remark to be matched by another.

Lipchitz reached under his seat with a grunt and produced an attaché case.

'And they ask me to drive at night with my eyesight,' he complained, handing Schlegel the case.

'US green. It seems we have a fairy godmother. Don't ask where it comes from.'

'I am bound to because your people don't have any.'

'I suspect it's dirty or the ultimate Jewish joke. I am just the messenger.'

'Me too. Who gave it to you?'

'The man didn't say, and we didn't speak, but I would bet my bottom dollar he's a Yank.'

'But they all cleared out or were packed off when the war started.'

'Not an unfamiliar story. But exactly so, which makes him interesting. If you happen to find out I would be curious to know. Be careful. They shoot the messenger.'

After Lipchitz left, Hans had trouble starting the car. He got out and fiddled under the bonnet while Schlegel sat in the back clasping the unwelcome case, picturing them stuck, with whatever plan he was part of in disarray.

What sounded like a motorcycle at speed tore down the main road.

Hans banged the bonnet shut and got back in, fastidiously wiping his hands. The engine started first time. Schlegel sat back, relieved.

Ten minutes down the long straight road, Schlegel saw flames ahead. Hans slowed down for the the burning vehicle, stopped and got out, pistol ready, followed by Schlegel, still clutching the case. The car must have left the road and smashed into the trees. Then he saw it was the Jewish hearse. Lipchitz was trapped in the cabin, his hair a halo of flame. Hans held Schlegel back, saying the tank could explode. He levelled his gun. The single shot starred the window and snapped back the burning head.

The man was beyond help was all Hans said.

They drove on. Schlegel sat staring at the back of Hans's severe head, asking himself if he had killed Lipchitz because the motorcyclist hadn't finished the job, or was he sparing him further pain, as stated? Had the business of their car not starting been a ploy? Was someone tidying up as they went along, in which case where did that leave him?

They went all the way to the other side of town, through empty streets, apart from an official motorcade with motorcycle outriders speeding in the other direction. Eventually Schlegel recognised the brooding shape of the Olympic Stadium. Hans circled it until they reached the high bell tower. He pulled up, turned to Schlegel and pointed to the top.

Schlegel got out, and looked up at the thin, concrete silhouetted, stretching up.

The entrance was guarded by two soldiers who behaved as if he was expected. Schlegel supposed the tower was an observation post. The door was open. The lift shaft stood in the middle of a large vaulted space.

The elevator ground its way slowly up, on and on, swaying slightly. Schlegel took out his gun and hid it behind the case, which he held to his chest. He persuaded himself Lipchitz's death was the result of an ordinary crash. He had complained about driving in the dark.

The cage at last clanked to a halt. No guard at the top or anyone waiting.

Several flights of exposed metal stairs carried him up to the roof. In peacetime it served as a viewing platform for tourists. He had never been up there.

After the strain of anticipation the anticlimax of finding the platform empty. Perhaps he was meant to leave the money for collection and go home.

He was briefly aware of the city in the distance, covered in moonlight.

He heard the lift go back down, taking its time, then it started to come back up, seeming to go on forever.

On the corner of the platform stood a low elevation with a concrete roof, to accommodate the stairwell. Schlegel crouched beside it, feeling foolish, thinking better safe than sorry.

Footsteps rang on the metal steps. The man was taking no precautions. Schlegel saw his outline pause, look around then go and lean on the far parapet, seeming at ease.

After a while, he said, 'Coming, ready or not. I know you're up here.'

It was Gersten.

'Let's not waste time. I am in harmless mode tonight. Can we be friends again?'

Gersten had known whom to expect. Did that mean he was higher up the chain?

Schlegel told him to stay where he was and put up his hands. He frisked Gersten, who protested he was not armed. Schlegel made him lift up his trouser legs to show he was not carrying a knife.

'Now you are being ridiculous. I was hoping you would tell me what's going on.'

Schlegel told him about Lipchitz.

Gersten sounded put out. 'Really?'

'I am not joking. What is your part in this?'

'Acting on orders.'

'Whose?'

Gersten seemed surprised he didn't know. 'Morgen's, of course.'

'Who is ordering what, exactly?' asked Schlegel, trying to keep a level voice.

'Nöthling's pig train in reverse. It's still standing in the goods yard. Back to Sweden with a consignment marked tinned peaches. They have a shortage, apparently.'

'What's in it for you?'

'I am surprised he hasn't told you, being his pet. I get a fresh start. Trieste. What are you being offered?'

The prospect of immunity made Gersten expansive. He admitted Metzler had got the better of him.

'Twice. First forging money I didn't know about. Then coming up with the perfect note. Who wouldn't be interested? Metzler's new star forger could produce fake money indistinguishable from the real thing.'

Schlegel didn't tell Gersten the money had been real. 'What about the accident?'

'What accident was that?' asked Gersten, all innocence.

'The warden Metzler shot was working for you. You were together in the east.'

'Oh that,' said Gersten, sounding bored.

'What about the accident at the slaughterhouse?'

'You are insistent. No idea. I delegated everything to Baumgarten and Reitner. Reitner especially. Barely controllable.'

'Is he responsible for the flayings?'

'You worked that out? I am impressed. I have no proof, but I suspected. I did my best to protect them.'

'By framing Lazarenko?'

'Lazarenko was the one who taught them how to do it. He was the first to have blood on his hands.'

He had been their expert in local atrocity. He knew how to dress and display killings with the correct Bolshevik trademarks.

'From the start we had information Lazarenko was secretly

working against us, but he was too good to lose and our general intelligence was poor so we ignored it. Nothing was black and white, you know that.'

'What about the accident at the slaughterhouse?'

'Sorry to repeat myself, but no idea. Ask Baumgarten and Reitner. Metzler paid, I told Reitner and they fixed everything on the ground. Any accident, they would have kept me in the dark.'

He looked at Schlegel and slowly recited, 'Men used to acting on their own initiative. Finer troops you couldn't ask for, and all that. Dangerous men. Keep your distance.'

He stared at Schlegel with apparent regret. 'Maybe I should have paid more attention. I was distracted. Greedy too. I was trying to recruit Grigor. He thought I was after him. I sent Abbas in waving a white flag. What a fucking disaster. Cuts off his cock, if you please. No wonder I was upset the day you and Morgen turned up. The woman too. He was supposed to listen to both of them. He wasn't meant to kill them. I thought he was going to be our pension fund. You have to agree, a man who can forge a perfect note is worth something. Isn't there any way we can keep this going? Why don't you come in with me?'

Schlegel's head swam. He supposed beyond a certain level this kind of switchback ride went on every day.

The latest safe train out was a mystery to Gersten.

'Haven't the faintest. They're involving me but it's gone up to a whole other register. US dollars! Where are they getting those, unless someone is giving them? Have we arrived at the stage of philanthropy? Buy in to save a Jew?'

He snorted and suggested they go down together.

'I'll take the case now.'

Schlegel was relieved to see it go.

'Split? Fifty-fifty.' Gersten laughed. 'For a moment you thought I was serious. Admit you were tempted.'

Gersten's hatchet-faced henchman waited obediently by the lift.

'Just in case of monkey business,' said Gersten smoothly. 'Nothing meant.'

He told the man to take the stairs.

With the lift doors shut, he said, 'I say we trade. Give me Grigor and I give you Sybil.'

'We have Sybil.'

'Ha-ha, no, dear heart, you don't. Who has been sleeping in your bed? Herr Valentine at Clärchens keeps me posted.'

Gersten paused, letting the implication sink in. 'So sweet.'

Schlegel took a swing but there was no room for the punch and Gersten was quick to grab his wrist.

'Pull yourself together. You'll get her back. Morgen is offering her a place out. That's fine by me. I bring her to the train, you bring Grigor. Straight swap. He'll work for us evermore and we will all be rich and happy. Time to put something aside for a rainy day. You and I will meet when this is over and sort something out. We should work together more. Have Morgen arrange to send you to Trieste. Frontier town, wide open. We could have fun. Relax. It will work out fine.'

Schlegel's apartment was empty, as though Sybil had never been. He crawled under the covers not bothering to undress. He smelled the pillow for a trace of the woman and found none. Despite his exhaustion, he fell into a deep and dreamless sleep.

# 56

Morgen looked at his watch and said they should be out of there in twenty minutes.

The train stood down the track. Schlegel saw steam, smoke and night. Next to the wagons stood the removal van, which screened the transfer from one to the other. It was all done so easily there might have been nothing going on. The only additional sound was hammering. Two to a crate. Schlegel wasn't sure if his own nerves would stand hours trapped in the dark, whatever hope lay at the other end.

There had been a last-minute panic over a missing export stamp, which had been obtained minutes before the office shut. Schlegel was struck by the discretion, the boring regulation of the bureaucracy, proving the legality of the false order, the lack of excitement, however much Morgen said the clock was ticking.

The day had started dramatically with Schlegel summoned to Haager's cell where Haager remained hanging from the bars by his trousers.

'Voluntary or assisted?' asked Morgen. 'Is this Gersten's work? The start of his clean-up?'

Schlegel stared at the grim figure of Haager, tongue lolling, eyes popping, white knees, varicose veins, ending in pigeon-toed feet. Had Haager been got rid of because it was feared he would talk? Was the story of Morgen's ruthlessness in Weimar going the rounds? Morgen said nothing other than to tell the guard to cut the man down.

Morgen remained irritable. Schlegel was forced to spend most of the day scrounging rudimentary food packages and chasing buckets for toilets, thought of at the last moment, and provided by the Grunewald railway depot, with the chit showing them as loaned for 'special consignment'.

Thirty-six 'pieces' for transport; eighteen crates, two to a crate, with extra ballast to correspond to the correct load of tinned goods shown on the dispatch sheet. Schlegel had no idea how it had been decided who should go. All he knew was he knew too much even knowing the train was sanctioned at the highest level. He'd had to liaise with Gersten on the telephone, as the man was nominally in charge, agreeing a time of departure, and so on, including the wagon numbers. The train would leave from what Gersten called the Nöthling siding. He would provide transport to the station and use one of his men. He made no mention of Sybil and Schlegel didn't ask.

Morgen drove just the three of them there, with Grigor handcuffed and surly in the back. Morgen told him his chances were good because Gersten still believed he was producing the perfect note. He thought it probably explained this latest round of shenanigans.

'You are of value to him.'

It was a dubious swap at best from what Schlegel could see. Morgen considered Gersten one of those men who had to introduce an extra little kick to everything, which might yet be his undoing.

When he asked about the side deal with Gersten over Trieste he was told not to be naive. When he said he thought Gersten was getting ready to leave and about to jettison his old comrades,

Reitner in particular, Morgen picked up on that and said, 'Really?'

He saw Sybil only briefly, during an almost wordless exchange. Gersten turned up with his hatchet-faced assistant, who took Grigor off. Gersten said he would walk Sybil to the train. Schlegel wanted to say Gersten couldn't be trusted, but Morgen had already left in a hurry. Sybil avoided his eye. Gersten smirked, looking high and pill-bright. He was wearing Lazarenko's coat.

Sybil stared away when Schlegel wished her good luck. He watched her walk off, carrying no luggage.

He was about to follow when he heard what no one had allowed for. Away in the distance the wail of sirens started to fill the skies. The first pinpricks of the searchlights appeared on the outer edges of the city.

Gersten turned back and shrugged, as if to say whatever else Morgen had in mind, his plans were spoiled. He walked on with a spring in his step.

Schlegel stood torn. He didn't like the way Morgen had disappeared, leaving Sybil with Gersten.

The sky was getting lighter by the minute. The sirens droned on. The train would have to go now or not get out. All that appeared to hold it up was Sybil, standing in front of the last open wagon. What Schlegel saw made no sense to him. She looked animated, happy even, in urgent conversation with Gersten. She nodded, agreeing. Gersten tapped his watch.

The hatchet-faced assistant took Sybil and they ducked down between the wheels and passed under the wagon. Gersten closed the door, blew on a whistle and waved the train out. Wheels slowly turned. By the time the wagons passed, Sybil and the man were gone.

A battery of lights came on over the other side of the embankment, making it almost as bright as day. Gersten turned and walked towards Schlegel, with the same easy spring, and gestured, showing empty hands.

Schlegel couldn't see what Gersten had to offer Sybil. Unless . . . he thought, struggling to make sense of what he had just seen.

He stood mesmerised by Gersten's approach. The chapstick came out of nowhere; the lips moistened; it was gone again.

The only reason for Sybil not to take the train was if Gersten had Lore.

Gersten looked as though he was about to shake Schlegel by the hand, to say no hard feelings, until at the last second he dropped his outstretched arm, and without breaking stride twisted and slashed upwards. Schlegel instinctively recoiled. He felt the thin draw of the cut across his cheekbone, saw the blade flash by the corner of his eye, narrowly missing.

Schlegel was left bent double from the shock. The blade had barely scratched the skin, a sign of the man's artistry. Schlegel could tell it hadn't been done to kill and was more a mark of farewell.

Elation, trepidation, a terrible sinking feeling; Sybil's heart beat wildly. She had difficulty breathing. She grew so dizzy she thought she would fall over.

She had never really believed in the train. It was no sacrifice not to be on it. Such a journey was beyond imagination, and in the back of her mind she had always discounted it. When Gersten told her, there hadn't been a moment's doubt. She dismissed all her obvious misgivings about the man's intrinsic untrustworthiness, duplicity and the punishment he had put her through, not telling her he had Lore, as well as using her right up to the last minute to get Grigor.

The whole episode would turn out to be another trap, she had no doubt of that. But seeing Lore was enough. They could do what they liked after that.

Gersten's assistant, with his dead eyes and irritating, persistent cough, evidently regarded her as harmless because he didn't bother walking behind her. She wanted to pick up a discarded shaft of wood and swing it at his head until she saw brains, but followed meekly because he knew where Lore was.

Past a foul slurry pit and a hangar-like building that stank of animal refuse, they came to an external flight of stairs. The man stepped aside to let her pass, close enough for her to see his look of cruel amusement.

Sybil went upstairs. She called Lore's name. There was no answer. She called again and heard a whimper. She found Lore lying mute on the floor, curled into a ball. Sybil kept repeating it was her, but Lore only wound herself tighter. Sybil had to use all her strength to unlock her body. She lay on top of her, trying to calm her, feeling her uneven breathing. She knew Lore's body as well as her own, yet it was somehow not her. She was aware of the thug's indifferent coughing. She grasped Lore's head and raised it to look at her and screamed.

The limousine stood parked discreetly under the glass awning of one of the markets. Schlegel drew back. People were in the car, a driver and two men in the back, one of them Morgen.

The man in the back nearest Schlegel wore a hat and civilian clothes. He did the talking, quietly and emphatically, in no hurry, as the sirens continued. There was no mistaking that white potato of a face, with its eyes as calculating as an adding machine. His official portrait hung in their building. In Nebe's office there was a signed photograph on his desk, sincerely, Heinrich Himmler.

Himmler said in his chatty, rather dull way, 'I want this place cleaned up tonight. A lorry-load of men will be here to assist.'

Morgen wondered how practical the Reichsführer was, with the small matter of an air raid imminent.

Himmler picked up a bound document resting on his knee.

'Published by the Ministry of Food and Agriculture.' He waved it in contempt. 'If it's supposed to be secret why commit to paper? Don't they know anything?'

He removed his spectacles and cleaned them with a silk handkerchief; he looked at Morgen with myopic eyes. One thing Morgen had learned about the man was he was frighteningly literal, almost childishly so.

Himmler sighed. 'Two years ago the same ministry instigated a policy of official starvation known as the Hunger Plan for those designated useless eaters, not worth feeding. Are you familiar?'

Morgen said he wasn't; always the safest answer. In fact, it was well known as the work of a clever idiot named Backe, one of those dangerous high-flyers who had acquired a name through daring academicism and currying Himmler's favour. From what Morgen had seen of Russia, the policy hadn't worked, not least because the local peasantry was endlessly cunning. Himmler had been blamed and now Backe was virtually a minister, from what Morgen had heard, and estranged from Himmler, who drew the line at the latest adventure of feeding human remains to pigs.

'Can you believe this? I quote: "in order to alleviate shortages suffered by our people". Next he will be suggesting we turn our glorious dead into sausages and we all eat each other. Do we wear bones through our noses? What if it were to get out that our reward for the fallen is to turn them into animal fodder?'

Cannon fodder to animal fodder, thought Morgen grimly.

Turning to look out of the window, Himmler said, 'This place is out of control. Feeding the dead to pigs. Boys being allowed to run around conducting executions. I am recently informed of a highly irregular practice involving sending condemned men from our own camp at Sachsenhausen to be killed at this . . .' He broke off and cast around with an expression of appropriate disgust. 'Meat factory. No more. You did a good job in Weimar. I will be sending you to other camps. The importance of our task is such that we must remain pure when faced with the greatest temptation. I am making you my conscience, Morgen.'

Who flayed? Schlegel asked himself. Gersten liked to cut; he had evidence of that. But he wasn't sure he did the flaying. He thought Gersten internalised. Perhaps knowing was enough.

Morgen was walking towards him and Schlegel wondered whether to give him an official salute, to show his contempt. A ground tremor signalled the crump of the first bombs before the report of the distant explosions.

'The deals one has to do with the devil,' growled Morgen. 'What happened to your face?'

One, two, three cuts. Down the arm. Cutting the Achilles tendon; painful that. The slow draw across the scrotum while reminding the man of what he had done to Abbas.

Gersten was in the steam room with Sepp, who was on the bottle. Grigor stood half-naked and defiant.

Gersten said he was about to embark on the psychological equivalent to making him come. He wanted him to admit there was no perfect note.

It took ten minutes. Gersten informed Grigor he had just made himself redundant. In an uncharacteristic fit of petulance he ground his heel into the man's hand, listening to bone snap, and announced, 'No more perfect note. A pity. I had high hopes.'

Gersten nodded at Sepp. Grigor was dragged to his feet and stood swaying with pain, unbowed.

'I will execute you myself. Face the wall.'

Grigor said he preferred to look at him.

'Then die like a dog in a ditch.'

Gersten stuck his pistol in the man's stomach and pulled the trigger. Grigor recoiled and Sepp kicked his feet from under him and clapped his hands in delight.

'Flay him,' said Gersten.

Grigor lay groaning, not yet dead.

Gersten watched Sepp, drunk and reeling, go about stripping Grigor of the rest of his clothes, wadding and chucking them aside, lugging the naked body with its floppy, useless cock – it couldn't be said to be Grigor any more – onto the trolley, hoisting it with the rattling chain, levering it so it hung over the boiling vat. The skin came off easily after scalding. Then the dismemberment, with the knack of letting the meat resist the blade before yielding to the cut.

Next door was sorting night. Reitner would be charging around like a man possessed, a very different sight from his blubbing over the boy.

Gersten knew the edifice was about to come crashing down. He was losing control. Time was running out. Reitner and the rest were crass, no play to their work, no instinct for the right question, no appropriate awe of the terror induced, no tenderness to their cruelty, no elegance of cut, only merciless glee.

Sepp had already come to him before the roundup, worried about Reitner's rampaging. A thing with a boy had got out of hand. No change there, but Reitner had previously kept disciplinary sadism within bounds, and never managed yet to kill one of his love boys, however much it had been on the cards.

Sepp turned to Gersten to get them out of trouble, as usual. Feed the body to the pigs, Gersten said. What's the problem?

Then he had an idea. Spread a little terror, stand back and admire. Borrow an old trick from psychological operations in the east. Disguise through obliteration and show, dress it up to look like something other than Reitner's drunken, maudlin cruelty. Blame the Jews. Baumgarten had been grumbling on about having to work with Jewish butchers. Make a Jew murder shrine and ship off the butchers before they could protest their innocence.

In the old days they had whipped women to death and flayed them after for public display: see how the Bolsheviks behave like beasts!

It remained his fancy from time to time still to relish the resistance and collapse of a mind and body, the mewling, sobbing and begging, the messy evacuations, moments of respite and generosity, learning to know, understand and appreciate that other inside out, his own failures, strange humour and compassion, the cradling before the breaking of the soul, and always afterwards secret desolation when the body was tidied away, with nothing to show for his artistry.

Reitner had loved the boy up whose arse he stuck the bayonet. Oh, for goodness sake! Reitner could live with that. They flayed the dead little fucker together, in the room Gersten was standing in, wearing butchers' aprons, Reitner snivelling to Gersten's caustic, weary commentary. He couldn't stand it when killers grew mawkish.

He relished how the simple fact of leaving the remains to be found grew into someone else's problem, with all the speculation and curiosity and everyone barking up the wrong tree. It made him feel like a real murderer rather than just another killer. Reitner was his blunt instrument, allowing him to appropriate and embellish, like an artist, becoming death's author, creating a story beyond anything Reitner's savagery was capable of.

Sepp lowered the flesh into the vat, with a slight hiss as it entered the water. The man was still alive and uttered a final blood-curdling, thrilling scream.

Flay and display. Gersten enjoyed the cutting, the way the epidermis lifted from muscle. He wished to practise and improve. The idea of murder as art – the individual act as opposed to so much senseless killing – was beyond Reitner and the rest, with the exception of Sepp, who was all brains and mush for stomach.

One bottle of schnapps, soon after the Reitner business, and the whole sorry story had splurged out in Sepp's tedious, drink-sodden account, layer upon layer. How Metzler's Jews had never left. How it was Reitner's idea to kill them. How the first time he pretended afterwards it was an accident and needed to be hushed up. How that brought Metzler sniffing, smelling a rat, arranging a transfer to the slaughterhouse, with the help of the interfering Jewish butchers. How it was Sepp's idea to stick Metzler in the steam room. How he wanted to get rid of him too, and the Jewish butchers. How Gersten warned him Metzler was off-limits (with the prospect of the perfect note in the pipeline). How the Jews that followed never left either, though Metzler watched them go and believed they had, not seeing the train stop down the line; change of plan, everyone out, lorries waiting.

Gersten hadn't known they were killing Jews on top of every-thing. It wasn't necessary. There was no shortage of bodies. It was the one thing there was a surfeit of. They were even shipped in by train.

Sepp explained it was a fallow period, with a break in supply from the east, a reversal of war, transportation difficulties.

The live cargo had dried up. Gersten hadn't been told about that either, how Reitner had a brother who worked in the big camp north of the city. Condemned men were being sent down so the boys could be inducted into the execution game. Reitner had in mind a killer elite.

But the camp was in lockdown after a prisoner escape, and in quarantine after a typhus outbreak. Nothing coming for three weeks. The boys were getting restless. Reitner told them the test of real mettle was killing Jews.

Reitner, the enterprising, no-nonsense NCO, exercised initiative in the face of a crisis; the constant how-to of solving problems; satisfying the economics of supply and demand. Two birds with one stone.

Of course they were all at it – as before – taking turns, Sepp got around to telling. Haager braining people with his stun gun. Baumgarten punching a man's lights out, taking pride in killing with a single blow. The sport of beheading chickens while doing the same to men, taking bets to see who would run around headless the longest. Even the gutless Sepp sneaked up behind people, shooting them in the neck. Chain whippings, hangings, everything short of crucifixion, though there had been a few of those in the east, thanks to Lazarenko.

Gersten had watched from the shadows on sorting nights. Boys and the men together, killing, killing, killing; the boys queasy at first, then looking forward to it, soon unable to get enough, with silly grins plastered over their faces.

'We all did it,' said Sepp. 'All the time.'

They sated their appetite and fed the results to the pigs. The perfect equation. Sometimes they worried about getting caught.

Gersten rationalised it for Sepp. 'They created a fierce legend for you. This is what happens when the legend comes home.'

Reitner was an increasingly loose cannon. He had taken it upon himself to get rid of Schlegel, a snooper he took exception to because of his nancy-boy white hair. He killed the wrong man instead, went around loosing off shots and failed to finish the job, so drunk that he temporarily passed out among the pigs too, a cause of subsequent hilarity.

Gersten watched Sepp go about his drunken business. He supposed he could shoot him or leave him for others to find *in flagrante*, a prospect that amused him more than shooting the man.

The first wave of planes passed over without incident, their target elsewhere. A single bomb fell on the outskirts of the yard. Schlegel heard its whistle then the dry explosion, followed by ringing hooves on cobblestone and the stampeding of a dozen horses that forced Schlegel and Morgen to seek shelter in the run Baumgarten had taken them up. They waited for the onslaught.

The promised lorry hadn't shown, forcing them to carry on alone or abandon the order. Morgen thought everyone would be hiding from the bombs anyway.

Plaster fell from the ceiling of the tunnel with the next explosion. The lights flickered, went out then struggled back on. Dismal before, the place was even more grim in a bombing raid. Morgen said he had no intention of dying there and preferred to take his chances outside.

He returned soon after, shaken after a close call, and proceeded up the tunnel, leaving Schlegel little choice but to follow. So much debris was coming off the ceiling it was like being trapped in a mine about to collapse.

Schlegel saw figures up ahead. Someone shouted, warning them to come no further. The tunnel plunged into darkness again, with the largest explosion yet, followed by what sounded like a rifle report and a bullet smacking the wall by Schlegel's head. He saw the muzzle flash as the firing continued, pushed Morgen to the ground and threw himself down. Morgen said he thought it was a Hitler Youth. When the lights came back on they would be sitting ducks. On the other hand, the kid was inexperienced, firing in the dark. Morgen was ready when the lights went on, lying as on a firing range, legs spread and using his elbows to steady his aim. The boy was flailing, trying to get his rifle up. Schlegel kept thinking Morgen was being too slow.

The lights flickered. Morgen fired twice. The boy went down, howling.

They hurried on. The boy thrashed on the ground. The other men wore prisoner stripes and were chained together. Schlegel pushed his way past following Morgen as darkness returned and he feared the men would turn on them as one. Boom! Boom! Boom! in the distance. Schlegel held his pistol, thinking how pathetic, compared to outside. The stink there was terrible, like the men were diseased and rotting. With the lights back, Schlegel turned and saw them stamping on the boy, who had stopped screaming and was pleading in vain for mercy.

The boys on the floor were being encouraged to drink, Gersten saw, as he watched the appalling theatre from a safe distance, in horror and admiration as Reitner, despite the crashing bombs, kept everyone at it, death's foreman screaming for overtime. Boys stood in line waiting their turn, stepping up to the platform, while others fetched from among the striped men by the door and, showering them with blows, forced them to strip. The boys dishing it out were as convulsed with terror as the men they beat. Fear ruled them all as the next shuffling man was driven forward, most assuming the pathetic gesture of covering their genitals. Another wave of planes passed over and Gersten thought best would be a fat five-hundred pounder in the middle of it all and not a shred of evidence, and Morgen and Schlegel's nasty little investigation blown to smithereens.

Some boys were crapping themselves at the imminence of death's door. Gersten had a flash of Haager admitting, to general hilarity, on a road in the middle of nowhere, that there was nothing like a warm turd in the pants to snap the mind into shape. There was only Reitner now. Haager and Baumgarten were conspicuous by their absence, Baumgarten, always expert at bunking off, looking innocent afterwards as he said he hadn't realised he was needed. Another thump as a bomb fell. Reitner was screaming for the boys to get on with it. Gersten had to laugh at such a magnificent and meaningless assembly line to death while the apocalypse banged around them. The boys took their turn. Faster! Faster! shouted Reitner. It was like the old days. An escort to bring forward. The dispatcher. No pit now, just two boys, anxiously looking up, waiting for the ceiling to fall in, as they dragged the body away. Kapow! The next one. One dispatching kid, more of a showman, did a Wild West imitation, blowing on the stun gun afterwards while a group stared at the spastic death throes. The next they forced on all fours and put him on the animal conveyor, and the dispatcher asked for a rifle.

Reitner, in his more lucid moments, was prone to banging on about how he wanted to pass on the crucible of his knowledge to the boys. The difference between when they started out was they were green, had to make it up as they went along, whereas now he was in a position to educate them in the legacy of the killing fields. Nerveless courage. Inhuman courage. Cruel hunters. The butchers. Gersten could see most of the boys were too stupid to learn, backward city kids barely in command of the rudiments of education. Where Reitner might once have been the cruellest of the brave, there was now only psychotic rage accelerated by drink. They were all the same. Sepp, lashings of the stuff, so far gone he had probably fallen into the vat. Haager spent his time trying to replicate that heady, summer moment when with bodies all around, the result of the hot pistol in his hand, he had stood with his fly undone, copiously pissing, while simultaneously drinking a whole flagon of beer, and the rest of them wept as they watched, helpless with laughter.

Across the floor, Gersten watched Morgen and Schlegel charge into the room and pause at the carnage, as well they might. Another prisoner fell, poleaxed. Reitner, worked to a frenzy, was rampant. Drunk and bellowing, he pulled down his tracksuit pants to reveal his erect tool, yelling, 'The state of hardness!' No one was paying him attention, apart from Schlegel and Morgen, who stared in disbelief.

Gersten suspected Reitner's work was done. He had passed on the killing virus, but badly, because the boys had no respect for their work, or for him. It was like watching the play of cruel frightened children. They would knuckle under because they were conditioned, but it was the obedience of imminent anarchy.

Exquisite confusion followed as the lights went out, leaving everyone shouting and screaming. One or two came back on, making a shadow play of the scene. Gersten pictured red sky above, huge flashes. Another round of bombs shook the walls, the perfect chaos outside matched by the internal carnage. They used to laugh at him because he didn't drink; who was laughing now? He moved forward, fast and controlled, pistol at his side. He took out one of the more hopeless lads, who looked in danger of scuttling off, shot him because the boy's head presented itself at an inviting angle. After that they all started firing. He would be lucky to get out alive; so be it.

He came to Reitner railing at the heavens. If he could see how stupid he looked, thought Gersten, passing behind, pausing to half-genuflect and pull the trigger for the bullet to pass through the soft hinge of the back of the knee to blow out the bone in front. Reitner gave an almighty shriek and went down, the agony spinning him in circles. Gersten would have finished him except he was distracted by Morgen and the tall, white-haired one charging around. The latter's silhouette gave him away. He fired off a shot and saw him hit, would have fired again except the rest of the lights came on. Another crash.

Schlegel was hit in the left shoulder. There was no blood. It had felt like someone had slammed his feet, leaving him with a puzzled image of fairground tests of strength, smashing a hammer down on a platform to try to make a bell ring. Someone had started firing, then they were all at it. Had he imagined Gersten slipping away down the tunnel?

Clutching his shoulder, Schlegel watched Morgen drag Reitner to his feet, which left him hopping on one leg, trying to protect his shattered knee. Another bomb, closer, and everyone froze. Reitner didn't look so tough now. The boys stood around, gormless.

Morgen barked at Reitner, 'Pull yourself together, soldier, and have them fall in.' Reitner made a feeble attempt to stand to attention. Schlegel heard the whine of stalling engines and the dive of a plane out of control. The boys lined up. One short of three ranks of six. A few tough ones, including the boxer and the boy he had beaten, trying to hold it together; a couple of spindly youths, including the ubiquitous shifty one, a fat boy with glasses, the ambiguous one that reminded Schlegel of himself; the rest making up the numbers. An anti-aircraft battery went da-da-da! The explosion that followed was in the air. It must have got the diving plane. Hooray! went one or two of the boys, and the boxer shouted, 'Death to the enemy!'

Morgen inspected the first rank. The boys instinctively stiffened. Reitner, propping himself on his hands, resting on his good leg, looked like a runner at the start of a desperate race. Morgen addressed the boxing boy and pointed to Reitner.

'That soldier can't carry on. What do you do with a soldier that can't carry on?'

The boy's eyes flicked sideways to the one standing next to him, who shook his head.

Reitner shouted, 'You shoot a soldier that can't carry on. You do not leave him for the enemy!'

Morgen talked to the boy again. 'But in this instance, in this place, what do you do?'

Reitner shouted he was forbidden to say. Their work was sanctioned. He was sweating like he was covered in glycerine.

Morgen snapped, 'Quiet, soldier.'

He changed his register to one of normal conversation, speaking to Reitner. 'Tell me, one thing I don't understand. Why did you have to keep the freezer and the morgue in town, not here?'

Reitner made a noise that Schlegel decided could only be the man attempting to laugh.

Morgen laughed too at the explanation. The premises were subject to regular inspection by the Department of Health and Safety, which had objected to a temporary morgue on an animal site. Morgen looked at the boys, who giggled too.

He stepped up to the boxing boy and snapped, 'Is something funny?'

The boy shook his head. 'No, sir!' shouted Morgen. 'No, sir!' repeated the boy.

Outside all the noise now came from the north.

Morgen told the boys he was in charge. Reitner was incapable of command. He asked again what happened to soldiers that couldn't carry on. Reitner repeated they must not tell. Morgen told the boxing boy he wasn't asking them to say, he was ordering them to show him. The boy bleated about the bombs outside.

'Do it,' snapped Morgen.

\* \* \*

The pigs were hysterical with fear. In the background the city burned. In spite of all the destruction, Schlegel could see little evidence of immediate damage. They made the strangest procession. Two lads pulled the trolley on which Reitner lay screaming. The rest straggled behind like boys on a nightmare school outing. Morgen made them pause to ask Reitner who had killed Keleman. Reitner refused to say, even when Morgen probed his shattered knee with the point of his pistol. Schlegel asked him to stop, saying it didn't matter now. Morgen addressed the boxing boy, who told them how Reitner had made them take the body to the pigs.

'And this one too,' he said, indicating Schlegel. But they had all been too drunk to finish the job.

'Not this time,' said Morgen.

Gersten watched from the room above the pigs, after being warned by his consumptive colleague, who wet-coughed into a handkerchief, complaining of the smoke and dust. People were below, he said.

Gersten knew he should get out but was unable to tear himself away.

The pigs were thrashing. Sensing human presence, they charged the rails, jumping up, some squealing, others keeping up a furious grunting. The boys were the tamest thing in the room, cowed. One or two started to cry. Morgen forced Reitner to stand. Reitner hopped around. Morgen offered him the choice of stepping voluntarily into the pigs. Schlegel could never tell when the man was serious. Reitner stiffened at a sight above him, and Schlegel looked up to see Gersten disappear from the window as Reitner, the veins in his neck jutting, screamed 'Judas!'

The accusation echoed round the cavernous space as the next wave of bombers rumbled in.

Morgen was already running. Schlegel followed, glancing back at the commotion around Reitner, who raised his hands as the boxer boy stepped forward, drew his fist to his shoulder and gave his hardest punch. Reitner half-fell under his broken knee. The sharp cry of pain was followed by the crack of the boy's uppercut, driving Reitner against the fence. He reeled from the force of the blow, swaying until the boy gave a shove, flipping him back among the waiting pigs.

One, two, three bombs. A proper appreciation of violence took time and control. No chance of that. Sybil and her friend sat on the floor clutching each other like babes in the wood. Catatonic. The friend not so pretty now, the job half-done. The plan – too late for that now; the plan had been to make a present of her to Sybil, as a sample of work in progress, before letting her watch the rest. He had never let anyone do that before, not by invitation, to see him do to her friend what he would then do to her. In fact, the friend didn't look so bad. He had kept himself under control. No, he hadn't. He hadn't meant to go to her in the first place. It had been after Schlegel and the tower. He had visited with the best of intentions, the bearer of good news. Sybil had kept her end of the bargain and delivered Grigor, so he would keep his, and as an extra surprise he would put them both on the train. Their strange love was love, after all. He wasn't narrow-minded. No, honestly, he said, seeing she didn't believe him. She spoiled it with that little hissing noise, made with teeth and tongue, more than her look of contempt, which he could have forgiven on its own. He hadn't meant to cut her, had meant to stop after a quick couple of signature marks. The punch spoiled it. By the time he was done there was no question of putting her on a train.

He had said to Grigor, 'There are some stories people are willing to tell and some they aren't. I am interested in you telling me all the stories you don't wish to tell.' He couldn't remember the name of the Jew actor who had once put his hand on his knee, who played the bug-eyed killer running around picking up kids and was reduced to screaming how drive overrode desire. Gersten wasn't so sure. Desire was everything. He had fancied exploring these thoughts with Sybil and her friend. He badly wanted to see if he could rouse Sybil into giving a decent account of herself. The other one he didn't care about, but Sybil he wanted to fight him, to die well. Had he really intended to let them both go? Yes, he had. Or at least he knew he would have no trouble convincing Schlegel. Some people were born to twist around your little finger.

Footsteps on the stairs, obliterated by the crunch of another bomb. Seconds only now. No time for fond farewells. Gersten took in the room. His colleague rooted in the corner, praying a bomb wouldn't fall on him, handkerchief across his face, stifling the hep-hep of his wet cough. Sybil and her friend pressed together, almost comic, so immobile they could have been garden statues. Perhaps he should sell novelty items after the war. The thought amused him as he shot his consumptive colleague, who gave a final cough wetter than the rest, spraying his handkerchief red. He was sorry to drag the girls apart. Sybil put up such a struggle that he was forced to kick her, hard. There was no time to explain that he was sparing her life. It was his present to her. The other one was past caring. He yanked her up and she came easily into his arms, to make a nice cushion as Morgen came blundering in. Gersten fired, off balance from the weight of the girl. The shot splintered the door frame, millimetres from Morgen's ear; a brief, fond memory of Lazarenko's body jitterbugging from the velocity of bullets. Gersten fired through the empty doorway to keep Morgen quiet. He dragged himself and the girl back towards the window. She was like a dead weight in his arms, hardly worth killing. He was about to discard her when Schlegel spoiled the moment by charging up the stairs, like an actor coming in off-cue, resulting in a scramble of frantic improvisation. Gersten switched to the blade, desperately sought the carotid artery with the hand he had around her throat and plunged.

Schlegel didn't recognise Lore, so terribly beaten, her face a horrible clown's mask. The nose was broken, teeth smashed, eyes swollen to slits, and someone had scribbled lipstick over her face and put make-up on, turning the face a ghastly, floury white.

Lore was like Gersten's marionette, tottering forwards as he gave her a huge shove and she came at Schlegel, desperately trying to raise her arms, the blood spurting from the tear in her neck. They collided in a terrible embrace, then got tangled up with Morgen, who was struggling to get past them to Gersten.

Schlegel glimpsed Gersten, who caught his eye, looking both appalled and amused by his destruction, before he turned and threw himself out of the window.

As the smash of glass filled the room, Lore's eyes fluttered open. It was like she was looking at something very far away.

Schlegel automatically ran and launched himself out of the window. He fell, hoping, and seconds later landed on the angled roof of the Jewish barracks, winding himself. He had remembered right; the roof was hard under the window. He had his gun where Gersten had chucked his aside for the blade.

He supposed Gersten had made such a mess of Lore. Having been there himself, he knew anything could go on in those deep pockets in Gersten's building.

He hit the ground. His shoulder was stiffening so he could hardly move his left arm. The sky was ablaze and bombs fell all around as he worked his way down the narrow gap between the barracks and the pig building. When he came to open ground there was no sign of Gersten. Schlegel retreated back along the corridor and checked the Jewish barracks, in case he was hiding there, a prospect more terrifying than confronting him in the open because Gersten was a master of confined space.

Schlegel was still inside when he saw Gersten through the window, trapped by explosions, standing exultant. When he saw Schlegel aiming from the doorway he ran off, not even with any urgency, as if to say he doubted if Schlegel could hit him. Schlegel fired and missed, and set off in pursuit.

One bomb dropped so close the blast left him staggering like a drunk.

The slurry pit was a stinking blaze of phosphorous. Planes were still coming over. Schlegel suspected Gersten was picking his way through the explosions, making for the railway embankment.

He was hit hard from behind. The force of Gersten's charge knocked him down and the gun flew from his hand. He waited for the slash of Gersten's blade. Instead Gersten was on top, pulling him over, straddling him, pinning his arms, making it impossible to move. The flames from the slurry pit gave his face a yellow glow. Gersten, with an eye for performance, looked around, admiring the devastation. He performed his sneaky trick with the chapstick.

'Always moist lips for a killing,' he said, relishing the absurdity, before holding the blade high to catch the light.

'Face to face, I say. Don't disappoint me.'

Schlegel knew he had only moments. His mind was blank. Not a single thing to say. Here goes, he thought, embarrassed to resort to her at such a moment.

'My mother remembers you as an actor.'

Schlegel saw the crucial instant of bewilderment, then the flattery register, long enough for him to dig his heels in and thrust upwards. He half-toppled Gersten, tried to push him off altogether, was hauling himself up when his frozen arm gave way, and Gersten was back on top, giggling as he pressed down on Schlegel's throat and lifted his arm high, turning to admire the blade. Holding it there, he looked back and said, 'There's no point if there's no glee, don't you agree?'

A single plane passed overhead. Bombs started to fall. It must be a stray, Schlegel thought, jettisoning its load. Gersten's blade would do its job first. Instead the blade fell. Gersten looked down puzzled at the hole that had appeared in the arm of Lazarenko's coat. He seemed more offended by the damage to that than the wound. Morgen called. Another shot. Gersten took it in the body, then he was rolling away and running.

Schlegel set off after, thinking he wanted to see the last of the man as he was blown to pieces in the inferno. Gersten zigzagged ahead, lurching. Morgen was calling Schlegel back, shouting it was too dangerous. The bombs created a corridor down which Gersten ran.

He paused to turn, inviting Schlegel to follow, then waved and ran on. The ground between them rippled like a carpet shaken. Gersten ran between walls of flame as the world raged, then the earth exploded and everything turned black and the last thing Schlegel remembered was being thrown through the air, to become the flying man, with the brief sensation that he would carry on rising, until everything below was reduced to insignificance and nothing mattered.

# 57

Spring turned to summer, a season once looked forward to now serving only as a marker for the deteriorating situation. Whispers that things could only end badly were countered by wild stories of extraordinary technological breakthroughs: a super-bomb, laser weapons, planes faster than the speed of light, secret underground factories where all these were being developed.

Dr Joseph Goebbels, in the sanctuary of his private screening room, watched a film archive print of the 1936 Alexander Korda movie *Things to Come* over and over, taking meetings with screenwriters, enthusing how its epic sweep and vision could be updated and appropriated.

'In the rubble of this film lies the future we will build for ourselves.'

He watched it alone late at night, in order to recite aloud the final speech, learned phonetically. Conquest beyond conquest. This little planet. Its winds and ways. All the universe or nothing. Which shall it be?

He told his wife, who was over her nervous collapse, how in the film in 1966 a chemical weapon dispersed from the skies, called the wandering sickness, was used by the unnamed enemy in a final desperate bid for victory.

'A wandering sickness!'

It was so German! Dr Harding and his daughter struggled to find a cure. With such little equipment, they had no chance.

'We have the equipment. This wandering sickness, what propaganda we will make from that when we inflict it on our enemies!'

His wife wanted to know what happened in the film.

'Hopeless! The plague kills half humanity and extinguishes the last vestiges of central government.'

Schlegel's mother's opening remark was, 'A broken arm, two broken legs and crutches, how on earth did you manage that?'

He couldn't be bothered to come up with even an approximation, so told everyone he had fallen downstairs during the raid. The bullet wound in his shoulder was disguised by the broken arm.

'You look lucky to be alive.'

During two weeks in hospital she was his only visitor. Of Morgen there was no sign.

Afterwards he sat at home and grew bored playing patience. He tried the theatre but his legs itched unbearably and with the plaster he had no way of scratching. Something as minor as that could bring on spells of panic. He adjourned to the bar early. When the others came out at the interval there was grumbling among those trying to get drinks about the space he was taking, in spite of his obvious disability. Everyone for himself now; no kindred spirit. In the bar mirror he saw the yellow suit, then Kübler, vivacious and laughing. She held his eye for a frozen moment in the reflection, then was gone.

His stepfather held a shooting party and insisted Schlegel come for the picnic and fresh air. It was pot luck, he said. No one bothered overmuch about hunting regulations now. He preferred to bag boar because so many were invading the suburbs.

Schlegel travelled in a van with the food while the men were out. His stepfather came in from the morning shoot in the company of a tall, stringy man with the palest blue eyes.

'This is Walter Fann. You can speak English together.'

Fann was a classic cowboy type whose level gaze made Schlegel think of the flatlands of the Midwest; eyes used to staring at distance. It seemed impolite to ask what he was doing there. He supposed some fellow travellers had stayed behind, and those married to Germans. He wondered if Fann was Lipchitz's Yank.

Fann had the usual American forthright manner and sales know-how. He could see Schlegel was curious about him. He had come from Switzerland, he volunteered, on an Argentinian passport, thanks to a Spanish mother.

Schlegel thought it unlikely given the man's Nordic looks. Sensing his scepticism, Fann said he was also travelling on a pass issued by the Vatican.

'And another for the Swiss Red Cross,' he said, laughing easily.

Schlegel supposed him about fifty, though he looked younger and in better trim than most German men his age. He showed no interest in Schlegel or his condition.

They ate ham and egg pie from his mother's recipe, and drank a dry white wine. Schlegel didn't say much. The men talked of sporting matters. He wondered about Fann and his stepfather. Before the war they could have been legitimate partners. Americans had developed numerous tax-shelter deals. Since the war these had been discontinued or reworked through neutral countries.

Fann didn't go back out in the afternoon, saying he had shot enough. He was reading Hemingway. *For Whom the Bell Tolls*. Did Schlegel know it? Schlegel wondered why Fann was not out with the guns again. Ten days ago if anyone had told him he would soon be spending his afternoon with an American he would not have believed it.

Fann read mostly, occasionally asked inconsequential questions, such as whether Schlegel 'had a gal', and Schlegel wondered if the man was sounding him out after all, and whether to a specific end.

Fann always checked that Schlegel knew what he was talking about. Henry Ford, for instance.

'You know who I mean by him?'

'Of course. Ford cars,' said Schlegel politely.

'Not just cars,' emphasised Fann.

He observed that he sometimes found Germans hard to read, so it was a relief to talk English.

Ford still had many subsidiaries there, despite the two countries severing diplomatic relations.

Schlegel supposed it was an American trait to spell things out.

The real reason for Fann being there was a surprise.

Fann said Ford wanted to make a donation from local company profits to eugenics research, which was a registered charity for tax purposes.

'You and we are leaders in the field, and until the war worked closely. Henry is looking to ways to reopen that channel.'

Henry!

Fann then had the nerve to describe himself as a simple kind of fellow, which was why he had consulted Schlegel's stepfather.

'He recommended that eugenics may have peaked, and isn't necessarily the best investment for its cultural return. What do you think?'

'It's odd,' said Schlegel carefully. 'I was involved in something the other day involving American investment where you would least expect it.'

'Where was that?' asked Fann neutrally.

'Foreign export. Illegal foreign export masquerading as tinned peaches.'

Fann changed the subject back to Hemingway and said he was an obvious kind of guy. Schlegel was sure Fann was Lipchitz's Yank. It didn't bear thinking about what his stepfather was up to.

He was left to surmise whether this money – due to be invested in racial research – was sidelined into the other operation. He suspected with Fann's introduction he was being shown something whose meaning would become clear only gradually.

He remained technically on sick leave, even after the plaster was removed. He suspected no one knew what to do with him. He found having to climb five flights using crutches had made him fitter. He tried not to think of Sybil. He didn't know if she was alive and had no idea where Morgen was to ask. Nebe kept his distance. Frau Pelz unnerved him by sending a get-well card.

Morgen resurfaced after some weeks via telegram, suggesting they meet at the Adlon for breakfast. He was late. Schlegel started without him. He ate something calling itself porridge oats that could have been put to better use as glue for advertising hoardings. The milk was watered down. The hotel, which had once prided itself on its bakery, now served a slightly superior version of the same cardboard as everyone else. No one, high or low, was spared its flatulent effects. During one of her hospital visits, his mother had been hugely amused to recount how at a recent dinner party an Argentinian diplomat had nearly caused an international incident by inadvertently releasing a huge fart during the soup course.

It was also widely said Adolf led by example and the climax of his speeches amounted to a cacophony of farting, which was why those immediately behind on the podium always looked so grim.

The boiled egg came with no salt. The elderly waitress had apologised that the coffee was not real and recommended the tea, which was. They were down to the last of their reserves. The tulips that decorated the room came from Holland, she said.

'You have to agree, they brighten the place up.'

Her tone was one of long sufferance, as though she had to spend all her time dealing with requests she could not satisfy.

People still dressed for the Adlon. A lot of senior uniforms and party badges were in, foreign journalists on good expenses, and the inevitable diplomats; the rest were new money.

In that studied enclave, a semblance of normal life remained persistent, if grave. Newspapers were scoured with intent. A vulgar, noisy quartet was frowned at. Schlegel guessed the men were on combat leave and in no mood for social niceties. One of their female companions was being groped under the table. Schlegel couldn't decide whether they were high-class prostitutes or society girls out for a fast time.

There was a lot he still couldn't make sense of. The section before he had lost consciousness remained a kaleidoscope of fractured images.

Morgen finally hurried in, altogether smarter, wearing what looked like a new suit. He sat down, didn't bother to apologise, and behaved as though they had parted as normal the night before.

The dining room was starting to clear. Morgen looked at his watch. 'Am I late?'

It required all his tact and charm to win the waitress round.

'Are you all right?' was all he asked Schlegel.

Morgen struck him as jittery. Nor could Schlegel understand

the point of the meeting. Morgen appeared to have nothing to say and spent all his time looking around and fidgeting.

'You don't know what to do with your hands.'

'What are you talking about?' asked Morgen, belligerently.

'You've given up smoking.'

'Giving up. Very observant, Mr Detective.'

'Short of the hotel messenger announcing it, I would say it's obvious to everyone.'

Morgen raced through his breakfast, slurped his tea, sat back in expectation then remembered there was no cigarette to be had.

'I must go,' he said, half-rising.

'For God's sake, man, light up.'

'I can't.'

'Then I'm going.'

'Look at the state of my hands.'

Morgen sighed, reached into his pocket and put an unopened pack of cigarettes on the table.

'Emergency supplies. Test of willpower. It works.'

'If you won't, I will.'

Schlegel reached for the packet and opened it. Morgen let out a groan.

'Light?' asked Schlegel.

'No. My willpower isn't that strong.'

Schlegel got matches from the waitress. The cigarette tasted foul.

'You do this to torture me.'

'Only to show you what a filthy habit it is.'

Morgen took the cigarette from Schlegel before he could stub it out.

'One drag.' The end sparked as he took in a huge lungful. 'Two drags.'

*     *     *

Equilibrium restored, Morgen held court in the empty dining room.

Gersten was being talked of as though he were dead.

'No body found but I am sure we haven't heard the last. I suspect Gersten is a Nosferatu. The Youth have been dispersed for re-education and are being assigned to anti-aircraft batteries. Baumgarten is missing. Reitner must be bratwurst by now. Sepp was picked up in the process of boiling Grigor. The flayings are now written off to a combination of Sepp and Lazarenko. Nebe is pleased.'

'What about Nöthling?'

'Haven't you heard? They arrested him and he hanged himself in his cell.'

That was news. Schlegel supposed nothing had happened because there had been no opportunity to follow up his entrapment using the Kübler woman.

'He was fingered by former Minister of Food and Agriculture Walter Darré, who is in disgrace and did it to try to get a foot back in the door.'

'Spanish Ricardo?'

It was what his mother called Darré, who was from Argentina. Schlegel said he had a reputation for being a terrific drunk.

'Absolutely,' said Morgen, lighting up. 'He keeps an elephant's foot in his study. Told me he didn't approve of stuffing animals, but it was all he had left of life in Buenos Aires. I said I didn't know they had elephants in South America, which he seemed to find funny. At any rate, he was a pushover after that in spite of a sticky start. He gave me a signed copy of his book, *The Farmer as the Animating Spirit of the Nordic Race*.'

'Read it?'

'Of course not. The man is so boring Adolf picked up a newspaper during one meeting. Darré showed me a photograph of them all in the first government. Adolf looking almost coy.

Goebbels like a ventriloquist's dummy, cupping his balls. A thinner Goering. Imagine, a thinner Goering. What a bunch.'

'What of Nöthling? He knew enough to embarrass a lot of people. Assisted suicide?'

'No. I think his vanity was offended to find he was expendable.'

'Are we allowed to talk about what went on the other night?'

Morgen looked around to check no one was nearby.

'Broadly speaking. In the heart of the beast it's business as usual, but the more perspicacious are starting to hold their fingers up to the wind. The days of grand disobedience are over.'

The term leadership vacuum was starting to be heard.

'Even as the work of zealous bureaucrats goes on, some at the top are starting to think of laying down the first markers for future negotiations and realignment.'

'I saw you in the car that night.'

'Keep that under your hat. Pretty breathtaking, I thought, that Heine should start to consider an alternative to the eastern route.'

It was the beginning of the redirection of the juggernaut, Schlegel supposed, a long process of wheel-turning. Morgen agreed siren voices were starting to be heard. Schlegel asked if he knew of an American named Fann. Morgen didn't and afterwards said it fitted what he was hearing.

'My enemy's enemy is my friend, and all that. It makes more sense to combine against the Bolshevik than fight each other.'

'And your analysis?'

'There will be no jumping ahead. The diehards will prevail, while a counter-movement of reverse negotiation goes on in the sidelines. This I hardly need point out is treasonable activity and there will be many watchdogs. At the same time, there comes a point when it is necessary to start thinking about survival strategies, also known as exercises in cynicism.'

It was the start of what would become known as strategic helping, as part of the laying down of future deals.

'First one must be seen to be aiding those most oppressed. Grotesque perhaps, but that is the way of the world. It seems some idiot has persuaded Heine to establish and preserve a Jewish escape line that in time may well become his own.'

'Any idea which idiot?'

Morgen smiled and stubbed out his cigarette.

'Come on, the Esplanade now. It's almost lunchtime. I have a surprise.'

Sybil sat alone in the lobby. She looked pale and ethereal. Morgen made a show of meeting like they were ordinary people and reintroduced Schlegel. Sybil offered the merest brush of a handshake, with downcast eyes.

Morgen appeared falsely jovial.

'Table for three,' he told the maitre d'. 'I have booked.'

Sybil appeared reserved, as opposed to withdrawn. She wore black. Many women did now. Most families had a death in them.

For the second time that morning, Schlegel puzzled over the purpose of the meeting. Sybil said little and Morgen busied himself with the menu, a pointless exercise as almost nothing was on it.

Schlegel made a futile attempt at conversation, asking Sybil where she was living now. With friends, was all she said. He stared miserably out of the window at the garden, thinking it couldn't be easy living like a ghost. He supposed Morgen had something in mind. Morgen insisted they bring an expensive bottle of wine from the cellar. Sybil did no more than sip hers and hardly touched her food. She looked terribly thin.

Morgen addressed her formally throughout, though he didn't say much. Occasionally he turned round, as if expecting someone. Schlegel considered making his excuses. Morgen smoked while eating, his hand circulating between ashtray, glass and plate. Once or twice, when Sybil wasn't looking, he gave her a look of forlorn pity.

Eventually he said to Schlegel, 'I thought Fräulein Todermann could come and work for us.'

'Instead of Frau Pelz? Yes, please.'

'She doesn't have secretarial skills, unless I am mistaken.'

Sybil gave a shake of the head.

'I expect we'll find something,' said Morgen airily.

Sybil looked neither grateful nor expectant.

She looked at Schlegel and said, 'I feel I am among the living dead.'

Schlegel stared at his plate. Morgen was standing up. Schlegel lifted his eyes and was horrified to see his mother. Worse, she had her friend in tow who had complained of losing her Jewish seamstress. Worst of all, Schlegel suspected Morgen had arranged it.

Sybil had gone rigid. She reached out under the table and gripped his hand.

'Darling, what a surprise. Don't get up. We'll join you for five minutes. I can see you are busy.'

His mother raised her eyebrows in the direction of Sybil. Her companion, staring at Sybil, asked if they knew each other. Sybil nodded imperceptibly, still holding Schlegel's hand under the table. He suspected his mother had noticed. She let go when they sat down. His mother was next to Morgen and smoothly took over.

She'd heard Morgen had been to see Walter Darré, whom she called Spanish Rick and explained why in an aside to Sybil.

Schlegel had trouble grasping the fact of the two women at the same table. He couldn't imagine what Sybil made of it.

'A little bit too cosmopolitan for my taste,' his mother went on about Darré. 'Speaks too many languages for a start and drinks far too much. Food and Agriculture, can you imagine anything worse? He was all for us going back to the land. Leave the beastly old cities and live in farming communes.' She turned to Sybil. 'I can say this because I am not German. They are hopelessly enamoured of the bucolic, and, like a lot of them who aren't of the blood, Ricky wants to be more German than German. Very fond of his uniform. I am told he doesn't look so impressive with his trousers down.'

She went on, unstoppable. 'He was no friend of Dr Goebbels, who regarded him as a complete flop and told me so in person.'

Schlegel sensed Sybil's flinch. This time he reached out and grabbed her hand.

Was his mother being indiscreet because she was drunk or did she just not care? Then it occurred to him. She was terribly nervous of Sybil.

She ran on and on, talking. She helped herself to one of Morgen's cigarettes and puffed on it inexpertly, saying how there were only about 180 people worth knowing in Berlin.

'Why don't you just say two hundred?' said Schlegel in exasperation.

'Because it's not that many, and you know it. And I am being generous at that. There are perhaps a further hundred outside Berlin, most landed with estates.'

Schlegel suspected her precision went down well with the elite. Her knowledge of etiquette and manners, combined with her own social compromises in consorting with the leadership, flattered those at the top eager to improve socially.

In the right milieu she was imperious. In the present situation she was grotesque. Even Morgen stared in astonishment at the sight of the woman in full flight. Sybil gripped Schlegel's hand harder until he felt his knuckles turn white.

His mother issued a succinct bulletin on the political

situation, saying there was a reformatory movement to get rid of the old Venetian-style corruption, snapping everyone into line for the new austerity. It was by no means a united front, but Goebbels and Speer were now seen as the new Lutherans.

She finally drew breath. Schlegel failed to get a word in edgeways and she was off again.

'Which reminds me, Spanish Rick boasts about having been to an English public school as an exchange scholar. He speaks quite good English as a result, but he's a terrific snob in an *arriviste* way. He said he attended part of Eton when he was talking about King's College Wimbledon, which is not the same. One only goes to Wimbledon for tennis.'

'Enough, Mother,' Schlegel said, and finally she stopped. They all sat there stunned.

'I'm sorry. I know,' she said.

She looked at her companion, indicated Sybil and said, 'I am sure we can find work for her.'

Schlegel stared at Morgen, who motioned that he should not interrupt.

His mother turned to Sybil. 'Spanish Rick is not entirely beside the point. I believe your mother is staying there. I am having a reading done tomorrow.'

'How do you know she's her mother?' asked Schlegel, unable to stop himself.

'Girls share information, darling. We went to Sybil for our couture and the men went to her mother, and now we're all at it.' She looked at Sybil. 'Isn't that right?'

'Yes,' said Sybil.

'I am glad you can still speak. I thought the cat had got your tongue.'

She was the only one who laughed. 'Well, I can see you're busy.'

She got up and addressed Schlegel rather than Sybil.

'She can stay in the summer house. The garden is quite private and she can work from there. What do you think?'

Schlegel looked again at Morgen, who appeared sphinx-like. Had all this been agreed? Five minutes ago he could have murdered the woman. Now he was supposed to treat her like a cross between guardian angel and benefactress.

Her mother gave him a smirk of triumph. 'We do what we can.'

She leaned down to be kissed. He gave her a single peck. She offered the other cheek.

'Come on, darling. Continental style.'

She shook Sybil's hand and said, 'The beginning of a fruitful acquaintance, I am sure.'

Morgen she addressed only as old rogue.

Schlegel was surprised to discover, whatever he thought of this impossible woman, he actually trusted her.

Morgen paid the bill.

'Satisfactory arrangement?' he said to Sybil.

Sybil nodded. Schlegel saw it would be a long time before she dropped her guard.

Nevertheless, outside she took their arms as she walked between them, holding her head higher.

'And what shall we do now?' said Morgen, reaching for another cigarette.

# Afterword

My fascination with Germany goes back to the late 1950s when I was an army brat posted with my family to the garrison town of Iserlohn, on the edge of the industrial Ruhr, to be part of the British Army of the Rhine. Even at the age of eight this upheaval raised interesting questions about winning and losing. Growing up in dreary post-war England resembled no sort of victory, more a state of shell-shocked exhaustion. Germany by contrast felt strangely arrested, strangely progressive (Mercedes, Telefunken), more technological and complicated, and interestingly scarred by its psychological burden, compared to our pathetic last days of Empire and deferral to the United States, which, nevertheless, in terms of its consumer disposables on offer, and constant promise of renewal, made it a Mecca for post-war generations. England in many ways remained a closed society but Germany was *hidden*, and therein lay its fascination.

Even at eight years old I already found the idea of losing more interesting (having by then decided I wouldn't be eligible for the Roman Catholic heaven of my upbringing). Years later I knew exactly what the lapsed Graham Greene had meant when he referred to success as failure deferred. I had no idea I would write, but that ambiguous terrain proved far more beguiling than the facts and dates dinned into us at school. As boys, our informal education was steeped in the *idea* of war, for at the time it seemed inevitable there would be another, involving us.

471

We grew accomplished (and pompous) on the subject, as one might in becoming an expert in languages (the Falaise salient, Verdun, the flight of Rudolf Hess, kamikaze pilots). We questioned the idea of military occupation no more than we did colonial imperialism. If I wondered why we were in Germany it was not articulated beyond agreeing it must be because we had won the war and, less certainly, to stop the Red Menace. It was the Cold War and a state of alert, a time when films would have such subtitles as, 'How I learned to stop worrying and love the bomb.' Ramped-up consumerism went hand-in-hand with the prospect of nuclear obliteration; no wonder we schoolboys took refuge in the patriotic trash and simplicities of the War Picture Library, celebrating easier heroics and being beastly about the Germans.

In the 1980s I spent long periods in what was then West Berlin and was again intrigued by the sense of recent (and current) history, far more than when in Britain. Germany made a point of emphasising its clean break from 1945 (which turned out to be not true at all), compared to us Brits limping on, dragging the coattails of the past behind (when in fact the Labour government of 1945 probably offered the cleaner break). On one trip to Berlin I happened to take a book called *The Last Jews in Berlin*. As Primo Levi later wrote, we all knew about the trains, which featured in every account, and what happened next, but I knew nothing of the before. I was reading some theory too, particularly an essay on politics by Gilles Deleuze, which considered history in terms of lines of migration and pointed out that life always proceeds at several rhythms and speeds. This variable offensive is no more apparent than in times of war. Later, I was equally struck by Don DeLillo's remark that history comes down to people talking in rooms. *The Last Jews in Berlin* blurred all the usual boundaries, to reveal a world of often impossible moral complexity and uncomfortable truths: how, for example, part of the twisted genius of the Third Reich was the way it solicited the cooperation of those it wished to destroy, first with the deportations and later in the camps. Both were the work of petty clerks as much as anyone, a bureaucratic nightmare out of Kafka. They were stark times, but the shading was infinitely complex.

The persecution of Berlin's Jews took place often right in the familiar heart of the city. *The Last Jews in Berlin* described a vanished world that remained horribly recognisable even as it was being twisted so out of shape: the city map remained the same as it had when Alfred Döblin wrote his street-specific 1929 masterpiece *Berlin Alexanderplatz* (except many street names had been changed to glorify the new regime). And then there were the Catchers. I'd had no idea that some Jews were turned by the Gestapo into agents to hunt down those that had gone underground. The most notorious of these was the glamorous Stella Kübler. At the time, *The Last Jews in Berlin* was the only reference to her that I could find. Yet vestiges of her lingered in the streets I found myself in: Kübler's beat scoured the theatres, cafés and bars of a part of Berlin I knew quite well. Down the years, her turning and betrayal retained a grim fascination when posed as the question: how would you or I have behaved under the circumstances?

Another book read at the time was Heinz Höhne's *The Order of the Death's Head: The Story of Hitler's SS*, which was the first time I came across the SS having its own equivalent to Internal Affairs, with reference to an investigative judge named Morgen who was put to weeding out corruption and sadism in the camps. As Höhne noted: 'It was an absurd spectacle; one or two "unauthorised" murders of Jews were investigated – by a whole squad of SS legal experts – inside the extermination camps where thousands were being murdered daily.' Morgen remained as much an historical obscurity as Stella Kübler; subsequent information adds little to the half-dozen pages offered by Höhne. The question remains unanswered whether he was a hypocrite or a man of conscience, or both. (The generous explanation might be that he did what he could, not without risk to himself, when most did nothing. Realising that any personal protest against state-sanctioned murder would go unheeded or punished, he took the more prudent and probably the only practical tactic of prosecuting individual transgressors within the interpretation of dishonour and the law.)

Details from both these books and other reading lodged in the memory: that the Gestapo used civilian removal vans (with a Jewish name) to transport their prisoners; that until 1943 those to be deported were summoned by private letter and reported voluntarily with their permitted baggage allowance to fill in their forms; that the Gestapo was suspended for corruption and an SS team from Vienna was brought in to instigate a mass roundup of remaining Jews. (Elsewhere, and perhaps most extraordinary of all, I read that free bottled mineral water was given to staff in Auschwitz. Mineral water in a death camp! In England we'd pretty much had to wait until the 1980s and the deregulation of the stock exchange when those coming into the financial sector from abroad demanded it. It took me years to stumble across the answer to the German story. The SS, covert but not particularly effective capitalists, had expanded into the soft-drinks market because Himmler thought Germans consumed too much beer and wanted to make the price of non-alcoholic drinks more competitive, so the SS ended up secretly owning most of the Third Reich's mineral water market, far more than was needed to achieve price leverage. For me, this sort of digression seemed much more revealing of the way things really worked than half-a-dozen volumes of traditional history.)

In the back of my mind, Kübler and Morgen twinned, as two contrasting individuals faced with an extreme moral dilemma. How had they reacted? Had they cared? Kübler apparently not; like many others afterwards she sought only to portray herself as a victim. So, again, what would you or I have done in their place? For myself, I suspected I knew the uncomfortable answer, being drawn to figures of transgression and disgrace. A third book read during my Berlin sojourns, picked up on the strength of its title alone, was *Black List Section H*, the autobiographical novel of renegade Irish author Francis Stuart, recounting his extraordinary life, which culminated in Berlin during the war, teaching at the University and broadcasting anti-British propaganda, for which he was lucky to escape later with his neck. Stuart lived a life of some privilege while Kübler was scurrying around the same part of town looking for people to betray; therefore the geography of their very different lives almost intersected. To have read Stuart's book in Berlin was to have a very clear sense of a past returned to haunt, and of lives lived during wartime, much of it still retrievable. *Black List Section H* remains a valuable documentary on the city's civilian history in 1943 when all eyes were turned elsewhere.

I never particularly had it in mind to write about Berlin at the time. I had made two films there, which satisfied my curiosity. I had also written what was ostensibly a London Soho novel, *Robinson* (1993) that was in fact based more on the experience of Berlin, which in the late 1970s and early 1980s offered enough distractions to test the border zones of anyone's identity. I later met Francis Stuart, who talked of the importance of drift in life, but not of how deep the currents were in which he had swum.

My novel *The Psalm Killer* (1996) had started off by asking the questions (after chancing across the term Ordinary Decent Criminals): what was the role of ordinary crime in sectarian Northern Ireland, and what percentage of police work was devoted to it? The questions were quickly overtaken by research, which, in terms of what was gifted, revealed a gold mine of mind-boggling paramilitary and intelligence complexity. But years later I found myself asking a variation of the same questions about Berlin during the war. What would have happened if an individual murder victim was Jewish, at a time when they were all deemed expendable? Who, if anyone, would have been assigned to investigate? I remembered Morgen. More to the point, I remembered that Morgen, after a mysterious interlude of punishment that had him sent to fight in Russia, had been just as mysteriously recalled to Berlin to work in the financial corruption section of the Criminal Police. He was told to sit on his hands and not cause trouble, advice he promptly ignored by investigating the commandant of a concentration camp for financial misdealing.

As with *The Psalm Killer*, the story became more complex than the simple questions that had provoked it. I thought again of persecution happening in familiar surroundings, and how soul crushing it must be to find where you lived all your life turned into an alien hostile space. More specifically, *The Last Jews in Berlin* told of a young Jewish woman, Ruth Thomas, whose 'designer clothes and patterns were not only well regarded in the garment industry but earned [...] badly needed foreign currency from sales abroad.' The book suggested other strands: secret trading between a parish worker from the Church of Sweden and the Gestapo, to free certain people from the SS – to 'buy them back' – then hide and eventually export them; reference to a people-smuggling operation using furniture crates belonging to a Swedish diplomat; mention of a Chinese forger and a female Hungarian fortune teller; an account of the demonstration at Rosenstrasse, and how Jews married to Gentiles and therefore legally protected were arrested in error, hence the protest. (One possible reason for their arrest, which was not gone into, is considered in Chapter 31.) Above all there was the depravity of Stella Kübler, who at the height of her activity was just twenty years old and known as the 'blond ghost'. She and her partner between them were said to have accounted for over 2000 Jewish arrests.

Elsewhere, the forger Schönhaus, mentioned by Gersten to Sybil in Chapter 46, was an actual forger who escaped from Berlin and years after wrote a memoir, *The Forger* (2007), with material on the Jewish art school scene, social life in general and a chilling encounter with Kübler, a friend from student days, who set up his arrest then, perhaps out of fondness, changed her mind. (It is the only record I could find of any humane gesture on her part.)

Morgen keeps his name, mainly because I felt I was chasing the man himself, and wanted to join up the dots of what there was, rather than trying to create a facsimile. In the context of an historical fiction it is sometimes more appropriate to speculate in the shadow of lives lived rather than just make stuff up. Francis Stuart got changed to Francis Alwynd, being not so much a portrait as an interpretation of cultural anomaly. Anyway I took liberties and, besides, Stuart had had the last word on himself in *Black List Section H*. The location of the slaughterhouse was nicked – there is no other word – from Alfred Döblin's *Berlin Alexanderplatz*, one of the great novels on Berlin or any other city; it was far too good not to appropriate.

The affair between Sybil and Lore owes something (quite a lot, actually) to the memoir *Aimée and Jaguar* by Erica Fischer, which tells of a housewife and mother of four who fell in love with a young Jewish woman.

I no longer remember where I read about an army surplus store being looted after the air raid, or cattle stampeding in the street, or there being photographs of the drowned in the reception area of the Criminal Police building. These are the kind of details you can't make up and, it is hoped, make the difference for the reader between theatrical brushstroke and something coming alive.

It could be argued that research is less interesting these days with more or less everything available at the press of a button. Previously obscure information – such as the Jews being forced to pay for their own transportation – is now instantly and universally available on Wikipedia. That said, the bulk of this research came from hard print, and more particularly foot-notes, which often prove more illuminating than the text and remain unavailable on the Internet, being the product of proper scholarship.

For their general use, the following books and reference maps, in no particular order, were helpful:

*Berlin 1910–1933* by Eberhart Roters (Wellfleet Press, 1982); *Creating Beauty to Cure the Soul: Race and Psychology in the Shaping of Aesthetic Surgery* by Sander L. Gilman (Duke University Press, 1998); *Ilse's Berlin: I Was There – 1926 to 1945* by Ilse Lewis (Authorhouse, 2011); *Hitler's Berlin: A Third Reich Tourist Guide [1937]* (WPC, 2008); *Berlin Allied Intelligence Map of Key Buildings [1945]*; *Pharus-Plan Berlin 1940* (reprint, 2013); *A Serial Killer in Nazi Berlin: The Chilling Story of the S-Bahn Murderer* by Scott Andrew Selby (Berkley, 2014) with material on serial killings, appropriated by Stoffel; ditto *Lustmord: Sexual Murder in Weimar Germany* by Maria Tartar (Princetown University Press, 1995). Peter Adam's memoir, *Not Waving But Drowning* (Andre Deutsch, 1995), has a section on growing up half-Jewish in wartime Berlin; *Spandau: The Secret Diaries* by Albert Speer (Collins, 1976) mentions the Horcher's restaurant story, as do *The Goebbels Diaries 1942-3* edited by Louis P. Lochner (Doubleday, 1948) which has an aside on the Nöthling scandal; *Eva's Berlin: Memoirs of a Wartime Childhood* by Eva Wald Leverton (Thumbprint Press, 2000); *Between Dignity and Despair: Jewish Life in Nazi Germany* by Marion A. Kaplan (OUP, 1998); *What We Knew: Terror, Mass Murder, and Everyday Life in Nazi Germany* by Eric A. Johnson and Karl-Heinz Reuband (Basic Books, 2005); *Nazi Terror: The Gestapo, Jews and Ordinary Germans* by Eric A. Johnson (Basic Books, 2000); *Ordinary Men: Reserve Police Battalion 101 and The Final Solution in Poland* by Christopher R. Browning (Penguin, 2001); *Germany Turns Eastwards* by Michael Burleigh (Pan, 2002); *Male Fantasies Volume 2* by Klaus Theweleit (Polity Press, 1989); *The Gestapo: Power and Terror in The Third Reich* by Carsten Dams and Michael Stolle (OUP, 2014); *Gestapo: Instrument of Tyranny* by Edward Crankshaw (Greenhill, 1990); *History of the SS* by G.S. Graber (Hale, 1978); *Behind the Steel Wall: Berlin 1941–43* by Arvid Fredborg (Harrap, 1944), in which a Swedish journalist reports from Berlin; *The Wartime Broadcasts of Francis Stuart, 1942-1944* ed. Brendan Barrington (Lilliput, 2000); *The Order of the Death's Head: The Story of Hitler's SS* by Heinz Höhne (transl. Richard Barry, Secker & Warburg, 1969), but specifically essential for introducing Morgen, as noted.

And the following works proved especially useful: *The Last Jews in Berlin* by Leonard Gross (Simon & Schuster, 1982) for reasons stated; *Berlin at War* by Roger Moorhouse (Vintage, 2011) has good detail (the filthiness of the food), plus Nöthling, Horcher's and Rosenstrasse; *The SS Dirlewanger Brigade: The History of the Black Hunters* by Christian Ingrao (transl. Phoebe Green, Skyhorse, 2011) has much on the psychology of atrocity and terror, referred to by Morgen in Chapter 52; *Aimée and Jaguar* by Erica Fischer (Bloomsbury, 1996) cf. p.107: 'girls were having pornographic pictures taken by Schmidt the photographer'; *A Social History of the Third Reich* by Richard Grunberger (Penguin, 1974) especially chapters on corruption, consumption, women and youth; *Swing Under the Nazis: Jazz as a Metaphor for Freedom* by Mike Zwerin (Cooper Square, 2000) and *Different Drummers: Jazz in the Culture of Nazi Germany* by Michael H. Kater (OUP, 1992) have fascinating material on jazz as a dissident but absorbed culture, with mention of a nightclub with telephones for calling between tables, as well as names (Mike Hidalgo, Kurt Widmann) featured in the book; Francis Alwynd's jazz ramblings in Chapter 10 would have come from these sources; *The Berlin Diaries 1940–1945* by Marie 'Missie' Vassiltchikov (Pimlico, 1999) offers a most detailed and impressive account of cosmopolitan life in wartime, the more fascinating for being from a woman's perspective, albeit elevated, as she was a white Russian *émigrée*. Vassiltchikov notes once the bombing started women took to wearing scarves instead of hats. She has a tiny cameo, appearing in Chapter 34 ('Schlegel had met her; a princess, no less, achingly beautiful'); *Eternal Treblinka: Our Treatment of Animals in the Holocaust* by Charles Patterson (Lantern, 2002); *The Taste of War* by Lizzie Collingham (Penguin Press, 2012): lots on pigs, and see especially the chapters 'Autarky and Lebensraum', 'Herbert Backe and the Hunger Plan' and 'Genocide in the East'; *Animals in the Third Reich* by Boria Sax (Yogh & Thorn, 2013 reprint) cf. p.54: 'The Sacrificial Pig'; *Jews in Nazi Berlin* by Meyer, Simon and Schütz (Chicago Press, 2009) includes a thorough chapter on 'Snatchers', the Berlin

Gestapo's Jewish informants, pp.249–267, with photographs of Kübler, who survived the war. She was sentenced to ten years of imprisonment by a Soviet military tribunal, then went to West Berlin where she was convicted for serving as accessory to murder but did not serve her term. She committed suicide at the age of 72 in 1994. *The Forger* by Cioma Schönhaus, (transl. Alan Bance, Granta, 2007) has much detail on the life and business of underground forgers.

In terms of fiction, Alfred Doblin's *Berlin Alexanderplatz* (transl. Eugene Jolas, Penguin, 1978 edition) presents the slaughter-house on a plate, in an astonishing documentary sequence (in an astonishing book) that spares no detail: 'hot steaming blackness, black red'. The slaughterhouse complex still exists, much knocked about, partly flattened, with some of the remaining buildings renovated into the usual retail parks and apartments. What that does to their feng shui one cannot imagine. Shed 27 is still there, derelict, with a relief carving of the head of a stone pig in the wall. Nobody nails Berlin better than Döblin, in terms of actual mapping and psychogeography, and if *The Butchers of Berlin* introduces any new readers to him then the exercise will have been worthwhile. The debt is (grudgingly) acknowledged by having Sybil read the book, which remains unnamed, although its hero Franz Biberkopf is in Chapter 23. Francis Stuart's *Black List Section H* (Southern Illinois University Press, 1971), as mentioned, formed the basis of Francis Alwynd's story, although the encounters with Sybil and Lore have no factual base. It was more the details and observations of Stuart's life in Berlin that were appropriated (the 'non-crease, unsoilable, turtleneck jersey' that gave him an un-Central-European air) and the fact he spoke English in Berlin throughout the war, almost without comment. Although, in retrospect, there was no reason for an Irishman not to be there at that time, as a neutral, Stuart's presence remained startling, and, for the purposes of this story, he seemed to belong with other real-life conundrums, such as an SS man in Internal Affairs and a woman who cruised the city looking to betray her own people. For the before and after of the period dealt with, and on Germany and Germanness, I reread Sybil Bedford's *A Legacy* (Penguin Classics edition, 2005) and Walter Abish's *How German Is It* (New Directions, 1979).

The following should be thanked for their help and/or hospitality during the writing of this book: Christopher Roth, Jeanne Tremsal, Georg Diez, Gabriele Mattner, Arno Brandlhuber, David Pirie, Liz Jobey, Lynda Myles, Richard Williams, Jennifer Potter, Iain Sinclair, Stanley Schtinter, and especially my agent Clare Alexander, for setting up and driving the project on, publisher Ian Chapman for having me back, Jo Dickinson for her clear advice and editing, and particularly Emma Matthews, for having to live with it.